Dawn of a Legend
The Silvan Book III

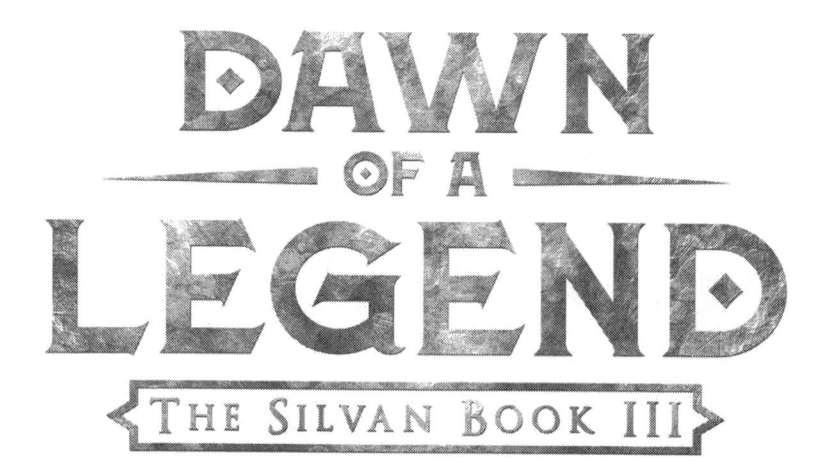

R.K. LANDER

Copyright © 2019 Ruth Kent (R.K. Lander). All rights reserved.
This work is registered with the UK Copyright Service: registration No. 284728079

Editor: Andrea Lundgren
Beta Reader: M.Y. Leigh
Cover art by Anastasia Znamenska (kaprriss)
Map of Bel'arán: Hector G. Airaghi

This is a work of fiction. All characters, names and events in this book are fictitious. Any resemblance to real persons, living or dead, is purely coincidental.

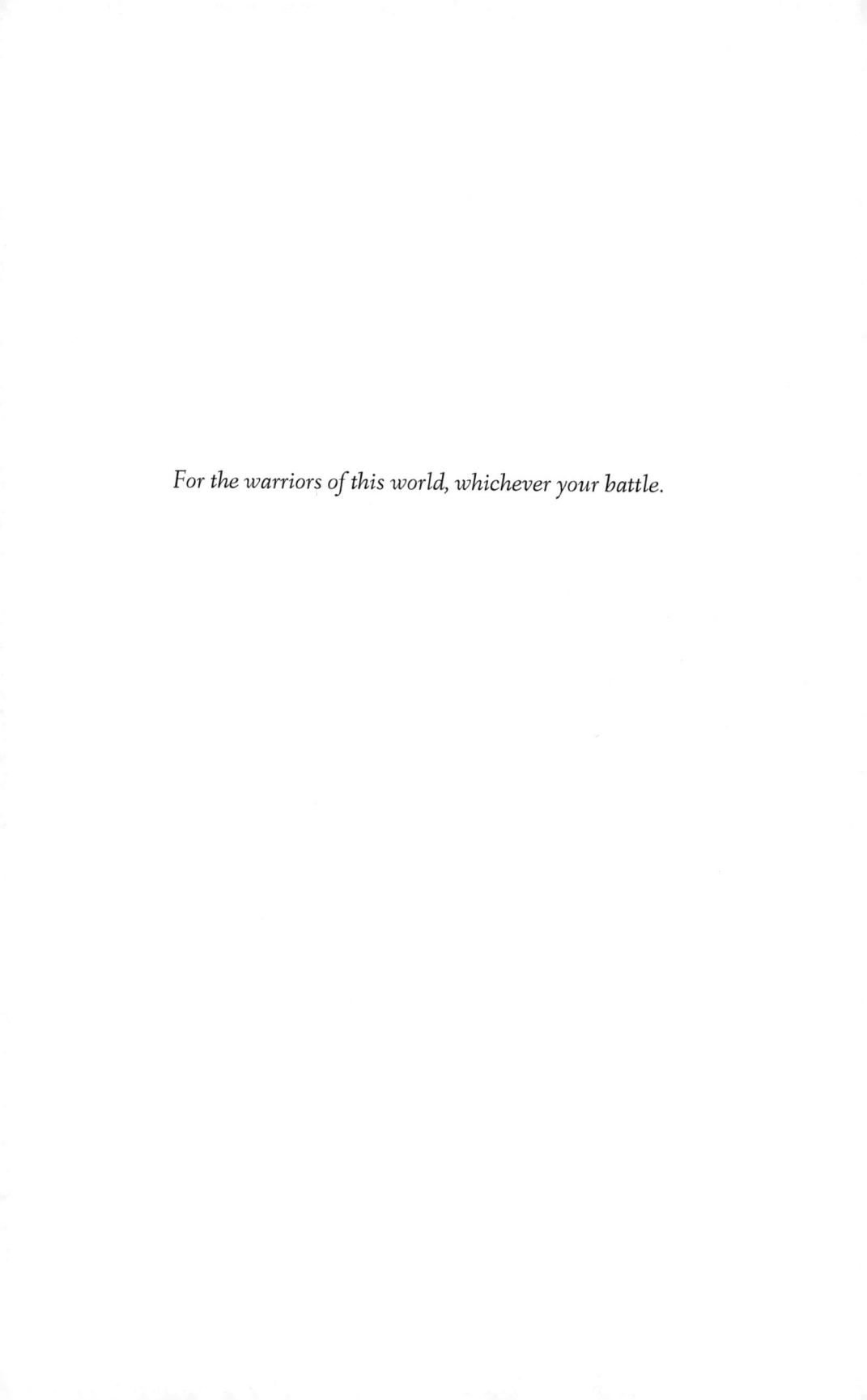

For the warriors of this world, whichever your battle.

Calrazia

Xeric Wood

Ea'Uaré

Sen'uar
Sen'olei
Abiren'a
L'an Taria
Ea'nanu

Everfern Wood

Oran'dor

Sen'garay

High Path

Cabo River
Court of Thargoden

Pelagian Mountains

Glistening Fa...

Port Helia

Pelagia

Dan'bar

Dan'su

Pelagian Sea

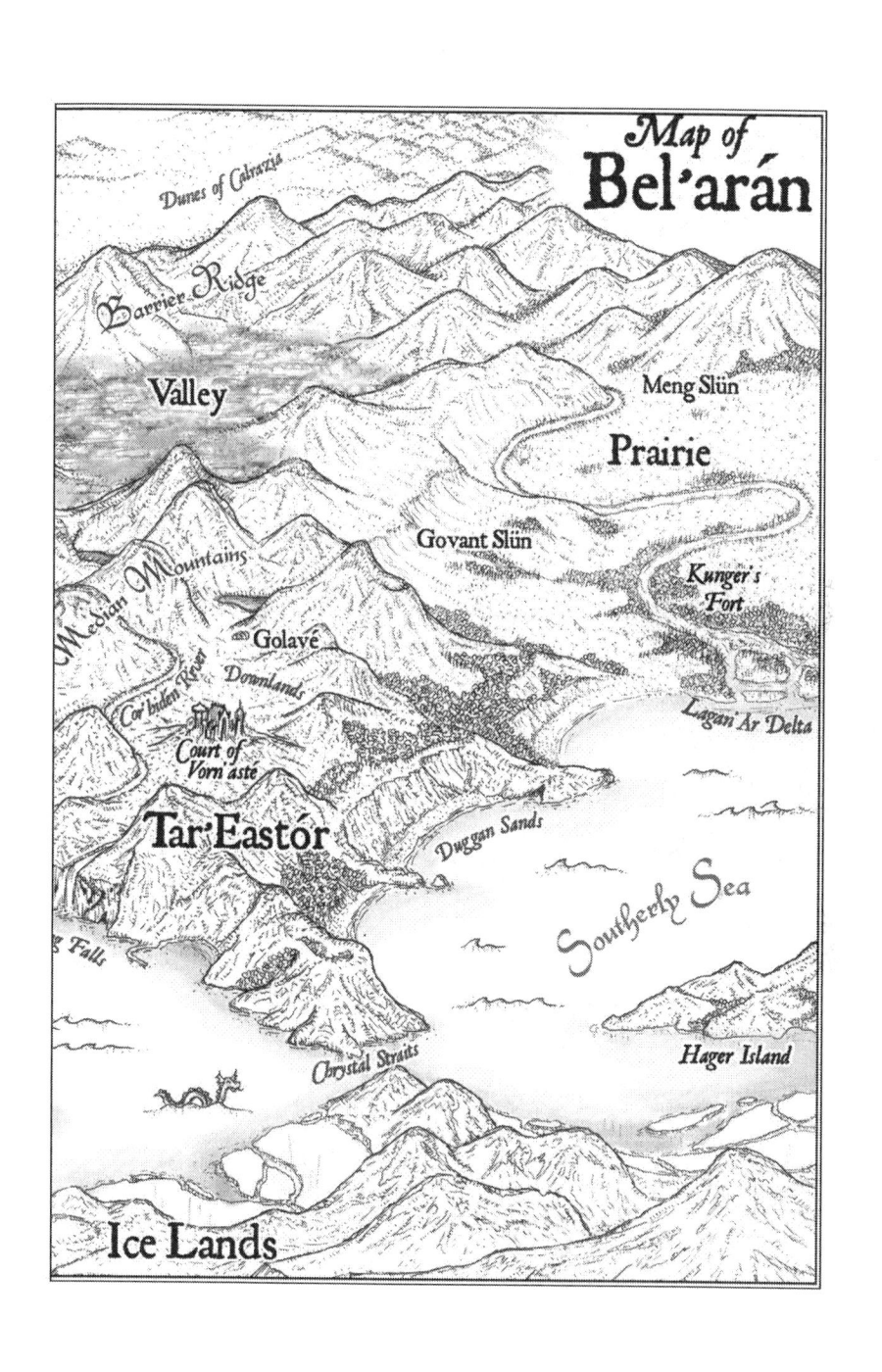

Map of Bel'arán

Dunes of Calrazia

Barrier Ridge

Valley

Meng Slün

Prairie

Median Mountains

Govant Slün

Kunger's Fort

Golavé

Corbulen River

Downlands

Lagan'Ar Delta

Court of Vorn'aste

Tar Eastór

Duegan Sands

Southerly Sea

Falls

Hager Island

Crystal Straits

Ice Lands

PROLOGUE

Beyond Araria

"Araria, city of defenders, city of the Ari'atór: Spirit Warriors. Few have seen its magnificence, for it is far to the north and bereft of trees, save for the Originals. It is hot, like the Xeric Wood of northern Ea Uaré, except it is sheltered from the ravages of Sand Lords by the Great Barrier Ridge, stone guardians of the Motherland. Beyond Araria, in a place only the Ari'atór can find, lies the shrouded land of Valley and within her mists, the Source, elven doorway to the Second Life. It is there that the Ari'atór Lainon rests."
The Alpine Chronicles. Cor'hidén.

A dark warrior stood breathless before a line of stone carvings, sword dripping with the red blood of mortals who had wished to be immortal.
Do not pass this place.
Dark chiselled features, slanted eyes and long, thick hair that

snaked around their heads in intricate twists, as if they were caught in an endless wind. Each of the eight figures, their features and weaponry clearly distinguishable, held one arm to the fore, palm to the front. A command to any human who sought to pass them by.

Behold the Last Markers. Turn away.

Beyond the stone sentinels was the land of Valley, and somewhere within lay a guarded passage that meant a new beginning for an immortal soul. But to a human, it was utter ruin, disguised as the promise of eternal life.

Turn away and live in grace.

But many mortals could not fathom the finality of death, could not fathom why there were immortals and mortals. What travesty of creation was this?

Pass and face death at the hands of the Ari'atór.

Death was a mercy for those who dared defy the Last Markers, for those who did not turn away. Survival would first turn these once innocent humans into Incipients, confused and unsettled souls whose minds would break down until they turned Deviant. That was when the rot would begin, and madness rose a victor. Immortal souls, mortal bodies and a twisted mind that sought nothing more than to sunder the lives of elves with unbridled hatred and relish.

That was Tensári's job, to slay those who would not listen, kill any humans who passed the Last Markers.

Tensári calmed her breathing and then turned away from her stone brethren and towards the waning pyres her warriors had lit to dispose of the bodies, the lives she and her patrol had ended.

She had met this group before. They had been rounded up and taken to safety, warned of what lay beyond, of why they should not pass. There had been a child with them, a beautiful hazel-eyed boy of perhaps eight winters. His smile had been wide and toothy, innocent to the horrors his parents unwittingly led him to, wondrous of the warriors around him, the Ari'atór with their dark skin, shiny blue eyes and their strange hair which he had wanted to touch. He was nothing more than ashes now, and she sent a prayer to Aria for the boy's soul.

"We ride home," she called, watching as her warriors mounted. As for her, she turned one last time, eyes focussing on some spot behind the statues. Lainon was there, still dead yet as close as he could be to her. She didn't want to leave, in spite of the stench and the chill that always surrounded this place.

One hand reached hesitantly, as if to stroke his soft cheek, see that rare smile he reserved only for her—but all her fingers felt was the cold air, as frigid as her own heart.

It had been one month since Lainon had died defending Fel'annár on the battlefield. One month in this strange place where nothing touched her, nothing except the memory of Lainon; that, and the growing resentment towards a young warrior with green eyes. Lainon had loved that boy, had died for him.

Had he been worth it?

She turned her back on Valley and faced her warriors. "Move out!" she called, striding to her horse and vaulting into the saddle. Tugging on the reins, she set a brisk pace home. With any luck she would have her warriors back in the city before nightfall, not that she cared for herself. No one was waiting for her. Lainon was gone and at best, Tensári would see him again, centuries into the future when she, too, died in battle and took the Short Road. For now, though, she was doomed to wait for his revival across the Veil, doomed not to feel him, to feel nothing at all.

Then they were home, and she nodded curtly at the warriors as their horses were led away, once more missing the lingering stares of her brethren. She never looked at them when she dismissed them because she knew what she would see in their bright blue eyes: pity—pity for an Ari'atór who had lost her soul mate, her Connate. Pity for a sundered soul, neither here nor in Valley, half dead and half alive.

Existing but not feeling, not living.

～

That night, Tensári couldn't sleep, not that she had expected to, and so she lay back upon her humble bed in a humble room, high in the towers that perched upon the loftiest mountain of Araria. It afforded her a shockingly spectacular side view of Aria herself, her face carved into the mountainside, large enough for the entire city and beyond to behold her impossible beauty. It was a reminder of their purpose, of the Ari'atór's implacable duty as holders of the faith, as protectors of Valley.

She stared at the wooden planks along the ceiling and then allowed her eyes to drift down the red sand walls and to the glassless window. Not yet dawn of another day of service, and yet she was empty—devoid of a purpose beyond mindless slaughter. She was angry with Aria, too, for ripping Lainon from her heart.

Her body felt heavier in her bed and she closed her eyes, the hazel eyes of an innocent soul floating before her sight. She felt lighter, full of air and wind, and there was suddenly nothing beneath her. Her body stood vertically, but the ground felt further and further away from her. There was a cold breeze against her face, currents pushing under her arms and lifting her twisted locks around her. Her dreams would be strange this night, just as they had been these past months.

She opened her eyes with a harsh intake of breath, for it was beautiful here in the heights. She wanted to cry for the majesty of this place, even though she had been here so many times of late.

She felt her body tilt forwards until she lay upon the wind, and then she was moving over the land she had helped defend for centuries. She flew over hills and high plains and then skirted the mighty mountains of Araria. She caught the shadow of herself upon the white slopes, wings flapping slowly, noisily, talons tucked beneath her for extra speed.

She squawked.

These mountains were the highest point of the land, and as she peaked the crest, she circled around. She could see buildings, characteristic halls of red stone and black marble. The Last City of Araria towered upon the mountain, carved into it in jagged spires of harsh beauty. She was inside that towering palace, asleep, but her spirit had been allowed to wander free—again.

She swooped down onto the high plains, just as she had done the night before and the one before that. She skimmed over the land, and it became greener the further she flew. There was light here, even though it was night-time. It was not sunlight, though, but *divine* light, for the Source lay just beyond. It was the golden light of a frosty morning, even at dusk.

Valley and the Source, the crossing from one life to another. It was the end of the Road, long or short, willing or through death.

For now, though, her dream would end here, as it had done these past months, and she braced herself for the familiar jolt of an abrupt awakening.

But the jolt never came.

She descended through the concealing cloud, and as she broke through the puffy humid towers, light exploded upon her face. It was bliss, and a tear escaped her eye. This was as close as she had ever been to the Source. It was eternal spring, never-ending life, a beauty so great it could never be described, only felt, and Tensári *did*, for the first time since she had been wrenched apart by the loss of Lainon.

Over green fields and lakes of crystal blue, the Ari'atór could be seen escorting a group of elves upon their final, joyous steps in this world, tiny dots upon the sprawling land. Tensári smiled, but she didn't stop, every beat of her wings taking her closer to the Source and the shimmering wall that separated Bel'arán from the other side.

She didn't expect to see a forest.

Despite her excitement, she slowed her pace, tilting her wings forwards so that she would descend. Talons extended before her, and she landed atop a craggy outcrop and admired the thick circle of towering trees and at its centre, the column of shimmering light that jutted into the sky, as far up as her eyes could discern. It was not a steady beam of light, for it sometimes pulsed and then shimmered, pearly streaks pulling at the thin, gossamer fabric of the Veil, and for a moment, movement could be seen on the other side.

Her eyes were drawn to the plain below, watched as the group of elves slowly walked into the forest while the Ari'atór who had accompanied them stayed behind, smiling as they disappeared into the trees. Tensári smiled too and then her eyes were drawn to another guard who stood with his back to her. He, too, watched his fellow Ari'atór, and Tensári's head cocked to one side in thought.

The guard looked over his shoulder, over and up, directly at her. His blue eyes shone with power and joy, and for a moment, a green shimmer passed through them. She felt too light, as if she would fall, but this feathered body was not hers: she knew she would not falter. He smiled and then turned his body towards her, his back now to the trees.

Lainon.

He lifted one hand and held it out to her, then placed it over his heart, and on his face was a message that needed no words, for it rang in her mind and flowed from her eyes.

"I love you. I have found myself."

He backed into the forest, but his smile never faltered as he disappeared, and a surge of thankfulness hit her so hard it was all she could do to spread her wings and *fly*, fly fast and furious. She banked away from the Veil Lainon had just passed through, free of her grief at last. She could feel his presence now, slipping into a place he should never have left. She felt complete again.

She soared, high, high into the clouds, fast and urgent. Utter joy exploding in her chest, love for Aria and the creations she had been born to defend, love for her Connate, Lainon, separated from her in body but no longer in spirit. His presence grew in her mind even as she flew fast and true, as if she *knew* where she journeyed.

But she *didn't*.

The mountain rushed passed her, under her, and still she leaned forward, challenged the wind to bring her down if it could, but it never would, for love had returned to her spirit and she had a purpose once more.

But what *was* that purpose?

The snow was thinning, giving way to bare rock and then sparse vegetation, and then lower, there were towering evergreen trees and rocky escarpments, but still, she did not stop, *could* not. This was surely Ea Uaré, the Great Forest, but why had Aria seen fit to show her this?

Lainon had been born here, in the small village of Abiren'á. Perhaps this was Aria's message: to find Lainon's folk and give them the news that he lived once more on the other side, even though it had been but a month since his fall.

But there was no time to ponder any longer—she was falling, plummeting to the ground, and she gasped, body jerking upwards until she sat, chest heaving and eyes wide, eyes that brimmed with grateful tears, for she could feel Lainon's presence, warm and safe, cradled in the protective arms of her mind even now when the dream had gone and she was awake.

It had *not been* a dream.

Aria had shown her, and Aria, spirit of nature, did nothing on a whim. There was a reason for her journey, one Tensári would now set out to discover, and there was only one who could help her: Commander Hobin, divine leader of the Ari'atór. She would seek his wise counsel, and then perhaps she too could live again, serve again and when the time came for her to sacrifice herself in battle, then she would do so willingly, knowing that beyond sacrifice would come paradise in Lainon's arms.

∼

Tar'eastór had the Inner Circle, and the colonising Alpine rulers of Ea Uaré had emulated that tradition. In Araria, though, the central seat of military power was a *cathedral*.

Tensári strode down the central aisle until she stood at a respectful distance from the raised platform at the centre of the main hall. Upon it stood a tall and powerful Ari'atór, strong arms held out to the side, head tilted backwards before the black marble carving of Aria.

He knew she was there, but Commander Hobin would not interrupt his praise of Aria, and so she waited, and she wondered how long it had been since she herself had given praise. She would, though, as soon as Hobin had heard her questions.

With the distant chime of a soft bell, Hobin lowered his arms and bowed his head. He turned, eyes just a little too bright. His connection with Aria was strong, and the echo of green Silvan eyes came to her in a rush of mixed emotions: curiosity, resentment...

"Tensári," said Hobin as he stepped from the platform and faced her, head cocked to one side as he read her face and the emotions in her eyes. A soft smile played about the corners of his mouth. "You bring news," he stated.

She wanted to explain, give her report as any worthy lieutenant would, but all that came out of her mouth was, "Aria be praised." She was shocked at how unsteady her voice had sounded, but Hobin was suddenly directly before her, his benevolent eyes of vivid blue boring into hers. They widened suddenly, and before she could ponder that, his arms encircled her and pulled her head to his chest.

"Aria has seen fit to bring him back to us soonest. I have never seen this, and I say it is justice, for he was Ber'ator. The deeds he sacrificed himself for have yet to play out, Tensári. His death was not in vain, and now, through your connection to him, he will have some ken at least of what he died for."

He knew her mind, not because he could read it, but because he was the most empathetic being she had ever known, ever would. She needed to know why Lainon had died; she needed to know that it had been worth it. That *Fel'annár* had been worth it.

"I have questions, Commander."

"And I will answer them if I can. Come," he said, releasing her and walking to another section of the grand hall. There was a square table upon which rested a map of Araria. Behind, books covered an entire wall, and in another corner, a mighty hearth crackled overly-loud.

"Did she show you? Did you see him pass?" murmured Hobin.

"I did. I did not know there were trees around the Veil, Commander."

"You have never been posted there; only our veterans work there, those who can no longer fight. They do not speak of that place, as you know, but Aria has seen fit to show *you* nonetheless."

"Then I am blessed. But I wonder. There are no trees in Araria; only there."

"They are the Originals, Tensári. Aria's first means by which she communes with us. They are all Sentinels, guardians of the Source. But come, ask your questions."

"Commander. I have dreamed this dream for a month, but only last night did the dream complete itself and Lainon came back to me. But it did not stop there."

Hobin turned briskly, a scowl on his face. "Go on."

"I journeyed on, past Tar'eastór and into Ea Uaré. It felt as though that is where I should be, but the dream ended. I am left with the certainty of some task I am to carry out. I think perhaps I am charged with telling Lainon's folk of his return."

Hobin's eyes studied his lieutenant, but he did not answer immediately. Instead he turned to the fire and crossed his hands behind his back. Tensári came to stand beside him, the warmth calming her growing sense of urgency.

"We have received missives from Commander Gor'sadén of Tar'eastór," Hobin said, his voice soft, her indirect question unanswered. "He requires our presence to discuss the increased Deviant activity we in Araria have not noticed. It is strange that the number of humans breeching the markers has increased but that Deviant kills has not. They are massing somewhere; we must confer with Tar'eastór, find out why this is happening. I am leaving in two days."

Tensári started. Their holy commander had not left Araria for many years save for the occasional patrol he would lead across the borders and into Tar'eastór. It was an unlikely event that merited a question.

"May I ask why you wish to travel personally, Commander?"

"It has been too long since last I spoke with Gor'sadén and Vorn'asté. Now seems a good time to re-establish our ties with our neighbours, and yet more than this, there is something in Gor'sadén's manner that tells me this is important. He is worried and I would see to this myself."

"I would accompany you, Commander. I do not know what Aria means to tell me, but I think perhaps there, I may find out."

"No. Your feelings and your thoughts are not yet clear, Tensári. You must give yourself time to think and to understand. You must learn to feel Lainon in your mind once more. And you must consider why you resent the Ber'anor for being the cause of Lainon's death. Because you *do*, don't you?" he asked carefully.

"But how am I to know the truth if I cannot ask him, ask the Ber'anor? He may still be in Tar'eastór."

"Yes. But you would accuse him, Tensári. All this is too fresh in your mind. Lainon has only just returned, and you are unaccustomed to the workings of Connates across the divide. You must rest for a while in Lainon's renewed presence, commune with Aria until you understand, until your anger is spent and the way forward is clear to you. Only then will I allow you to return and to follow Aria's bidding."

Tensári wanted to reject his words, convince him that he was wrong. She didn't need time. All she needed was to ask Fel'annár why Lainon had died, ask him why he had needed the protection of the Ari'atór—whether he had been *careless*.

Hobin was right. She *would* have been angry. She *was* angry, even though the joy she felt at Lainon's return had pushed that anger to the back of her mind.

"I must prepare to leave." Hobin had not given her answers as she thought he might, but he *had* given her a mission, one she began to accept as a necessary step before returning to Tar'eastór. She would venture out into the wilderness to think. She would commune with Aria, understand her mind if she could, interpret the vision she had had. She would learn to connect with Lainon, just as surely as he would be doing from the other side, and she would reach the source of her anger, understand it, quell it if she could.

"Thank you, Commander, for the freedom you give me to seek answers."

Hobin turned to her, his strange eyes dancing from one side of her face to the other. She bowed from the waist, turned, and left the cathedral with the light of purpose blazing in her blue eyes, and Hobin watched her. His smile was gone, and his face seemed carved from black marble, firelight setting his blue eyes aflame. It would soon be time for Tensári to shine, but first, Hobin had his own mission to accomplish, Gor'sadén's request aside. If Fel'annár was still in Tar'eastór, then Hobin needed to know if he knew, whether the Silvan Ber'anor had the slightest ken of what he was—and what was requested of him.

Tensári's black-clad figure disappeared in the halo of light from the other side of the doors, and Hobin spoke softly, not quite loud enough for anyone to hear.

"May you find that path, Tensári, just as Lainon once did."

ONE
EVER PRESENT

"It was a time of turmoil, for the Deviants came in hoards, attacking our villages with the simple purpose of razing them to the ground. The brave warriors of Tar'eastór were over-taxed, patrolling for weeks on end, and with them was Fel'annár and The Company. There had once been eight, but now there were seven, for Lainon of the Ari'atór had been lost defending Fel'annár from a Deviant scimitar.
His absence was ever present."
The Alpine Chronicles. Cor'hidén.

~

The thud of an arrow piercing flesh, a cry of pain from an elven warrior who was thrown to the floor with the force of the bolt.

A roar of anger, a plea for aid, the scream of a defeated soldier, the desperate sounds of elves and Deviants locked in combat, fighting and dying in the frigid cold. But Fel'annár did not flinch, even though he stood in the midst of the chaos. He *couldn't*; he was the only master archer left, the only one who could eliminate the Deviant snipers that were picking off their warriors.

He sighted his next target, stance perfect; it *had* to be. His arm did not waver, it *could* not, and his heart did not feel; it *must* not. He would not allow that, and when the last sniper was down, he whipped out his long and short swords with a morbid sense of satisfaction and moved closer to Captain Comon and The Company's position, where the fighting was at its worst.

The shriek of polished metal upon rusted iron grated on their ears, but it did not deter the Alpine warriors of Tar'eastór, even though they had been fighting almost constantly for the last weeks. They bore down upon the rotting mass of Deviants that had thought to surprise them, their elven faces twisted into snarls of hatred for an enemy that was relentless, ruthless.

"Behind you," warned Fel'annár as he moved closer to his captain to engage another Deviant, whose massive scimitar swung unnervingly close over his head. Shocked, he flipped backwards to gain space and time and then moved to the side and scored a blow to the Deviant's shoulder. But that only served to enrage it. Roaring in unbridled wrath, the beast bore down on Fel'annár with such strength it sent him stumbling backwards. What was *wrong* with him? Yet even as he asked himself he knew the answer: he was tired, his concentration slipping, and this opponent was not going down easily.

Swivelling his right sword to the left, he whirled around and sliced into its other side, garnering another unearthly shriek that vibrated painfully in his ears.

He moved in from the front this time, but the beast's counter blow was so strong it was all Fel'annár could do to keep his sword from flying out of his sticky hand; he was off balance once more, and the nascent tingle of dread began to take hold of him.

Fel'annár raised both blades and brought them down upon his enemy, but they were blocked, and for one strange moment, bright green eyes locked with the cloudy but challenging gaze of the

Deviant. There was hatred and cruelty there, as there always was; he had expected that, but Fel'annár hesitated, for there was something more, something he could not place. His brow twitched in confusion, but before he could ponder it any longer, the handle of the Deviant's blade caught him in the side of the head with a heavy thud, sending him stumbling backwards and then, to his utter horror, to his knees. He was down, and he desperately blinked to clear his reeling mind, not fast enough to avoid the boot that crashed into his mid-section, sending him gasping to the floor. It was all he could do to roll out of the way as the scimitar came down upon him, missing him by mere inches, a blessing in disguise, for the beast had placed so much weight behind the blow that it overcompensated. Fel'annár had just enough time to plunge both swords into its mid-section.

Gasping, he fell alongside the dead Deviant. He groaned as he tried and failed to get his feet below him, and the shouts of victory around him seemed muffled and far, far away. He stopped where he knelt, shaking his head once more before trying again—and promptly crashing to the ground. Something wet trickled down the side of his head.

A strong hand clasped his forearm and hoisted him aloft, but he reeled to one side and the hands were back on him, steadying him. He could not tell where he was; he could feel his feet below him, but it felt as though he was lying down—his eyes were deceiving him, and his stomach flipped miserably.

Someone took his arms, and he felt himself lifted, the tips of his boots dragging over the ground until his saviours stopped and he felt the solid earth beneath his back. He stared upwards, into a treeless sky, breathing too fast. *Damn it*, he cursed bitterly. His mind was working just fine, if only his eyes would cooperate.

"Hwindo . . . how many?"

Squinting at the fat, swimming digits that danced before his eyes, he tried to focus on the fuzzy objects, and his stomach roiled. With a groan he closed his eyes and the world began to spin. He bent to one side and retched.

The strong hand was back, pushing him down to the ground. He could feel the pressure on his back again, yet his eyes told him he was sitting up. He knew what would come now, and so he lay still, eyes open, bearing their involuntary movement as best he could. It would pass; it always did.

He felt something soft press firmly against the side of his head and then someone was bandaging. Every so often they would crouch beside him and touch him, speak to him. "Don't sleep," they would say, and he would not; he knew the chances of not waking after a concussion. He wondered if it was Sontúr, but turning to look would hurt, so he lay there, one hand absently stroking a shrub just beneath the thin layer of snow.

The Deviant's face was before him once more. He saw the gleam of malice and morbid enjoyment, one he had seen so many times, and yet it had suddenly changed into an emotion that he could not place. But then it had walloped him on the head and Fel'annár had killed it. Those rotting eyes had dimmed and its life had ended before he could solve the mystery. To Fel'annár's fuzzy mind, there was something very wrong about how the Deviants were acting, but he could not focus. All he knew was that something had changed, something important, and the incessant song from the trees was perplexing to his confused mind.

Nim'uán. Beautiful monster.

But how can a *"monster"* be *"beautiful"*?

He might have slept but couldn't be sure.

"Fel'annár?" came the familiar voice of Ramien. "We'll be back at the barracks soon; I think we have *all* had enough," he said softly, wistfully, only just loud enough for Fel'annár to hear. There was no answer, though, for Fel'annár's skull had begun to hammer between his ears, every thud a wave of eye-watering agony that stole his breath. It was all he could do to control his breathing and his treacherous voice that begged to be freed so that it could express the pain he felt.

When next he woke he saw leafless boughs swaying softly over his head, heard the sounds of bubbling water and clinking cups, murmuring voices around him. His eyes slowly focussed on the sky beyond the winter trees, and he remembered how it was he had come to be here.

They had been sent out a scarce week after they had arrived from their previous patrol, a patrol Fel'annár would never forget. It had been his first time battling in the heights, the first time he had seen Incipients. The first time he had lost a brother.

Lainon.

They had returned, but he had barely had enough time to recover his strength before they were riding and fighting once more. The forces of Tar'eastór were hard-stretched; they had been needed in the field, and in truth, Fel'annár had been glad of it.

No time to think of what he had lost, of *how* he had lost him. Lainon's death had been so very strange.

His heart was so heavy it hurt and in his mind was nothing but confusion for what was happening to him—this uncontrolled gift of his that was becoming stronger, that was changing and developing, manifesting itself in ways he had not anticipated. It still frightened him, that lack of control. Lainon had known that.

But Lainon wasn't here. He'd gone to Valley.

They had only meant to be on a week's tour, but by the time they had regained the ground they had lost to the enemy, one week had become two, with only fleeting visits to nearby villages. By then, the late winter avalanches had threatened the outlying villages, and the patrol had stayed to help.

They had all suffered injuries, were battered and bruised, tired and hungry, mentally exhausted. They had taxed their strong bodies as far as they were able, and now, Captain Comon was leading them back. He would deliver his report on enemy numbers, movements and engagements, information Commander Gor'sadén would then use to plan their ongoing strategy against the Deviants. Fel'annár wondered if he would be able to give voice to his own thoughts about what he had seen and felt—and then he wondered whether they would even *believe* him.

Deviants felt nothing but hatred, didn't they?

Deviants weren't *beautiful*, were they?

And still the song went on in his mind.

Nim'uán. Beautiful Monster.

The following day, they broke camp and took the western road to Tar'eastór. Fel'annár bore the riding with a clenched jaw and narrowed eyes, for the sun had come out, reflecting on the crystal white snow and setting his head to pounding like the summer drums of the Deep Forest. Every time they stopped, Sontúr would provide him with a steaming cup of some repulsive herbal tea which would ease his head for a while at least.

Two days later, they were out on the High Plains, fast approaching the wooded ascent that led to the citadel of Tar'eastór. The broken patrol of Alpine and Silvan warriors kicked their mounts into a canter, but still they were mostly silent, for service such as theirs came at a high price. There was no desire to speak of meaningless things, no inclination to humour or song, for they could think only of the heavy losses they had suffered: twelve immortal souls they had all known well. Captain Comon would now break the hearts of their families, their soulmates, and their children. He would solemnly hand over the swords of the fallen so that they might be passed down through the generations, their wielders remembered.

Hot water and fresh food awaited, sleep and perhaps oblivion. He should have been content, but with their arrival at the citadel, his own, studiously-buried thoughts would be back: Lainon, Handir, the imminent missives from King Thargodén of Ea Uaré.

Fel'annár's eyes strayed to his right, still expecting to see his dark warrior brother Lainon close by. But he didn't; he had died, defending *him,* and he swallowed the lump that had formed in his throat, closing his eyes lest his emotions betray him. His only comfort came from a tiny part of his mind where he imagined Lainon's blue light had lodged itself, the light that had detached itself when the

Ari'atór had taken the Short Road. Funny, he pondered, because that light, that place in his mind felt brighter, bigger for reasons he could not yet fathom. Still, it calmed his anxious mind and the pounding in his head.

They had stopped to rest, and Sontúr was back with his concoction. It was hot enough to make him wince, and now, as they continued on their final leg back to the city, Fel'annár remembered the enigmatic Ari'atór commander, Hobin. When Lainon had passed on, the commander had called Fel'annár '*Ber'anor*.' He didn't know what that was, but he knew that, should he ask Idernon, he would find out. But he hadn't asked, because there was something about that word, something about the way Hobin had spoken it that had given Fel'annár reason for pause. And then Lainon's cryptic last words came back to him, about completing some task together with Prince Handir, his half-brother. He had not understood those words and had spent hours pondering their meaning. But to no avail. All he had been able to do was break the news of Lainon's demise to Handir, tell him what Lainon had said. But the prince in his grief had said nothing, and the meaning of those last, precious words had been lost.

"Fel'annár."

His eyes snapped to Idernon beside him, only now realising that he had been sitting askew in the saddle. He straightened his back, and the Wise Warrior nodded. Forcing his mind back into the present, one last thought came to him—the missives that would surely arrive from Ea Uaré and, in them, the king's dictates. Was he free to return to Ea Uaré? Was he repudiated? Exiled even? Would the king want to meet him? Would *Fel'annár* want to meet his *father*?

A deep breath later, he shook his head to rid himself of his incessant questioning. He felt Idernon beside him and Ramien behind him. He could hear Galadan and Galdith's quiet banter and Sontúr, whose brow would surely be riding high on his forehead at the bawdy words of Carodel's soft melody. The Company, his brothers, the only elves who knew him well, knew his secrets and his ambitions, even his fears. They followed him as a warrior would a brave captain, and he relaxed into their strong and steady presence, even the one in his mind.

Fel'annár didn't need a family he had never known.

He already had one.

~

Prince Handir, second son of King Thargodén of Ea Uaré, sat at King Vorn'asté's breakfast table, enduring the calculating stare of his mentor, Lord Councillor Damiel. The king, too, watched him with the same questions in his eyes; Handir knew what they were thinking, could see it all too clearly. He had made a mistake, and the question was, would Handir remedy that, now that Comon's patrol was approaching?

The missives from Thargodén had arrived just days before Fel'annár had been sent back out on patrol. There were messages for the king, for his chief councillor, and his commander general, and Handir had delivered them personally. But the two scrolls addressed to Fel'annár remained upon his desk in his rooms. Untouched. Undelivered.

He should have sought the boy out, should have given him the messages. But he hadn't. He *couldn't*.

Lainon would be angry with him.

He was angry with *himself*.

He was still reeling with Lainon's loss, unable, as yet, to understand how he, Turion and Aradan would continue with their plan to restore Ea Uaré without the Ari'atór, the instigator of their undertaking. In order to cease the ever-growing racism and stop the Silvan people from turning their backs on their Alpine king, they needed Fel'annár on their side so that the king would be stirred back to life—so that he could rule again as he once had and pull back their nation from the ever-growing schism between Alpines and Silvans. And yet Lainon had hinted at more, had implied that there was more to

Fel'annár's participation than the return of the king. And herein lay Handir's problem.

What had Lainon seen in Fel'annár beyond a young warrior with a promising future and some heightened sensitivity with trees? He was just a boy whose existence had embittered his own…

He stopped himself. It would do him no good to walk the road of resentment. He had already done that; it had served no purpose. Instead, he reminded himself of the reasons that had brought him, Aradan, Turion and Lainon together. It was for Ea Uaré, his forest home, and for its subjugated people. He did it for his father, his duty as a prince. He did not have to *like* the Silvan boy.

Whatever it was that Lainon had seen in him, Handir had always assumed it would be the Ari'atór who would deal with Fel'annár, explain his part in the scheme. Now, though, that task fell to Handir. But how could he make Fel'annár see the merits of helping them if there was no empathy between them: no *trust*. Handir was a prince and Fel'annár was a warrior; there was nothing else between them except for a sad story.

But the facts remained. He had two days before Captain Comon's patrol was due back, and then he would tell Fel'annár he had a message from his father. When the shock had passed, he would tell the boy of their plan.

Handir pushed his hands into the ample sleeves of his robes and left the dining hall, to where he did not know, did not care. He felt empty, alone save for the timid friendships he had struck up with a few of his fellow apprentices, and of course with Lord Damiel himself. But there was nobody who knew him well; no one who loved him as Lainon had.

It was cold, and lazy snowflakes drifted from the leaden sky. He pulled his hood over his silver locks and wandered into the busy courtyard, blissfully anonymous for a moment. It would soon be time to return inside for the council session programmed for late morning, and the sour, arrogant features of Lord Sulén invaded his mind.

Lord Sulén, his father's third or perhaps fourth cousin, was proud of his distant ties with the royal family of Ea Uaré, a circumstance he was all too ready to remind his fellow councillors of during the countless council meetings Handir had attended during his tutorship with Councillor Damiel. Sulén had taken to calling Handir "cousin," and Handir had hidden his dislike behind his well-studied mask of placid indifference. But it was Sulén's unyielding respect for *Band'orán* which had first drawn Handir's attention to him, that and the fact that he was Silor's father. Handir had resisted the urge to shut the fool's mouth on more than one occasion. Instead he had stepped back to listen and observe. Soon enough he understood the situation for what it was. The lord's son, Silor, *was* a fool by Pan'assár's account, but his father was *not*. Sulén's staunch alliance with Band'orán suggested he had something to gain, and the questions begged to be answered.

What had Band'orán promised him? And in return for what?

Heaving a deep breath, he turned to watch a group of weary travellers grind to a halt beside the stables. He caught glimpses of long, grey hair: Pelagians, he mused, but then a head of deep auburn emerged from the crowd. Handir stared, blinked, and then cocked his head to one side. Greens and browns, suede and leather, all muted tones save for a long colourful scarf with the all-too-familiar patterns of the Forest.

Handir turned to her, watched from afar as she exchanged heartfelt goodbyes, and when she turned, Handir froze. Light blue eyes locked with warm honey and he remembered. Hazy summers high in the boughs, mischievous plans upon the banks of the Calro River, a clumsy kiss under a twilight beech. But she was walking, feet tentative and eyes wide, and then she was striding, cloak billowing around her high boots. Her gape faded into a smile, and then her lips spread wide until all her teeth shone and she opened her arms, satchel falling to the ground.

"Handir," she gasped and then reached out to him, clutching at his velvet cloak and encircling him in her embrace. Handir's half-frozen arms slowly wrapped around her, his grasp becoming tighter as his mind finally caught up with his eyes. Only one word made it past his slack mouth.

"Llyniel."

He stood there with her, relishing the feel of familiar hands, that face he knew so well. Here was an elf who *did* know him well, who understood him like no other could.

Theirs was a legendary friendship, forged during the innocence of youth, shaped by the duress of life at court in Ea Uaré. He had kissed her once and both had gazed upon one another in silent accord. It had not felt right, and yet from that moment, although they knew they would never be lovers, a bond was formed, one that would never be sundered. A decade had passed since she had left Ea Uaré, unable to endure the racism and discrimination against her people, and Handir had been duty-bound to stay at his father's side.

And as suddenly as she had left, so had she re-appeared, just when he needed her the most. She was standing before him, incredulous tears in her eyes, and for one strange moment, Handir wanted to cry for the joy in his heart, for the relief of her presence. Her wise counsel and her loving Silvan heart would give him the courage to stand tall and see his duty done.

He had an uncomfortable job to do, a friend to grieve for and enemies to outwit. Aria had seen fit to take Lainon from his side, but so too had she brought Llyniel to him, and Handir thought that he could, perhaps, endure it all.

∼

After a stunned, almost desperate parting, full of promises for a prompt reunion with her inseparable friend, Llyniel had made her way to the Healing Halls of Master Arané. It had been a long journey from Pelagia, the island home of the Sea elves, *her* home for the last ten years.

But Llyniel was no Pelagian. She was Silvan—well, *almost*.

Princess Maeneth had taken up permanent residence there after the departure of the queen of Ea Uaré, and Llyniel had journeyed with her, as yet a junior healer. Serving under Master Healer Tanor, she then become a head healer, a step closer to her dream of becoming a master. And then, a singular opportunity had arisen.

Tar'eastór had called for healers willing to collaborate with the famed Healing Halls of Master Arané. Battle was escalating and Llyniel was eager to gain more experience, but it was the promise of knowledge that had endeared her to the idea.

Her pack sat more heavily upon her back now, and the bundle in her other hand was slowly slipping from her grip. Still, she followed an attendant as he led her down the well-lit corridors of the residential wing of this legendary place of healing.

She was impressed, and, had she not been so tired, she would have stopped to admire the wall paintings that seemed to span the entire height of the walls. The greatest of all physicians were immortalised upon the dark stone, candle-lit faces staring down at their ailing patients, expressions schooled but eyes so very expressive. Beron and Canoréi, Penat and Yerái could be seen reading books or mixing potions, embracing a grieving lover. This was Llyniel's passion: this was her place in spite of her lofty birth. This was why she was here, to learn, to become a *master* healer in the most revered of all the Halls of Healing.

She walked into the room she had been assigned and waited for her attendant to light the candles. It wasn't a large or luxurious room, but it was clean and functional, if a little dark. Llyniel thought it would suit her just fine, although Handir would be horrified, she smirked, pampered prince that he was. It was not that she didn't appreciate comfort and luxury—she wasn't stupid, but neither was she perturbed by simplicity. She was Silvan, after all: *half*-Silvan. In any case she would surely spend most of her free time with her life-long friend, and *his* quarters would surely be fitting an Alpine prince. She would soon find out at the afternoon meal, albeit she had no idea how to find him. Handir, though, had assured her that he would find *her*, and so they had parted, each with a disbelieving smile at having found each other. A spark of excitement came to her eyes at the prospect of news from home, of family they both had not seen in years—one for duty, the other for shame.

She sat at the small writing table and pulled out a large, leather-bound tome. She placed it reverently upon the scuffed surface and then dragged a single candle closer. Opening it at a place she had marked, she smiled at the many illustrations that littered the pages. There were untidy notes all over them, some words underlined while others were circled.

Deciduous tree bark, the most fascinating subject, one that had captivated Llyniel for many years.

No sooner had she arrived at the Halls, than she had presented Master Arané with her letters of recommendation from Master Nestar of Ea Uaré and Master Tanor of Pelagia. Arané had read them with interest, and then his eyes had pulsed wide when he read of her expertise with tree barks. It was an emerging speciality, one he seemed enthusiastic to pursue. He had gladly accepted her services in exchange for a fair wage and these quarters.

By rights, Llyniel could have claimed quarters at the palace as a lady of Ea Uaré. But she wouldn't, for to do so would be to accept her rightful position, use her family name and *that* she could not do, because her father was a *coward*.

She had asked for hot water and then sunk below the steaming surface of her bath tub. It was a luxury she had not enjoyed for weeks upon the road, and she had wallowed in it for far too long, had almost fallen asleep. But she was eager to learn the lay of the Halls and so, dressed now in the black robes of a head healer, she went in search of someone who could help her. She would visit the store rooms, inspect the herbs, roots and perhaps barks that could be used. She would learn what mixtures were already prepared, the instruments they had. She would ask of their protocols and the chain of command, all those things a good healer should know. Only then would she be reunited with Handir, and she would remember.

She would remember the family she had walked away from—and *why* she had left it all behind.

∼

Just beyond the first outposts of the great mountain citadel of Tar'eastór, the shrill squawk of carrier birds echoed over the open plains of eastern Ea Uaré. With the forests of the Silvan people behind them and Tar'eastór looming before them, three birds flew in perfect formation, soft leather harnesses strapped upon their backs, ornate feathers ruffling in the cooling breeze.

It was still winter, but no clouds lay before the sun, and as they flew, they relished in the warmth upon their feathered backs—until three arrows flew in rapid succession with flawless precision, piercing their breasts. They plummeted lifeless to the ground in a bundle of majestic green and brown feathers, their once vibrant eyes now dull and vacant.

"Well?" asked Silor as he came to stand over his companion's shoulder.

Slinging his field bow onto his back, the archer crouched and roughly flipped one of the dead birds over. Holding it with one hand, he used the other to open the sealed flap and pull out the protected messages. Unfolding the parchment, he read.

"Military Code. These are not King Thargodén's missives. Your lord father will be most displeased," murmured the archer.

Silor paled and then straightened his hunched shoulders. "How can you be sure? Can you understand that?" he asked, one long finger pointing to the unintelligible symbols.

"Not entirely. These codes change with every season, but this here I *do* recognise. It is General Huren's seal."

"Can you tell who it is addressed to?"

"No, but I would assume it is for Commander Pan'assár. It will be a report, no doubt, on the state of the land in his absence."

"Very well. See that Pan'assár gets it," said Silor, his mind racing ahead to when he would have to tell his father of his failure. They had been expecting King Thargodén's missives for many weeks, but so far, all they had intercepted was personal correspondence and now this: military code. There were only two possibilities. One was that the king had not sent anything, and that did not seem likely. The second was clear. The messages had slipped through their fingers, through *his* fingers, and found their way into the prince's hands.

"I will find a way to deliver this to Pan'assár, and good luck with *Sulén*," murmured the archer.

"*I* will deal with *Lord* Sulén. You must make sure no carriers make it past the borders of Tar'eastór. Use your contacts, Macurian. If the king's missives are already in the city, the prince will soon be sending his own correspondence to his father. It must not arrive in Ea Uaré. When you have it, you must deliver it to me."

"My lord," bowed the archer and then watched as his companion left, wrapping his luxurious cloak around his slim frame and making for his tethered horse, the symbol of the house of Sulén briefly visible as he strode away.

An hour later, Lord Sulén was, indeed, profoundly disappointed and had once more made it clear to his son, dismissing him with a cold wave of his hand. He stood now, together with Councillor Ras'dan before the hearth in his study.

"How did those missives slip by us, Sulén? Surely Thargodén does not suspect?" asked Ras'dán.

"Thargodén? No. He is finished, remains on the throne thanks to Aradan and Rinon. It is *Handir* we must watch."

"Do you think *he* suspects?"

"I have no doubt of that," said Sulén as he walked towards the windows, his silken skirts swishing over the fine carpet. "We must warn Lord Band'orán. If those loyal to Thargodén, perhaps even Handir, have managed to avoid our Shadow warriors, then he may also find a way to intercept *our* correspondence. We cannot allow that to happen."

"It won't," assured Ras'dan.

"Do not underestimate Handir, Ras'dan," said Sulén, turning from the window and coming to stand before his fellow councillor. "He is here tutoring under Damiel himself, and that is no simple *royal right*: you know Damiel. He will not be cowed into taking disciples, not even our own lordly sons, not unless they have already shown merit."

Ras'dan nodded, and Sulén turned to a mural of the Great Forest Belt, Ea Uaré as the colonisers had found it centuries ago. His own father, together with Ras'dan's, had ridden with Or'Talán, had loved him before they had despised him for betraying his Alpine heritage, for forgetting who it was that had helped him in his quest for new lands to rule. He had taken it all for himself, had left the Silvans in their forests and ignored the pleas of his faithful lords. *Band'orán* would not deny them their right to land and lordship, though. The sons of those great warriors would claim the boons their fathers should have enjoyed. Thargodén was a king that was crumbling under the weight of grief for some Silvan whore he had engendered a bastard with. It was not worthy of an Alpine king, and Band'orán knew this—they all did. The *future* king of Ea Uaré would put it right, with Ras'dan and Sulén's help, and when that happened, they would make the journey their fathers once had, take up the rule of the outer lands and rid the Forest of the vermin that infected it.

Sulén would be his own master—at last.

TWO
THE FOREST SUMMIT

"*It was the beginning of Thargodén's return. An official decree was sent to the furthest reaches of Ea Uaré and beyond, to Tar'eastór, the Motherland. Fel'annár, our Green Sun, was Ar Thargodén, a crownless half-blood lord to the Alpines but a warrior prince to the Silvans.*"
The Silvan Chronicles. Book V. Marhené.

∼

Band'orán had loved his brother Or'Talán. And then he had hated him, from the tip of his extraordinary silver mane to the hem of his kingly mantle.

Pale hands, smooth and manicured yet strong and demanding, reached out and followed the outline of the portrait beneath his fingers, not quite touching.

Brother. King. *Bane*.

This king's son, Thargodén, his own nephew, would have ruined their kingdom with his unnatural love for a Silvan peasant had Band'orán not prevented it.

Unnatural.

He smirked at the rhetoric he would use at the summit. He had mastered the art and could so easily seduce the powerful lords with his talk of racial superiority, of the *lesser* Silvan elves.

Forest vermin.

How easy it was to plant ideas in other people's minds, repeat them over and over until they became law, never questioned but simply assumed. Alpines were better than Silvans because they had built larger, more complex constructions, because they had written the Warrior Code or because they had jewels with which to trade. To have money is to be respected—to have power is to be coveted.

A knock on his study door brought him back to the present, and Band'orán's appraising eyes landed on Barathon, his only son and at his side was Lord Councillor Draugole. Barathon wore the uniform of a royal captain, and in his mind, Band'orán sneered at the boy's as yet undeserved pride. He knew nothing of command, but he *was* who he *was*, and Alpine princes must rule and command: that was Barathon's destiny. He would learn.

As for Draugole, he too knew of Barathon's shortcomings, had taken it upon himself to guide the boy in the art of statesmanship. Whether that was at all possible remained to be seen, but if anyone could achieve such a thing, it was Draugole. The councillor was no warrior, but he *was* deadly in his cunning; it was why Band'orán had sought him out all those years ago, when his plan had first begun to form in his mind.

Standing, he straightened his back, dark robes hanging perfectly around his powerful frame. Draugole and Barathon instinctively stiffened, for there was something intrinsically commanding in Band'orán, something innate he shared with his dead brother, yet where Or'Talán had inspired respect, Band'orán kindled fear.

"Father?"

Band'orán simply nodded and gestured to the seats before the fire while he turned his back on them, eyes staring unfocussed into the flames.

"And so the Forest Summit begins," he murmured. "I would have your assurances that everything is clear in your minds, that our collaborators are aware of what is required of them."

"As far as it is possible without knowing the king's mind, my lord," Draugole said. "If only we knew for sure that he knows that the Silvan bastard is alive, then I could have better prepared our collaborators, could have told them before it is made public. But without that surety we cannot disclose such information willingly."

"If the king *does* know, they will *certainly* be surprised," said Barathon.

"*Surprised?* Yes, but in what *way,* Barathon? Will they accept him? Reject him? Will the king make a stand in his favour? Disown him?" The icy grey eyes bore into those of his son, familiar notes of disapproval, sarcasm, and pity.

It was Draugole who rescued his young friend, as was so often the case.

"We cannot know, but it is our job to ensure that they take the news in a way that is favourable to *us,*" began Draugole and Band'orán turned his judgemental eyes on Draugole, nodding in approval.

"Continue, Councillor."

"It is an outrage, of course. The presence of a half-blood son is to be censured, his misbegotten status used as proof of King Thargodén's infidelity, of his faithlessness. We can rile our followers' belief in the purity of Alpine blood, the inferiority of the Forest Dwellers. We can bend it to our gain, my lords."

"Indeed, Councillor, and that is what we must achieve today. If the king knows and wishes to recognise the half-blood, we make our stand against any concession the king may grant and we must work hard to garner the support of those who are indecisive. Do you see how it must work, Barathon?"

"I do, Father—Lord Draugole."

"My lord," continued Draugole. "I am not convinced of our crown prince's convictions with respect to your endeavours. Our considerable efforts to draw him towards our beliefs and goals yield results that are often times unclear. His disdain for his father *is* clear, of course, and as such, I doubt any concessions from the king to his bastard son will be taken kindly by Rinon, but I am unsure as to whether he can be drawn completely away from his father."

"He is *ambitious*," said Barathon as he shook his head, "and his arrogance worries me. I cannot see him meekly obeying your dictates, Father. When the time comes and our plan has been executed, he will want to rule for himself."

Band'orán smiled. "If Rinon does not bend to what logic dictates, he will bend to *me*. He loves his younger brother, Handir, but above all other things, he loves his twin *sister*."

"Maeneth? You would use her against him?" asked Barathon.

Draugole's eyes sharpened and turned to Barathon. "An official invitation to some such event the princess cannot turn away from, perhaps even her own brother's coronation. She would not miss that, and once she is here, there are many ways for us to show Rinon that she is *vulnerable*. He may have to step down, forsake his royal rights to the throne in deference to the greater experience and wisdom of his uncle. After all, Rinon is a warrior more than he is a legislator. There would be no shame in that. Everyone has a weakness, Barathon. For Thargodén it is grief, and for Rinon, it is his twin. We only need Rinon for as long as it takes to prise Thargodén from the throne. After that, none of it matters. He will be in our hands."

Barathon turned to his father, who was staring impassively back at him, his irritation at his son's naivety well-buried. "But what of Handir? Surely he will not sit by and watch all this. He has a shrewd mind, Father, and he's close to Lord Aradan."

"True," said Band'orán. "But you see, Handir is far away, and the return journey is fraught with dangers for one not trained in the ways of a warrior."

Draugole's smile was soft, sad almost, and respect danced in his eyes. Barathon was slower to understand, but when his father's meaning finally sunk in, Draugole saw the first stirrings of fear. He couldn't blame the boy. His father was nonchalantly speaking of the assassination of his own blood, of a child who had sat at his knee.

"Heed me now," continued Band'orán, "we have spoken of whether Handir has informed the king about the half-blood, but it is just as important to understand whether the *Silvans* know. It is something I strongly suspect, and if they *do* indeed know, they will claim him as their lord, use him to gain the king's favour, to rally their people, and that is something we cannot allow. That boy must not be permitted to step foot inside Ea Uaré, because they will protect him, as I suspect they have been doing for fifty-two years."

"And our allies in Tar'estór?" asked Draugole.

"Sulén knows what is expected of him, Draugole. It should not be hard to dispose of him; Sulén knows what is at stake and is well-motivated to comply with my wishes. Once it is done—once Prince Handir meets with an unfortunate group of bandits and King Thargodén, already fading with grief, hears of the demise of his two younger sons—he will surely take the Long Road to Valley."

Band'orán smiled, but it did not quite reach his silver eyes, which were strangely devoid of emotion. They were his shield, his protection against those who would look too deeply and perhaps glance at his own grief, catch a passing glimmer of oddness in his soul. He could not let them see his simmering hatred, his lust for the power to change destiny—a power only kings could wield.

∼

The Silvan caravan had arrived at the city gates not two days ago and had set up their tents, their cooking pits, and even their training circles. There were makeshift pens for their animals, and even now, bakers were kneading dough for the day's bread.

Thargodén's impressive stone gates lay close enough for the Silvans to see the guards high upon the walkways, helms gleaming under the winter sun. Beyond the battlements, spires and domes jutted skywards, powerful and imposing, so foreign to one from the

Deep Forest. This strange architecture did not seek to emulate nature as Silvan designs did. Instead its purpose was to *contrast* with it. It was not ugly to look upon, but it *was* unnerving, a stark reminder of the differences between Silvans and Alpines.

Today, the first Forest Summit would commence, and it fell to two Silvans to give voice to the entire forest, a forest of people who had been subjected to Or'Talán's authority centuries ago when he had crossed the Median Mountains from Tar'eastór and colonised the land. They had been indignant at first, but soon enough, Or'Talán had endeared himself to them. He had no intention of subjugating them, he said, but of helping them to move forward in peace and equality. His strong leadership had led to the creation of a mighty army, in which Silvans and Alpines had fought and commanded equally, one that had successfully kept the enemy at bay for many years. But that had changed the moment Or'Talán had forbidden his son, Thargodén, to marry Lássira of Abiren'á. That was when the true prejudice had started, when the disdain and the discrimination had begun to hold the Silvans back.

Band'orán had started it, and perhaps now, Erthoron of Lan Taria and Lorthil of Sen'oléi could finish it.

The soft crunch of boots, and Erthoron and Golloron of Lan Taria turned to face Lorthil and Narosén of Sen'oléi. Village leaders and Spirit Herders sat before the fire in companionable silence while Golloron prepared them tea.

It was times like these when Erthoron wondered at the wisdom of their native political system. Having a group of three ruling elves for each village had many advantages in times of peace and harmony, but that was no longer the case. The time had come to force the king's hand, force the Alpines into understanding that something had to change, and yet they lacked that one figure, that leader who could speak for them all, rally them all. Their enemies at court, the Alpine purists, knew this. It was the Silvans' one disadvantage, and only one elf could remedy that.

But he was not here.

"Finally," began Lorthil. "The time has finally come."

"Yes," answered Erthoron slowly. "But we must be cautious, brother, for while there is reason to rejoice at this new opportunity, things will surely worsen before they improve; keep this firmly in your mind, Lorthil. The consequences of what we do now may be disastrous, to our people and to *him*."

"I know," smiled Lorthil, holding up an appeasing hand. But allow me this one moment," he said slyly, before turning his eyes to the trees. "So many years of silent contemplation, the decades of patience. It has not been easy, and the simple promise of our secret hope stepping into the light . . . no more deception or skulking in the dark, no more *lies*. I am not alone in these sentiments, Erthoron."

"I wonder. I wonder how things have been for young Fel'annár. He must surely know . . ." mused Lorthil.

"I believe he must," said Erthoron thoughtfully. "And I cannot help but wonder whether he can forgive his people for having deceived him his entire life."

The four elves turned their eyes to their small fire. It had been a necessary evil, something they had learned when Lássira had been murdered. Still the facts lay like bitter milk on their tongues. How they had tried to convince Amareth to tell Fel'annár of his heritage before he had ventured into the world in search of his dreams! But she had been adamant, and their silence had endured. Amareth did, indeed, hold her secrets, and Erthoron wondered if she would ever reveal the entire story of what had happened during the weeks after Fel'annár's birth.

"There has been no news from Lainon, in spite of his promises," said Erthoron. "This concerns me, and I wonder if Aradan is as much in the dark as we are about what is happening in Tar'eastór. We must seek private counsel with the chief advisor during the summit. It is entirely possible that he *has* had word but has not been able to safely inform us."

Lorthil nodded, accepting a mug of hot tea from Golloron while

Erthoron sighed deeply, brows furrowed as he reached for his own mug and continued voicing his thoughts.

"We must instil upon our people the need for caution, Lorthil. We cannot walk into Thargodén's court showing anything but mild interest, at least until he has openly explained his reasons for calling the summit, until he clearly acknowledges Fel'annár's existence." The Silvan leader cast his eyes over the colourful sea of tents that were dotted around the flat land before the city gates. Soft singing floated around them and the ever-present rhythm of drums pulsed in the background. Wherever he looked, his people smiled, their chatter quick and animated.

"I understand them, Erthoron," Lorthil said. "If the king does proclaim Fel'annár as his son, it will be difficult to contain our people's enthusiasm, difficult to hide the fact that we have always known who he was. The king may not take kindly to that," he warned and then drank.

"Perhaps not, and neither will *Band'orán*." Erthoron snorted. "Once his existence is made known, there can only be two outcomes. Success or failure: the return of *all* the noble Silvan houses at court and the reinstatement of the warlord, or rebellion. And yet it is difficult to contemplate a revolt with no central leader," he added, shaking his head. It will be all too easy for anger to lead us astray, Lorthil, and then who will pull us all together? We should create a council of our own, perhaps, with one visible leader."

"That takes time, my friend," said Lorthil, stabbing at the fire with a twig. "And yet we must at least contemplate it. The alternative is to submit to the will of those Alpine purists, and I will *die* before I see my forest lost to *them*." He adjusted his position on the ground, and Narosén watched him closely.

"And I. But will our people feel the same way? Will mothers and fathers risk the future of their children for a *dream*?" asked Erthoron wistfully.

"It is not a dream, Erthoron. It is our *right*. And here we are, full circle. We need Fel'annár here with us. You have known him since he was a child and may feel he is still too young and inexperienced to accept such a heavy burden, but *my* people, Erthoron, they remember the fire and the fanfare of Sen'oléi, and so too do we remember Sen'uár. My people believe in him. Leadership is in his blood, my friend. Those tales have spread throughout the land and our people wait now, to proclaim him as our leader, our *warlord*. I do not think we can silence them now, even should we ask."

"You both know that Fel'annár may not wish for this," said Golloron softly. "He is a warrior; the wiles of court will not interest him. All he ever wanted was to be a captain."

"But our proposition is not exactly one that would keep him at court. It is more a representation, if you will; it will not interfere with his calling as a captain. Besides," said Lorthil as he stabbed at the fire with the now charred remnants of his stick, "if he *does* accept, he will be more than just a *captain*. We must make Fel'annár see the merit in this plan we have—it is paramount to our people, *his* people. These are *our* lands, lands that harbour *guests*, guests that are free to stay or leave but not to impose their ways, not to eradicate our culture or belittle our people. We must not allow it. Not anymore. We have stood by silently for long enough."

Erthoron nodded. "I wonder what Handir, Aradan, and Lainon will think when they learn there is more to this than they had originally thought. They seek to restore the king upon his throne by gaining the consensus of the Silvans, but I do not think they understand the price of that consensus. I hope they will realise that this is the only way for the Silvans to live peacefully with the Alpines," said Erthoron, his gaze drifting sideways and to the trees beyond.

Narosén threw his tokens onto the floor and then pushed them around with his fingers, twisted locks hiding his painted face from the fire's glow, but then he sat up straighter, as if someone had whispered in his ear. The others listened, tuning their senses to the husky whispers of the trees.

"The forest is alive," said Golloron, and beside him, Narosén closed his eyes. Erthoron could only wonder what the Spirit Herders could hear, what they knew and did not say. All *he* could see was the gleam in their brilliant blue eyes, and the soft breeze that played with their dark, beaded locks.

Yet if Erthoron were to express his thoughts, he would say that something carried on the air, as if the Forest held its leafy breath, restless roots swirling beneath the loamy ground, searching for a way up and into the light, just like the Silvan people did now.

The Forest slept no more, despite the winds of winter. Awake now, it would surely no longer be silenced.

⁓

Crown Prince Rinon rapped on the king's door, nodding curtly at the guards as he passed inside and waited for his father to address him. Aradan stood at the king's side, his formal robes of state lending the councillor an air of authority. The experience and wisdom that always sat behind his eyes was reflected now in his attire, and the occasion called for no less. However, if Aradan was splendid in his finery, the king was beyond description. Rinon watched the attendants working on the finer details of the king's hair and crown, adjusting the fall of his mantle and the sheen of his jewels as he stood, back to the door. Rinon bowed even though he knew the king would not see.

And then the monarch turned to face him and Rinon's heart sped out of control. A blast of raw power slammed into his iron defences. He faltered.

"Crown Prince Rinon."

"My king." Rinon allowed his eyes to drift over the elf he had not seen in over half a century. *This* was Or'Talán's son, his own father. A *king* stood before him, not some grief-stricken elf with a fading soul that Rinon told himself he despised. He could not help the unnaturally long stare, and then barely managed to contain a flinch when the king finally spoke.

"Come," said Thargodén, gesturing to the hearth. "Sit with me before we begin the summit. Aradan," he invited with a tilt of his head.

Rinon nodded curtly and then sat in an armchair beside his father, eyes lingering on the monarch's hand as he poured wine. The familiar, rough-cut emerald hung from his index finger as it always had, a symbol of the Alpines of Ea Uaré. It was an odd piece, for of all the jewels the king had at his disposal, he chose to wear *this* emerald. It was irregular and unpolished and it looked broken to Rinon's eyes. But his father was fond of it, and Rinon never bothered to ask why. Still, he grudgingly admitted his father looked quite stunning, powerful in his jewels and brocades, as natural as a squirrel in its fur, and a surge of unwanted pride rolled through him.

He brushed it off.

"Have you ventured past the walls this morning, my prince?" asked Aradan, accepting the goblet the king held out to him.

"I have, Councillor. It is a heaving mass of Silvan colour. Uncle Band'orán will be *ecstatic*."

Thargodén's mouth tightened, but he said nothing.

"Your summons has been a great success, my king; all the village leaders have come, each with their Spirit Herders and foresters. Even Miren's village is represented, and for that she is driving me to insanity," said Aradan.

The king smirked. Aradan's wife was a character not easily forgotten. Daughter of one of the few remaining noble houses of the Silvan people, the tribal leaders of Sen Garay, the woman was prone to filling silences with her incessant chatter. She was a breath of fresh, Silvan air, so long as one did not expose himself for too long. Still, Thargodén envied his friend for his lovely wife. She was such an unlikely match for his intellectual councillor, but Thargodén understood that attraction all too well. That natural wildness that hung about the Silvans, their unashamed display of emotions and passions, their giddy love of life had been equally irresistible to him.

And then his thoughts of Miren and, ultimately, of Lássira led him to think of Aradan's absent daughter. She had left with harsh words of censure, and Aradan never spoke of it.

"The appearance of my youngest son and my acceptance of him *will* be made known," said the king suddenly.

Silence settled around the three elves. Aradan already knew this, but Rinon stared disbelievingly at his father.

"You cannot be serious. Publicly announce you have a bastard son? Recognise that you were unfaithful to your queen?" he asked, his incredulous face searching his father for signs that he had misunderstood.

"You think they will not find out, Rinon? They say he closely resembles my father. It will not be difficult to draw conclusions considering the public nature of my involvement with Lássira. It is better they hear it from me rather than be left to discover him by chance. That would give them the impression that I do not care."

Rinon stared at his father and then turned his head to the crackling fire. Aradan watched him closely, analysing the prince's feelings he did not hide well.

"Does the boy have a name then?" asked Rinon after a while, as if he did not care.

"Fel'annár," said Thargodén simply.

"Well, you don't get more Silvan than *that*," he scoffed.

"You do not approve, of course," said Thargodén with a twitch of his lips.

"I do *not*. What warrior of renown is named after a *flower*, by Aria!"

Aradan stifled his bubbling humour and turned back to the king as he continued to brief them on his intentions.

"I cannot name him *prince*, as he was not born to the queen. And yet I must acknowledge him, and there will come a time when you will meet Fel'annár, Rinon. I will expect you to comport yourself as befitting a crown prince," he said, eyes lingering meaningfully on his son.

"I cannot foresee that, Father. I cannot foresee how I will feel when I see him. One thing I *can* say—I will not welcome him as a long-lost *brother*. I am sure you can appreciate this," he said.

"So long as you do not disgrace yourself, Rinon."

Aradan saw the spark of hurt in Rinon's eyes at the king's words. He *did* care, he *did* want the love and attention from his father that had been denied him since the queen had left, but it was beyond him to show his need. He was too proud, too much like his grandfather.

"I have passed a royal decree," continued the king. "He is named a Lord of Ea Uaré."

Rinon nodded slowly while Aradan stood.

"I should be leaving, my king," said the councillor. "I must pave the way for your appearance this evening." He nodded at father and son and then glided from the room. Thargodén watched him leave, wondering if he had sensed the king's desire to speak personally with his son. It would not surprise him at all.

"Rinon," he began, turning to face his son, studying him for a moment before continuing. "Whatever you may think, in spite of the years of neglect, never doubt my love for you."

Rinon was taken aback by his father's sudden turn of conversation and was reminded of the events from just weeks before. It had been a pivotal day in which the king had told him of the Silvan boy, his bastard child and Rinon's own half-brother. He and his father had argued, and yet strangely, the years of silent anger and regret had snapped, leaving them both swimming upon strange tides. The king had once more begun to rule the land, and with that change, so too had he begun to demand a change in Rinon.

He had tried to comply, but still, you cannot eradicate years of anger, cannot mend the hurt that had been done after one single moment of truth, one simple admission. It would take much more for Rinon to trust his father as he once had, *love* him as he once had. But that did not stop his tongue from disobeying his mind. The king had, indeed, changed, but so had Rinon.

Turning in his chair, Rinon looked squarely at the king. "I cannot change years of bitterness. I was old enough to see the damage you did to my mother, to my brother and my twin sister. Handir was not entirely aware, but Maeneth and I *were*. I tried to minimise our mother's absence, explain it away when my own heart was breaking, and I *hated* you for that," he said harshly. "Now that I know some of the details, that my grandfather started all this by prohibiting your love for the Silvan woman—now that I know the extent of your love for her and my own mother's prior knowledge of it, my rational mind can understand these things, but the damage was done, and I acted in consequence. It has made me who I am. It has made me *how* I am." Rinon's words had simply tumbled from his mouth, and he desperately tried to hide his own surprise.

"And can you change that? With time, can you come to love me once more?" asked the king softly.

Rinon's eyes felt too full, and he screamed at himself to not show how much the king's words meant to him. He would not allow his father to see his weakness—he had not earned it.

"I can try," he said as he stood, pulling on his ceremonial uniform until it was perfectly straight. "I have duties, my king."

"You may leave," murmured the king, watching as his eldest child once again closed the door that led to his heart and strode from the room.

He knew that his crown prince would still fight him as surely as he knew Rinon would fight the Silvan boy, for in *him* was the physical evidence of his father's disgrace, his mother's betrayal, and his own ensuing bitterness.

But Thargodén would cling to the hope that, perhaps someday, he could redeem those empty years of fatherly neglect.

He had to. His children were all he had.

～

Thargodén's court was brimming with councillors and legislators, lords and ladies, commanders and merchants, all of them decked in their most distinguished attire, heavy jewels on display for the first time in many years, for through the cycles of Thargodén's grief, there had been no events worthy enough to don them.

It was a sea of bobbing, blond heads, dotted only sparsely by the occasional brown or auburn mane of a Silvan—that is, until the Deep Forest arrived and the din was silenced, replaced now with curious whisperings as village leaders, Spirit Herders, and foresters filed into the Great Council Hall, chins jutted defiantly. Their brown and honey eyes danced over the strangeness of the Alpines, for to *their* eyes, they seemed alien to this land, so far removed from the natural simplicity of the Silvans even though they resided here, in what they *thought* was the heart of the realm. Most had never even *seen* the Deep Forest, had no understanding of how wrong they were about that.

The Alpines in turn, watched the Silvans, eyes registering their heavily decorated braids, hair adorned with flowers and vines, coloured cord and river stones. Some smiled in distant interest while others smirked, leered and whispered words of disdain.

Aradan watched the interaction from afar, a thoughtful look on his face. The truth was that any hope he had held to, that agreement and consensus would be found, was fast dwindling, for there was no common ground that he could see. The living land and the ruling lords were not one and the same. It was a recipe for strife.

Turning, Aradan spotted Turion, dressed magnificently in the formal uniform that marked him as a member of the Inner Circle—an Alpine Captain. General Huren, Pan'assár's second and acting commander general, was at his side, talking with an Alpine merchant. Aradan gestured to Turion, and soon, the two elves were greeting each other warmly. They had barely met before that day when Turion and Lainon had revealed the existence of Fel'annár, yet since then they had spoken often of the situation in the Forest, of Fel'annár and of their plans to restore a strong king upon the throne. They had not always agreed, but they had come to respect one another. Friendship came easily after that.

"How are things at the barracks, Turion? Is city life agreeing with you, or is the great open calling you home?" he asked with a smirk.

Turion returned it. "Well, a bit of both I suppose. Aye, I miss the young ones, but this was the price I paid so that Fel'annár could pursue his training, so that our plan could be set into motion—that is payment enough," he smiled, and Aradan nodded. Indeed, that was exactly what the captain had done, a boon that General Huren had wrought from him in exchange for leading Fel'annár on his first patrol.

"What an event," said Turion absently as he watched the elves around him.

"Aye," said Aradan. "It promises to be *interesting* at the least." His comment was more than a little evasive, and Turion turned to him, askance.

"There has been little forthcoming knowledge on the summit, Lord Aradan. The warriors are anxious that perhaps something has happened, while the lords reckon new trade routes are to be opened. Yet it is the *Silvans* that puzzle me," he said with a frown.

Aradan turned to the captain and studied him for a moment. "How so? What do they say?" he asked.

"That is the point. They do *not*; they say nothing—they simply smile, as if they know something the rest of us do not. Something strange is happening, and I would wager on the truth of it." He turned now, his eyes sparkling with a challenge, and Aradan nodded.

"Turion, we know that Erthoron knows, and from what you say, it is possible that he has told his people, in which case, our king's announcement will only be a surprise to the Alpine lords and ladies. Now our king is joyous, but I cannot help thinking there will be more opposition from our Alpine people than we had originally anticipated. Band'orán has been most productive in his slow poisoning of our once tolerant society."

Turion cast his eyes around the crowds, unable to refute Aradan's worries. "He is publicly recognising him then," he murmured, and Aradan nodded. "That, at least, is encouraging and I wonder, if it is enough to bring him back to us." He shook his head, as if to refute his own words. "Look at them. Our people look upon the natives of this land as if they were trespassing. What travesty is this, Aradan? What have we done to create this land of ignorant bigots? How has it been tolerated for so long? It is an infection I do not know we can cure, and the Inner Circle is riddled with it. Even if Thargodén *can* react, find himself and be the strong king he once was, I wonder if it is not already too late."

Aradan studied Turion, tried and tested commander—Alpine and yet immersed in the culture of his forest home, truly comfortable amongst the Silvans, just like he himself had learned to become. Turion possessed a natural wisdom that Aradan could not help but admire. The commander surprised him with his next words.

"Our missives for Tar'eastór have had ample time to arrive, and yet no answers have been sent, or perhaps they have and were intercepted," said Turion, his eyes landing for a moment on Band'orán across the Hall. "Still, we must trust Prince Handir and Lainon to prepare Fel'annár. The poor boy has no idea of the storm that awaits him."

Aradan nodded slowly. "I only hope that Handir can come to terms with his brother's existence, not blame him for his mother's departure, his father's fall. I have written long and thoughtfully to him, but such questions oftentimes do not adhere to cold reasoning, Turion. Rinon is a good example of that."

"Lainon will help him. I, too, have written in similar terms to our Ari'atór," said Turion.

Turning to the sound of guards snapping to attention, the two elves looked to the open doors of the great Council Hall, where the king now stood—resplendent.

Magnificent.

It was his first formal engagement since his return from the depths of his grief, and the Hall fell abruptly into silence. An elf gasped, the sharp sound lingering, its underlying emotion mirrored by those who looked on. Even the Silvans stood rooted, hands poised upon their mighty wooden staffs. It had been many years since they had seen King Thargodén Ar Or'Talán. Aradan's heart thudded, its rhythm strange, and his skin pulled tight and cold. Turion lowered his head in respect.

A shimmering silver vest of thin, exquisite armour lay over a sky-blue shirt of fine silk and a skirt of muted violet that reached down to his calves. His cloak was a striking green, so long it hung behind him and pooled upon the polished floor in a short trail, like moss spilling over stone, and upon his head of silver hair lay the crown he had not worn since the queen had left, hugging his face and cheekbones as would a lover's hands.

At his hip sat a mighty sword Aradan knew had been Or'Talán's, and as the king began to walk down the centre of the hall, one hand rested on its pommel. Upon his index finger was the rough emerald Thargodén had never removed.

The people bowed low, even the Silvans, faces still and expectant. If Thargodén had been looking to make a statement, he had certainly achieved his goal.

The crown prince was at his shoulder, decked in the ceremonial uniform of a royal captain, ice-cold eyes fixed to the fore. Only Aradan knew what lay in his mind, the turmoil of incompatible emotions: hatred, love, rebellion, deference. He was the perfect target for Band'orán, one he would not let go of easily, but then again, Rinon was no easy foe. His one weakness was his emotions towards his father, a weakness Band'orán had been trying to shape to his own advantage for many years. Aradan was still unsure as to his success.

Arriving at his throne at the end of the hall, the king turned and sat, face placid, eyes *alive*. Rinon stood to one side, the picture of a duteous prince despite the doubts in his mind, and Aradan silently commended him.

Three loud, dull thuds marked the commencement of the summit, and it fell to Aradan to inaugurate the talks. With a nod at Turion, he moved into the centre of the Hall with practised confidence and turned his eyes to the Silvans on one side and then to the

Alpines on the other. Opening his arms in a gesture of welcome, he launched his powerful, well-seasoned voice, carefully modulated words capturing the attention of all.

"My lords, ladies, warriors and merchants, Ari'atór and foresters, subjects all. Please be welcome to the court of our King Thargodén Ar Or'Talán.

"Today, we commence the first Forest Summit, one of many, to be celebrated every three years. Its purpose?" he asked somewhat theatrically, "to bring together the representatives of the Alpine and Silvan people, to share our concerns, our needs, to solve our problems and lend aid, wherever it may be needed, so that Ea Uaré may vanquish its foes and be great once more, that she prosper to the best of her abilities. For this, we have called upon you, good elves of the Great Forest Belt. Together we will pave the way for a better land, a more just and prosperous society."

Here he stopped and waited for the timid applause to dwindle, studiously ignoring the blank stares of the Silvan leaders. He could not blame them for their scepticism.

"Today, our King Thargodén has an announcement to make. Afterwards, an inquiry into the state of the land will be heard and documented so that tomorrow, we may begin the talks."

Turning, he gestured to the king with a deep bow. All eyes shifted to the shockingly beautiful figure who stood in a rustle of silks and moved towards Aradan.

Lord Band'orán cast a sideways glance at his son, Barathon, and his close friend, Draugole. Band'orán was good at many things, but he excelled in the art of masking the truth. And the truth was that he had been lax. He had not foreseen this, for Thargodén was not the broken king he thought to usher onto the Long Road to Valley. It was surely the appearance of the bastard child that had brought him back, rekindled his flame, his desire to live and to rule.

"My lords, ladies, warriors and merchants, Silvan village leaders, Spirit Herders, and foresters, I welcome you warmly to my court," began Thargodén, eyes steadily scanning the crowds, gauging their emotions, their reactions. "The news I bring you today is cause for joy, joy I hope you, too, will share with me. I must announce to you the existence of a fourth royal child, son of my blood, son of the House of Or'Talán. I publicly recognise this child as my son and grant all privileges and titles save that of '*Prince*.'"

The king was forced to stop, for the steadily rising voices rapidly turned into a full-blown din. There were words of genuine shock and curiosity, others of outrage. There was instant speculation and brash judgement. But *all* of those voices were Alpine. The Silvans stood before them in silence, a knowing smile upon their faces, smiles that slowly widened until their teeth shone in the early evening light and all attention fell upon them.

It was the precise moment in which Erthoron and Lorthil realised that their people would not heed their plea for caution. They had not *wanted* to feign indifference, had not *wanted* to wait any longer. One voice cut through the silence.

"All hail The *Silvan*!"

A mighty cheer rang out loud and clear, wooden staffs banging upon the stone floors, a rumble of Silvan defiance. Another voice shouted over the rest.

"All hail Fel'annár Ar Thargodén!"

The cheer was louder now as the Silvans raised their clenched fists as one. Aradan's fine hairs stood on end, his eyes falling on a confused Thargodén, a disapproving Rinon, and a carefully controlled Band'orán.

The Alpines stood frozen with indecision while Aradan's mind worked frantically. He knew that Erthoron was aware of the child, but the entire Silvan party were not only simply aware but exuberant, *proud*. They had called Thargodén's son by his *name* before the king had had time to do so.

They all *knew*, not because Erthoron had just told them, but because they had *always* known, realised Aradan, and now, the Deep Forest would be tossed into a heaving sea of strong wills and demands. More than ever, this absurd rivalry between Alpines and Silvans would come to a head, with Fel'annár in the very midst of it.

Those Silvan staffs of ancient wood beating against the stone floors had been a proclamation of Silvan defiance, and it shook the floor beneath their feet. There was no going back.

Either Fel'annár was welcomed by the Alpines or the Silvans would rebel.

THREE
HOMECOMING

"The heart is a stubborn fool. It denies the truth, is blind to reason. All it can do is feel, but it doesn't think at all. It can lead to the greatest of deeds, but so too can it lead to cruelty, hatred, and resentment. Only the reasoning mind can put those feelings into perspective."
On Elven Nature. Calro.

~

The battle-weary patrol had been navigating the surrounding forests for an hour, climbing the boulder-strewn slopes that led upwards and to the mountain citadel of Tar'eastór. King Vorn'asté's seat of power loomed above them in the afternoon gloom, and at last its mighty gates were groaning and then creaking as the slabs of wood and stone opened inwards, enough only for Comon's battered patrol to file into the courtyard, silent and grey under the sorrowful, respectful gazes of those citizens brave enough to be out on this cold, wet winter day.

Fel'annár's gaze fixed upon the statues that decorated the battlements, each one separated by a space just large enough for an archer to fit and fire a bow. They were warriors, but what had always drawn his attention was that they were all different. Some held one long sword, others two. Some were archers and others were standing with no weapons at all save for their hands. He would ask Gor'sadén who they were when time permitted.

"Fel'annár."

He startled and then turned to Prince Sontúr, who rode at his side.

"Ready for another taste of Arané's foul potions?"

Fel'annár mustered a crooked smile but said nothing, and the haggard warriors dismounted. One crumpled to the floor, but Arané's healers were already there to pick him up while others walked amongst the group, sharp eyes assessing, analysing. Across the courtyard, a new patrol was preparing to leave, watching them respectfully as they mounted, their eyes drawn to the number of unclaimed swords strapped to Captain Comon's horse.

"Fel'annár," called Comon. "Report to the War Room tomorrow morning. I would have you explain your *skills* to the commander."

"Aye, Captain. Sir, I have—I would speak with you about that. There are details which I believe are important. A song from the trees I would discuss."

"Can it wait?" asked Comon, his eyes glancing over to the awaiting group of elves Fel'annár knew were the family, friends, and children of the fallen. He averted his gaze, unable to watch. He would have to, though, one day when he was a captain.

"Yes, Sir."

Comon nodded and then turned to his patrol, raising his voice over the din. "You have all served well. Rest while you can, for the enemy does not. Tar'eastór is grateful. Dismissed."

The patrol saluted as one, but for The Company, it took a moment for them to understand that they had been *thanked*. They were unused to praise, and for one, wonderful moment, Fel'annár realised that it didn't matter who he was or what he looked like, and he wondered if such a simple thing would ever be true in Ea Uaré, whether he would ever hear these simple words of praise given by an Alpine captain to his Silvan troops. It bolstered their sense of purpose, their sense of duty to the realm and its people. It made the hardship worthwhile.

It had indeed been an arduous few weeks. Fel'annár had been their scout, had warned them of encroaching danger thanks to his ever-evolving skill. He had fought for three and had decimated the Deviant archers with his unparalleled archery. The warriors had welcomed him, if a little warily at first, and then heartily as he had endeared himself to them with his questions and his diligence and his Silvan humour. Ramien had come to the rescue of many an Alpine warrior with his massive axe and hands that spanned the width of a human head. Ferocious in battle and generous in his good humour, he was loved. Galdith, too, had earned their respect with his agility in battle and his Silvan tales at night, and as for Carodel, his irreverent songs had lifted their hearts at breakfast and then later, after the battles when he would sing the ancient lays of hope and love. Galadan was an enigma, stone-faced and unflinching. He was a lieutenant yet even so had served as a warrior, had helped Sontúr in his duties as healer. As for Idernon, he was the odd one, but his knowledge had been a source of inspiration and entertainment. The troop had taken to asking him the strangest, most unlikely questions, but the Wise Warrior had always answered. Little had they known that at times, Idernon had lied just to give them an answer, but only The Company could tell that he *had*.

Releasing his feet from the stirrups, Fel'annár dismounted carefully, trying and failing to land softly and avoid the lance of pain that shot through his temples.

"We are well enough, Fel'annár," said Galadan. "We return to the barracks to bathe and eat. You go to Arané, and join us when you will. You don't have to feign health anymore." The Alpine lieutenant of The Company sought Sontúr's gaze, his silent request for the prince to keep an eye on Fel'annár understood, and Sontúr nodded curtly back at him. Fel'annár was too tired to notice, and so he hung his throbbing head and followed Sontúr and the flow of healers and injured warriors to the now familiar doors of the Halls of Healing.

Inside, it was warm, and Fel'annár shivered at the contrast. An assistant ushered him in the direction of the recovery area, and Fel'annár made straight for the roaring fire. Slowly, he lowered himself to his knees and held his frigid hands to the fire, under the scrutiny of the patients already there, mostly warriors sporting minor wounds they had gained upon the training fields or on previous patrols. They watched as he warmed himself, observing the soft shake of his hands, the way he sniffled miserably and blinked a little too often. They saw the wear on his uniform, the fading bruises and scratches upon his face, and the blank stare in his extraordinary green eyes.

"Silvan," called one warrior. "How goes it in the north?" he asked, for there could be no mistaking where he had been serving these past weeks.

Fel'annár turned and met the warrior's gaze squarely, his eyes steady, emotionless. "It goes ill, Warrior," he said softly before turning back to the fire, sniffling again.

"Fel'annár? Warrior Fel'annár?"

"Here," he said, still facing the fire. The sound of his name being called rang differently, and something triggered in his mind. That was no *Alpine* accent. He turned where he knelt only to look up into the concerned eyes of a healer. But her concern rapidly turned to utter shock. The mug of steaming herbal tea in her hands jolted, not quite enough for the liquid to escape and burn her. Fel'annár briefly wondered if his eyes had lit up without him realising, but he soon discarded that idea. No one was running from the room.

She was Silvan. There was only one other reason for her reaction. She had recognised him as a scion of the House of Or'Talán, first king of Ea Uaré.

"Drink this, Warrior," she ordered, pushing the mug into his reddened hands and visibly collecting herself. He wrapped his freezing fingers around the hot mug and then drank it down, relishing in the feel of it as it warmed his frigid body. His eyes, though, lingered on the healer, wondering what she was thinking even as he told himself he was too tired to care one way or the other.

"Go to the baths at the end of this aisle; you know the way I assume? Get out of those clothes and into the tubs. I'll not be long."

He nodded, questions accumulating in his mind. Where did she come from? Were there other Silvans in Tar'eastór? Had she come with messengers from Ea Uaré? But she was busy and all he could do was watch as she left, and when he had lost sight of her amongst the wounded and recovering, he turned back to the fire. Swallowing down the rest of the concoction, he stood on shaky feet.

"Recover your strength soonest, Brothers. There is much to be done," he said softly, his eyes meeting them all and then walking away under the respectful gazes of Alpine warriors who knew nothing of the discrimination against the Silvan fighters of Ea Uaré. They only knew what the others were saying: that this young warrior had fought well, that he listened to trees—that he was the *worthy* grandson of Or'Talán, first Alpine king of the Silvan lands of Ea Uaré.

～

"He's back."

Gor'sadén, commander general of Tar'eastór, looked up from his desk and to Pan'assár, who stood on the balcony, leaning over the vertiginous rock face below, blond hair fluttering in the frigid breeze.

"The Silvan. Comon's patrol has just arrived," clarified the Forest commander.

"Are they all right?" asked Gor'sadén, snapping his book shut and getting up to join his friend. Blue eyes looked down upon the battered patrol far below, his own question answered.

"As well as a warrior can be, I suppose, after serving in these times," said Commander Pan'assár. "They have been away for longer than expected," he added as he watched Comon dismiss his warriors and then Fel'annár as he walked into the Healing Halls.

"Captain Comon will have news," said Gor'sadén as he turned back inside. "We must understand why Deviant activity is so high. It is disturbing, Pan'assár; we need more intelligence. We need to speak with the Ari'atór." Gor'sadén raked a hand through his unbraided hair and turned back to his desk. "I have sent out messengers to Araria. They should have arrived by now, but it will take the Ari'atór some time to get here. You know, something tells me this is not a simple increase in the number of humans seeking immortality. Something drives them, Pan, something we have yet to understand."

"I remember Galadan commenting on something to that effect after the attack on our convoy. Their tactics were too advanced, too orchestrated to be random, he said. I would accompany you to hear Comon's reports tomorrow. The sooner the Ari'atór get here, the better. If anyone can say what this is, it is the Spirit Warriors."

Pan'assár walked towards his friend. "And I have received a message from General Huren. He says Deviant activity in Ea Uaré is *normal*."

Gor'sadén nodded. This was *not* a widespread phenomenon then, just as he had suspected. Whatever it was, it was happening in Tar'eastór and perhaps in Araria. He turned towards the fire, feeling Pan'assár just beside him.

"The *boy* is in the Halls of Healing. You'll be visiting him, I suppose."

Gor'sadén closed his eyes. He had thought his friend was over the sarcastic comments and open hostility towards Or'Talán's illicit, half-Silvan grandchild, yet even now, the odd comment would escape the commander, as if he could not help but belittle him, an irresistible urge to debase him. Gor'sadén's only solace was that compared to but two months ago, Pan'assár was almost complimenting the boy.

"I will visit *Fel'annár* when he has rested. Tomorrow, if he is still in the Halls. Will you not visit *your* warrior, Commander?" asked Gor'sadén, jaw clenching in irritation.

"Of course," replied Pan'assár evenly, knowing he had riled his friend. "Prince Handir will surely tell the boy of the arrival of missives from the Forest and the singular information they contain. Once that is done, we shall see. Despite what you may think, I *am* proud of my soldiers."

Gor'sadén nodded. He *did* want to see Fel'annár, but he also needed to tell him that Pan'assár had agreed to giving him a test, one which, should he pass, would allow him to become an apprentice of the Kal'hamén'Ar. Gor'sadén could only hope Fel'annár was not too badly wounded, because there would be no second chances with Pan'assár. If the Forest commander could avoid Fel'annár becoming an apprentice, a Kah Warrior, Gor'sadén knew he would play his hand and use every advantage he had. And yet the last time they had spoken of the Kal'hamén'Ar, Pan'assár had been adamant that they should not hide Fel'annár's trial. It would not take place publicly—that would go against the Warrior Code—but it *would* be announced. It was time for their young warriors to remember the Kal'hamén'Ar, to dream that perhaps, one day, they too could earn the honour of becoming a Kah Warrior and weave the Dance of Graceful Death.

Gor'sadén could see the advantages of bringing back the ancient art. It had almost passed into legend with the breaking of The Three, the death of Or'Talán and one of the last remaining Masters of the Kah. Perhaps he was wrong, mused Gor'sadén; perhaps Pan'assár was *not* as reticent as he seemed. Perhaps it was that stubborn pride that marked his character which was impeding him from finally accepting Fel'annár as a potential ally and not a shameful enemy to be scorned and discriminated against.

~

Fel'annár's clothes were sodden, his fingers so unresponsive he fumbled with the clasps and buttons until frustration drove him to pull too hard. Stopping with a sigh of frustration, he calmed himself and started again, slowly unfastening his quiver and placing it upon the table, his eyes roving over the poor state of his weapons. There had been no time to clean them after their latest skirmish and after, he had not been able.

Next, he unbuckled his pauldron and chest protection, scratched and scuffed leather and metal falling with a heavy thud. Then came his vambraces, which he set respectfully beside his quiver, and soon he stood naked and filthy. Raking one bare forearm over his brow, he stepped into his bathing cubicle and immersed himself in the steaming tub. He promptly ducked under the surface, feeling his hair as it floated around him. It was bliss and he took his time unravelling his thick, twisted locks, running his fingers through the now loose strands after what seemed like months.

Reaching for the soaps that stood upon a nearby ledge, he scrubbed at his scalp again and again, even though his fingers hurt, and then began on his body, almost obsessively. Releasing the filthy water, he rose and stepped into the next tub down, the water clean and fragrant. He wanted to stay there, weightless and warm, but he would surely fall asleep, so he pulled himself out and wrapped a towel around his waist. Padding into the main hall, he picked up another towel on his way and dried his hair.

He caught his own reflection in the window as he passed, and he stopped mid-stride. He had become stronger during this last patrol. Although he had already been well-muscled, the planes and ridges were now more acutely defined. And yet he had learned something of the limits of that strength, had learned that he was not indestructible. He could have died out there—he had allowed tiredness and distraction to lower his defences and had almost paid the highest price.

He needed a comb, but his pack was nowhere to be seen. He turned in search of help only to find the Silvan healer standing not far away, practiced eyes roving over his body, and for the first time he could remember, he felt the inexplicable need for clothes.

"Here. Use this bed for today," she said, handing him a long linen shirt.

"I can't stay, Healer. It's not necessary."

"You are a *healer*?" she asked with an arch of her auburn brow. That accent...

Fel'annár opened his mouth to speak, but she promptly cut him off.

"You suffered a recent concussion. It is protocol—you know this. Don't argue and waste my time."

He wanted to defend himself, but all that came to him was a lame smile, the first in many weeks, for she sounded like home. That lilting accent and the bluntness in her tone, the bossy manner of a concerned healer who would brook no compromise.

"You're Silvan," he mumbled. The healer looked up at him and then smiled. It was not soft and endearing but mischievous and just a touch challenging.

"Oh, aye, I'm Silvan, and if you know anything about Silvan healers, it's best you still your tongue, Warrior. Sit down."

And Fel'annár did. He wanted to tell her that *he* was Silvan, too, but she wouldn't believe him, and in any case, he was distracted by her lovely eyes. He was drawn to her, like a soft bed in the night, like the smell of pea soup on a hazy Sunday morning. He didn't understand—all he knew was that she was fresh and clean, her eyes sharp and keen, lips full and soft.

She sat next to him on the bed and reached out to prod at his head. He watched her, saw how she, too, watched him from the corner of her eyes. "A sword hilt?" she asked.

"Aye. A lucky strike."

"Well, I'm sure its wielder paid the price."

It *had*, but he wasn't giving her the details. Instead he fell into the soft, silent melody that seemed to wrap around her, a protective embrace he too wanted to feel. It was a melody that spoke of the Forest, and his heart ached. A strong hand rested on his shoulder, and he lay back. The same hand swiped his damp hair to one side and lingered there for a while. His eyelids felt heavy as the herbs he had drunk began to numb his aching body and his conscious mind. The last thing he remembered before deep slumber took him was the brush of a soft hand over his face, a caring healer's hand; it surely didn't belong to the commanding Silvan that would be looking down on him now. He felt safe, and for a fleeting moment, his worries faded and there was blessed peace before oblivion.

Tomorrow he would continue to ponder the questions that assailed him mercilessly: what was this strange message from the trees? The spark of emotion he had seen in a Deviant's eye? How could he explain it to Captain Comon in any understandable way when he didn't understand it himself? And what of his powers? They had evolved, grown stronger and more diverse. *Fear* had begun to stir in his mind, fear of how much more there was, fear that he might not be able to control it. And then he remembered his father, the one he had never met. Lainon had said there would soon be news from the Forest, news that had the power to change his life completely. Lainon's face floated before his mind's eye, and for a moment that fear was tempered.

But how his heart ached for his lost brother!

This Silvan healer had reminded him of home, of where he came from. He didn't know if he could ever return, and even though he loved that place, he was no longer sure he *wanted* to.

∼

Dawn had long-since passed. Fel'annár had slept for longer than he had done in weeks, and his stomach growled in protest. He wondered if he would still be in time for a hearty breakfast at the barracks and perhaps escape the bland gruel he knew they would serve here in the Healing Halls. The barrack cooks always indulged the warriors on their first day back from patrol; he knew what would be sitting upon the long tables even now—fluffy eggs and *sausages*.

Sitting stiffly on the edge of his bed, he took a deep breath and turned his head to the footboard. His uniform lay neat, clean and pressed, and beside it a new under-tunic. Propped against one side of the wooden frame were his weapons. He would find time to care for them later.

His gaze wandered down the long aisle of beds, half of which were occupied. Conflict was escalating, and questions needed to be asked. Indeed, even now, Captain Comon would be briefing Commander Gor'sadén on the events of their tour in the mountains, and Fel'annár had his own thoughts to add, even though he had yet to straighten them out in his own mind. Emotions in a Deviant's eyes, the song from the trees—if it all sounded strange to *him*, he knew it would be hard to believe for those who did not know him well, except perhaps for Gor'sadén. He had been present when Fel'annár had felt the return of Tar'eastór's queen; he had seen the Winter Sentinel bloom, seen his own, unnerving transformation. Still, a commander cannot base himself on anything but hard facts to take his decisions, and what Fel'annár had to say was not . . . *logical*.

Despite his good night's sleep, he was bone weary. His muscles ached, and his head thumped in time with his heart. Standing, he pulled on his battle-worn uniform, leaving the outer jerkin unbuttoned, and hastily braided his hair. He was not on duty, but he hardly had any clothes of his own, not that it mattered, for without coin, there was nowhere to go save for the barracks, and neither he nor The Company had a penny between them. What was important now was food, real food at the barracks.

He cast a guilty gaze around the Halls and then grabbed his two weapons harnesses, thinking to make a sly escape. Straightening, he came face-to-face with Prince Sontúr. All thoughts of eluding the healers and their gruel crumbled before the acutely arched eyebrow of his friend.

"Just where do you think you are going?" he asked with a smirk. Sontúr was dressed as a prince today, silk and velvet garments vivid and clean, his grey hair immaculately braided, but his face was pale, eyes puffy and just a little slanted.

Fel'annár's lip curled, but it was almost a smile as he slung his harnesses over his shoulder. "Are you going to *stop* me?" he asked with feigned anger. Sontúr's brow arched even higher on his forehead.

"I came to *rescue* you, you fool. I have spoken with your healer. She says you are free to leave." After a while he added, "She's *Silvan*, you know."

"Yes, I had noticed," said Fel'annár, rolling his eyes.

"And she's lovely."

Fel'annár nodded. She *was* lovely and he wondered if Sontúr had plans. He turned to look at his friend, and Sontúr grinned, holding up both hands as if in surrender.

"Now, now. I'm just saying."

"Do you know if she rode in with company? Has there been news from Ea Uaré?"

"Not that I know of. She must have ridden in with the Pelagians my father spoke of, in which case she's only been here for a day."

Fel'annár nodded and then clapped a hand on his friend's velvet-clad shoulder. "Sausages," he said challengingly, and for all that Sontúr was a prince, he loved his sausages as much as the rest of The Company did. It was time to leave this place that smelled of herbs and tinctures, but Fel'annár cast his eyes around the Halls one last time, in case he had missed something—but the honey-eyed Silvan healer with a sharp tongue and a soft touch was nowhere to be found.

∽

Breakfast at the barracks was far too noisy, but the hot food was enough for Fel'annár to endure it. The Company had tried and failed to engage him with idle chat, but his mind was not at the table—it was in the war room where he knew the commanders would be. He had much to think about, things he was not sure they would believe. Still, he would try, even if it earned him a cold, cruel sneer from his own commander general. Instinct told him it was important, and he had learned not to ignore it.

"I've no idea what to do now. We've been away for so long, and suddenly I'm free and penniless in Tar'eastór," said Carodel and then packed a hunk of bread into his mouth, cheeks bulging as he chewed.

"Penniless in Tar'eastór," snorted Galdith. "There are plenty of things to do without money, Carodel."

"Ah yes, let's see. A *picnic*. What say you brothers? There is nothing *better* after a spree of Deviant slaughtering: a basket oozing culinary delights, a sultry amble through the woods, or perhaps a *swim* and a merry song to welcome the spring!"

"Carodel, you *fool*," muttered Galadan before adding, "I'm sure our commander will provide us with our wages; in fact I'll mention it to him."

"We've yet to experience the city taverns. The others visit regularly, yet the pockets of us poor Silvans are filled with nothing but our own kneecaps—no coin to be found at all," moaned Carodel.

Ramien laughed loud enough to turn heads, but he couldn't care less. It was true, after all.

"Fel'annár."

He jumped, almost toppling the sausage from his fork, and the Wise Warrior frowned. "I and Ramien will accompany you to Captain Comon. Later, perhaps, we could watch the blade masters. They are on the fields today, or so I've heard."

"Yes, of course," mumbled Fel'annár. He was listening, had heard everything they had said, but still he was tired, something he did not want to admit—tired and utterly distracted. Once he'd given his report, he told himself he could relax, sort out the mess in his mind and in his heart. There had hardly been time to mourn the loss of Lainon, and then their gruelling tour had been so arduous it had taken his mind off his lost friend. It was only when he stopped that he remembered the dark Ari, his unconditional support and his strange death. He would never forget that moment, and he thought perhaps that, one day, he would understand what had transpired the moment Lainon's light had passed through him. It was then that Commander Hobin had called him *"Ber'anor."*

He banished the word from his mind.

"Fel'annár—hello—is the Whirling Warrior home?" asked Galdith, and Fel'annár batted at the hand that waved before his eyes. The Company smiled, but it was fleeting and soon, they had agreed to meet after Fel'annár, Idernon, and Ramien returned from the War Room at the Inner Circle.

Striding over the thin sheet of melting snow, they crossed the courtyard and then passed the guarded doorway into a singular building of black stone and dark wood. It was a four-layered, circular construction, peculiar in itself, but what truly drew Fel'annár's attention was the lack of windows. It was a cave above ground, he mused. Still there was beauty in it; it took skill to design this perfect circle and achieve the smooth, polished surface over such a vast expanse of stone. It must have taken centuries to construct, he realised.

This was the Inner Circle of Tar'eastór, the heart of military command. Passing the armed guards at the entrance, they began to navigate their way towards the War Room. All they had been told was to take every corridor to their right. By the time they had taken three, they began to hear voices, voices that grew until they were loud enough to grate on the ears, and sharp needles of pain stuck into Fel'annár's brain. He pinched the bridge of his nose and promptly remembered the bruise that sat high on his cheek.

"I hope Captain Comon is not in *there*," muttered Idernon half-heartedly behind him, but a passing lieutenant confirmed that he *was*. They had arrived at the closed doors of the War Room, and so the three friends sat on a wooden bench a little further along the corridor and waited.

And waited.

Sometime later, Ramien's head was tilted backwards, leaning against the cold stone behind, eyes closed, and Fel'annár's head had fallen onto one of his friend's enormous shoulders, mouth slack. As for Idernon, he stood peering at a wall mural of the Battle of Prairie.

"There you are," came a voice from above. Ramien snorted loudly and Fel'annár startled, only now understanding that he had fallen asleep. He stood a little too fast and Ramien's arm steadied him while Idernon turned to face Captain Comon.

"Yes, well," said the captain with an arch of his brow, eyes focussed on Fel'annár's crumpled tunic.

Fel'annár looked down at himself and then pulled hard on it, smoothing a hand over his hastily braided hair as he fell into step with Comon. The noisy crowd of captains and lieutenants was gone, the corridor now silent, and the three Silvans and one captain passed through the solid oak doors that led into the War Room. Comon spoke as they made for the centre of the Hall, and although Fel'annár listened, he was acutely aware of the strange perspective of the room. The back portion of the hall was raised, so much that he could only see the elves that stood there from the waist up.

"Our commander has questions," said Comon matter-of-factly, unaware of the wonder in the eyes of the Silvan warriors as they scanned their surroundings.

There were no windows, no natural light at all, but the white-orange glow of candles illuminated the place well enough to guess, at least, at the height of the vaulted ceilings above them. Standards and flags of different colours and symbols hung like velvety stalactites from the heights, dampening, if only a little, the click of their boots as they walked. A crushing sense of history descended on Fel'annár, only now truly appreciating just where he was. This was where it had all started—where the Warrior Code had been written and ruthlessly upheld, where the greatest warriors on Bel'arán had sat strategising, moulding the defences of the Motherland, masterminding the colonisation of the Great Forest, his own home.

They stopped at the steps that led up to the raised half of the floor. Fel'annár could see Gor'sadén and Pan'assár's heads in the distance. To the left were two others and a little further away, two more, and although they all stood in different places, all of them were looking downwards, to the floor.

Fel'annár was curious beyond words, and as they took the first step upwards, all eyes turned on him, staring weightily at Fel'annár, remembering Or'Talán, perhaps, as he used to stand with them centuries into the past.

Gor'sadén nodded a curt greeting and then gestured with his head that the three Silvans should climb the four remaining steps. Pan'assár watched impassively, light flickering oddly in his cool eyes while the other captains watched and wondered if what their warriors were saying was true, that this *Silvan* was some kind of mage warrior.

With each step Fel'annár took, what lay beyond them slowly came into view. His eyes pulsed wide at the looming spectacle, and he heard Idernon and Ramien's soft exclamations behind him. There was no scuffed and worn table upon which a curled map lay; no carved figurines of warriors and Deviants, no stone markers to show rivers and villages. Instead, the entire floor jutted upwards in three dimensions, a floor that had been sculpted and moulded over years of painstaking work, work that told of a skill beyond Fel'annár's ken. His mind struggled to quantify his astonishment, because over and above the workmanship, to walk upon a sculpted map, to feel the land beneath your boots, to touch the caves and crags, the high passes and the valleys—it made strategy come to life, he realised. It gave a sense of what you fought for, what you were up against. It was sheer brilliance, and Fel'annár was in awe of the very idea.

Eyes roved hungrily over varnished mountain ridges and etched gorges, painted forests and coloured lakes and rivers, and around every feature of the land, a narrow walkway allowed strategists and tacticians to walk comfortably from one place to the other. Here stood the entire realm of Tar'eastór, and at the very end, to the far north was what Fel'annár could only assume to be the Last Markers, stone statues of Ari'atór, one hand held out to the fore, a silent order to stop. He peered closer, realising that every sculpture was different and he was once more reminded of the statues that stood upon the ramparts.

He was gaping, he knew it, but how could he not? He wondered if they had such a carved map in Ea Uaré. They *must* have, he thought, for most of the Forest commanders were Alpine; they would have stood in this very room themselves. They would surely have mirrored this building, this map.

"I asked Warrior Fel'annár to report to me this morning regarding the information he has gleaned from the *trees*." Comon straightened almost imperceptibly, eyes travelling over the captains and two commanders, thinking perhaps that they would laugh at him. They didn't, though, and instead, their eyes landed once more on Fel'annár.

"And why has he not shared it with you already?" asked one captain.

"Warrior Fel'annár was in the Healing Halls until this very morning, Captain. He did wish to speak with me. It was I who told him to wait until today," he clarified, closing the gap that separated him from the others.

"You may already know that he is what the Silvans call a *Listener*. This is the second time Warrior Fel'annár has patrolled with me, and I do vouch for the veracity of that claim; this *ability*, however, seems to be evolving. He has successfully scouted for my patrol without having to ride ahead, a great asset as you can all imagine. I cannot help but wonder if there are other Silvans with this capability that could be put to great service." Comon's eyes briefly looked at Pan'assár, but his face was unreadable. Quiet murmurs ensued, and Fel'annár resisted the urge to fidget where he stood.

"Fel'annár, tell us what you have perceived. What do the trees say?" finished Comon.

He had wanted to speak with Comon privately, but he had not been given the chance. And then he realised that perhaps the captain had done this purposefully so that the commanders could ask their questions directly, so that it would be easier for them to believe. Then again, perhaps it had simply been about Comon being embarrassed to speak of what he perceived as *magic*.

"Speak, Warrior," said Gor'sadén.

"Sir, I have heard a strange song from the land these last weeks. I hear it even now, although it is calmer, quieter than it was. It speaks of some new danger." His eyes slipped suspiciously to the other captains behind the commanders, knowing they would not believe him.

"What new danger?" asked Pan'assár slowly.

His eyes snapped to the commander. "They have named it *Nim'uán*."

"*Beautiful monster*," murmured Gor'sadén with a frown.

"Who is '*they*'?" asked Pan'assár.

"The trees, Sir. They often refer to Deviants as monsters. It is the *beauty* that has me perplexed."

"And your thoughts?" asked Comon.

"Sir, I cannot say. Perhaps a sub-species of Deviant? The implication of *beauty* would imply they are not so rotten, or perhaps that they rot at a slower rate. It is a passing strange thing to think. Then again, it may not be a Deviant at all—some new beast, perhaps."

"This is an unexpected development," said Comon.

"Forgive me, Captain. I had meant to speak with you about it yesterday."

"I know. But there were priorities."

"Sir, there is one more thing." His eyes were darting from one elf to the other as he grappled for the words he needed to make them understand. "It's much more subtle and open to interpretation, and I cannot be sure . . . but I've seen something in the enemy's eye, a spark of some emotion that was never there before, except once. Commander Pan'assár, you may have heard of the Deviant leader of the attacks on our escort on our way here . . ."

"The one that screamed?"

"Yes, Sir. I saw it in *his* eyes too.

"What did you see?" insisted Pan'assár. "Your best *guess*, Warrior."

"I believe it's . . . *hope*." Even as he said it, he was surprised at the word he had chosen.

"*Hope?*" repeated Gor'sadén.

"Yes, Sir. *Purpose* beyond mindless killing," he said, eyes unfocussed, ironing it out in his own mind even as he spoke.

Silence followed Fel'annár's words—he had expected nothing less, for his report was strange at best. He had not been sure of his thoughts until the moment he had given voice to them, and it unnerved him, because there was no reason for it. It was knowledge beyond reason, and he knew what the commanders would be thinking.

"I thought your ability was to listen to the *trees*. How can you perceive emotions in *Deviants?*" asked Pan'assár.

Fel'annár nodded. "Sir, my ability concerns the energy around us. This energy is channelled by trees, essentially. Sometimes, I hear and feel what trees do, and other times they feel what *I* do. As to how I could perceive an emotion, I can only conclude that perhaps it was the trees conveying that thought to me. I cannot say for sure, Commander."

"How can you *know* this?" asked a captain as he stepped forward, a frown of confusion on his face.

"I don't know, Captain."

"So you could be *wrong?*"

"I could be. But I never *have* been, so far."

The captain remained silent, mouth pressed into a tight line. Fel'annár knew he was sceptical.

"So if you capture this energy from trees, the closer you are to them, the stronger this connection? The more precise information you can glean?" asked Gor'sadén.

"I believe so, Commander. That's the way it's been so far, but in all honesty, this gift is unstable, Sir, in that there are new facets still revealing themselves to me. I have no way of knowing how this ability will change; there may be further developments I cannot foresee."

Gor'sadén held his gaze for longer than was comfortable. Fel'annár had given himself away, he realised. Gor'sadén had seen his *fear*.

"Warrior, step closer. Can you show us where you felt these

sensations?" Pan'assár's calm words, not Gor'sadén's. Fel'annár was surprised yet no less enthusiastic about being invited to step onto the map—in fact, given the chance, he would have pulled off his boots and allowed his bare feet to wander all over it. He wanted to reach out and touch it all like a child with his first bow.

"Here was where I first sensed the song of the Nim'uán," began Fel'annár, pointing to an area just north of Crag's Nest. "The song was just as strong here, on the opposite mountainside, and yet at Queen's Fall, precisely where the fighting is at its worst, the song was at its weakest."

Gor'sadén's eyes lingered on the lands surrounding Queen's Fall. This was indeed the focal point of the fighting, and it seemed strange to him that this *song* would not be at its highest where the conflict was.

"It is possible that, whatever this *Nim'uán* is, it comes from around Crag's Nest, where the song was at its highest and where the fighting is not so bad," murmured Gor'sadén as he walked along the pathways, Pan'assár and the captains behind him.

"Which would indicate that the Nim'uán is not in the same place. It is not fighting with the Deviants. This is either a momentary coincidence, or there is a diversion tactic in place," said Pan'assár.

"We have scouted the caves at Queen's Fall as well as we can with so much conflict, but they continue onwards and downwards with little to no natural light," said the captain. "But the dangers of going any further are too great. Once the thaw begins we *can* block those entrances, *but* we would be destroying the natural habitat of many of our indigenous species. However, the caves here, at Crag's Nest and the opposing rock face here are familiar to us. We have had no cause to revisit them—until now."

"Could the Deviants be massing in there? Would it be possible for them to hide in there and sustain themselves? Air, water, food . . . " asked Pan'assár. "Perhaps this is the reason the fighting is happening at Queen's Fall, to draw our attention away from this . . . *muster* . . . if it can be called that."

"Unlikely," answered a captain. "As I said, we are familiar with those caves. We do not think they are large or deep enough to hide any substantial number of Deviants, and Deviants need food. They are not cannibals. Commander," continued the captain, his eyes landing on Fel'annár for a brief moment before turning back to Gor'sadén. "How can we be sure that Warrior Fel'annár's claims are accurate? We are basing our conjectures on *his* word alone that this *Nim'uán* even exists."

Gor'sadén turned to him, and when he spoke, it was softly. "You have my *word*, Captain."

The captain nodded, his eyes straying back to Fel'annár, who in turn was staring at Gor'sadén. A wave of utter gratefulness washed through him. All his fears of not being understood, of being taken as a fool were gone—because Gor'sadén, Commander General of Tar'eastór, believed in him, answered for him, trusted him implicitly.

"All right. Here is what I believe we must do," said Gor'sadén. "We send a reconnaissance party out to these two areas, where Warrior Fel'annár heard this song more clearly. If this Nim'uán is there and not in the conflicted area around Queen's Fall, then we need to know what it is doing. This patrol should try to avoid conflict and concentrate on mapping the enemy's tracks, watching for signs of activity, a supply line, anything that would suggest Deviants are inhabiting these caves. If they *are*, then we must seal off the entryways and be done with this thing." He turned and then walked upwards to Queen's Fall on the map. "However, I am wary. This is where the conflict is taking place and where the Nim'uán is *not*. If Commander Pan'assár is right, and there *is* a diversion tactic in motion, there *is* a reason for it, something that is happening and that the enemy endeavours to hide from us. Commander Pan'assár?"

"Commander, I suggest this Nim'uán is on the move and does not wish to be seen. And if it doesn't want to be seen, it is because it has a surprise in store, either that or it is frightened. But that does not seem likely according to Warrior Fel'annár's report of a new *threat*.

Perhaps it is waiting," murmured Pan'assár, and Gor'sadén turned to watch his friend. Pan'assár had always been a brilliant strategist.

"How long until we have those reports?" asked Pan'assár.

"Journey time, mission time—perhaps two to three weeks. Warrior Fel'annár, the slightest hint that something is happening, however remote, however *unlikely*, you will report immediately to me," ordered Gor'sadén.

"Sir."

"Comon, we need those reports. Reinforce the western and eastern flanks around Queen's Fall, and send another patrol to the area this Nim'uán may be using for whatever he does not want us to see. Our reconnaissance team may need their support."

"It will be done, Commander. Sir, the captains are eager for news."

"Brief them, Comon, but heed me, *all* of you. The Nim'uán is not to be mentioned. Our official stance is that Deviant activity is increasing and that we ride out to investigate. There is no point in alarming our people for the moment. From today, we are on Alert Three, but if the presence of the Nim'uán is confirmed, we will move to Alert Two. No overnight leave is to be granted. I want all our resources ready to ride out at short notice should the need arise."

"Sir," said Comon as he saluted.

"Thank you, Commander, Captains. We will resume our talks tomorrow."

The captains left the high crags, valleys and ridges of Tar'eastór and walked passed Fel'annár with a nod of recognition while the two commanders approached more slowly, Gor'sadén's eyes searching Fel'annár.

"Has Prince Handir spoken to you?" he asked, and Pan'assár turned to listen.

"No, Sir." A sinking feeling pulled at his guts. There was really only one reason the prince would speak to him—there was news from Ea Uaré.

Gor'sadén nodded. "You are free of duty for the next week at least. See that you make good use of the time. You may be out in the field again before long." With a nod, he dismissed Fel'annár, who saluted and then left, Idernon and Ramien right behind him, and once they were outside and away from the lingering stares, Fel'annár's head turned to his friends.

"The *map!*" he exclaimed excitedly.

"It is as beautiful as it is practical," agreed Idernon. "I can see the merits of standing on the map you are studying rather than pointing to features on parchment. For example . . ." But he stopped mid-sentence, because Fel'annár was no longer listening to him, despite his initial enthusiasm. He stood stock still, as tense as a drawn field bow, hands balled into stony fists at his side.

"What is it?" murmured Ramien, eyes darting around them.

"I don't know," said Fel'annár, for his skin was tingling and the fine hairs on the back of his neck prickled. His eyes darted from left to right, but there was nothing out of the ordinary that he could see.

"Fel'annár?" insisted Idernon, urgency beginning to tinge his voice.

"I don't know, Idernon. A threat, perhaps."

Idernon breathed deeply, his body stiffening as it prepared for attack, one hand over the knife at his belt. They were in the courtyard before the Royal Palace and barracks, under the bright light of day, surrounded by civilians and warriors alike. Even so, Idernon did not doubt Fel'annár's words and neither did Ramien.

They passed the outlying barracks, the Healing Halls and were soon at the fences, beyond which the warriors trained.

"It has passed," said Fel'annár, visibly relaxing.

"Do you know what sort of threat it was?"

"No. It could simply have been an unfriendly gaze." But Idernon was not appeased. He had seen his friend's reaction. It had not been some simple, disapproving stare. The threat had been real. He needed to speak with The Company, because while they had been away, something had changed, and the threat was no longer silent and hidden—it was moving, hunting. It was walking under the sun, even though its identity still lay in the shadows.

~

Shadow. Secret warrior: covert and highly skilled in many arts, but this he had *never* seen. The bastard, as Silor called him, had sensed his presence from afar. He had made no noise, he was sure of it, had not been seen, he would swear to that. All he had done was take up his position behind a nearby tree and prepare his weapon—however the boy had known. Macurian had underestimated him, and he wondered if Silor had told him everything he needed to know. He already knew where the Silvan went, who he went with, the people that mattered to him, but how had he known there was a danger?

He would need to strike fast, unexpectedly, but he would not do so until he was sure of success. Should he fail, the boy's allies would be warned, and that would make his job so much more difficult . . . and Macurian had never once failed to carry out a mission, certainly not one as well-paid as this one.

He turned in search of answers, his objective playing over and over in his mind.

Stop the bastard from returning to Ea Uaré.

FOUR
THE MISSIVES

"The things we do to protect ourselves are often misconstrued, for few dig deeper than the significance of words. It is what lays between them that is important. It is in the empty space between words where the truth resides."
On Elven Nature. Calro.

~

Lyniel had seen the first great king of Ea Uaré, Or'Talán.

Only it *wasn't* him—she knew that. He'd been slaughtered by Sand Lords before she was born. Still the elf she had seen was identical save for the colour of his eyes, had the exact same face she had seen in her history books, had seen countless times back home, hanging upon the palace walls. There could be no mistake. That warrior was a royal scion, but he was too young to be Or'Talán's son. He was the son of Thargodén, or Band'orán, albeit that did not seem likely. He was Handir's cousin, or his *brother*—and he was shockingly beautiful.

"When were you going to tell me?"

Handir stiffened where he stood, his hand momentarily stopping, the glass decanter in his hand perfectly still before he slowly continued to pour two glasses of wine.

"About what?" he asked, unsure whether she had seen Fel'annár or whether she had heard of Lainon's demise.

"About your cousin. Or is he your *brother*?"

Handir scowled and then turned. "As soon as I had time to. The patrol rode in earlier than expected. I would have warned you."

"Yes, well, get talking, Han. Who is his father? And his mother?" she demanded, flinging herself into a cosy chair before the fire, auburn hair flying around her head unchecked. "Is he your cousin or your brother? And pour me some of that *wine!*" she said.

Handir laughed in spite of the situation, and Llyniel smirked. Her frustration and impatience were getting the better of her, and that sometimes led her to ask too many questions all at the same time, until it became so obvious that she would stop and then laugh at herself. But the moment soon passed, and Handir could not hide his hesitation. He needed to find a way of telling her only the essential elements without opening the door to her questioning.

She watched him closely. She was good at that; indeed Handir was sure she already knew he would not tell her everything.

"You remember the affair between my father and the . . . Silvan woman from Lan Taria?" asked Handir as he placed the glasses on the table before them, shuffling closer to Llyniel, brow pulled together in thought.

"Lássira, yes. My mother once mentioned she had the most extraordinary eyes. Your *brother* then. You're saying he's half *Silvan?*"

Handir nodded curtly, and of all the things Llyniel could have said or done, she *giggled*.

He stared back at her in disbelief. "Only *you* could find humour in such a convoluted situation, Llyniel."

"Convoluted? What's so *convoluted* about it? Your father loved that woman; any Silvan will tell you *that*."

"They loved each other so they had a *child*. Can you see nothing off about this? Do you think it is that *simple?*"

"I do *not* think it is simple, yet neither is it hard to understand." She sighed, cocking her head to one side. "I can see this affects you deeply, but I am your *friend*, Handir. I'm not judging you by saying it's not convoluted. *Love* is not convoluted. If they had a child it was purposeful; children are never mistakes. The question is—what *was* that purpose?"

"Llyn, whatever the purpose, Band'orán will not want him in Ea Uaré. My father's position on the throne is already compromised. Can't you *see* where this will lead?"

"I can well imagine. How well do you know him?" she asked, taking the wine to her lips and drinking deeply.

Handir shook his head. "Hardly at all. We have spoken only once, and that was when he came back from his last tour. He had news to share with me." His voice fell away, and he turned his head, battling to control his grief. Llyniel didn't know. He heard the rustle of her tunic and then felt the warmth of her hand on his shoulder.

"What news?" she asked softly.

"Lainon is dead." He hadn't meant to blurt it out but he *had*, and her grasp grew weak for a moment, only to squeeze stronger. One hand cupped his cheek and turned his head to face her.

"Sweet Lainon is dead?" she murmured, tears pooling in her eyes and then spilling over the long lashes of her bottom eyelids. He watched them for a moment, marvelling at how easy they had come. His own tears were still stubbornly inside, their freedom denied by his ingrained sense of propriety. Alpine princes didn't cry; it was a sign of weakness, and yet to the Silvan people, it was a token of empathy, of nearness and harmony. Crying was not frowned upon. It was cherished.

She stood and walked towards the windows and the magnificence of Tar'eastór beyond, blurred now by her grief but still beautiful.

"I remember when we were children, running amok in the palace, old enough to know we were a bother, young enough not to care, and Lainon was always there, somewhere in the distance, watching but never scolding," said Llyniel. "Then later, when we were older and we talked of weightier things, still he was at your shoulder, silent and duteous. I saw you many times together, when you thought yourself alone with him. The guard became a friend, a brother even, and you would relax. You would tell him *everything* and he would listen, more than your true brother, more than your own father. You loved him, and my heart aches for the tears you cry on the inside. I am glad I'm here, Handir." She turned back to the room and to the lonely prince who still sat, his gaze lost somewhere off to his left, a rare sign of vulnerability.

Handir couldn't speak, and so he swallowed thickly and nodded, reaching for his wine and drinking. Llyniel sat beside him, reaching for her own glass and observing the exquisite carvings around the base for a moment.

"What happened?" she ventured.

"He died saving Fel'annár in battle. That is his name."

She frowned, shaking her head. "Why was he with Fel'annár and not with you?" Handir turned to her, and Llyniel watched him closely.

"I reassigned Lainon—to *him*."

She leaned back, and Handir could see she was, perhaps, beginning to understand. Handir already resented Fel'annár for what Lássira had done to his family, and now, he needed to come to terms with the fact that Lainon had died because of Fel'annár himself, because Handir had sent him. The Silvan had told him briefly of what had transpired, that Lainon had not died because Fel'annár had been careless. They had saved *each other*. He had no reason to doubt that, but still, for Handir it was all too easy to do just that: to find blame in Fel'annár.

And to feel guilty for reassigning Lainon.

"You must be curious," murmured Llyniel after a while, eyes locked on Handir, watching his reaction closely.

But Handir didn't answer.

"You are curious, and you do not *want* to be. Am I right?"

Handir breathed deeply and wrenched his eyes away from hers. "You know you are. I do not rightly know why I should even care what becomes of him. His mother was the reason my mother took the Long Road to Valley; you must still remember that time. I cannot forget that, I am reminded of it every time I look at him. Why *should* I care?"

"Because your heart tells you that you must. It is that simple, Prince. Your mind rebels against your heart and that is always a battle that cannot be won without consequence."

"It feels wrong to care—a betrayal, if you will."

"Your mother would not have you punish her husband's child, Han."

"No, she would not." Handir had not thought of it that way. But *he* was not his *mother*. "It is *me* who cannot accept, Llyniel."

"Because of the hurt his mother caused yours?"

"Yes," was Handir's somewhat clipped reply.

"And what of the hurt done to *her*? She and your father were lovers before your mother was ever introduced to Thargodén. They were wrenched apart unnaturally, Handir. Your father and Lássira loved each other—what choice did they ever have? If they *were* soul mates, to part from each other would be like trying to kill yourself by holding your own breath."

Handir watched the woman he felt closer to than his own sister and locked gazes with her. She had the uncanny ability of synthesising things; *he* did, too, but where Fel'annár was concerned he had failed where *she* had seen it so very clearly. Llyniel leaned forward, her brow drawn together in a frown.

"What I *don't* understand is why he's *here*. Or are you going to tell me that is coincidence?

Her questions were becoming uncomfortable, because to answer her now would open up *other* questions he did not want to answer. His hesitation cost him.

"Handir, tell me what it is you hold back."

He had not told Fel'annár of the missives, of the plan, and in all conscience he could not tell Llyniel until he *had*, and even then he would think long and hard about whether he even *wanted* to tell her. It was dangerous, and of all the people in this world, he would shelter *her* from harm. She was passionate about her Silvan roots, ashamed of the Alpine side of herself. Should he tell her now of what they had planned, he knew she would not step away. He knew she would make herself indispensable in some way. It was in her blood, the blood she had inherited from her lordly father.

But Handir's rational mind told him he had no right to keep it from her, no right to protect her. She didn't *need* it.

Handir smiled but it was far away and a touch sad. "There is so much to say, my friend. But for now I need your trust and . . . your *patience*. There is something I must do before I can tell you."

She cocked her head to one side, but she could see Handir's determination. There was no use in insisting, so she nodded slowly. "All right. So long as you *do* . . . tell me."

Handir nodded. He would, indeed, answer her questions, as soon as he had told Fel'annár of the plan.

∼

That afternoon, the blade masters stood talking quietly with the other weapons instructors, eyes occasionally straying to where Fel'annár, Idernon, and Ramien sat watching the warriors spar. Although he was free for the next week at least, Fel'annár had come down to the fields to watch in the hope of catching one of the masters train. He was restless in spite of his lingering tiredness, incapable of enjoying his freedom, for the strange song of the Nim'uán was still there, even though it had dwindled. But there was something else, some unknown feeling that lurked on the fringes of his consciousness. Whether it was good or bad he couldn't say, and he wondered if he should get himself to the gardens, to the Sentinel that had blossomed in winter. Perhaps there he would find answers.

"Pity Pan'assár can't be moved to allow Gor'sadén to take you as an apprentice of the Kal'hamén'Ar," murmured Idernon as he watched the more advanced warriors.

Fel'annár smiled wryly. Too much time had passed since the commander had told Fel'annár he would try to wrangle his friend's consent. He had expected Pan'assár's negative—still he had managed to get his hopes up all the same.

"It was a dream, brother, one my mixed race will not allow to become a reality. Even so, perhaps I can take the test for Blade Master while we're here."

"You never know, Fel. Pan'assár has changed since we've been here. I can tell you that much. He seems *happier* I think. Even Galadan agrees, and he knows our commander better than any of us."

"I'd never use the word '*happy*' to refer to our commander, Idernon. He's worse than Galadan with his stony face, and he certainly doesn't hide his disdain for the Silvan people. I can't help but wonder why."

"Why not? There's nothing new in that, Fel'annár," spluttered Ramien. "Why are you surprised, after all this time?"

"I've been here long enough to realise just how close our commander was to King Or'Talán, who, by all accounts, was revered by the Silvan people. Why *would* Pan'assár hate them?"

"Yes, you have a point." Idernon scowled, mind racing as the silence dragged on.

Fel'annár broke it with a completely unrelated question. "Did either of you see that Silvan healer?"

There was no answer, and Fel'annár pressed on. "Sontúr said she travelled with a group of Pelagians."

"Pelagians?" exclaimed Ramien.

"I haven't seen any Silvans since we've been here. I suppose our folk reckon they won't be made welcome. It's a pity they think it's like that here, too," said Idernon. "They can't be blamed, mind."

Fel'annár listened to the words that Idernon continued to speak but their meaning did not register, because before his mind's eye was a mischievous smile upon a glowing face surrounded by hair of deep brown silk and a liquid-honey gaze. She was a mystery Fel'annár found himself wanting to solve. Her simple presence was like a beacon that led to the Forest. She reminded him of his home, a home he had sometimes wondered he even wanted to return to—a place of discrimination and injustice, a mother who had lied to him his entire life, his own countrymen who had deceived him purposefully. Here, he was valued as a warrior, had made a tentative friend of the mighty Gor'sadén. He had a life here, if he should choose to stay. But all it had taken was the fleeting presence of a bright Silvan soul: that lilting accent, the richness of her dark hair, and the open simplicity in her eyes and on her tongue. She reminded him of why he loved the Forest so much, in spite of the suffering it had brought him.

Ramien's elbow was digging into his ribs. Fel'annár wanted to punch him, but the warriors on the field had stopped their exercises and bowed. Prince Handir was approaching, and Fel'annár's stomach fell into his boots.

Standing and straightening their uniforms, the three Silvans bowed.

Handir's weighty gaze landed on Fel'annár, and for a moment he simply stood and watched, until Fel'annár shifted his weight to his other leg.

"Fel'annár, I must have a private word." They were the words of a school master to his pupil, proper and formal, yet there was no compromise in his tone. His statement *was* an order.

"My prince," nodded Fel'annár. His mind raced at what Handir would say, for it seemed to him there was a spark of pity in his eyes. That morning, Gor'sadén had asked him if he had spoken with the prince—whatever this was about, Gor'sadén knew, and if *he* knew, then so did Pan'assár, he wagered.

Handir gestured that he should accompany him, and so prince and warrior walked away under the curious gazes of the warriors while Idernon and Ramien followed at a respectful distance. One was a prince, a statesman clad in velvet and silk, and the other a

Silvan warrior despite his outward appearance. Fel'annár was taller than his princely brother, broader across the shoulders, more powerfully built, whereas Handir was slim and pruned to a fault, decorated as was befitting an Alpine prince. And yet none who looked on could deny the kinship between them, even though one had warm blue eyes and the other, preternatural green eyes. Still, the silky silver locks of Handir contrasted with the wildness of Fel'annár's indomitable mane of plaits and Ari twists. Culture and prejudice separated them as starkly as their features marked them as brothers.

There was silence for most of the time it took them to arrive at the prince's private suite of rooms on the upper levels of the Royal Palace. Idernon and Ramien knew better than to follow Fel'annár inside the guarded doors, and soon enough, the two brothers were alone, wrapped in a shroud of awkward silence.

"You are not on duty, Fel'annár. For what I have to say you are free to talk with me as you see fit." Handir's voice was low and studiously devoid of emotion.

He fleetingly admired the boy's ability to command himself. At fifty-two, such an inexperienced elf should be somewhat overwhelmed by his current circumstances . . . apprehensive, at least. But the boy simply stood with his hands behind his back and stared at him expectantly.

What was going on in his mind, wondered Handir. Was he really as calm as he looked? Or was he simply good at hiding his emotions, as Handir himself was?

He wanted to know, *needed* to know what Lainon had seen in this boy, why he had even suggested that Fel'annár could help them in their plans for the restoration of the Forest. Handir did understand from a practical viewpoint, because Fel'annár *was* who he *was*. He represented the Silvan people in that they believed Lássira should have been queen and not his own mother. Perhaps it was that simple, he mused—but the thought was fleeting, because Lainon would not have based all their efforts on a symbol, not when a symbol could very well turn against them. Lainon had seen something in Fel'annár *himself*, and Handir needed to know what it was.

He poured wine for them both and then turned to the Silvan, holding one goblet out to him, gaze firmly anchored on his brother's strange eyes: the same legendary green eyes they said The Silvan's mother once bore. Fel'annár looked at the glass and then at Handir, who gestured with his hand that he should take it. Fel'annár nodded his thanks, and Handir, for the first time, saw emotion: surprise.

"On your arrival from your previous foray, when you told me of . . . of Lainon's departure, Lainon's final words, the words you did not understand and . . ."

Fel'annár's hand froze, goblet half-way to his mouth. "You know of what he spoke?" he asked quietly.

"Yes, yes I know. And it is time that you, too, knew."

Fel'annár took a step forward. "Tell me, Prince. Those were Lainon's final words; you should not have kept their meaning from me."

Handir watched The Silvan closely, just as Aradan had taught him to do. There was an intensity about him, a need to know, and a spark of anger Handir wondered if the boy would let loose. He was bold for suggesting his prince had erred.

"You may feel . . . *overwhelmed* by what I will tell you now."

"I have been overwhelmed since Lainon told me who my *father* was not four months past. How much more you can *shock* me, Prince, is questionable."

Handir nodded, and for a moment, he was sure that his own surprise had been visible. The boy was forthright and just a little sarcastic. He drank slowly from his goblet while Fel'annár stood rigid and expectant.

"After your arrival at the city barracks for recruit training, Lainon came to me and delivered news that shocked me. I had a brother, a *Silvan* brother, he said, born of the woman who had been my father's lover." From the corner of his eye he could see the boy listening intently, and he turned to the fire, increasing the distance between them.

"I hated my father, questioned my mother's decision to leave, despised *you*," said Handir with an arch of his brow. "Everything I had thought had happened between my father, Lássira, and my own mother was called into question, for you see, my father has spent the last few decades inside a shell, distancing himself from his surroundings. We thought it due to the departure of our mother and the ensuing scandal of his infidelity with *your* mother. We thought it was for *shame*, for had he not precipitated the queen's departure with his faithlessness? It was surely for this reason that the queen had abandoned her adolescent children; there was no other reason that could merit such a thing," he said, eyes now riveted on Fel'annár, watching his reactions. But The Silvan simply stared coolly back at him.

"After the shocking revelation of your existence, I came to understand that the king's grief was due to something *else*. It was not the absence of the queen, my mother; it was the loss of his soulmate —*your* mother," he said quietly.

Fel'annár's cold gaze widened, ice melting instantaneously, his shield of protection suddenly gone, and in its place was raw surprise, and to Handir's utter shock, the onset of quiet empathy.

"And yet it was not my father's *infidelity* that sent my mother away," he said softly. "It was not even Lássira; it was *you*. It was because Thargodén had created a *child*."

Handir had expected fiery defence and anger, but all he saw was sadness. Fel'annár's eyes filled with unshed tears, and he abruptly turned to the door.

Handir suddenly felt ashamed, and when next he spoke, it was kind, but his words were not the ones he had meant to use at all.

"Fel'annár, it is what you *represent* that hurts, not *you*."

Fel'annár visibly started, but he did not speak as he turned to face him once more.

"I'm sorry," whispered Fel'annár at last. "I'm sorry, I—I never had a mother to lose but you . . ."

Handir stepped back, as if he had been slapped. He had never considered the situation from that perspective. He, at least, had *had* a mother to remember fondly, in spite of the ensuing anger at her departure. But Fel'annár was bereft of that bond, had no memory at all of the woman who had given him life.

"I don't know what happened, Handir, am woefully ignorant of the nature of my mother's relationship with . . . with the king. I know only what Lainon has told me. He said they met long before the king took a queen and his children were born, that they shared deep love and that King Or'Talán forbade it."

"Yes," said Handir, nodding and then turning back to the window, taking a sip of his wine. He needed to distance himself from those eyes, from the grief he had briefly captured: they were the eyes of an orphan.

I never had a mother to lose . . .

"That is the short of it, as much as I myself know," continued Handir as he shifted and forced himself to return from where he had all but fled. "I discussed the issue with Lord Aradan, chief councillor to my father. He suggested that the prohibition was political, that the circumstances at the time must have merited such a drastic decision, one that heralded a political union between Thargodén and an Alpine lady of high standing, my mother."

"It seems harsh, but then," said Fel'annár, turning to Handir with a humourless chuckle, "she was nothing but a Silvan commoner, unfit as a bride to a future Alpine king."

Handir turned to face him. "This is a complex matter, Fel'annár. You should keep your mind open, not condemn King Or'Talán on the basis of such rudimentary knowledge."

"You think I am *wrong*?" said Fel'annár, voice stronger. "You think race and standing had nothing to do with my mother's disgrace? Because of it, my own early childhood was marked by unanswered questions and ruthless mockery, for *look* at me, Prince. An Alpine face on a child raised as a Silvan from the Deep Forest. All the people I ever loved were in silent collusion to keep the truth from me. Even our village library was emptied of any book that contained the face of Or'Talán. I have been misled all my life, judged from the moment I had knowledge of myself."

"Do not use your anger against *me*, Fel'annár. I do not doubt it had much to do with all that. You apologised because your mother was the reason *my* mother left, and I would return that gesture by asking you to forgive my grandfather for doing what he felt was right. He was not one of *those* elves, Fel'annár, he did not discriminate against the Silvan people, did not see them as inferior in any way despite the obvious differences between us—and neither do I, neither does Aradan, and neither did Lainon." He had come to stand before Fel'annár, aware that he had allowed his emotions to show, and for one moment he did not care at all. He watched as Fel'annár's anger washed away and the battle to contain his emotions began once more. At last Handir had seen it, seen the Silvan's weakness.

Family was Fel'annár's weakness.

"Even if you leave me out of this puzzle, Handir. What of *love*? My mother and the king were one. That bond cannot be undone in spite of one elf's will, in spite of the absence of a marriage. King Or'Talán condemned my mother to eternal grief, and he did so consciously."

"And my father still pays the consequences, Fel'annár. I ask only that you keep your mind open, that you remember the lack of knowledge that we have as to my grandfather's motivations."

Fel'annár was silent, and Handir knew the boy was listening to him. It was time to press on to why he had brought Fel'annár here in the first place.

"So you see, Aradan, Turion, Lainon and I devised a plan, Fel'annár. We knew the knowledge of your existence would not remain a secret for long; your face gave you away to Lainon and would have done to my father's entire court had you not left the barracks. This was the first part of our plan, to get you away with Lainon and Turion to *protect* you while Aradan and I paved the way. You know of racism in our lands, but perhaps you are unaware that it was Lord Band'orán, our great uncle, who first instigated it. Our lands were not like this under Or'Talán's rule. This downward spiral into injustice is but one generation long. It is Band'orán and his manipulation of our institutions, of the Inner Circle, his slow but relentless poisoning, his talk of inferiority and hatred that have led us to this point, and I would be one of those to stop him. His treachery runs deeper than even those closest to the king imagine."

Fel'annár stood wide-eyed, and Handir could not blame him. Handir was telling him a tale of treason, disclosing information that was sensitive, dangerous and restricted. He could only hope this was not wrong; he could only trust that Lainon had been right about Fel'annár.

"You think they will turn against our king? You think I can do something to stop that? This is nonsense. I was not raised a prince. I have no knowledge of politics or scheming."

"Our king has proclaimed you a *lord*, a *Silvan* lord. The Silvans that were denied a queen will want the prince that could not be. Silvan son of an Alpine *king* . . ." said Handir forcefully, coming to stand as close as he could to a disbelieving Fel'annár, eyes sharp.

"A *lord*? Why? What for? Just so that you can *use* me?"

"As for my father, I cannot say, although I suspect he does this to protect you, to give you grounds to fight against the rivalry you will undoubtedly come up against in the Forest. But as for me, *yes*, I would use you, just as would your own people, Fel'annár. Why do you think they deceived you? Why do you think they shielded you? Emptied their libraries?"

"I am a warrior . . ."

"You are the son of a *king*! Yes, you are a warrior and I would not see that change—Gor'sadén is adamant you should be allowed to train in the Kal'hamén'Ar, and I do not seek to wilfully stunt your dreams, none of us do. We still have time here, time to learn and for you to train. *Think* about it, Fel'annár. Think of the possibilities: to help us and set your people free once more, not from their ruling king who loves them well but from the dictatorship of the powerful who would take the throne for themselves and subjugate your people for eternity. We mean to give the Silvans back their sense of pride and purpose. We mean to return to them their identity, Fel'annár, and *then* there will be peace once more under the grace of our father's rule. You *can* help us do that."

After long moments of silence, Handir understood that Fel'annár would say no more, so he turned to the missives that sat upon the low table before them.

"Here, this is from Captain Turion, and this . . . is from your father. Read them, later, when you are alone and your mind is free to wander."

Fel'annár locked gazes with Handir, hand slowly taking the two scrolls from the prince. "This must not have been easy. Thank you—for telling me."

Handir once more hid his surprise. "Go, Fel'annár, go and think, with an open mind and the good of our people in your heart. When you are ready, if you ever are, come back to me. Perhaps then we can carry out what Lainon bid us do together. He believed in this plan and, Aria as my witness, so do I."

"It was *this* then? Lainon spoke of *this plan*? To stop this racial madness? To reunite the cultures of Ea Uaré as they say it once was?"

Handir smiled softly and nodded. "Lainon was a king's man, Fel'annár, loyal to Thargodén like few others. He knew what it would mean for Band'orán to take the throne, the ruin it would bring to the Forest and its people, and so do I. It cannot be allowed to happen. We both can avoid it, with Aradan and Turion's help. If you wish to think we would *use* you, then you are right, but *using* you does not mean we wish you harm. A king uses his warriors, Fel'annár, and still he loves them. Captain Turion would never have accepted his part in this if it would bring harm to you, and I do not need to tell you of Lainon's thoughts."

Fel'annár breathed deeply and looked to the floor, his extraordinary eyes drifting over the exquisite rug under his feet. The Silvan was once more in control of his emotions. He was a tough lad, thought Handir, like Rinon in a more humble way—in a *Silvan* way.

Handir startled when the door clicked and a figure drifted into the room only to stop mid-stride. He saw Llyniel's embarrassment at having interrupted, but it promptly turned to curiosity and then suspicion. He had told her there was something he needed to do before he would speak to her, and the light of understanding flared in her eyes. She smiled, and Handir mirrored it while Fel'annár watched them both.

There was a spark of complicity between them, and something else that could not be denied.

Fel'annár saw love in their eyes.

Irrational anger, the urge to leave before it could be confirmed, and he turned to Handir, affording him a curt bow, and as he passed Llyniel on the way to the door, their gazes met. He wanted to stop, ask if they were lovers, or perhaps glean the truth from her open gaze. But he didn't, and with a somewhat stilted gait, he left, the two scrolls Handir had given him clutched a little too tightly in his hands.

Llyniel turned to Handir, eyebrows lifted in surprise, but there was a gleam in her eye that Handir could not ignore. She had been patient, just as he had asked of her, but she had sensed that *this* was what Handir had been waiting for, this discussion she had interrupted. It could not be avoided. He had tried, but she had been adamant. She wanted to know, and with no further excuses in his mind and the encouragement in his heart, he turned to her.

"Have lunch with me. There are things we must discuss."

He saw the spark of satisfaction in her eyes. If only she knew just how much he was about to change her entire life.

∾

Fel'annár walked from the Royal Palace, Idernon and Ramien silent at his back. He did not return to the barracks but to the plains beyond and a copse of trees Fel'annár often visited. They beckoned to him now, their reasons yet hidden from him. The song of the Nim'uán echoed softly in the mountains, but there were other whispers of some new knowledge that danced and giggled at him from just beyond his awareness. Damn Handir—for the news he had delivered and the loving gaze the prince had directed at the Silvan healer. Anger warred with deeply hidden emotions that clamoured at the doors of his conscious mind, feelings of family and love, all of them unfamiliar. He had told himself a thousand times that he didn't care.

He was a *fool*, and Handir had surely seen that.

Fel'annár sat and rested his wrists on his knees, eyes following the red ball of fire as it sailed lower and lower and then caressed the jagged horizon. Of a sudden it seemed to accelerate, as if it could not wait to navigate the night and appear once more in the morning sky. His own life, he mused, was dipping below the horizon, vanishing before his eyes, careening almost out of control towards a new life he had yet to comprehend. What lay on the other side of night was, as yet, a mystery, just like what was written in the scrolls that lay heavily in his lap.

He didn't *have* to open it.

He could just rip it all to pieces and walk away, returning to the life he knew.

He looked down at the one he knew was from King Thargodén, his father. It was time to face it, time to stop his absurd denial. He *did* care who his father was—he always had. He pulled the two ends of the parchment open and allowed his eyes to admire the well-penned letters, words he had never thought to read from a father he had always told himself was dead.

Fel'annár Ar Thargodén

Come to me as my son, a lord and in peace upon your return to Ea Uaré.

There is much to speak of, questions you will have and that I, in turn would ask you. The years between us lie heavy, ripe with grief and ignorance, and I ask only that you agree to sit with me, if only for a while so that we may speak . . . and perhaps understand.

I have asked your brother, Handir, and Lieutenant Lainon to assist you for the time that is left to you in the Motherland. Use it well, for upon your return there will be much joy but also much concern for what some believe you represent to your mother's people. You must be ready.

I am told you are a warrior, have heard of your deeds at the Battle of Sen'uár. You wish to be a captain, as my own father was before me, before he was commander general. You carry the blood of kings, and yet I ask but one thing of you: that you come to me as my son, a lord and in peace upon your return. There will be no other impositions, Green Sun.

His father wanted to meet him, knew about what he had done, about his dreams. He had not expected it, or perhaps he *had* but had not dared believe it. He was strangely pleased, but he didn't *want* to be.

The king asked for nothing, he said, only that Fel'annár should accept his position as lord and agree to meet him. But what did being a lord imply? He would need to ask Sontúr about that, but whatever it meant, he would only accept it if it didn't interfere with his military career. But then, was he even free to reject it? He didn't think so.

That night, his questions kept him awake, and so he wandered into the deserted common room at the barracks and lit a single candle. He knew The Company had spoken amongst themselves, for they left him alone—even now as he sat at the empty table, the two scrolls sitting upon the scuffed surface. They knew the short of it, knew Handir had brought him news from a family he never thought to have, but Fel'annár could not yet bring himself to speak of it. With his heavy head propped against the palm of one hand, he turned his face to the window, watching as the stars floated across the sky, their path predictable, unlike his own. He was to be a lord, a warrior amongst princes and politicians that would stand against Lord Band'orán, Or'Talán's brother. He could not fathom how it could be done, and yet Handir was adamant that he could play some part. It seemed an insurmountable feat, and he wondered if this was his duty or whether he was allowing himself to be lured into a web of intrigue he would do best to steer clear of.

He watched as the sun peaked over the jagged horizon. Its presence comforted him enough to step back and see his options more clearly. Fel'annár had seen Handir's conviction; he knew the prince was risking his position, his favour at his father's court in order to carry out his plan. As for this *Lord Aradan*, Fel'annár knew nothing of him at all, save that he was the king's chief councillor, and as such would be a valuable ally. Now Captain Turion he *did* know and trusted him implicitly, as he had Lainon. *They* were in this plan, believed in it. *Fel'annár* believed in it—he was Silvan: how could he not see the merit of it? And yet Fel'annár could not see what *he* could possibly do to help.

Handir surely saw the circumstantial merits. He did, too. He was a son of the king, half Silvan, the fruit of Thargodén's love of a Silvan woman who should have ruled at his side. Fel'annár was a representation of something Handir thought could be used, just as the Silvan people would use him, for had they not protected him for this very reason?

Fel'annár was shaking his head even as he pondered the question. He had always lived his life with one underlying ethic. Deserve what you have, earn what you own. Whatever you have and whatever you are, it should be because you have worked for it, you have merited it by your deeds, and not for "who you are."

He could not reconcile that belief with what Handir was asking of him.

Fel'annár's eyes landed on the as yet unread scroll, and a soft smile played around his lips. *Turion.*

Of all the things that had happened to Fel'annár in his admittedly short life, the coming of Turion was one of the best. He could not have had a better captain on his first patrol. It was thanks to Turion that Fel'annár had begun to understand himself, and that had changed everything—it had changed him irrevocably. Turion and his great friendship with Lainon... he would need to find the courage to sit and pen a letter to his captain, explain the circumstances of Lainon's death, conjure words of comfort he was not sure he could find.

He pulled the scroll open and read, eyes sharp and gleaming. He smiled as The Company came to sit beside him, chairs scraping over the floor.

"Good news from home?" ventured Galadan.

"Personally, it is not bad, at least."

"And that smile on your face?" pointed Ramien.

"Is for Turion. He is serving in the Inner Circle. He promised General Huren he would, in return for commanding my first patrol into the Forest. He balks at it, but I can tell he's not discontent." His smile faded. "I must now tell him that Lainon has gone—they were great friends, just like us, Ramien."

They were silent for a moment. Only Idernon was brave enough to ask the question they had all been waiting to ask. "Fel'annár, tell us what the king says."

Green eyes darted to Idernon, and he was quiet for a moment. With a soft nod of his head, Fel'annár spoke for the first time about his father.

"He has publicly recognised me, has proclaimed me a *lord*."

Galdith sucked in a breath. "How did your brother feel about *that*?" he asked, even before he had thought about it, and the eyes of The Company were upon him.

"Sorry."

"It's all right. Our conversation was not easy, but I cannot say it was bad. Handir is conflicted, and I understand that. My mother inadvertently ruined his childhood."

"As his grandfather ruined yours. Where's the difference?" asked Galdith curtly.

"There's *none*. That's the point, Galdith. I cannot begrudge him his feelings against me, just as he does not begrudge mine. We *understand* each other, I think. We are both victims of the schemes of others."

"Well then, that's a weight off your shoulders, brother," said Ramien, slapping Fel'annár on the knee. "You've not been exiled and now you're a *lord*. It'll all get better from here—you'll see," smiled the Silvan giant and Fel'annár smiled.

But there was something in it that seemed off to Idernon. There *was* more, he realised, more to that first conversation between brothers that Fel'annár had not said. He hid something, as surely as Idernon was wise. It was not the shock of being proclaimed a lord nor the bewilderment of reading his father's words for the first time; it was not even the song from the trees. There was something about his friend, as if he struggled to understand something.

Idernon knew Fel'annár better than most. It was not the first time he had kept things to himself. He did it when he didn't understand something. He would chew on the puzzle for as long as it took, and only when he was ready would he share it. Handir had said something to Fel'annár, something that even now was distracting him.

It will all get better from here, Ramien had said, and Idernon dearly wanted to believe him. But belief was not Idernon's strong point, and the mists of doubt and suspicion descended upon him like an overly-heavy blanket on a hot summer's night.

FIVE
BECOMING

"The child with a thousand questions had gone with that last sunset, and in his place stood a young warrior lord, poised upon the cusp of dawn. It was the dawn of discovery, of his own understanding of a world that was taking shape before him—in spite of him."
The Alpine Chronicles. Cor'hidén.

∾

"Fel'annár." A deep, commanding voice none could confuse. The Company made to stand from the breakfast table and salute, but Gor'sadén held up his hand. Breakfast was sacred, and Lord Damiel beside him agreed. The commander general and chief councillor took a seat in front of Fel'annár and observed him for a while.

"You look tired," said Gor'sadén.

Fel'annár studied the commander's face for a moment, eyes momentarily straying to Lord Damiel before answering. "Sleep eluded me."

Gor'sadén arched a brow and then leaned forward with the intention of asking Fel'annár a question, but *he* was already speaking.

"I have spoken with Prince Handir," said The Silvan, a challenge in his eyes, but Gor'sadén's face was utterly straight even though his eyes danced from one side to another. "You already *knew*, I assume." The hint of sarcasm was not lost on the commander.

"We did," said Damiel softly. He cast his eyes around the table and then back to Fel'annár, cocking his head towards the door.

"I will be at the Sentinel, brothers," said Fel'annár. The Company nodded, watching as he left with the two lords.

"There are things he has not told us," stated Galadan, and Idernon turned to meet the lieutenant's stony countenance.

"I know. And I wager it has to do with his conversation with our prince."

"He holds back, Idernon. I can see it in his eyes. He struggles with something."

The Wise Warrior considered Galadan's words, but he said nothing. His own observations had been confirmed by Galadan, the oldest and one of the wisest amongst them. There was something new in Fel'annár's eyes, something neither of them recognised.

~

"Why didn't you tell me before I left?" asked Fel'annár. Gor'sadén could see he was uncomfortable in the presence of Damiel. He did not know the councillor at all and certainly would not trust him.

"The missives arrived shortly before you rode back out on patrol. There were messages for my king—hence the news was made known only to his closest collaborators. It was not our place to tell you."

"And Prince Handir saw fit to leave me out of it. Why that surprises me is perplexing," muttered Fel'annár as the three walked along the garden path.

"He is just as conflicted about everything as you are, Fel'annár. I believe he needed time to think, to accept, just as you do now, I wager," said Damiel.

Fel'annár said nothing, and Gor'sadén knew he wouldn't comment on that. Damiel was close to Handir, and Fel'annár would perhaps think his words would make it back to the prince.

"Your father accepts you, gives you his name," ventured Gor'sadén.

"Yes," was the only answer he received. It wasn't enough.

"Well, does he say anything *else*?"

Fel'annár shot him an exasperated look. "I am to report to him no sooner we arrive in Ea Uaré. He says I have nothing to fear, that I will be welcomed."

Gor'sadén nodded slowly, sparing a fleeting glance at Damiel; getting Fel'annár to speak of the missives was like gleaning water from an autumn leaf. Under different circumstances he would have spoken privately with his young friend, but Damiel's presence was necessary.

"Fel'annár, I see your hesitation. I know you know more than you say, and that is all right. You can trust us . . . I hope you know that," coaxed Damiel.

Fel'annár nodded, even tried to muster a smile, but it was stilted and Damiel returned it. Trust was to be earned, not requested—this Gor'sadén knew. Damiel was underestimating Fel'annár, and Fel'annár had sensed that. It was a small mercy that the reason for Damiel's presence was finally made known.

"Fel'annár," began Damiel carefully. "Protocol dictates that Tar'eastór should formally recognise you as a lord, as the son of King Thargodén. To that end King Vorn'asté requires your presence in the council chambers tomorrow, when he will read your father's decree. There are sundry matters of protocol that you must know, arrangements for your attire and living quarters, and . . ."

"My *living* quarters? I am a warrior, my lord; my place is at the barracks."

"Not any more, Fel'annár. Lords do not reside at the barracks."

Fel'annár stopped and turned to Damiel. "And why not? If they're warriors, wherefore this preference? I'm a lord through the dictates of *others*. I do not choose this. I wish to stay at the barracks."

"You can't," said Damiel simply, stepping towards Fel'annár and looking into the boy's unnerving green eyes. He cocked his head to one side, a gesture Gor'sadén had seen many times. Damiel did it when he was reconsidering his tactics. "You cannot change our rules simply because you do not like them. Debate them if you will—I personally would enjoy the challenge—but for now you must reside in the palace. There are reasons, Fel'annár, circumstances that will arise that you cannot foresee. You must trust those older and wiser than yourself to guide you." He gestured to the path, and the three were walking once more.

"All this is new to you," continued Damiel. "Your life is being changed by the will of others; I can see your resistance, how you struggle to maintain control, to find your own path forwards. I will help you with whatever you may need, and I know Prince Handir will do likewise, but for now, Fel'annár, go with it; do not swim against an incoming tide."

Fel'annár scowled at the imagery and then nodded slowly. But he was a warrior—he could not help but fight for what he thought was right, no matter the odds. Still it was clear to him that he could not go against King Thargodén's wishes, as clear as Damiel's veiled order that he should reside at the palace.

"I just need to straighten things out in my own mind, my lord. You have had an entire month to ponder the questions pertaining to my heritage. I have had one *day*, strange though that may be, given I am the protagonist. Those *older and wiser* than me must realise it is not quite enough. I have decisions to take, things to consider. I accept your counsel, my lords, but I am my own elf. I, too, have expectations, dreams I have never renounced and never will."

Damiel reminded Gor'sadén of Sontúr just then, for one brow rode high on his forehead. The councillor had not expected Fel'annár's sarcasm, and the commander was secretly glad that his young friend had surprised the old fox.

"Then I am sure this is all a question of negotiation; life often is, Fel'annár. I will see you after lunch to brief you on the ceremony."

Fel'annár bowed and then startled when Damiel returned it with a soft, knowing smile, and when he was gone, Fel'annár turned to Gor'sadén.

"He is . . . *intense*," he said, and Gor'sadén chuckled.

"Yes, that is one way of putting it. He skewers you with those shrewd eyes and reads into your very soul. He underestimated you, I think, but be careful *you* do not underestimate *him*. He is a master of the art of politics, Fel'annár, a true asset to our king. Handir is lucky to have him as his mentor."

Fel'annár nodded and then started once more on the path, Gor'sadén watching him from the corner of his eye. He realised that he felt proud. The boy had stood his ground as a warrior would before Damiel's onslaught but so too had he listened. It was time Fel'annár was rewarded with something he *did* want.

"I have news."

Fel'annár half turned his head to Gor'sadén. "More?"

"Yes, but this is *good* news, Fel'annár. I have secured for you a test . . . with Pan'assár. If you pass it, he will allow you to become my apprentice in the Kal'hamén'Ar."

Gor'sadén was suddenly alone, and he turned to Fel'annár, now behind him, standing rigid in the middle of the path, face no longer pulled down in lingering irritation at Damiel. Instead he scowled in confusion, and then his forehead smoothed over as he began to comprehend just what Gor'sadén had said. But his tongue was tied and he could not speak, and so the commander began to explain.

"Take advantage of the days ahead, for Pan'assár will not allow this easily. He will fight you personally, and you must impress him in every way that you can."

Fel'annár's dawning understanding promptly turned into growing panic. "I can't beat him, Gor'sadén."

"No, no you cannot, and that is not the purpose. But you *can* show him how good you are—you can show him how good you will *become*, with my training." The commander allowed himself a smile. "I trust in you, child, and now, you must trust in yourself. You must have the faith you will need to see this done."

But Fel'annár did not react to the words. Instead he stared back at Gor'sadén as if he had grown spines for hair.

"What is it, Fel'annár?"

He blinked. "I just . . . you reminded me of something Lainon once said." He shook his head. "*Why* do you trust me?" he asked then, his brow drawn together in confusion, but his eyes hungered for an answer.

Why *did* he trust him? Gor'sadén considered himself a good judge of character, and he thought that perhaps it wasn't about Fel'annár's skills as a warrior or his abilities with the trees—it wasn't even about his face or the blood in his veins. It was something unique to Fel'annár. It was an intuition. Gor'sadén simply knew he was not wrong.

"You ask a difficult question. My only answer is that my heart tells me I should. Is that enough of an answer?"

Fel'annár's head leant to one side as he considered the question. And then he smiled.

"It is a good answer," he said, "a *Silvan* answer."

Gor'sadén raised his eyebrows, for the boy's face had transformed once more. He stood looking back at him with a toothy grin, and the commander wondered what was going through the boy's mind, for it looked almost as if he had discovered something—*found* something.

"And the Kal'hamén'Ar? Do you *want* to do the test?" It was a rhetorical question, of course, an attempt to understand Fel'annár's mind. They had gone from speaking of the test to the wherewithal of Gor'sadén's trust in him.

Fel'annár walked up to him, his eyes swimming with some emotion, some power Gor'sadén could not fathom. There was an intensity in his gaze that was hard to endure, and he resisted the urge to step backwards.

"I could never have imagined meeting you, knowing you, being worthy of your *trust,* let alone having the chance to train in the Kal'hamén'Ar. I do not rightly know which I value most." His words trailed off, and Fel'annár stared back at him expectantly while Gor'sadén struggled—and failed—to hide his surprise . . . and his joy.

He was beginning to understand. The boy had never had anyone he could look up to who would teach him, push him to his limits, praise him for his successes and encourage him when he failed, not until Lainon and Turion had taken him under their wing. But Lainon had died and Turion was far away. Gor'sadén, though, was here.

"Forgive me," came Fel'annár's soft words. "There is a storm in here," he gestured to his head. "Handir's words, my father's words, Lainon's absence, and now, the Kal'hamén'Ar." He didn't mention the Silvan healer—the way she had looked upon Handir, the way the prince had gazed back at her.

"Don't let your father's words deter you from your goals, Fel'annár; don't let Handir's resentment change who you are. You have an important decision to take. If you want this, if you truly want me to teach you the ancient art, I *will*. All you have to do is convince Pan'assár and then it is *you* who must trust *me*. Can you do that?"

There was no hesitation in his voice, no reserve on Fel'annár's face, and Gor'sadén smiled even before Fel'annár spoke.

"I trust you," he said. "Your friendship means . . ." The boy stopped, strange lights dancing in his eyes. His left hand moved to cover his right, and Gor'sadén looked at them for a moment, registering the slightest of tremors, and then his eyes were back on Fel'annár.

"What is it?"

Fel'annár shook his head. "Nothing," he lied, releasing his hands and flexing them, eyes momentarily glancing at the trees further away.

Gor'sadén was not convinced, but that intensity in his young friend's eyes was back and he thought perhaps that he should not push him.

"Tomorrow you become a lord and the day after, you fight for the right to become my apprentice, a Kah Warrior."

"I won't let you down."

"I know." And he did; he knew it with a surety he had seldom felt. A change was coming to his own life, one he grasped with enthusiasm. It was time for Gor'sadén to shine once more, as he once had with the Three, but his purpose, beyond training Fel'annár, was yet to be revealed.

∼

Handir and Llyniel sat at the table in the prince's quarters, sated after their private lunch and nostalgic of younger, more innocent days.

But it was time to tell Llyniel what he had held back from her. Since that afternoon when she had interrupted his conversation with Fel'annár, he knew he could postpone it no longer, and so he turned to his friend, her honey eyes already resting on him, cool and expectant.

He breathed deeply. "Heed me, Llyn: what I have to say must not be spoken of with anyone else, I *mean* it. When I tell you, you will understand why. This is no game I speak of now, but something which may turn dangerous for us both. If you truly want to know, you must accept the risks."

Llyniel frowned, one hand reaching out to cover Handir's. "If *you* are in this and it is dangerous, then I will stand at your side and bear that danger with you. But you already knew this. Tell me."

She had been patient only because she'd seen the gravity in Handir's eyes when he had asked her to wait, and she had. But when she had inadvertently interrupted Handir and Fel'annár, she began to suspect. Why had Handir needed to speak with Fel'annár? What did that have to do with her question of why Fel'annár was even here in Tar'eastór?

"Captain Turion, Lieutenant Lainon, myself and . . . and *your father*, we have a plan. We mean to confront Band'orán and rid our forest of his taint."

Llyniel's eyes grew wide, and she leaned backwards slowly, breath caught in her chest. She didn't understand. Her father was a *coward*, had never stood up for her people, for her *mother's* people. Handir's words made no sense, and yet his eyes told her he did not lie.

Even as a child, she remembered her mother's sad eyes and the eternal apology in her father's eyes. She remembered her own frustration, at first unaddressed, and then, later, she remembered her anger when she had given voice to her concerns. All she received from her father was a measured call for calm and patience. *Patience? How can you stand in the presence of racial discrimination and ask for patience?*

As soon as she had taken the grade as junior healer, she had packed some scant belongings and joined the royal caravan bound for the south-western Port Helia, the southernmost tip of Ea Uaré. She had travelled the villages there, perfecting the art of healing, learning of herbs and shrubs, of *tree barks*. She had come into herself, discovered her own voice, her own convictions. And then she had secured a position in the Healing Halls of Pelagia under the tutorship of Master Tanor, earning the title of head healer.

She would never go back to Ea Uaré, not while King Thargodén continued to do nothing, while Chief Councillor *Aradan* did nothing. Her dream of serving as a master healer in Ea Uaré together with Master Nestar would never become a reality, but that would not stop her. She would become Master Healer, wherever she was.

She shook herself out of her memories and listened to Handir's unlikely tale. Indeed, for the next hour, Handir explained their plan. She interrupted him with her own questions, and he answered them as best he could, but he had seen the moment when shock had turned to disbelief and then steely determination to be a part of it, just as he knew she would. He had involved her in his dangerous scheme, but he could not find it within himself to regret it. From the moment he had seen her at the stables, he knew he would have to tell her. Llyniel was a healer, a good one, or so they said, but she possessed another trait. She was brave and acutely aware of her people's suffering. It had driven her away from Ea Uaré, away from her parents, and yet perhaps now there was a chance that she could return, that she could see her father, Councillor Aradan, for what he truly was—a brave and intelligent soul who, above all things, revered Handir's own father, the king. He was *not* a coward; he was a king's man. He had done everything to keep Thargodén on the throne, even unto the loss of his own daughter's regard.

But his decision to tell Llyniel had not only been to honour her wishes or because he felt she had a right to know. There was a part of him that wanted to see her reunited with her father, an elf Handir respected, loved even as a father. And then there was that selfish part of himself that rejoiced at the prospect of her help and support. She would bring balance to his own, admittedly volatile thoughts with respect to Fel'annár. She would keep him focussed, ground him, counsel him like no other could, except for Aradan himself. It was selfish of him, but he *had* warned her of the dangers, had tried to dissuade her from wanting to know. But she had not cared for the danger, and he was so very glad that she hadn't.

His happiness was soured by the memory of how Fel'annár had left their meeting, of how he had looked at Llyniel as he passed her. Handir had seen anger and then curiosity, and the spark of suspicion was seeded in his mind.

∼

Lord Damiel had visited Fel'annár after lunch and accompanied him to what was to be his new suite of rooms, not two corridors away from Prince Sontúr's living quarters. He explained the short ceremony that would take place the following day and assured Fel'annár that all he had to do was stand before the king's council and look lordly. He would then utter two words, and miraculously, Fel'annár would become a lord. The evening would bring with it a small celebration at the king's table, where Fel'annár would dine in the presence of princes and kings. He comforted himself in the knowledge that Sontúr, at least, would be there.

Once Damiel had finished his explanations, Fel'annár had named his own condition for moving into the palace. In truth he had been sceptical that Damiel would accept and had been pleasantly surprised at the lack of objection. The Company would have their own room beside his, and although it was only one suite for the five of them, still, it was a luxury for any base warrior to have his own bathing chamber and the finest soaps and oils good money could buy. He had then wrought from Damiel the promise of finding more beds to accommodate them all.

Ramien ran the tips of his fingers over a skilfully-carved chest of drawers, eyes travelling over the gauzy drapes and the floor-to-ceiling windows behind. And then he turned and smiled, lumbering over to the roaring fire.

"This hearth is as big as the one in our village hall where Carentia roasts the chickens."

"And there's another one in the bedroom," said Galdith, smiling as he ran into the bathing area, where Carodel was already opening jars of colourful liquids and soaps, inhaling their aromas noisily.

"Ah brother!" exclaimed Idernon. "You were a genius to wrangle that boon from Lord Damiel, not that we mind the barracks. But someone needs to watch you, and we cannot do that when we are there and you are here."

"That's true," said Fel'annár, smiling. He sat on a cushioned window seat and looked out over the jagged grey horizon, listening as his brothers chatted merrily about his suite of rooms, and although Galadan's voice could not be heard, he knew he would be watching it all from one corner.

The royal tailor was due any moment, and, after a knock on the door, Fel'annár stood as Galadan opened it. It was not the tailor; it was Prince Handir. The chatter ceased, and The Company bowed low to their prince.

"Fel'annár. A private word if you would."

"Of course, my prince." He nodded at The Company, who filed out of his new rooms and to their own adjacent suite. Ramien, though, stayed outside Fel'annár's door, for it was his turn to guard it.

"You have seen Lord Damiel," stated the prince as he sat the parcels he had brought with him on the table before the hearth.

"I have. He has told me how it will work tomorrow."

"There are some details that need to be addressed—specifically your presentation. As a lord of Ea Uaré, a *Silvan* lord."

Fel'annár's head cocked to one side. Handir was scheming, he thought, and his defences slipped into place.

"What details, my prince?"

"The question of how you will present yourself. You are a Silvan lord."

"And am I not also Alpine?"

"That you are. And do you wish to be presented as an Alpine lord?"

"I wish to be presented as what I *am*."

"Well then, should we dress you as an Alpine, as a Silvan, or as something entirely *different*?"

"I am both. It would make sense to dress as *both*, although I fail to see how an Alpine tailor would capture *that* idea."

Handir smiled, and Fel'annár swallowed thickly.

"I had anticipated that," said Handir, and Fel'annár was not surprised at all. "An example, if I may," he said. Fel'annár nodded and then flinched backwards when Handir reached for the honour stone at the end of his braid.

"This is a symbol. It is a *prohibited* symbol, an Honour Stone."

Fel'annár's eyes narrowed. He would not remove it, whatever Handir said.

"Why do you wear it, if you know it is not allowed?"

"Because it was given to me in love and respect. Why would the

Alpine commanders of our army forbid such a thing unless it was to repress us, annihilate Silvan culture until it's nothing but a distant memory of times gone by?"

"Well-said, Warrior. And so you wear it to *show* that you disagree," continued Handir. "You wear it to remind others that you are Silvan, and that this custom must not be lost. I have seen others of your company wearing them; your circle of warrior rebels, it seems."

"You would disapprove?"

"On the contrary. I applaud the initiative."

Fel'annár blinked. Handir was inciting him to break the rules, encouraging him to influence others to do the same.

"You are surprised," ventured Handir.

"Yes. I thought this dressing and faffing a necessary evil, but I see, now, your point in this."

And Fel'annár did, but Handir was pushing him to accept what he thought should be Fel'annár's role in the plan, and anger began to surface. It wasn't that Fel'annár could not see the merits in that cause —in Lainon's plan—but he had already told Handir that he would think about his own role in it. He would not be manipulated into participating and certainly not unwittingly. Not by Handir, not by Damiel.

Handir reached for the wrapped parcels he had brought with him, tearing the paper and revealing the contents. Fel'annár stepped forward and reached out for the sumptuous cloth, holding it up before him.

"You wish me to wear *this*?"

"I do."

His eyes roamed over the peculiar pattern of the deep green tunic, and after a moment of silence, he dropped the garment and turned to his prince.

"Then it will be as you *command*, my prince."

Handir bristled, because beneath the servitude was rebellion. Fel'annár would not do this because he accepted his role in the plan, even though he wore his honour stone for all to see. It made sense to

Handir that, as a self-proclaimed Silvan, he would wear these garments, but Fel'annár had seen his mind, read his intentions, and had made it clear that he accepted Handir's request because it was an *order*. Handir had achieved his goal, should have been satisfied, but for some strange reason, all he felt was disappointment.

~

That night, Fel'annár lay in his new bed in his new suite of rooms, the mellow orange glow from the hearth softening the darkness.

Tomorrow, he would be presented as a lord, and once that was done, he would endure the pomp and then prepare himself for his test for the Kal'hamén'Ar. Perhaps then, his life would return to some semblance of normalcy. He would lead the life of a warrior, even though he would be stuck here at the palace and called a lord.

Tailors had come and gone; books on Silvan lore, Alpine politics, and the workings of a monarchy were left piled up on his shelves, from Handir no doubt. He would be dressed and pampered and then taken before the king while he read King Thargodén's decree. After that, Fel'annár would endure a formal dinner at King Vorn'asté's table.

As for The Company, while Sontúr and Fel'annár dined with the lords, they would visit the local taverns. They had invented some hare-brained story that their outing was, in fact, an advance reconnaissance tour to register the land before Lord Fel'annár braved it. He snorted in mirth for the first time that day; he was glad they would get some time to themselves, that Carodel would finally live his dream of visiting the Alpine inns with more than his own kneecaps in his pockets at last. It was Sontúr who had proposed they meet later, and Fel'annár could only smirk at the state in which he would surely find them.

But then his traitorous mind led him to Handir and King Thargodén, and he knew, then, that sleep would not grace him. He crept from his bedroom and into the living area where Galdith was snoozing lightly. He turned, catching Fel'annár's gaze and standing.

"Peace, Galdith, I mean only to take a stroll."

He said nothing and simply picked up his weapons harness and strapped it on, following Fel'annár as he left the room. Passing the barracks, they veered left to the familiar and by now well-used copse of trees.

Handir had manoeuvred things in such a way that, whatever happened in the proclamation tomorrow, Fel'annár would be forced to make a political statement. He had walked into that trap himself, and although it had irked him at the time, now that he thought about it, it was not so bad. An impression had promptly turned into a suspicion. Damiel knew of the plan, and together with Handir, they were scheming to bring Fel'annár over to their side. Handir was his brother, but he was also a statesman, a good one. Everything he did was for his father's realm, and Fel'annár did not doubt that he would do anything to safeguard it, even at his brother's expense. Is that what Or'Talán had done? he asked himself and then scowled at the invading thought.

And then his father's words of conciliation replayed in his mind.

Come to me as my son, he had said, even though the missive had not been signed. It would be for security reasons, thought Fel'annár, but then he wondered. Had it been because he did not know *how* to sign it? For what would he say? *King Thargodén? Your father?*

"Father," he tried, the word strange in his mouth, and he wondered if a day would ever come when such a simple word would leave his mouth, not in anger but in love.

Looking up at a towering spruce, he sensed a presence high in the boughs. Only a Silvan would while away the time in a tree. With a nod at Galdith, he climbed, wondering which member of The Company it would be.

He scurried up the bark, pulling himself skywards. He could see someone sitting against the central trunk, and he froze. It was too late to slink away, not that he wanted to, but he would not have interrupted her privacy had he known.

"Healer?"

A sudden rustle of cloth and then a waterfall of auburn hair as she looked downwards. "Warrior."

"Am I intruding?" he called back.

"It is not my tree. Come up, Silvan." She watched as he accommodated himself on a branch opposite hers, his long legs stretching out before him.

"I couldn't sleep," he said simply.

"Well then, two sleepless Silvans," she smirked. "You are from Lan Taria?"

"Yes, and before you say it, I know I don't look Silvan."

"No. But you *feel* Silvan," she said, and Fel'annár's smile widened. No one had ever said that to him before.

"And you?" asked Fel'annár.

"Sen Garay."

"Ah. My friend Carodel is your countryman."

"Carodel? Surely *he's* not here!"

Fel'annár's eyebrows arched, a soft smile on his face. "You know our Bard Warrior?"

"*Know* him? He was the terror of our village. A naughty one, I tell you. He was never without a lover, using that lyre of his to lure his victims," snorted Llyn, and Fel'annár laughed out loud.

"That's the one," he said, briefly wondering if she, too, had been lured. "I am Fel'annár," he added, feeling the need to introduce himself despite the stupidity of it. She surely knew who he was by now.

"Llyniel."

Fel'annár watched as her gaze seemed to lose focus, as if she were remembering something. "You miss home," he ventured.

"I miss the Forest, but I was brought up in the city, at court," she said somewhat sourly.

"You didn't enjoy it?"

"I am *Silvan*. How could I? So few trees, so few friendly faces, always separated from my cousins in the Forest. It was sweet enough when I was a young child. I have no siblings, but I grew together with the king's children. They are my brothers and sisters—Handir especially though."

Fel'annár tried his best not to show his confusion at her comment. The way Handir and Llyniel had looked at each other did not strike him as fraternal, and yet she had just suggested that was what she felt for the prince.

He needed to know. He needed to be sure.

One strong hand smoothed over the branch he sat upon, movements careful and rhythmic, and Llyniel's eyes focussed on it. He pulled his hand back.

"Sontúr says you arrived in the company of Pelagians," said Fel'annár.

"I spent the last ten years there, serving under Master Healer Tanor. I am preparing a theory on deciduous tree barks and their uses in the healing sciences."

Fel'annár's eyebrows rose. "I've only ever used them to light campfires."

Llyniel smiled. "You'd be surprised; they can save lives."

"I believe you. Still, ten years in Pelagia is a long time. You must have family," he said, leaning back against the trunk, trying his best not to seem overly interested in her reply.

She stared back at him for a moment, and Fel'annár knew she had understood the underlying question. She was deciding whether to deflect it or answer it. "I am busy with my studies for now. It's not easy to become Master Healer at my age, Fel'annár. It is a highly competitive thing to train under one of the great healers, and to work with Master Arané is a dream. There is little that could deter me from staying here, for a while at least." Her eyes were drawn once more to Fel'annár's hand, which was once more stroking over a branch. "I do wonder, though, what's going on back home."

"Why do you say that?" asked Fel'annár, a suspicion beginning to form in his mind.

"Well, for one, I've heard a most unlikely tale, Fel'annár. You are Handir's half-brother. If that news has permeated in the Forest, I can only imagine the scandal and hearsay that must be flying everywhere."

She was blunt in the purest of Silvan fashion, but she seemed to realise it had made him uncomfortable.

"Just . . . ignore me," she said with a rueful smile, even as she flapped one hand in front of her own face. "It's no slight against you."

Fel'annár's head cocked to one side, smiling at her antics. His suspicions were stronger now, and he wondered just how much Handir had told her, whether she knew about the plan. She was blunt in her Silvanness, but so was he.

"What else has Prince Handir told you?"

She shrugged. "He has told me who you are—that, and of Lainon's death."

Fel'annár averted his gaze. He knew that she watched him, but he couldn't hide his grief, and for some reason he did not feel the need to. He just hoped she would not press the issue.

She did not.

"I have missed this, being up here," she said. "There are few trees in the Pelagian Isles, and here, thank Aria, we have this copse and the surrounding forests at least."

"It's a small mercy to us Silvans. I've travelled the surrounding lands and found many wooded areas. But there's nothing quite like the Deep Forest." He smiled fondly, gaze turned inwards and to his memories of Ea Uaré. He had always wanted to travel to Ea Nanú and see the giant trees, but that, too, had been prohibited to him. His soft, nostalgic smile faltered, and he turned back to Llyniel, inexplicably glad that she seemed so at ease, so confident here in the heights.

"We could take a trip to the forests of the Downlands, just be Silvan for one day," said Fel'annár with his winning smile. She arched an eyebrow at him.

"Being *Silvan* implies many things, Warrior. Which one are you referring to?"

"Whichever one you wish," he said, smile widening. "I mean we *could* just sit in the trees, talk of trees, eat . . . in the trees, that sort of thing."

She snorted irreverently, and Fel'annár grinned back at her, glad she had not taken offence. He felt stupid—again— but he couldn't help it. He was driven by his need to know how she felt about Handir, how she felt about *him*.

"I am a good Silvan lad, Llyniel. My aunt taught me well." It was half the truth, but he didn't want to scare her away.

"We should take Handir. The fool knows nothing of the Forest, all that he is prince of our lands." Her eyes stared back at him, watching him for a reaction. She must have seen it, because she smirked back at him. She knew what he had meant by his comment about *being Silvan*, just as she knew he had no intention of inviting Handir.

They talked then, of Handir's and therefore Fel'annár's imminent return to the Forest. He told her of the ambush on their way to Tar'eastór and then of his plans to take the test for Blade Master. She told him of her theories on deciduous tree barks and of her dreams of becoming Master Healer. They shared tales of childhood in the villages, of how she had wanted to spend more time there but had never been allowed to while he told her of how he had never been allowed to travel *anywhere else*. Their talk was easy and relaxed, amusing and empathic, interesting and so involving that they had become oblivious to the passage of time.

"It's cold, and I have duties tomorrow. I am pleased to have met you, Fel'annár of Lan Taria. You have brought the Forest back to my heart for tonight at least."

He smiled and then watched as she returned it, her eyes straying to his lips for just a moment before she turned and began to navigate the trunk. She stopped and looked up at him, a lop-sided grin on her face. "I will think about that outing. *Being Silvan* for a while does not sound so bad," she said, and then she was gone. Fel'annár stared after her, his mind only slowly registering what she had just said. She had understood his meaning perfectly.

She *was* interested in him.

But the shadow of doubt still lingered in his mind. She had known Handir since they were children, and Fel'annár had not missed that look of complicity when Llyniel and Handir's gazes had locked. He had seen love, and for all that he tried, he could not shake the idea that Llyniel and Handir were lovers, or perhaps had been at one time. But then Llyniel had not rejected Fel'annár's proposal and he did not think she would play Handir for a fool.

Still, she had a dream, just as Fel'annár did. She wanted to become Master Healer; he wanted to be a Silvan captain. She would stay in Tar'eastór while he returned with Handir to a conflicted forest. He laughed at himself, shaking his head at his own stupidity. What was he *thinking*? He had proposed a Silvan fling in the trees and she had suggested she might be interested. There was nothing more to it, and here he was musing over the fact that they would soon part ways.

Still, he would tread carefully. Handir might be interested in her, and perhaps even Llyniel did not realise it. He tried to imagine what a relationship between her and the prince would mean in the Forest, the way Handir had painted it to him. Aria forbid he held feelings for a Silvan commoner. The Alpine purists would surely not allow it, and if Fel'annár had things *his* way, neither would *he*.

SIX
WARRIOR LORD

*"Appearances can give a first impression that is difficult to change.
Only a remarkable word or a remarkable elf can change them. Handir
knew this and played it to his advantage. He had put much thought
into his brother's attire . . . and none at all into his feelings."*
The Silvan Chronicles, Book V. Marhené.

~

"I'll be gone all day, brothers. I won't see you until we retire," said Fel'annár as he stood before the hearth in his rooms, his sleeping breaches hanging low off his waist, damp hair slowly drying.

"So when do you get your fancy clothes?" asked Ramien.

"I already have them. Prince Handir is adamant I present myself in the *proper* fashion." He cast his eyes over The Company, daring them to poke fun at his expense.

"Just—don't let him manicure your hands, Fel'annár," pleaded Galdith. "You're a *warrior*—you're supposed to have hands like crunchy leaves and nails as black as squirrel droppings."

"I'll have no say in the matter, Galdith. I'm a puppet in the hands of our prince."

"So you are saying, Galdith, that a warrior may not have a manicure because then he will not be a warrior?" asked Idernon.

Galdith turned to the Wise Warrior and held his challenging gaze with one of his own. "Yes—that is *exactly* what I am saying."

Idernon's eyebrow arched acutely, but he said no more. Instead he turned to Fel'annár. "I wouldn't miss our Fel'annár all lordly in his finery," he smirked, eyes glittering.

"You'll have to make do with the end result," said Fel'annár. "Go, and enjoy your day," he added with a smile. "And your evening." He smirked at Carodel, who sat polishing his boots. He knew Idernon would fret about who would guard him, but the truth was, Fel'annár needed time to himself—to think.

Idernon nodded. "You'll stay inside, with Sontúr and Gor'sadén?"

"I will," he said, and then watched as they filed out of the door. He turned back to the fire, relishing its warmth on his bare skin, but someone was returning.

"Fel'annár." It was Handir, surely come to ensure that he was preparing himself in the proper fashion. He did not expect to hear *Llyniel's* voice.

"Have a care, soldier. Half-naked warrior lords are highly coveted around these parts," she drawled. He could almost hear the smirk on her face and he turned, trying and failing to mask his surprise even though his own lips curled upwards.

He bowed at Handir and then turned to face her. "I am quite capable of protecting myself," he answered with a smirk, eyes roving over her form.

She no longer wore the straight, black robes of the healers but a simple yet elegant blue dress that accentuated her body, her auburn hair half up and half down, accentuating her long, naked neck of smooth, creamy skin. His fingers tingled at the thought of ghosting his way from her ear and downwards . . .

"Fel'annár."

He snapped from his imaginings and looked at Handir. His own smirk vanished in the wake of the prince's darkening gaze.

He was jealous.

"I know you two have met, although not formally," said Handir with practised calm. "Lady Llyniel of Sen Garay, this is Lord Fel'annár of Lan Taria."

"My lady," said Fel'annár with a bow. He had not realised she was a noble. Not so incompatible with Handir, he mused. His eyes darted around for a shirt to cover himself, and Llyniel smiled a *naughty* smile. Fel'annár could not help the twitch of his lips at her audacity, in spite of Handir's visible irritation.

"Forgive me, I was not expecting company," he said.

"Well, I am sure Llyniel has seen it all before," said Handir somewhat curtly, but there was a gleam in his eyes and Fel'annár wanted to scowl at him.

"Listen to me, Fel'annár," began the prince, his tone that of a superior to his servant. "Take your time dressing, be mindful of what you represent. Today you become a lord of my father's realm—you become a lord of Ea Uaré. That privilege comes with duties."

"I understand my duty, my prince."

"Good. I am aware you find this tedious, that you would rather be elsewhere with the warriors."

"You have already explained I have no choice in the matter, my prince. If it is the will of my king, I will obey."

"It is. However, it would be desirable that you, too, saw the merit in this."

Fel'annár knew what *"this"* meant. Handir was pushing him to accept his part in this grand plan, and his eyes slipped to Llyniel. But she simply stared back at him and Fel'annár knew that she knew, that Handir had told her. But then why *wouldn't* he? She was special to him, Fel'annár could see it in the prince's glittering eyes, hear it in his imperious words, feel it almost as a tangible barrier he wove around her. He was protecting her, he mused, protecting her from *him*. And then another thought pushed its way to the fore. Was she trying to seduce him to help Handir garner his acceptance of the plan?

Fel'annár remained silent and Handir turned to Llyniel with a gesture. "We will leave you to prepare."

Fel'annár bowed, eyes lingering thoughtfully on the noble healer as she walked out the door. Once they were gone, he turned back to the fire, alone with his thoughts of politics, of duty, of his attraction to a woman Handir did not want him to have, a woman that perhaps was playing him, luring him into a plan he was not convinced he should accept.

~

"You *fancy* him," said Handir as they walked down the corridor and back to his suite to await the summons from the king. "Have a care, Llyn. He is a warrior."

"Don't be a fool, Handir. From what I've heard and seen, *everyone* fancies him, but that doesn't mean I want to *marry* him, does it?"

"No," said Handir. "So what *do* you want to do with him?" He turned to meet her squarely. He had not meant for it to sound funny, but to Llyniel it had, and he rolled his eyes in exasperation of her Silvan humour. She swiped him across the shoulder, laughing as he batted her hand away. The prince played along with her mischief, but she had not missed his anger. It was something she would need to address with him, for although she did not take kindly to it, she knew it was born of love for her.

But Handir's question stubbornly remained in her mind. What *did* she want to do with Fel'annár? She smirked. Handir was right, she did fancy him; it was hard not to, and a thrill of excitement coursed through her body at the thought of his proposal to *be Silvan*. But Handir was also right in that Fel'annár was a *warrior*. Should she allow herself to feel anything more for him, that fact might well bring heartache, even grief, something that would interfere with her plans of becoming Master Healer, of helping Handir with Lainon's plan.

Lainon's plan, she mused. She herself had readily accepted to help in whatever capacity she could, and she failed to understand why any Silvan would not. She had seen the honour stone in Fel'annár's hair, had heard how the others referred to him as The Silvan. It was not because he did not understand the merits of it. She could see that he did. His resistance came from somewhere else, perhaps from his feelings towards Handir, a half-brother he would see as the reason his mother was denied her soulmate, the reason for her absence.

Llyniel and Handir had once kissed, and then both had said it had not felt right. Llyniel briefly toyed with the idea that Handir had lied, that perhaps he had said that to help her reject him. But it was a fleeting idea, because Llyniel knew Handir better than anyone else. His was not the love of a suitor; it was not unrequited love. It was the fierce love of a brother who would never be satisfied with Llyniel's choice, especially if that choice was his half-brother—one he had yet to accept.

∼

Fel'annár did not recognise himself at all, for a lord stared back at him in the full-length mirror, a lord the likes of which he had never seen. But Fel'annár was a *warrior*. He felt bare without his leather vambraces and his pauldron, his chest protection and his harnesses.

Handir had been busy, he realised, had clearly given much thought to these designs—designs he had never seen before. He briefly wondered where they came from. A spark of resentment towards Handir washed over him, for forcing the issue, an issue he knew Fel'annár had yet to accept, but even so, the result was strangely pleasing. He would have done this himself, given the chance, for this attire was beautiful—political statement though it was. The form-fitting tunic reached down to his booted calves, and the front was slit up past his knees. One sleeve reached down past his wrist while the other was cut at the shoulder, revealing his Master Archer band and the strong muscles of his arm. Over his bare forearm was a skilfully-crafted bracer running from elbow to wrist. It was Alpine in its military opulence, Silvan in its masculine allure. Alpine and Silvan, just like himself: an open challenge to the Alpine purists back home.

He felt comfortable.

An attendant had been sent to braid his hair, and he had asked him to braid it in the way Galadan had once shown him: Silvan side braids, a central Alpine braid, and the Ari locks gathered around his crown in honour of Lainon. Amareth would be proud, he smirked. But Lainon would have rendered a better result. Something swam over his vision, and he blinked to clear whatever it was that had collected there. It was not the first time it had happened to him recently and he thought he would ask Sontúr about it. Had he been looking in the mirror, he would have seen a wisp of blue pass over his right eye.

Three knocks on the door and Handir entered, decked finely as a prince of Ea Uaré, and upon his head was a golden headdress, woven into his hair at the sides. Fel'annár straightened and then bowed.

Handir's eyes travelled the length of his half-brother, reticent, perhaps, to admit that he cut a fine form indeed.

"Is my appearance to your satisfaction, my prince?"

Handir had been trained in the art of subtlety and his face remained devoid of emotion as he observed the results of his research on Silvan history. His eyes ran over the braids in Fel'annár's hair, understanding their meaning, and then he saw the Master band on a strong arm, an arm that had killed many Deviants in service to his realm and Tar'eastór. A wave of admiration hit him unexpectedly, and he quelled it, gave it no importance beyond that of a job well done.

"It is. Come."

No sooner had they left the room than Fel'annár realised The Company had not yet left. Instead they stood chatting and laughing and then turned to prince and warrior—only to fall utterly silent, as if they had been caught stealing nut cakes. They had surely thought to tease Fel'annár in his finery, but now that he was before them, all thoughts of childish banter scattered. All they could do was stare on as the brothers left, bound for the king's council chambers. It was the last time they would see Fel'annár as a simple warrior. When next they met, they would owe him deference as a lord of Ea Uaré.

As they continued towards the council chambers, Handir watched as all those they passed stopped to stare while others bowed in respect. But it was when they came to stand upon the threshold of the council chambers that Handir's skin tingled and the true weight of his brother's presence slammed into him, taking him completely by surprise, as if a blindfold had been ripped from his eyes, eyes that had not wanted to see, to admit just how much Fel'annár looked like Or'Talán, how much his presence affected those around him, for they stared openly, unashamedly, even those who had been trained to hide their thoughts. It wasn't just his similarity to Or'Talán, though. It was his compelling presence, his commanding essence. There was a surety about him, something magnetic that drew others to him. Was this what Lainon had seen in him?

"Prince Handir of Ea Uaré, Warrior Fel'annár of Ea Uaré." A powerful voice rang out over the din, and the heavy doors banged shut behind them. The path towards the king's throne began to open before them, but the people moved too slowly. Lords and ladies, councillors and advisors lingered before them, eyes on Fel'annár's face, his hair, and the odd fashion of his clothes. Those further behind moved from one side to another for a better look at the new lord, and for a moment, Handir did not envy his half-brother at all. He turned his head to read his expression, but it was not as he had suspected. There was no distress, no anger, no challenge in his eyes. What Handir saw was not a boy overwhelmed by his circumstances; he saw a warrior lord, powerful and proud.

He recognised the blood of princes.

Handir walked towards the dais, feeling Fel'annár's bare shoulder close to his. Strange that he should feel proud to present his reluctant brother at Vorn'asté's court. But the fleeting thought was ruthlessly quashed as they came to stand before the steps that led to the king's stone throne. To one side stood Commanders Gor'sadén and Pan'assár, magnificent in their shining armour. Both were Kah masters, but only one of them bore the purple sash that said it was so. On the other side stood Lord Damiel with Prince Sontúr and then Lady Llyniel who waited for Handir to join her.

The king rose and accepted a scroll from Damiel's jewelled hands and, with a cursory glance at his guests, he began the day's proceedings.

"My ladies, lords and councillors, it is my duty as king to read the words of my fellow ruler, Thargodén Ar Or'Talán of Ea Uaré. I read, literally, his decree, to be read before his own ruling council during the celebration of the first Forest Summit."

Fel'annár scowled. He had never heard of a Forest Summit, and for some reason his eyes slipped towards Llyniel. She too was confused, he realised. Something had happened in their homeland, some political event they had no knowledge of.

"I, Thargodén, son of Or'Talán, second king of Ea Uaré do proclaim that Fel'annár of Lan Taria is my son, born of Lássira of Abiren'á, daughter of Zendár Ari'atór."

There were murmurs of shock, but Fel'annár heard none of them. His mother was the daughter of an Ari'atór, he was the grandson of an Ari'atór...

"Also do I proclaim that Fel'annár of Lan Taria is named Lord of Ea Uaré, his rights and privileges to be debated at High Court."

Vorn'asté lowered the scroll and fixed his eyes on Fel'annár. "Fel'annár of Lan Taria, do you accept this honour from your king?"

He could not speak, and his eyes slipped once more to Llyniel, who was staring back at him. It was not pity in her eyes but empathy. She felt for him, had seen his shock, and he wanted to reach out, touch her, but instead he stood riveted, eyes moving to Handir beside her, but in the prince's eyes, all he saw was silent expectation.

"I do." The words had slipped past him, and he suddenly wanted to pull them back, but he couldn't. He had done exactly what Damiel had asked of him. He had swum with the tide and could no longer turn back.

"I, Vorn'asté Ar Caren'ár, seventh king of Tar'eastór, proclaim that this here is Lord Fel'annár Ar Thargodén. Be he welcomed in our realm."

A mighty thump of a staff against the floor echoed around them, and slowly, voices began to rise. Fel'annár let out a rush of air and looked around—for anyone to anchor himself. He found Sontúr, who was walking towards him, eyes searching and perhaps understanding.

"You didn't know?" he murmured.

Fel'annár shook his head, still in shock at the revelation.

The prince's sparkling grey eyes searched and found Prince Handir, but no words crossed his lips. They weren't necessary.

Censure, confusion, *dislike*.

"Come, away from this crowd and to somewhere quiet."

Fel'annár simply nodded, but his passage to the now opened door was blocked by Handir and Llyniel.

Sontúr stiffened. "Have you not done enough, Prince Handir?"

"I have done my duty."

"A prince has a duty to his own *heart*, Handir; where is *yours*?"

"I didn't know he was ignorant of his origins."

"You could have asked. He didn't even know who his *father* was until just months past. Had you cared, you would have suspected."

Handir stared back at Sontúr, jaw tightening, but with Llyniel's hand on his back he stepped to one side and then watched as a silent Fel'annár left with a fuming prince, and just behind them were the commanders. Pan'assár nodded at his prince, but Gor'sadén stared at him with cold blue eyes as he passed.

"It was not my intention, Llyniel."

There was censure in her eyes, but there was something else, too, and Handir did not like it.

"I do not want your *pity*, Llyniel," he ground out, and she turned to face him.

"And yet you have it."

She left his side and Handir was alone amongst the crowd of Alpine councillors. Alone as he had been since Lainon died.

Alone.

～

Fel'annár was walking, striding through the hallways, unaware of those who stared after him and Sontúr. Was this connection to the Ari'atór a reason why he had this skill with the trees? And did Zendár still live? Did he have Silvan family in the Deep Forest apart from Amareth? And if he did, why had they never visited? Had that, too, been deemed dangerous?

"Where are you going, Fel'annár?"

"Away, anywhere but in there."

They were outside, walking briskly along the pathways that led past the Inner Circle and then skirted around the training grounds. Not even the sparring warriors were enough to draw Fel'annár's eyes away from the path ahead of him, and soon they were in the more remote areas of the public gardens. Fel'annár's steps slowed until he stopped and turned to face Sontúr.

"My mother was from Abiren'á, she was the daughter of an Ari'atór. My grandfather's name is, or was, Zendár. I wonder if he, too, is dead."

Sontúr sighed heavily. "You knew none of that. It is unfortunate indeed that your brother did not see fit to check with you before that decree was read; indeed I must wonder if Thargodén did not ask him to do so. It seems callous."

"Callous, yes. But then he is a prince on a mission. Why did I expect anything else?"

"Because he is your *brother*. It is logical to assume he would feel something for you."

"Well, he doesn't. Better for me. I don't *need* a brother; I don't *need* a father."

"But you want them all the same." A deep, husky voice that was not Sontúr—and both elves turned to Llyniel.

"You do not *know* me, my lady," said Fel'annár. "You don't know what I want and what I do *not*." His tone was far from the one he had used the previous night up in the trees when they had talked and laughed.

"I do not mean to offend, Lord Fel'annár. But you are ignoring the truth, and you do not need *me* to tell you this."

"Then why tell me at *all*?"

"Fel'annár, I come on behalf of one I have loved my entire life..."

"You would come in defence of *him*? Because he is your *lover*, your *what*?"

Her countenance changed so suddenly that Fel'annár bit his tongue and watched as she walked towards him.

"You do not know me at *all*, my lord."

Fel'annár recognised his own words to her just moments before, and he nodded slowly in apology.

"You come on behalf of one you *love*," began Sontúr. "But he has not even the slightest of consideration for his own brother. He kept those messages from their rightful owner, he did not bother to tell him he has family somewhere in the Forest. This prince that you love is a frozen block of *ice*."

"Sontúr," said Fel'annár, turning to his friend and placing a hand on his forearm. "Give me a moment, will you?"

Sontúr's glittering eyes moved from Fel'annár to Llyniel, and then he nodded curtly.

"I will be nearby."

"Thank you," said Fel'annár, watching as his friend turned to leave, not before pinning the Silvan healer with a look that brooked no argument. She, however, simply stared back at Sontúr defiantly before turning to Fel'annár.

"Handir assumed that you knew."

"He never bothered to think about it."

"No, and for that he is sorry."

"Then why is *he* not here?"

"Because to come to you, now, would be tantamount to acknowledging you as a brother, not in words but in deeds. He is not ready for that, and I wager you aren't either."

"And I never will be, if he does not show me his heart."

"Has he seen yours, Fel'annár?"

"No. I have hidden that from him. But then it is not *me* asking *him* to trust me."

She said nothing. Fel'annár didn't want to be angry in her presence, and his steely gaze softened.

"I apologise. It's just . . . a delicate subject, that's all."

"I know a little of your story, Fel'annár, and I think perhaps that I understand in some small way."

Fel'annár turned expectant eyes on her. He had assumed that Handir would have spoken to Llyniel, but just how much of his private life had the prince revealed to this woman, a stranger to him?

"I can only imagine that, for someone who never had a family, every last detail of who you are is important. You know so little."

"And now you know as much as I, Lady Llyniel." He should have been angry at her for delving into his personal affairs, for presuming she would be welcomed to do so. But he could not express anger because, strangely, he did not feel it, not towards her at least.

"I *do* understand you a little, Fel'annár. You and I have much in common."

"How so?" asked Fel'annár with a frown.

"Silvan mother, Alpine father . . ."

Fel'annár started. He had not expected that. To look at her dark features, her accent, and her open ways, she was pure Silvan, the exact opposite of himself. He was momentarily distracted by the highlights of autumn hues in her soft hair.

"You look Silvan," murmured Fel'annár, and she smiled.

"And you look Alpine. Is that why they call you The Silvan?" smiled the healer and Fel'annár could not stop his traitorous mouth from spreading into a smile of his own.

"That is the short of it." His smile turned lop-sided. His anger was gone; it wasn't important.

Llyniel's smile widened, and a sparkle came to her eye. "You know, I have known Handir since I was a babe. I was raised at court with the royal family, as you know. They are the siblings I never had. Handir and I share a singular friendship, Fel'annár. We know each other so well, love each other so well, not as soul mates do but as twins perhaps; as Prince Rinon is to Princess Maeneth."

Fel'annár stood searching her eyes and found only truth behind them. But a question begged to be asked, and he was in no mood to ignore it. "And does Handir feel the same? How can you be sure he does not harbour feelings for you?"

Her eyes lingered on Fel'annár, and then her gaze turned to the side. "You have my word, Fel'annár. His love for me is that of a brother, and it is fierce." She smiled sadly. "Perhaps you will see in Handir what I do, one day. Perhaps you, too, will call him *brother*."

"He doesn't want that, Llyniel. His intentions with regards to me are not those of a sibling."

"He wants you to help him, help *us* in this cause, yes. Handir wants this for our country, Turion seconds it, and blessed Lainon started it all. And as for Aradan, he is my *father*." She watched him register the information before continuing. "Do not undermine our intentions, Fel'annár. It is no small thing that we set out to achieve, and while we do it, who is to say that you and Handir cannot come to better understand each other?"

"Tell me truthfully," said Fel'annár, "has Handir sent you to help garner my acceptance? Is that the sum of your interest in me?" There was a sadness about him, a gleam of despair in his eyes he had not been able to mask.

"No. No, Fel'annár. Why would you assume my actions are about Handir? They are *my* actions, *my* beliefs, everyone else be *damned*. I left my home, my beautiful forests because every day was torture to me, watching my people suffer discrimination and mockery, watching my mother bear the snickers of those pompous Alpine ladies. Not once did she fight back, Fel'annár, not once did my father, *Lord Chief Councillor,* put them in their place. This plan will succeed, or I will leave Ea Uaré *forever*. But these are not the reasons why I am here, Fel'annár."

Fel'annár stood wide-eyed, watching the fiery Silvan woman whose passion for the Forest ran deep. She was *not* here on Handir's behest. She was not here to persuade him to join them in this plan.

"Then why? Why *are* you here?"

She stared back at him, and Fel'annár saw her hesitation. She seemed to be searching, perhaps to conjure a lie, but no, it was not deviance he saw in her eyes. It was confusion.

"I just . . . I don't want you to think badly of Handir, Fel'annár."

He watched her, standing so close he could reach out and kiss her if he so desired, and he did desire it. He felt his body lean forwards, begging his mind to give in and take what he wanted. His eyes wandered over her face, and for a moment he wondered what it was that made her irresistible to him. This was no simple desire for pleasure; there was something deep in his soul that pulled at him, like a strong wind high in the boughs. He was moving in spite of himself—he was losing control.

He blinked.

"I . . . I will see you later at the king's table, Lady Llyniel." He bowed, his gaze intense, almost commanding, and then he was gone, and as he strode back to the palace, his mind raced far ahead of his feet. She was a distraction to him, another reason for him to lose control, another reason not to want to leave Tar'eastór . . . because she would be here.

Yet in spite of his denial, in spite of all the reasons why he had stopped himself from kissing her, his heart felt triumphant.

She was not Handir's lover. She never would be.

That night, as Sontúr and Fel'annár walked towards the music and the still distant conversation, the prince couldn't help wondering why his friend was not cowed by his new circumstances at all. He wasn't nervous, unsure, uncomfortable even, in his new clothes. Instead, his step was steady and confident, and he realised that this was in his blood, a natural ability his friend simply fell into without realising.

Standing now upon the threshold of the great dining hall, Fel'annár took a moment to gain his bearings. He had never seen the hall so full, so finely decked, and neither had he seen so many jewels sitting ostentatiously upon the fingers and necks of their proud owners. This was a *"small celebration"* or so Lord Damiel had said, and Fel'annár couldn't help but wonder what a true Alpine feast would be like. It would certainly be very different to the Silvan celebrations and festivals he had experienced in Lan Taria. *They* were held outdoors, under the trees, to the beat of heavy drums, under colourful lights that dripped from the boughs. There was dancing and roasting meats, circles of story-tellers and trysting in the shadows. Here in Tar'eastór, it was pomp and opulence, courtly dances to the soft rhythm of stringed instruments and educated voices. It was rich and it was proper, while in the Forest it was wild and tribal.

Fel'annár followed Sontúr as he navigated the space between tables until they were before the king. *His* table spanned almost the entire far wall. With a bow, the prince occupied his place at the king's right, and Fel'annár was ushered towards a chair beside him. On his left, was Lord Damiel, and opposite, sat Handir and Llyniel, side by side. Fel'annár first bowed to the king and then to Handir, before sitting and allowing his eyes free rein. They roved over the immaculate table, the utensils and decorations, the delicate crystal glasses and jewel-encrusted candelabras. He had never seen such luxury. He was gawking, he realised, and straightened himself in his softly-padded chair, scowling at a sniggering lord further down the table, who promptly quieted and looked away.

He felt eyes upon him, judging, wondering, comparing. There was nothing new in that, and Fel'annár bore the scrutiny as naturally as he almost always had. Opposite him and a few chairs down, a young lord stared, an open invitation in his eyes. Fel'annár arched an eyebrow at him and allowed his eyes to continue their travels. Further along, a lady smiled and offered an encouraging nod while another stared, eyes smouldering unashamedly. He nodded coolly and then turned back to his immediate dinner companions.

And then there was Llyniel.

He had not allowed himself to register her presence until the protocol was done with. She would have distracted him and he would have made a fool of himself—and then Handir's judgemental eyes would be upon him. He was fascinated by the length of her eyes, not slanted like the Ari'atór but so very big, an exuberant splash of colour upon a palette of creamy smoothness. The slight curve of her nose and the marked ridges of her upper lip . . . he must have stared for too long, for Sontúr's next words startled him.

"Here, try this sweet wine from the temperate valleys of the Downlands," said the prince, pushing the decanter towards Handir. Luckily, Fel'annár didn't have to pour his own glass; he wouldn't have known which one to use.

He drank, the fiery liquid sliding down his throat and setting his nose to tingling. "It is wonderful," he murmured, admiring the deep amber liquid and how the light caught on it.

"Wait until you try the human brandy later," smirked Sontúr. "My brother Torhén has been asked to barter for some before his return from Prairie; *that's* the good stuff."

"I will be sure to try it," smiled Fel'annár for the first time since he had sat at the table. His eyes, though, strayed back to Llyniel, who smiled back at him and then to Handir at her side as he spoke with Lord Damiel. Their eyes were fixed on someone who sat a little further down the long table. Fel'annár followed their line of sight to a large elf in overly colourful clothing, and beside him, to Fel'annár's shock, was Silor.

Their eyes met. Silor's head tilted backwards until he looked down his nose, and Fel'annár simply watched him, eyes cool and hard. Funny, he thought. Until just recently, Silor was spewing orders and treating him like a kitchen scullion instead of a warrior, yet now, Silor was the son of a lord where he himself was the son of a king. He turned away from the once trainee lieutenant, wondering if Pan'assár would ever allow him to return to command training. He resisted the urge to snort at his own question.

Sitting back in his chair, Fel'annár's eyes and ears continued their journey. He admired the finery, listened to the rich vocabulary and charming laughs. He watched eyes, too, eyes that spoke of ambition and renown, of lust for power and position, of shrewd machinations and subtle invitations. There was a dark game playing out beneath the glittering surface—this was Handir's world of intrigue, this was Llyniel's childhood, the one she had grown to despise.

His gaze strayed back to Silor, who was now talking with other young lords around him. He could not hear what was being said, but their body language told Fel'annár it was something they believed passionately in. Even the big lord beside Silor was listening and nodding from time to time.

"Who is that lord, sitting beside Silor?" he asked Handir. The prince turned from Damiel and then followed Fel'annár's gaze down the line of lords and ladies.

"That is Lord Sulén, Silor's father."

"He looks rich."

"Oh, he is," said Damiel. "A very influential councillor."

"I don't like him," murmured Fel'annár, and after a while, Damiel answered.

"Neither do I."

"He is King Thargodén's third or fourth cousin removed," said Handir, speaking directly to Fel'annár for the first time. "Unfortunately, we are related to him."

"Thank you for *telling* me, my prince," murmured Fel'annár.

Silence descended on those close enough to hear, but Fel'annár was not going to apologise. Indeed he felt better for it.

"And what does Sulén think of the situation in Ea Uaré, I wonder," asked Llyniel quietly, breaking the tension-thick silence.

"I don't think it matters to him, my lady," said Damiel. "Power and wealth move that one; I doubt he has any other convictions."

"Silor was pushed through the ranks fast enough," said Fel'annár. "He was a trainee lieutenant on our journey here. Not anymore though."

"Well, he is the son of an Alpine lord, Fel'annár," said Llyniel. "You know how it is in our realm, do you not? It is not about skill or potential but about race and money." She did not seem concerned at all that Commander Pan'assár might be able to hear her, and Fel'annár rather thought that he could. She was bold to the point of insult, and he did not think that was wise. Indeed Handir seemed to agree, one hand covering hers as he spoke, much quieter than she had done.

"That is the unfortunate truth." Handir's eyes landed heavily on Fel'annár, who stared back at him. There was no hatred, no callousness in his brother's eyes—rather, there was an underlying softness just below the practised veneer. Whether it was an apology he could not say, but Fel'annár was sure he had not seen it before. Handir was showing a small part of himself. It was a minute concession that Fel'annár chose to value all the same.

It was Sontúr who broke the awkward moment once more with a complete change of subject. "So are you ready for the Kal'hamén'Ar tomorrow, Fel'annár?" he asked with a smirk, knowing full well the impact his question would have. He wasn't wrong. Indeed, conversation at the king's table lulled, and although Pan'assár continued his conversation with Gor'sadén, both commanders had one ear on the other conversation.

"I am ready," said Fel'annár confidently.

"Every patient in the Healing Halls is talking about it," said Llyniel.

"Everyone in *Tar'eastór* is talking about it," added Damiel. "There have been no new Kah warriors for many decades now. As far as I know, only Commanders Gor'sadén and Pan'assár are left. The rest are dead, their portraits hanging from the walls of the Inner Circle, their statues guarding the crenulations upon the walls."

So that was what those statues were, mused Fel'annár. Kah warriors, dead and gone but never forgotten. A sense of responsibility and pride settled over him, and he remained silent, until Llyniel spoke to him.

"You surely can't beat *him*," said Llyniel, gesturing to Pan'assár further along the table.

"No, and that is not the purpose, Llyniel. It is about showing the commander my potential to become an initiate of the Kal'hamén'Ar. I am not expected to beat him but to show him I am worthy of the honour." He couldn't help turning his head and looking at Pan'assár. He was surprised to find the commander staring back in his direction.

"Well, don't get your hopes up, Silvan," she muttered, and Fel'annár turned back to her. He shrugged—because he had nothing to say. She was familiar with Pan'assár, resented his treatment of her people, and so did Fel'annár. Silor had reminded him of that, but he had not been able to help it. He *had* gotten his hopes up, even though he knew it was unwise.

Fel'annár said no more on the matter, and soon, the diners engaged in varied conversation. Handir told Fel'annár of the council and its workings and the extent of the king's right to overrule, or otherwise, its dictates. Llyniel spoke somewhat stiffly with Councillor Damiel, who knew her father well, and as for Sontúr, he spoke with his father about the trade agreements Prince Torhén was currently attending in the mortal lands of Prairie.

As for Fel'annár, he listened, and he learned. He had expected to be bored, but in truth he found it interesting, fascinating even, had enjoyed almost every minute of it, and his prior misconceptions made him feel childish. He smiled and shook his head minutely and then plucked the last stuffed mushroom from an ornate plate before him and popped it into his mouth.

Further down the table, Lord Sulén contained a sneer and turned to Councillor Ras'dan. "The boy plays the lord. Prince Handir has dressed him as a child decks his favourite doll. How he uses the bastard to his own gain!"

"I wonder what it is he pursues," pondered the councillor. "Gain merit in his father's eyes, of course, but why? Rinon is heir—what has he to gain by delivering the Silvan to the Forest Dwellers? There is something we are missing."

"Maybe he actually *believes* it," mused Silor, almost to himself, and Ras'dan turned to him, face rigid, eyes frigid. "You have much to learn, young lord. Heed your lord father: no one goes to such lengths on a whim."

Silor said nothing and then jumped when his father's words were whispered in his ear.

"How much longer must we endure his presence?"

"We wait for the opportunity, Father. It is not easy to catch him unawares."

"Every day that passes is a day in which the Silvan gains allies. We cannot allow him to continue influencing others the way he does. Look at them, Silor. See how they watch him? And what do you think they say?"

"Some will remember Or'Talán, wonder if he is like his grandfather."

"And what else, my son?"

"They will wonder what will happen upon his return to the Forest."

"Yes. They will wonder what he will be to the Silvan people. They are curious, Silor. You cannot wait because, for every day that passes, he endears himself to others. He is skilled in that—he is *dangerous*."

As much as Silor hated to admit it, his father was right. He had seen that trait in the Silvan on the way to Tar'eastór, when he had still been trainee lieutenant. His jaw tightened.

"I will see to it, Father."

Sulén leaned back in his chair, gaze drifting to Ras'dan opposite him. A subtle nod and a passing glance at the Silvan, who laughed freely at something Prince Sontúr had said. He would give Silor a little more time, but Band'orán had been clear in his dictates, and Sulén would not fail him. The stakes were too high. This was the moment they had all been waiting for, a return to the days of old. Alpine glory would be restored, and Ea Uaré would be theirs to rule —Band'orán upon the throne, himself as his chancellor, and his son as a royal prince, second only to Lord Barathon, who would be *crown* prince.

This was his family's right, an heirloom earned centuries ago, one only Band'orán had acknowledged.

He, Sulén, would not fail the future king of Ea Uaré.

SEVEN

THE TEST

"The Dance of Graceful Death had become a symbol of the past, a reminder of bygone glory. Those who had danced and died stood immortalised as statues upon the ramparts, their portraits hung upon walls in the Inner Circle. It was the ultimate skill, born by the greatest of warriors in service to their king. They said it had died with Or'Talán's passing, but it was Or'Talán's grandchild who would rekindle its flame."
The Alpine Chronicles. Cor'hidén.

~

Since his arrival in Tar'eastór, Pan'assár had gone from racially biased, distant and uncaring to accepting—albeit grudgingly—that he had not been fair, that his ordeal at the Battle Under the Sun and Or'Talán's horrific death had made of him a lesser commander, a lesser elf. His friends of old, King Vorn'asté, Councillor Damiel, and especially Gor'sadén, had all looked upon him in disappointment, but it had been Gor'sadén who had forced the issue and made him break, made him talk of that horrific day and the scars it had left in its wake.

He wanted to return to what he had once been. He missed the looks of pride and respect in the eyes of his warriors, the ones he saw Gor'sadén harvest every day. But still he was hindered by his own unyielding pride. He had admitted it all to himself but not to others. He had not asked forgiveness and wondered even if he could. The Silvan's face had been Pan'assár's downfall; Fel'annár embodied his ghosts, fed his hatred, his need to place blame and purge his own lingering anger, and however much he tried, he could not see Fel'annár for who he was, would always be reminded of the past.

"They arrive by the dozens, even though they know they cannot watch."

Pan'assár snapped out of his musings, eyes landing on his friend, who stood in the centre of the training arena.

"That is not why they come," said Pan'assár as he drew a cloth over his blade once more, blue eyes catching a glint of sunlight from a window high up on the stone wall of the training circle. The doors were still open, waiting for one elf to arrive, but once he did and the test started, they would be closed and guarded.

"They come to taste the moment, Gor'sadén. They come to be a part of history; whatever the outcome, they will be the first to know. You said it yourself—the return of the Kal'hamén'Ar is a good thing, a part of our glorious culture. It will encourage the troops to aspire to greater things," he said, one hand running down the velvet of his purple sash. "I stopped using this symbol many years ago," he trailed off, eyes slipping to Gor'sadén's own sash and then his hair and the intricately buckled braid that hung from his temple. It was the Heliaré, symbol of a Kah warrior, one he too had worn—until Or'Talán had died and he had cut it off.

"You, though, have never lost your way, have you?"

Gor'sadén held his friend's inquisitive gaze, registering Pan'assár's veiled admission of failure.

"Will you allow me to weave your Heliaré?"

"Perhaps," said Pan'assár. "After the test and the verdict is given . . . we shall see."

"Despite what you may think, Pan'assár, you *do* deserve it. You are *still* a master."

Pan'assár bit his lip. He wanted to say that he didn't, that he had failed Or'Talán, failed his warriors, allowed himself to be poisoned by the toxic words of a bitter lord who sought nothing but power. He had been so far gone it had ceased to mean anything to him anymore. Now, though, he could feel his resentment slipping away, and he wondered. Could he bear the symbolic weight of the Heliaré? Could he wear it and feel proud once more, without remembering his past failures?

"You and I have yet to serve a purpose, Pan'assár. Something comes, and I am not referring to this *Nim'uán*. You and I must be ready." The commander's voice was soft, and yet it echoed strangely off the walls, affected Pan'assár more than perhaps it should have, and his mind rebelled against the odd sensation.

"You speak like an Ari'atór," said Pan'assár, his upper lip curling.

"You dislike the Spirit Warriors?"

"No. I dislike their divine ways, their omens and their ill-founded beliefs. They speak of signs, of songs on the wind—things I do not understand, just like you do now," he said, throwing his head back and taking a long drink from his flask. "I wonder if there are any Ari'atór in your line."

"I have that honour; a distant uncle, three or four times removed, I believe. And yet if you had seen and heard the things I have these past months, if you had seen a tree blossom in winter, seen the eyes of a young warrior ignite with some inner fire. If you had heard words that none could know save for our king . . . you *would* understand. And like me, you would not be able to explain it."

"But I haven't, so I can't."

Gor'sadén's brow rose acutely. This was almost the Pan'assár he remembered—and loved. He was irreverent and practical to the point of insult. All that was left to achieve was his acceptance of how wrong he had been with Fel'annár. How wrong he had been to treat the Silvan warriors the way he had, to have allowed Silor and so many other young lords to climb the ranks of command on the sole strength of their family name. Only when Pan'assár could put voice to these things could he regain that sense of honour and dignity that had once shone from his sharp blue eyes, from the very pores of his skin.

"Close the door," he called to the guards, and even as they banged shut, Pan'assár took off his boots and his tunic until he stood in nothing but his black breeches and the purple sash that once more marked him as a Master of the Kal'hamén'Ar. He had his doubts, but he *had* promised to give the boy a trial. He would not go back on his word.

"Spar with me, brother, and go easy on a lost master. I have not danced for many years."

Gor'sadén smiled, and then he bowed respectfully, watching his friend as he did likewise.

Outside the doors, all conversation died out as the first ringing clashes of legendary swords met. The warriors listened, and fire came to their eyes. They longed to be on the other side, to marvel at absolute skill, but it could not be. They would have to wait and, if luck prevailed, they would one day watch the Dance of Graceful Death in the only two ways it was allowed: at a king's behest or on a field of battle.

∽

The world was upside down; long silver locks pooled on the ground around Fel'annár's hands while the soles of his feet felt the warmth of the late-winter sun. His arms, though, did not shake, even though his muscles stood out in stark ridges under smooth skin. He lifted one hand from the ground and held it out to the side. Both legs, perfectly aligned, followed the direction of his arm while the rest of his body moved to the other side to compensate for the shift in weight.

Handir was far away, his father was in Ea Uaré, and Llyniel did not occupy his mind as she had done for the past few days. It was him and his body; his *mind* was in control, not his emotions.

"How long will he stay like that?" asked Galadan. He, Galdith, and Sontúr had never seen Fel'annár's strange training routine, and Idernon took it upon himself to explain what it was he was doing.

"These routines are taken from the Kal'hamén'Ar. He learned them on his own, back when he thought the art had died. It was Tensári who set him right."

"Is it not prohibited to perform the Kah in the presence of those who are not masters?"

"The sequences of the Dance are prohibited, unless performed before a king or on the battlefield, but this is preparation. These are the techniques a Kah master will use to train their bodies and their minds. These preparations are not secret."

"I don't understand this need for secrecy," said Galdith as he watched the spectacle.

It was Galadan who answered. "The sequences of the Kah are highly orchestrated; they are dangerous to any who do not understand the underlying principles and how to deflect an attack. Only a Kah master can teach a Kah apprentice—none other can engage in such practices—in the same way a child is not allowed to touch a sharp blade or a novice warrior is not permitted the honour of charging in the front line of battle."

"How does he *do* that? It must hurt," mused Sontúr.

"It used to," confirmed Idernon, "but he has done this so many times now that it is second nature to him. He had to hide it, though, always secreting away while Ramien and I covered for him. He knew the attention it would garner him, attention that would almost always be hostile." Idernon's eyes were unfocussed while Ramien looked to the ground as he remembered. "He has come a long way to earn this moment, this chance to become great. He deserves this, and we can only hope Commander Pan'assár does not undermine the years of diligent training, make his sacrifice meaningless."

"He won't," said Galadan, his voice strong. "He is a warrior, Idernon. He will not act dishonourably in matters of the Kal'hamén'Ar."

"I am glad you are convinced, brother," said Sontúr. "I, however, will remain sceptical until it is over and I can see for myself that Fel'annár was given a fair chance, whatever the outcome."

There was no sound when Fel'annár's bare feet touched the ground, and he stood upright in one fluid movement.

"It is time."

Fel'annár knew that the test had been publicly announced, but he had thought it would all be conducted quietly and discreetly. Yet even as he and The Company navigated the corridor that led to the training arena, he knew his assumptions had been wrong. The place was teeming with warriors, and more were arriving by the moment. They collected around the closed doors where Fel'annár knew the test would take place, talking and waving their hands about, speaking of tactics and movements, of what they knew, or thought they knew, of the Kal'hamén'Ar. The Ancient Art was returning to Tar'eastór, whether or not The Silvan passed the test, for others would now surely be allowed to dream that they, too, might be found worthy and taken as apprentices.

With a steadying breath, Fel'annár walked towards the uncharacteristically guarded door, and once there he knocked and then turned to face The Company. Silence had fallen, thick and expectant, and Fel'annár's eyes fell first on Ramien and then on Idernon, his companions through a lifetime of preparation for this very moment, even though he had never understood that until now. They smiled, understood the words that did not leave his mouth, and with nothing but shining eyes, they spoke to him of strength and hope. *They* believed in him, and now, all Fel'annár had to do was believe in *himself*. With a resolute nod, he turned and walked through the now open doors. They groaned and then banged shut behind him.

The arena was empty save for the two commanders. Gor'sadén walked towards him, his expression guarded, no sign of his customary smile.

"Fel'annár. Are you rested?"

"I am, Sir."

"Are you ready then?"

"I am."

Gor'sadén stepped to one side, and Pan'assár came into view. He wore nothing but his black breeches, and around his waist was the purple sash Fel'annár had never seen him wear. He had heard stories of Pan'assár's greatness, every warrior in Ea Uaré had, but he had never seen the evidence of it—until now. It was just one more part of the puzzle that Pan'assár represented to him.

He breathed deeply, a strange feeling of finality descending over him, and for some reason it made him sad; it was almost as if he were saying goodbye. The chubby face of a child came to his mind's eye, sparkling eyes and a cheeky grin, mouth covered in crumbs. But then the vision of himself as a child was replaced by Pan'assár's angular features as he came to stand before him, far too close for comfort on any day, but it seemed to Fel'annár that the Forest commander had never truly looked at him, had always seemed to avert his gaze if he could help it. He did it even now.

"Commander Gor'sadén has asked me to consider your candidature as an apprentice of the Kal'hamén'Ar and I have conceded to put you to the test. Only if you pass this test will I consent to his request to train you in the ancient art." The commander looked to the ceiling for a moment before his unfocussed gaze was back on Fel'annár. "I must tell you, now, that I do not believe you will pass this test."

Fel'annár blinked, his heart jolting at the commander's words.

"How does that make you feel?" he asked, turning away from Fel'annár, the muscles in his back rippling menacingly beneath the soft, pale skin.

After a moment, Fel'annár found his tongue, unsure of whether to truly speak his mind or simply go with what he thought the commander wanted to hear. He was suddenly reminded of a similar situation with Turion back at novice training. He opted for the truth.

"I am disappointed, Commander."

"Why?"

"I am disappointed that you do not think me capable."

"Why should I? You are fifty-two years old; you are half Silvan. Silvans know nothing of the Kal'hamén'Ar." He turned back to Fel'annár. "Now, how does that make you feel?"

Fel'annár stopped himself from speaking without thinking. It would be all too easy to show his anger, but then, wouldn't the commander see it anyway? And then it occurred to Fel'annár that Pan'assár was purposefully goading him, that perhaps the test had already started.

"Youth or race should not be a reason to be excluded, although I understand it is unlikely I would have the necessary skill . . ."

"What else?"

"I am disappointed that you feel being Silvan is a reason to doubt my skill." Fel'annár stood defiant, and still, after what he had said, the commander's gaze seemed off centre, focussed on some object behind him. He could see Fel'annár, but he did not *look* at him, he never had, realised Fel'annár. Still, there was something dangerous in the commander's eyes, and Gor'sadén's words came back to him.

"He will not make this easy for you . . ."

"Ready yourself, warrior," said Pan'assár. "Do not hold back; I won't."

Turning, Fel'annár unbuckled his jerkin and then removed his shirt below, revealing bare skin and the band of Master Archer sitting over his right bicep. He wasn't sure if he was required to, but Pan'assár was bare from the waist up, and Fel'annár imagined that was what the test called for. Arranging his clothes neatly on a bench, he removed his boots and then reached up and secured his hair into a single tail.

It was the hardest thing he had ever had to do: overcome the knowledge that he walked into this test with the surety of defeat. He had always held back in his sparring, in his training, because it garnered him unwanted attention. Now, though, all he could do was show everything that he had and remember that victory was not the purpose; all he had to do was sufficiently impress the commander.

He had trained for this, all his life had been dedicated to this, one moment.

"Silvans know nothing of the Kal'hamén'Ar."

But they *did*. He was Silvan, and although he was no expert, he did know something of it, more than most Alpines. But that didn't matter now, nothing mattered except the strength of his muscle, the clarity of his mind, and the sharpness of his own senses.

"Select your weapons," said Pan'assár with a tilt of his head. To one side of the arena, a weapons rack stood dripping with long and short swords. Some were thin and curved while others were shorter and broader, but all of them were exquisite, and he ran his fingertips over the hilts. He wanted to pick them all up, feel them in his hands, feel their weight and guess at their origins and whether they had been wielded in battle.

Taking note of the weapons Pan'assár held in his hands, Fel'annár chose a long, curved sword and another shorter sword. Gor'sadén's eyes darted sideways to Pan'assár, who was watching Fel'annár's every move.

With one weapon in each hand, Fel'annár turned and walked into the centre of the ring until he stood before the commander, while Gor'sadén stood where he had from the start, to one side, feet firmly planted on the ground, his own purple sash caressing the tops of his boots.

"Present arms," said Gor'sadén, and no sooner had he spoken than Pan'assár held his weapons before him, like some spiny insect from Calrazia, poised to jump and sting its victim.

Stepping backwards, Fel'annár pointed the long sword at the commander and then held the shorter blade over his head, the tip pointing in the same direction. He held his position and fixed his eyes directly on Pan'assár. Just as he had expected, Pan'assár's eyes seemed unfocussed, and ultimately, Fel'annár understood it was not because he was Silvan—it was because he was *Fel'annár*.

When Pan'assár moved, it was so quick that Fel'annár was hard-pressed to dodge his strike. He avoided the tip of Pan'assár's long sword by mere inches, leaning so far backwards that he almost lost his balance.

Shaken, he danced sideways and then brought his sword around to the front, but Pan'assár was no longer there, and he turned, adjusting his stance. He had been taken by surprise, had underestimated the commander's speed and agility, but there was no time to think, because a short sword swung past his face, catching his cheek with a glancing blow that stung like ice on heated skin. Bringing his own blade up and outwards, he parried one blade and then ducked under Pan'assár's long sword. He tried to penetrate the commander's side defence, but his long sword clashed violently against Pan'assár's, the vibrations running painfully through his bones and up to his shoulder.

Whirling around, he tried again but was parried all too easily. A foot against the side of his ankle and he was on the floor, but there was no time to wonder how that had happened. All he could do was roll out of the way of the swinging blade that was surely meant to take his head off. He kicked his legs over his head and flipped to his feet, bringing his swords before him once more, but Pan'assár was back before he could blink. Too fast and he was on the floor once more, a short sword hurtling downwards. He kicked out, catching the commander's blade—and by some miracle he did not lose his own. Fel'annár grappled to his feet.

Do not think; do not feel.

A whispered breath, a calm sea, a gentle breeze... Heartbeat, the flow of blood through veins, the strength of skilled muscles. Peaceful, acute perception.

Harmony.

Metal clashed with a violent clank, and Fel'annár pushed the invading blade to one side. He stepped back and resumed his stance, moving in to attack from the right. Parry and loop around. Again, and again, and then he had it, the rhythm.

One, two, three, *strike*.

Every attack was parried, just as he parried every attack, and soon his body was moving in circles. Forward, backward in a rhythm of four, the flow fuelling his own capacity to concentrate, to focus only on what was important—the blades in his hands and in those of his opponent.

A strange song echoed off the distant walls around him, of crashing blades and harsh breaths, of an ancient drum that beat in his own heart, as if he could hear the Kal'hamén'Ar dances of old at the king's court. Music enveloped him, heavy drums and the minor notes of a lone flute. It snaked around him, and he was whirling this way and then that, blades impossibly fast in his hands.

Something cut the air before his mouth, and he leaned backwards and then spun around. Jumping, he twisted into the air so that he would land on the other side of his opponent. He ducked low to avoid Pan'assár's blade slicing towards his throat and then swiped at the commander's feet with his long sword. Pan'assár jumped, and then, with a move Fel'annár could not comprehend, the tip of Pan'assár's short sword cut painfully into his skin, just over his heart. He staggered backwards, eyes pinned on the commander's face, wondering if he would call an end to the test now that he had scored a blow, but Pan'assár was coming for him once more, slashing both swords so close to his chest that Fel'annár flipped backwards and then sailed into the air, twisting sideways and out of their way.

He stood gasping for air. He had almost been defeated. The music had gone and he had lost his rhythm. He needed to regain it, to *focus*.

Pan'assár attacked. Fel'annár parried. Fel'annár attacked, Pan'assár dodged, but they slowly slipped into a rhythm, and before he could even register it, the music was back in his mind, the rhythm of four commanding his feet and his blades, better than it had before, and the true battle began.

Pan'assár's eyes were on the Silvan's face, somewhere to the right of his nose, but he did not *see* him, had never *wanted* to. Instead, as his body performed the Dance, he realised the boy was good, better than he had ever expected him to be. Gor'sadén had been right. Why he chose that moment to finally allow his eyes to focus on Fel'annár's, he could not say.

He would regret it in hindsight.

They were Silvan eyes, forest eyes, but a sliver of brilliant blue passed over the deep moss green irises, and it was Or'Talán who was before Pan'assár, no longer in the training arena but in northern Ea Uaré, upon the arid sands of the Xeric Wood, years into the past. He was at the Battle Under the Sun once more, staring into his brother's eyes for the last time, and a stinging blow ran the length of his forearm. He whirled out of Fel'annár's reach, and when he faced him once more, it was the face of a Sand Lord that glared fiercely back at him. Pan'assár lunged forward—a flurry of three combinations and his opponent was staggering backwards. He once more heard foreign shouts of glee: how they had mingled with the cries of pain and outrage from Or'Talán, his own raw screams as Pan'assár tried to cut through the enemy line and save his friend!

His arms were moving, whirling in skill, fuelled by anger, yet still his opponent was standing and then jumping high into the air. A whoosh of heavy metal as blades were brought down over his head, and he crossed his own swords above him, meeting those of the enemy, and then pushed outwards. He had expected the clatter of falling metal as he disarmed his opponent, but it did not come. A heavy thud sounded behind him instead, and Pan'assár swirled around and brought his swords up to face his adversary.

The blows came hard and heavy, his own breath ragged, but still he could not reach Or'Talán. Desperation drove him now, and all reason was abandoned. He was moving forwards in a frenzy, gaining ground at last, his enemy cracking under his thunderous onslaught. But then the Sand Lord was gone and his own face stared back at him in shock. He was fighting *himself,* and his long sword arched around, stopping just inches away from his opponent's chest—his own chest. He staggered backwards, away from the blades that swung before him, and then he froze.

Breath came in mighty heaves of air, sweat poured down his face, his chest, eyes wide as his mind struggled to understand what had happened. The hot sands of the Xeric wood were now the cool dirt of the training arena, the shouts and screams faded away to nothing but harsh breathing, and the elf before him was not himself but Fel'annár Ar Thargodén.

A hand on his shoulder and he whirled around, the face of Gor'sadén just inches from his own, sword drawn, but he said nothing. His friend simply gestured with his head that he should move away, and he did, his mind slowly emerging from the mists of history, the faces of the Sand Lords, the Silvans, Or'Talán and himself fading away, and in their place was realisation and the onset of understanding.

Pan'assár knew what he had to do.

He needed atonement.

~

"Fel'annár."

He couldn't answer. He couldn't catch his breath, his chest and stomach heaving too fast, sweat pouring from him in fat drops. He had crashed painfully to his knees, and now, his head was too heavy to look up at the elf who stood over him, looking down on him in concern—and *shock*.

With a groan, Fel'annár shifted his legs beneath him and slowly stood, but even then he was bent at the waist, not quite able to straighten his body and regain his breath.

Gor'sadén was not surprised at all at the state he was in. Pan'assár had almost killed him, had exerted himself to his limits to bring Fel'annár down, but he had not been able to break his defences until the very end. Pan'assár had been formidable in his glory years—still was—but he had lost the edge he had once had. What Gor'sadén could not explain so easily was how Fel'annár had managed to survive for as long as he had. Not even *he* had understood the extent of the boy's talent, and he had certainly not expected to see such precise aerial work. That was a speciality few had ever adopted, for it required a physical prowess that went far beyond the norm.

Gor'sadén had seen the murderous intent in his friend's eyes at the end, knew he had lost control, and he had drawn his own sword, had been on the brink of stopping Pan'assár, even injuring him so that he would stop, but as luck would have it, Pan'assár had stumbled backwards and stopped himself.

He watched now, as Fel'annár finally stood straight and faced him. Gor'sadén couldn't help the wince that escaped him. One cheek was cut and bruised. There was a long scratch over his chest, and his knuckles were bruised and bloodied. He looked like he had just come back from war, and perhaps he had, from Pan'assár's personal war.

"Are you all right?" asked Gor'sadén.

"Yes. I'm all right," he managed, breath still coming too fast. His eyes drifted to the edge of the ring where Pan'assár stood rigid, his back to them and his weapons still firmly in his hands.

"Is *he* all right?" asked Fel'annár.

"He will be, I think," murmured Gor'sadén thoughtfully.

Whether Pan'assár had heard them, neither could say, but he moved then, placing his weapons upon the stone bench and reaching for his tunic. He was still looping the clasps as he strode towards Fel'annár and Gor'sadén. Something had changed, realised Fel'annár. Something in his expression—and then he had it. Those summer-blue eyes were wider, brighter. They were alive with some fire behind them that was a force he had only ever seen in Gor'sadén's eyes. They were upon him, focussed on him, *seeing* him for the first time, but there was no sneer upon his pale lips.

The silence stretched on except for Fel'annár's heavy breaths, which stilled with Pan'assár's words.

"You have my acceptance to train in the Kal'hamén'Ar with Commander Gor'sadén, but there is something you must know."

Fel'annár let out a rushed breath. His knees were trembling, and it was all he could do to anchor himself firmly to the earth below his feet.

"By allowing this, I am allowing you to become a dangerous weapon . . . and yet here is my dilemma. I do not trust you. I do not trust your loyalty to King Thargodén, and so I warn you, as Gor'sadén is my witness, if you move your hand against my king, either directly or by participation in some scheme to harm him, physically or otherwise, I will kill you."

Fel'annár could not answer. His tongue clove to the roof of his mouth, but his mind worked frantically. Pan'assár would never kill him because Fel'annár would never betray his king. But then a spark of anger flared in his heart. Why did Pan'assár always have to think the worst of him?

"I accept your condition, Commander. There will never be cause for that, but I will tell you this." He took a step forward, his anger fuelling his bravery. "Sir, you will never trust me—if you cannot *look* at me. You will never be sure of my intentions if you do not *see* me. You will never count me as an ally if you do not *listen* to me."

"No. No, I will not. Still, in this one test I have seen a part of you I had not expected: humility and the blood of a warrior. These two things I do not doubt, for wherever your loyalties lie, a warrior you *are*."

A powerful wave of emotion hit Fel'annár so hard he swayed. The anger was gone, and his knees felt weak, but it didn't matter, for he suddenly wanted to lower himself to the ground, and so he did. He sat upon his heels and looked up into the forbidding eyes of Pan'assár and then at Gor'sadén who came to stand at his friend's shoulders.

"I will not fail you, Commanders, and I will not fail our king. You have my oath, and my understanding that if I should ever falter in this, you will take my life. But you will *never* have cause to."

Pan'assár looked down upon him for the first time with emotions that were not disdain or disapproval. There was curiosity . . . and perhaps respect. He nodded curtly. "Gor'sadén, he is all yours." He turned then and left the room, leaving Fel'annár kneeling, alone before Gor'sadén.

The long days of lonely training in hidden glades, the sweat and tears he had spent to mould his body, to quicken his reflexes, to stretch his limbs—the dreams that had fuelled his ambition, the mockery he had endured to be the best that he could be at almost fifty-two. He remembered it all, and his head bent, eyes filling with hot tears. He didn't care, for the tears were of relief, of joy beyond expression, of pride in himself for this one thing he had achieved.

Gor'sadén crouched before him. "Look at me, Fel'annár."

Slowly, he raised his head, eyes shimmering like water under the full moon.

"I will speak with Captain Comon. You will still be a part of his patrol, but you are freed from routine training. For today, go, bathe and rest. Tonight, after the evening meal, come to my quarters in the palace. There is much to discuss."

Fel'annár nodded slowly and then collected his feet beneath him, rising slowly together with the commander. He could not quite mask the grimace of aching limbs and bruises. Pan'assár had been merciless in his onslaught, and then Fel'annár had seen a glint of some madness in the commander's eyes, one that had almost cost him his control. Still, he was in utter awe of Pan'assár's prowess, and the strange clouds that had descended upon him began to dissipate, replaced by a budding sense of joy.

Straightening, he reached for his tunic and worked his painful way into it. Turning back to Gor'sadén, he bowed respectfully for longer than was necessary, for he was so very grateful, and the commander seemed to understand—indeed he returned it.

As Gor'sadén straightened, he stepped forward and took up a braid that curved around his apprentice's ear. Releasing the leather thong, he opened it and then ran his fingers through the rippled hair. With deft fingers he began to weave and then loop and buckle and when he had finished, he tied it off with the leather and stood back. "I will find a suitable clip for you tomorrow, but for now, this should stave off the questions from your fellow warriors. They will recognise the Heliaré, symbol of the Kah Warrior.

"You fought bravely, beyond my expectations. You are worthy of the Kal'hamén'Ar." He gestured to the door, and with a nod and a slowly spreading smile, Fel'annár left, leaving Gor'sadén alone with a thousand hefty thoughts in his mind and amongst them, he wondered what it was he had seen. Wispy tendrils of green, blue, and purple had chased after Fel'annár's blades like autumn leaves after a galloping horse. He had seen it in those last moments of desperate fighting. It was, perhaps, a simple trick of the light striking metal, but a suspicion began to form in his mind, one he would put to the test when Fel'annár's training began in earnest.

～

The doors to the training arena slammed shut behind him, and Fel'annár stood before the heaving mass of silent warriors. The Company were at the very fore, and Idernon and Ramien stepped closer.

"Well?" asked the Wall of Stone, his voice booming around them. But Idernon's eyes were trained on the *Heliaré* at Fel'annár's temple —symbol of the Kal'hamén'Ar.

"You have passed the test."

Fel'annár raised his chin, gaze latching on to Idernon and his knowing eyes, eyes that slowly wrinkled around the edges, and the Wise Warrior smiled. He could not help it. Fel'annár's awe, the shock and perplexity on his face at Pan'assár allowing him to become Gor'sadén's disciple—he could hardly believe it himself, and soon, Fel'annár too was smiling, so wide it split his face apart, dimples appearing on his cheeks, and yet when he spoke, tears pooled in his eyes.

"Yes."

Galdith roared in Silvan delight, and soon, Fel'annár Ar Thargodén had disappeared under a sea of blond, auburn, and grey hair. The onlooking Alpine warriors were cheering too as they watched the odd bunch of Silvan and Alpine warriors, their prince amongst them, and the spark of some new challenge burning in their eyes, and from inside the training ring, Gor'sadén listened. Power surged from the soles of his feet, up his spine, and to his head, and in his mind he knew—knew that something important was looming on the boundaries between impression and reality—and that, whatever it was, it would change him inexorably.

～

The news that Fel'annár had passed the test travelled from captains to warriors, from warriors to teachers, bakers, councillors and stable hands. The healers, too, came to hear of it, and Llyniel listened to their excited chatter with a smile on her face and no small amount of pride for her friend's feat.

She followed Mestahé down the floor-to-ceiling shelves that lined the walls of the large store rooms which sat one floor below ground, directly under the Halls of Healing. That morning, they had found the locked doors open, the bolt hanging loose from the wood. Someone had entered during the night and had taken supplies. According to Mestahé, it was not the first time it had happened, but even so, Arané had cursed rather colourfully. He had then sent Mestahé to find out what had been taken so that arrangements for their replacement could be made and Llyniel had offered to accompany him and continue her own study of Tar'eastór's stock of herbs and tinctures.

While Mestahé made his list, Llyniel wondered who might have done such a thing. There was no shortage of healing supplies, in fact the city was full of apothecaries. She made a note to look at Mestahé's list when time permitted, thinking that perhaps there was something rare and expensive that somebody needed, or that somebody would sell for a handsome price. For now, she trailed her fingers over the jars and baskets, eyes registering the herbs and mixtures, the roots and plants, most of them known to her, although some were not. These were the ones she took note of and would later study. For now though, it was time to return to the halls, finish her duty round, and then visit Fel'annár for the first time since that moment in the forest when she thought he would kiss her, had hoped that he would.

But he hadn't, and perhaps it was just as well. She would congratulate him, see his proud, smiling face, see to him if he was wounded, and then she would rush to Handir's rooms and lunch. She would have just enough time.

Once they had finished in the supply rooms, Llyniel made her way to her own rooms and changed out of her robes and into a simple blue dress. Throwing a few basic supplies into a basket, she made her way to Fel'annár's suite of rooms.

She had assumed that Pan'assár would find a way to foil Fel'annár's bid to become a Kah Warrior. She had been wrong, but she wasn't about to berate herself for it. She had known Pan'assár all her life. He was cool and sarcastic, so utterly monotonous in his face and bearing. Always stiff and frozen. There was no life in him, no passion except for when he spoke of the Silvan people. For them he always had a sneer and a cutting word. Perhaps something had changed in the commander, or perhaps Fel'annár had simply been too good for him to find an excuse to fail him.

She wanted to know what had happened, congratulate him on a feat she had not thought possible.

Arriving at Fel'annár's rooms, not far from where Handir himself was housed, she knocked, and then heard the sound of a bolt sliding open. A Silvan warrior appeared in the half-open door.

"Can I come in?"

"Healer," he nodded, opening the door for her.

With a grateful nod, she entered but then stopped, not having expected to find Fel'annár in the company of others, one of whom was Prince Sontúr. They had crossed words the day Fel'annár had become a lord and had yet to clear the air.

The warriors stood together, laughing and joking around while Sontúr tried to dab a wet towel against Fel'annár's bruised face. He noticed her standing there before any of the others.

"Lady Llyniel," was all the prince said, but Fel'annár's head turned to her, and Sontúr huffed in exasperation, cloth dripping over his hands, not that Fel'annár noticed at all.

"Fel'annár, forgive me. I just came to see if you needed anything. I heard you passed the test."

The room was utterly silent, The Company watching Llyniel and then Fel'annár.

"I did." His smile widened, and she thought it must hurt, for his face was battered. The silence, though, lingered for longer than was comfortable.

"I thought you might need my aid, after facing our commander, but I see you are well-tended to." She nodded slowly at Sontúr, who returned it just as coolly.

"I . . . forgive me. Lady Llyniel, these here are Idernon, Ramien, Galdith and Galadan," said Fel'annár, watching as his friends bowed to her. Then he gestured to Carodel. "And of course you are familiar with Carodel." His lips twitched, and she smiled at the dumbfounded Silvan warrior with a lyre in his hands.

"I am, indeed, familiar with Carodel. We are both from Sen Garay, although we have never met."

Carodel had the good conscience to blush, and Llyniel repressed the urge to snicker at him. Still, she was ill at ease. Sontúr had been barely civil with her, and the others stared at her for entirely too long. She cleared her throat.

"Well, if you don't need anything . . . congratulations, Warrior. I am glad I was wrong about Pan'assár."

"So am I," said Fel'annár.

She nodded and then turned to leave.

"Llyniel."

She turned back, watching as Fel'annár walked slowly towards her and then looked down at her. She saw regret there, regret perhaps that he was not alone, but so too did she see gratitude. Funny that she could read all these things without the necessity for words.

He smiled apologetically. "I will find you tomorrow," he said, nodding resolutely.

"Good." Her eyes strayed for a moment to the warriors behind Fel'annár, and then she left, the contents of her basket untouched. Galdith watched as she navigated the candle-lit corridor and then turned, bolting the door shut, eyebrows riding almost as high as Sontúr's.

Carodel's eyes were fixed on the door and when it was clear the healer had left, he launched one arm into the air. "Oh, for the love of a *healer*! She was . . ."

"*Shut* it, Carodel," said Fel'annár with a grin.

"*Aaaaiiii*," yipped Ramien, a high-pitched Silvan exclamation, and while Fel'annár took the heel of his hand to his forehead, the rest laughed bawdily, clapping him on the shoulders and delivering playful punches to his arms. He bore it all good-naturedly because all of a sudden, life had turned so very sweet.

And while Fel'annár celebrated his victory in his rooms, Llyniel wandered down the corridor, her untouched healing supplies in her basket. She didn't care, though, had all but forgotten the uncomfortable silence and the assessing eyes. Fel'annár's bruised but smiling face lingered in her mind, looking down at her, the promise of something in his eyes. She would make sure he did find her tomorrow.

She did not see Handir until his words snapped her back to the corridor and the present.

"Visiting the *warriors*?" he asked with an arched brow.

She looked up at him. "Congratulating Fel'annár on a mighty feat, as you will no doubt agree," she said carefully, falling into step with the prince as they made their way to his rooms for lunch.

"I am surprised, I'll give you that. I had thought Pan'assár was simply going through the motions, indulging Gor'sadén to at least give the boy a test. But I always thought he would fail him, find some excuse."

"Perhaps Fel'annár is simply too good." She shrugged.

"Perhaps." Handir glanced sideways at her as they walked. "Was he *alone* in his rooms then?"

She scowled and faced him. "And what if he *was*?"

"You won't heed my warning then? Llyniel, he is a *warrior*, he could die at any moment, yet more than this, he is dangerous to know, Sister. Distance yourself from him while you still can. I will not *allow* him to hurt you and . . ."

"*Don't!*" she ground out, turning to face him, forcing him to stop. "You will not *allow*? Is this a royal command, *Brother*?"

Handir breathed deeply. "Well, you know I love you, and *no*, this is *not* a royal command. It is me, *Handir*, warning you to step away from him. He has already almost died once since we have been here, just as he almost died out on patrol when Lainon had to protect him. He paid the price of loving that warrior, Llyniel, and of all the people in this world, you are the dearest to me. I would not see you grieving over his death. It is my *duty* to keep you safe if I can." He stepped closer to her and placed a hand on her arm.

"And it is your duty to *respect* me. To trust me to do what I must. You will not interfere with my feelings for Fel'annár, whatever they may be." She breathed deeply, closing her eyes to steady herself. "I know your heart, Handir, but this aversion you have for Fel'annár —*that* is the real issue, not my attraction to him, not because he is reckless as you seem to be implying. You warn me away from him because you cannot stand your best friend becoming intimate with a half-brother you do not accept."

She was angry, but now, so was Handir.

"Think what you will. *Delude* yourself if you must, but do not ask me to stand by and watch you hurt yourself. I cannot do that."

She lifted her head, held his glittering stare and returned it with one of her own.

Handir bowed his head and looked to the floor for a moment.

Pressing his lips into a thin line, he offered Llyniel a sad smile. "I don't want us to be angry at each other. Come, let's talk over lunch."

"I am not hungry, Handir."

His smile was gone. He nodded, regretful eyes lingering for a while, watching as she turned away from him, leaving him with her angry accusations echoing in his mind.

∼

Later that evening, Fel'annár made his way to Gor'sadén's chambers, his face still smarting and his mind on his meeting with Llyniel tomorrow. But so too were there questions he needed to ask Gor'sadén. How had Pan'assár moved so fast? What strategy had he used to break his defences in the end?—and why had he stopped?

He knew Pan'assár would not have killed him, but he had doubted that for one alarming moment. He glanced backwards and to Galdith, who nodded back at him, and Fel'annár damned the day he had given voice to the threat he had felt on their return from patrol. Since then he had hardly been left alone without a guard, and he wondered if it was not all a little exaggerated. Trees were not always precise in their warnings. He did not always understand them well.

He knocked on the door to Gor'sadén's private suite of rooms, and soon enough, it opened. Galdith took up his place outside, and Fel'annár placed a hand on his arm as he stepped inside and then closed the door.

"Fel'annár, come and sit by the fire, and before you do, you are not on duty; we are equals here."

Fel'annár smiled but could not help the respectful nod. He sat and then accepted a glass of wine from the commander and took a sip, enjoying the warmth from the hearth.

"Your new status is the talk of the entire palace—and the barracks, I would assume."

"They recognised the braid, my lord."

"Aye, the Heliaré. The Kal'hamén'Ar was almost extinct, but that does not mean the warriors of Tar'eastór have forgotten."

Fel'annár nodded, his eyes drifting to the dancing flames.

"You fought well with Pan'assár; I had not realised you had some skill with aerial work. We should exploit that," he said, taking a sip of his wine. "He did not make it easy, did he?"

"No!" snorted Fel'annár. "About that . . ."

"You have questions, yes."

"Will you answer them?"

The commander did not answer straight away, and he swirled the wine in his goblet as he considered his words. "No. I cannot do that. Pan'assár will answer them or no one will."

"Then they will go unanswered, for certain. I am still surprised he even allowed me to test for the Kal'hamén'Ar. Have you ever noticed that he cannot even *look* at me?"

"All I ask of you, Fel'annár, is to keep your mind open as to his reasons, and as for accepting the test, that is because, despite what he may feel or think of you, he is a warrior, a Kah Master."

"But he did look at me in the end, and it almost cost him his control, didn't it?" asked Fel'annár softly, looking into his goblet and not at Gor'sadén. "I wonder what it is that he saw, when he did, finally, look at me."

The commander stared at the boy's profile. He wanted to tell him, but it was Pan'assár's story to tell—if he ever would. Gor'sadén would not betray his friend's confidence to anyone, not even to Fel'annár. But none of this was the reason he had asked Fel'annár to join him this evening.

"He may yet surprise you, tell you one day."

"I doubt that."

Gor'sadén stared back at Fel'annár. "You are sceptical, and that is a fault."

"Can you blame me? I don't think you have ever been discriminated against, Gor'sadén. If you had, it would not be so easy for you to criticise my scepticism."

"Perhaps not. Yet still, it is a fault. It benefits no one, serves only to justify your anger. You must rid yourself of these negative thoughts, not feed them."

Fel'annár turned to Gor'saden, allowing himself to digest his mentor's words. Wisely, he kept quiet, for admitting fault did not come easily to him—another fault, perhaps.

"And you are angry, aren't you?" said Gor'saden.

When Fel'annár finally answered, his voice was a little strained and his jaw was clenched, eyes staring into his goblet.

"Yes."

"That is a start," came the quiet words. "A little advice, Fel'annár. You are good, very good, and at your age that is almost unheard of, but heed me. You are not perfect; you do not *have* to be perfect. Do you understand me?"

Gor'saden's words took him completely by surprise and he froze where he sat.

"You do not have to be perfect."

"You have never seen it that way, have you?" asked the commander. "I first began to understand when I saw your temper—so like Or'Talán's—it gave you away. You strive for perfection in order to be *accepted*. When you are wrong, it irks you, because it leaves you open to criticism, and you cannot accept that because you have spent your entire life thinking that you don't deserve it . . . because you have had too much of it."

Gor'saden's words reverberated in his mind, his skin alive with raw emotion, and still, his mind screamed at him to reject the words: they weren't true, Gor'saden was *wrong*.

But he wasn't, and Fel'annár knew it. Still, he could not say it. Anger stirred in his chest once more.

"I ask only that you think on my words, Fel'annár. They are meant to help, not to hinder. Now, I have things to say about your apprenticeship, things you may not know."

Fel'annár turned to Gor'saden, grateful that the commander had seen fit to end the uncomfortable moment. Still, only Gor'saden could have spoken to him the way he had, like a father guiding his wayward son.

"I have spoken with Captain Comon. He is aware that I have taken you as an apprentice, as is every other commander in this army," he added with a smirk. "Admittedly I have done nothing to contain the news. The return of the Kal'hamén'Ar is something I believe will renew us all, motivate our warriors to strive for greater things, as it once was centuries ago. And yet that is not to say this will be flaunted; it won't. Our training will be carried out beyond the Inner Circle and the fields. Out of sight to the uninitiated. Do you understand the reasons why?"

Fel'annár had read about the prohibition in the Warrior Code, but he could not say that he understood, and so he shook his head.

"The Kal'hamén'Ar is to be contemplated in the Dance, or on the battlefield, nowhere else. Your preparation, your physical and mental training is not secret. It is the moves and their combinations that must not be revealed. Centuries ago, Kah Warriors trained openly upon the fields, and those who had not yet made the grade as an apprentice would often emulate what they saw. One warrior broke his neck as he practiced the *Gorahei,* and another accidentally ran his opponent through the chest as he tried to perform the *Den'ab*. There were other, less serious incidents, until it was finally written into the Warrior Code that all training should be carried out in a place where only other Kah Masters or apprentices could see."

The commander's gaze lingered for a while before he turned to the fire. "You are to wear the grey sash of a Kah Apprentice with your uniform but you must bear the Heliaré at *all* times. All this is law, Fel'annár. You must not go against it."

"I won't, Gor'sadén. But tell me, why does Commander Pan'assár not comply with this law? He wore the sash for the test, at least but where is his Heliaré?"

"That is not for me to say. Suffice it to say I believe you will see him wear them, one day."

Fel'annár nodded. It was a part of Pan'assár's story that

Gor'sadén would not speak of. It was related to why the commander had lost his control, why he would not look at him, why he did not wear the Kah symbols.

"It is also law that an apprentice can only become a master if he or she is proficient in three weapons. You are already a bow master, but you must think on your other two weapons of choice—one, though, must necessarily be blades, and you must soon decide on the other." He stood and walked to the fire, eyes unfocussed. He still remembered his previous apprentices, recalled the day he had asked them of their weapons of choice. Benolá and Semu'lán, Cavena and Por'ya. They stood in stone now, upon the crenulations of the city walls, and in his heart, in a place he revisited fondly from time to time.

"The Master teaches but so too does he guide," continued Gor'sadén, swallowing the bittersweet memories. "Our relationship will not be that of a weapon master to a warrior. It runs far deeper than that, Fel'annár. It is why I previously required the permission of both Pan'assár and my king to carry out this task. You see, it is my duty to teach you the Kal'hamén'Ar, but in doing so, my obligations extend to you as a whole. I will train your body and cultivate your mind. I will teach you to synchronise them so that they work together in harmony. You will be a priority to me, as much as my own duty here as commander general. The time that is left before your prince must return to Ea Uaré is insufficient to fully learn, and so, should circumstances permit, I must return with you to the Forest in order to complete your training."

Fel'annár's head snapped to the commander. "How is that possible? Who would take over your responsibilities here?"

"Comon is my second. If circumstances allow, if this new threat of the Nim'uán can be neutralised, then he will take over for the time I am away."

"And if it is too dangerous for you to leave, what then?"

"We wait. You return and I will follow when I can."

Fel'annár's heart was racing in his chest. Gor'sadén would travel back to the Forest with him. He would have his mentor at his side to face whatever it was that awaited him in Ea Uaré.

"I never realised. I feel like a fool for taking so much for granted, for not understanding how much it would affect you. I can't even understand why you would do such a thing, give up so much in order to teach me."

"And there you have it. Who are you to be taught, you ask. Why would I wish to teach you. This is why you strive for perfection, because you feel imperfect—because you think perfection will make you worthy. I am giving up nothing, Fel'annár. It is a great honour to train a warrior in the Kah; it is written in the Warrior Code, yet more than this it is etched upon my very soul. I would see this honourable art come back. I have everything to gain . . . we all do. There are many enemies to face, both here and in the Great Forest. Our warriors must be the best they can be and then some. Bringing back the Kah will inspire them to greatness and as we walk that road, I will show you your imperfections, make you a better elf."

Fel'annár listened, nodding at the things Gor'sadén said, but above all he struggled to contain his joy at the prospect of having Gor'sadén at his side.

The commander turned from the hearth to face Fel'annár.

"In order to do this, you must know what I will expect from you, what I want from you in return."

Fel'annár stood, worry stirring in his chest. Perhaps there was another test he must pass. He nodded.

"I want *everything*, Fel'annár. I want your best effort with the blades. I want your honesty, your sad story, and your childish dreams. I want your cries of pain and your tears of bitterness. I want your self-doubt and the anger you think you hide so well. I want to see your defences so that I can smash them to pieces and see *you*, you who hide behind your walls and your armour. I will break it all to pieces and reconfigure you, set you upon the road of a warrior, upon the path of the captain you want to be—and more if I can."

Fel'annár could feel his eyes straining wide, wet and hot, could feel a searing tear burn down his cheek, but he could not bring himself to care. He was suddenly adrift, floating above unknown territory as deep blue eyes of ancient wisdom watched him, as if they could read his thoughts.

Gor'sadén stepped back, satisfaction in his eyes while Fel'annár sagged where he stood.

"Will you give me everything?" asked Gor'sadén.

Fel'annár bowed his head in respect, and when he faced Gor'sadén once more, a smile graced his bruised face.

"I will," he said, words echoing oddly in Gor'sadén's ears. He nodded and then returned to his chair before the hearth. He did not expect Fel'annár's next question.

"Does your father live, Gor'sadén?"

"No. He died in battle. He was a captain under the rule of King Car'enár, before he too fell and his son Vorn'asté was invested."

"You must miss him."

Gor'sadén wondered what a fatherless elf would know of such things; or perhaps it was precisely that he *didn't* have a father to miss that he understood so well.

"Every day. He was sometimes harsh in his expectations for me, demanding of what I did and how I did it, but I learned to understand that it was for the faith he had in me, the pride he held for me. It was love that drove him to push me, make me what I am. I don't think anyone else believed in me quite as much as he did, except for those of The Three," he said. "I cried the day he fell, but the memory of him carried me to new heights. In honour of him I became lieutenant, then captain, general and then commander."

A soft smile graced his face as memories raced through his mind, memories Fel'annár had brought to the surface with his questions. Only when he had stopped speaking did he realised he had disclosed far more than he had intended. His gaze fell on Fel'annár once more, and what he saw there took him to sudden realisation . . . of why Fel'annár had asked that question in the first place. He watched as his pupil rose and then knelt before the fire, carefully feeding it with another log. He turned to Gor'sadén from where he knelt.

"Will you do that for me?"

Gor'sadén was struck by the intensity in Fel'annár's eyes. They were open, he realised, unguarded, revealing unashamedly what lay beyond. All his weaknesses, all the things he had always hidden: his yearning to belong, to feel loved, to know he was cherished. It was a rare gift, he realised, an act of utter humility. Fel'annár was giving him *everything*, and Gor'sadén felt privileged beyond his ability to express with words.

This was what Fel'annár had missed his entire life. That older, wiser figure to guide him, one that would see his faults and not blame him for them, would not judge him as weak. His recent conversation with Fel'annár in the gardens rushed back to him.

"Why do you trust me?" he had asked. *"I won't let you down,"* he had vowed.

A sense of responsibility slammed into Gor'sadén, and then came the tingle of nascent realisation. This was what he had sensed. This was the feeling that had been growing in his mind, the feeling that something important was about to happen, that he would be needed to serve some *purpose*. That purpose was before him, kneeling with his back to him once more, stoking the fire but with every sense trained on the one behind him. This bereft child had come to understand what it was to have a father, to realise what he had never had, what he had always needed.

Will you do that for me? were his words, but what Fel'annár truly asked was whether Gor'sadén would be as a father to him.

Gor'sadén had never had children. He had always been too busy with his calling as a warrior. But to look at this extraordinary boy, to understand him as Gor'sadén had come to do . . . his heart was reaching out. He wanted to protect him. He wanted to make him the best elf he could be. He wanted to feel proud of him, brag that he had, in some small way, been responsible for his successes and achievements.

"Yes, I will do that for you." He smiled as he uttered those words, glad that Fel'annár's back was turned away from his watery eyes, unaware of the soft smile on Fel'annár's face and the resolution in his unfocussed eyes.

This was the start of a new era, a return to the glory days of the warriors of Tar'eastór. Gor'sadén would make this son of Thargodén, the son he chose for himself, a warrior the likes of which Elvendom had never seen.

It was the dawn of a legend; Gor'sadén would see it done.

~

In the early hours, Fel'annár and The Company sat in a remote corner of the public gardens. Sontúr had led them here, claiming they would not be disturbed. How he could possibly know, Fel'annár couldn't say but Sontúr seemed confident enough they were free to oaf around without restraint. He laughed now as Galdith imitated Silor's arrogant bragging.

"As trainee lieutenant, under Commander Pan'assár *himself,*" he said, eyes wide, one eyebrow riding high on his forehead, "Silvan warriors do not come *close* to us Alpines," he shouted, throwing his arms to the heavens. They all snickered, all except for Galadan. He had been entrusted with teaching Silor the ways of a lieutenant by Pan'assár himself. Silor had learned nothing, because he had always known his future position had nothing to do with his skill—with his ability or his motivation to serve. It had been a futile exercise from the very beginning. It was a travesty, and Galadan could find no humour in it.

Ramien poured wine down his throat. He swallowed and then let out a mighty gasp, wiping his sleeve over his mouth.

"You're drunk!" Fel'annár snorted as he swiped another bottle of the wine from Idernon's lax hands.

"So are you, Fel'annár, soon to be apprentice of the Klamenen . . .

Arrr." Ramien shrugged his shoulders and then burped for so long that Galdith sent peals of laughter into the night air.

They laughed and slapped their thighs, for Ramien had never been able to say the word. "Ramien, just say Kah. Everyone else does," explained Galadan in mock irritation.

"All hail Lord Fel'annár, apprentice of the Arrr!" shouted Galdith and then chuckled at himself.

Carodel shuffled where he sat and soon, his new lyre weaved a soft melody, and Fel'annár smiled, wondering where he had gotten the instrument when his original one had been lost in the battle on their way to Tar'eastór.

"Lind'atór, Bard Warrior of Sen Garay. What would we do without you, brother?" said Fel'annár.

"Um . . ." He smiled as he played. "And what would we do without Hwind'atór, Whirling Warrior?" asked Carodel with a smile.

"There is that," nodded Fel'annár seriously. "But then I would not be here were it not for the Wall of Stone—or the Wise Warrior," he said with a grin.

"And what of Galadan, of Galdith, and Sontúr?" asked Idernon. "Are we to call them by those stuffy names alone when the rest of us have been honoured with a *warrior* name?"

"It's hardly fair," said Sontúr, while Galadan and Galdith stared expectantly at Fel'annár.

"Well, that must be remedied!" proclaimed Fel'annár as he grabbed the open bottle of wine sitting on the grass. "Now let me see . . . Galdith." He stroked his chin with his hand. "Do you not think that Galdith of Sen'uár has the face of a *boy*?"

The others laughed, but Galdith was indignant. "I do *not*! I am a veteran warrior you Silvan lackwit!"

The rest jeered, but Fel'annár had not finished. "You have the face of a boy, but in battle, it scrunches and warps out of all shape and becomes a thing of nightmares. Have you not noticed? The innocent boy becomes a fire-spitting demon, and he is terror incarnate. I say Galdith is fierce of face—he is the Fierce Warrior."

Galdith's mouth was open in a silent "oh" while the rest stared at him, as if they were seeing that transformation only now. Idernon nodded. "That is a just name. All hail the Fierce Warrior!" he shouted.

"*Hail!*" they replied, even Galdith who laughed and then drank once more. "At last!" he proclaimed. "I am a true brother of The Company! But what of Galadan and Sontúr?" he asked, and the rest leaned forward.

"Galadan, too, has a trait you may have noticed. He is stone. His expression ever the same whether he drinks or fights. It is only the fire or ice in his eyes that speaks of his thoughts. But it is with anger that his transformation occurs. I say Galadan is the Fire Warrior, for the flames that dance in his eyes."

"All hail the Fire Warrior!" shouted Galdith.

"*Hail!*" they answered, while Galadan, quite uncharacteristically, stood and bowed theatrically.

And then all eyes were on Sontúr.

But Fel'annár was scowling. "And now, I confess I am torn. I cannot rightly say what Sontúr will be. He is Alpine, of course, a prince, a warrior, and healer, but none of these things make him unique."

"That eyebrow of his is uncanny," said Ramien as he pointed at the prince. "Gives me the chills."

They laughed.

"But I can hardly call him the Eyebrow Warrior!" scoffed Fel'annár as he took another swig from the bottle.

"Please don't," said Sontúr with his characteristic arch of the brow in question. "And if you drink any more of that stuff, Ramien, you will be swinging through the trees like one of those forest bears I have seen in books!"

"No tree would hold him!" laughed Carodel with a flourish of his lyre.

Ramien wagged his finger at Sontúr. "You Alpines have no idea how to navigate the trees. Can you even *climb* one?" he scoffed and then took a sloppy swig of wine.

"Of course I can, you Silvan troll. We Alpines are alike to the red squirrel: fast and adept, sure-footed even upon the most slippery of barks."

The rest of the Silvans jeered and mocked his words in jest, and Fel'annár smiled at their antics.

"Red squirrel, eh? Well, in the Forest we have black squirrels, this big," said Ramien, showing them the length of his wrist through to his elbow. "Now *they* are skilled in the trees, even if the trees do not welcome them. They shake them off if they can, lest they bite through to the very *sap*, and if, by chance, they are allowed to latch onto your feet . . . heed me, Alpine, they will bite through to the bone, boots or not."

Sontúr's eyebrows rose as he laughed. "Squirrels do not fall from trees, least of all Alpine ones," giggled the warrior healer as he drank, and Ramien leaned forward.

"Show us! Show us how Alpine squirrels traverse the trees!" he said with a challenge. "Two coins he falls on his noble arse!"

The rest of The Company roared in drunken laughter, imagining the undignified image of Vorn'asté's princely son rubbing his backside. Indeed, Fel'annár fell backwards into Idernon's lap, holding his middle as he laughed scandalously.

Sontúr stood and bowed, perfectly serious and lordly, save that he keened to one side for a moment before rectifying his balance.

"Oooohhh!" they shouted as they pointed at him and laughed even harder.

"You have no idea what an Alpine squirrel is capable of, therefore I move to enlighten your ignorant, Silvan preju—prejudice," he corrected. "Watch, and learn . . ." he drawled and then disappeared into the nearest tree.

The Company was silent for a moment, frankly impressed that Sontúr had been able to pull himself into the tree so fast for one so inebriated.

"Where is he?" asked Carodel, his eyes searching the darkness.

"I don't know," said Galdith, his head moving from side to side.

"Shshs—listen," said Idernon, trying to track Sontúr by the rustle of leaves, but there was no sound, and he frowned.

"Is he already at the top? I can't hear the leaves," he said, puzzled.

There was a sudden thud as something black fell hard upon the forest floor and then a groan of miserable pain.

A mighty snort escaped Ramien, but Carodel elbowed him in the ribs.

"Sontúr?" asked Idernon. "Is that you?"

Silent expectation.

"Yes," came the breathless groan, and laughter erupted once more, loud and raucous.

Galdith tried to talk through his laughter, only half successful. "He, he latched on to that—that low hanging branch and—*froze!*—like a fruit bat—that's, that's why we didn't see him!!!" he roared. "He was but ten feet from the ground, and still . . ."

Ramien tried to control his wheezing, "You owe me—two coins!! His arse will be as black as his cloak tomorrow!!!"

∽

They had fallen asleep in the gardens and then crawled to the barracks as discreetly as they could. It was closer than the palace, and so both Sontúr and Fel'annár decided it would be safer if they were to have breakfast with the troops. Fel'annár had missed that.

Straightening their clothing and brushing their hair, they made for the noisy hall and found a table for themselves. They were surprised to see the two commanders sitting close by.

But their surprise was quickly replaced by evil expectation as Sontúr sat next to Ramien, his face blank and noble, if a little pale, the perfect mask of a young and handsome lord. Yet when his body touched the bench there was the hint of a grimace, and that was all it took for the Silvan warriors to snort and then wheeze in mirth.

Fel'annár desperately tried to cover his treacherous mouth as Idernon hooted even though he had tried to muffle it.

All eyes fell on them, some askance while others in immediate understanding and a few with a smile of their own. It was clear the lads had been out the previous evening and some such mischief had occurred involving Sontúr and The Company.

"Well, are you going to tell us what happened?" asked Gor'sadén in mock irritation.

"Suffice it to say, Sir," began Fel'annár, his voice a little strangled, "that Lieutenant Sontúr earned his warrior name last night. He is," he struggled to finish his sentence, "he is Rafn'ator—the Winged Warrior!"

Scandalous laughter exploded at The Company's table as chair legs scraped over the floor and the warriors convulsed in uncontrollable hysterics, Ramien hitting the table over and over again, clay bowls thudding in time to his fist.

Gor'sadén chuckled while Pan'assár desperately tried to stop the corners of his mouth from twitching.

"Do I want to know what happened, Lieutenant?" asked the commander, turning to his prince.

"I, eh," began Sontúr, "I was explaining about the kinetic qualities of—of Alpine squirrels!!!" he shouted and then slumped over the table in laughter.

That was all it took for the commanders to work out what must have happened. Gor'sadén threw his head back and laughed as noisily as the rest of the warriors, slapping his leather-clad thighs. This, in turn, brought a rare smile to Pan'assár's face.

"Children!" he muttered.

EIGHT
A SILVAN STORY

"There is power in unity—this Band'orán knew. The Silvans had no central government, and that was a singular advantage to one who sought to impose his own laws upon the natives. The Silvans, though, had once had a warlord, but that figure had been outlawed with the coming of the Alpines. Now, Band'orán's only threat was the prince the Silvans were denied. He was but a child, a child the Silvans would use as a symbol: their own claim to power."
The Silvan Chronicles, Book V. Marhené.

~

The Forest Summit was reaching its apex, and today, Erthoron and Lorthil would convey their requests to the king. They knew these requests would be debated, that they would need to be voted upon, and they set out to put forward their reasons to the very best of their abilities.

They sat within the semi-circle of councillors, and opposite sat the king and crown prince. There was a public area at both sides which, on any normal council day, would be almost empty. Today, though, they were brimming, one side with the many Silvans who had ridden in from the Deep Forest while the other was made up of Alpine nobles and merchants.

The king would listen to the opinions of his councillors and visiting dignitaries, but would not give his own opinion while the debate was ongoing. That was Aradan's job. The king *would*, however, give a speech before voting took place. A strong king would always achieve the results he desired because his councillors were with him, trusted him and voted accordingly. Today, though, was the first vote they would take after Thargodén's *return*, and Aradan was not so sure the king would have his way. Band'orán had been busy in his absence. But then that was *his* job. Aradan would exert himself as he never had before to communicate the king's will, convince those councillors who had moved towards Band'orán's position to come back to Thargodén.

It was going to be hard for Den'har, the Council Master, to enforce the principle of equilibrium, allow everyone a turn to speak, to refute, to defend, and to correct false inferences, because it meant giving voice to the Alpine purists—it meant listening to their racist ways and their discriminatory words. Still, the freedom to speak was a sacred principle to Aradan. It was the only way that a nation could prosper, could serve the people it harboured in all their wonderful diversity. Should that freedom be used to spread hatred, Aradan wanted to believe that those responsible would, sooner or later, lose their right to speak, because no one would follow them, no one would respect them enough to back them in their destructive ways. Wishful thinking, perhaps, but then Aradan told himself that was exactly what politics was about; it was why he loved what he did.

"Lord Band'orán, you have the floor," shouted Den'har. Aradan's gaze momentarily landed on Turion, who nodded encouragingly back at him while his right hand sat calmly over the pommel of his long sword, as if he stood upon a hill, watching his troops organise themselves for battle.

"My Lords, I, and I am sure many of you, wish to express our displeasure at the king's official stance concerning the bastard child Fel'annár," he began amidst gasps from his fellow councillors and the crowds of Silvans over to one side. But not everyone was outraged at Band'orán's choice of words, for there were nods of agreement and words of approval from the more conservative lords. The king, though, sat placidly upon his chair, his face completely devoid of emotion.

"The Silvan has already been proclaimed a lord, but I move to limit his rights and functions at court. Specifically, I move to vote that his lordship be limited to a mere token. I do not say *honorary* title, as that would be like rewarding infidelity and mixed blood; it is not worthy of an Alpine king." Band'orán's eyes were now trained challengingly on Thargodén, yet still, the monarch sat like stone upon his ornate throne, and Rinon's face was just as blank.

"Let this Silvan lad serve in our army, for I have heard he is an acceptable warrior. Aria knows we need competent archers. But any inclusion in these hallowed council halls will be deemed an insult to our departed queen, a reminder of King Thargodén's *indiscretion*, a reminder of how he has dishonoured this land and his noble father, our great king, Or'Talán."

Aradan saw Band'orán's speech for what it was. He was using the brother he despised to glean the council's approval. Or'Talán was revered, and his brother used that love to his own personal gain. His blood boiled. He could not allow this, could not continue to hold his silence. It was why Aradan had lost his only child. She had left, gone in search of a fairer land with fairer rulers, where elves were not afraid to act on their beliefs, where chief councillors were brave enough to face the likes of Band'orán. Thargodén had made his way back from his years of oblivion, but so too had Aradan taken an oath. He had promised to make Thargodén great once more, and to do that, the time for patience and caution was gone. He buried the heartache of his absent daughter and forced himself to concentrate on Band'orán and his slowly emerging tactics.

"Councillor Vardú!" called Den'har. A dark-haired woman, one of the few Silvans on the ruling council, stood.

"I am outraged at your words, Lord Band'orán. I will not discuss my king's *personal* affairs in these public halls, as you seem so willing to do, but you speak of '*half-blood*' as if it were a curse, a taint upon your Alpine heritage."

Band'orán smiled sadly at her from where he sat, and her eyes flickered wide. She stepped backwards, in shock that he had not refuted her words, that he had so openly defined himself and that no one would stand up to him. And Aradan watched her as if she were Llyniel.

"Councillor Band'orán!" called Den'hár.

"Well, you are Silvan, Lady Vardú. You defend the boy, and there is honour in that. But tell me in all truth, what has he done to deserve a lordship? What has he done to merit our respect, our deference?"

Den'hár nodded for her to continue, but she was interrupted by a Silvan voice from the public area.

"And how many of our *captains* deserve the uniform they wear?"

"Order!" shouted Den'hár, banging his staff against the stone floor.

Band'orán chose to ignore the comment and rounded on the Silvan councillor. "Tell me, Lady Vardú. What has he done to deserve such an honour?"

"He is who he is, Lord Band'orán. As you are a lord for the blood in your veins. What have *you* done to deserve the power *you* wield?"

"*Aye!*" shouted the Silvans.

"I serve my king, here at council. I protect these lands by helping to decide what is best for our future."

"And Fel'annár is a warrior, he too serves this land, protects it with his life."

"*Aye!*" they shouted again, and Den'hár called for silence once more.

"And are we to make lords of *all* our warriors, Lady Vardú? Come —you can do better than that," he smirked.

"Lord Band'orán, unless I have sorely misinterpreted our king's intentions, this summit is to bring us *together,* to find common goals, and instead you spit your hatred for my people as you always do. I am deeply saddened that so few of my fellow councillors have not spoken out against such provocation."

There were murmurs all around them, but Band'orán was quick to use his rhetoric.

"Calm yourself, my lady. You cannot serve on this council if you cannot control your emotions," he drawled, knowing full well how it would rile her.

She stood as if he had slapped her, and she turned accusing eyes upon her fellow councillors. But they would not look at her, and her expression turned from one of anger to sadness. She wanted to shout at them, shake them awake, scream in their faces that this was *wrong,* but she stood alone before a demon. But then one voice broke through the silence.

"Councillor Aradan."

"Lord Fel'annár is a child of the Forest, born to Lássira of the Silvans," said Aradan pointedly, "and King Thargodén of the Alpines. You insult one you have never met, one you do not know the worth of—under the simple pretext of being a *bastard*. Tell me, Lord Band'orán, are there no *worthy* bastards? Are all bastards evil and inept, deserving of the most deplorable insults? Are they not, then, elves to be judged with the same measure as any other? Is it simply who they are born to that matters to you? Are you that . . . *prejudiced,* my lord?" he finished with a smile that was not friendly at all.

A mighty cheer went up amongst the Silvans; indeed many Alpines were nodding their heads in approval of Aradan's words, albeit they were surprised that Aradan had been so vocal.

"Lord Band'orán."

"Indeed, there are rules and laws that govern our lives. As elves we have legislated and passed them. They are there for a purpose, and in this, Lord Aradan, you must concede. A child born outside the bonds of matrimony cannot be heir to a king, cannot be a prince of the realm, for to allow it—what then, is the point of matrimony? Why would a king secure for himself, and his realm, a queen that is both noble and honourable if he is then free to impregnate the first elf that takes his fancy?" he said theatrically, and the gasps were back, some Silvans even rising to their feet in protest.

"I do not mean to offend, my lords, only to illustrate my point," said the councillor calmly. "Laws exist for a reason. The Silvan child must not be given a vote at court, for to do this would be to infringe upon those laws," he concluded and then sat.

"Lord Erthoron."

"My Lords," he began in a voice that was both sad and frustrated. "This," he gestured to Band'orán, "is the reason the Silvan people are discontent." He paused, looking slowly and carefully at the councillors around him. "This . . . *discourse*, this disdain, the sarcasm and the patronising words, the overt insult and the unveiled sneers. Had this child been *Alpine*, 'bastard' would become 'illegitimate'; 'child' would become 'son'; indeed had he been Alpine, you may well have taken advantage of his existence and turned him to your own racist ways if you thought there was some personal gain to be had." His finger pointed straight at Band'orán.

Band'orán looked on, impassive, but Aradan was not fooled. Or'Talán's brother was not as skilled as he believed himself to be, and on the inside, there was no doubt that his anger was on the brink of boiling.

"You speak against an elf who shares your blood, Lord Band'orán, you speak against your own nephew and your king, and you speak against the Silvan people. You call him 'Silvan', but he is half Alpine. You say he is a passing warrior when we Silvans know he will be the greatest warrior of our time. You take every advantage to mock and to scorn and to disqualify, and I will tell you what *we* think, my lord. We think you are *scared, scared* that with the appearance of this new Silvan lord, your dreams of Alpine dominance, your own ambitions for power and wealth will be *dashed!*" he shouted, and the roar that followed his words was inflamed and angry.

Aradan closed his eyes; this was not going according to plan, for the Silvan people had been awoken and Band'orán had done nothing but add timber to the already roaring fire. He had few doubts that this had been Band'orán's plan all along. It was a game of provocation which he would smooth over with words of reason and rhetoric, only to start once more. The question was—what was Band'orán pushing for? Did he want the Silvans to lose control? Did he want them to react negatively so that the councillors would rally against them? So that Band'orán could justify denying Fel'annár a vote on the council? It seemed likely to Aradan.

"Lord Falagar!" called Den'hár.

"My lords," he shouted over the din. "Let us please calm these harsh words we throw at one another. We should be discussing whether or not Lord Fel'annár should have a vote on this council. This Alpine–Silvan confrontation is as destructive as it is unnecessary. There is no reason for it, and I bid you all *stop* it. We all do that which is best suited to our skills, to our very nature. The Silvan people care for the Forest, harvest her bounty, nurture Aria's creation. You care for the trees and replant when they are lost, and that is a noble thing. We Alpine command our militia, because that is in our blood, our history. We legislate the land, for we have held great kingdoms and have the experience to do so efficiently. This, too, is noble. Can we not simply accept this reality and move forward?" he asked sincerely.

The Silvan area was quiet, but there were baffled expressions, looks of confusion and disbelief at Falagar's false assumptions, however good his intentions had been.

"Lord Lorthil."

"I thank you, Lord Falagar, for your sincere words," replied Lorthil. "However, although I appreciate your good will, you are nevertheless wrong in your assumptions. Think you there was no strife under the trees before the Alpines came from abroad? Think you we lived in chaos, incapable of ruling ourselves? We have spent millennia here, under the trees, and then more together with the Alpines—in harmony in the beginning under the rule of King Or'Talán. Even if you *were* right, my lord, even if you Alpine *do* come from a war-faring culture, do you not think that centuries are enough to learn? Do you not think our brave warriors capable, in all that time, of commanding a patrol as well as any Alpine? Tell me, then, why there are ten Alpine captains to every one Silvan captain when seventy percent of our troops are Silvan, my lord? And tell me, also, why there are no *female* warriors in our army?" There was a roar from the Silvans, and murmurs of outrage from the Alpines. The councillors, though, were divided. "Tell me," continued Lorthil, "why our music does not play in your halls, at your feasts. Tell me why more Silvan councillors do not advise the king? Tell me why our books of lore are not read in your schools, or why our villages are raided systematically by Deviants or Sand Lords without the necessary number of troops to protect us. Tell me, do you seek to purposefully exterminate us?"

The Alpines to one side flapped their hands at what they considered an absurd question.

"Lord Barathon!" called Den'hár.

"Lord Lorthil," began Band'orán's son. "You exaggerate, of course, and I understand you do this to rally your people. I, too, could rally my own, and where would that get us, tell me? Our commanders are just, and if they choose an Alpine captain over a Silvan one, then that demonstrates their professional opinion. It is not discrimination; it is common sense."

There were murmurs of agreement from the Alpines, and Barathon was encouraged.

He continued. "You claim for yourselves a Silvan lord who will speak for you, return to you what you consider was lost, but that is not the answer. The answer lies in understanding the truth. We all excel in certain things, as Lord Falagar has already suggested. We Alpine are good warriors and commanders, and you Silvan are excellent troops and archers. The land finds its own balance, naturally, without the intervention of anyone. Let things lie, my friends; let us take the burden of rule so that you may enjoy your forests and your lore. It is as it should be."

There were nods of approval from many of the councillors, and Aradan curbed his exasperation as he watched the Silvans carefully. There could be no mistake in what he saw. They had started the summit warily, and then with the proclamation of a new Silvan lord, they had started to hope that something would change. Aradan had seen it in their eyes, that spark of anticipation and excitement. But it had promptly turned into sadness and then quiet, smouldering outrage. Band'orán and his son Barathon would not go unanswered, though, and Aradan braced himself as Erthoron stood to speak.

"My Lord Barathon," said Erthoron, walking slowly back into the centre of the circle. "Will you now tell us what we are *good* and *bad* at? Like a mother to her wayward child? You speak of common sense, and so, *here*, I will *give* you some. Why are Alpine councillors dictating what the Silvans can and can't do in their own homes? *Common sense* would suggest it is because you think we cannot do it for ourselves. *Common sense* would imply that you do not want us to participate in the ruling of this land. Common sense tells me there is a *reason* for that, and that reason, my lords, is as plain as the lust for power I see in your lord father's *eyes*. Common sense? *Pah!* You have *none*."

Murmurs rippled through the councillors and the visitors, and even some giggling could be heard—and not only from the Silvan spectators. Barathon stood red-faced and seething, but he could almost hear his father's voice, demanding that he comport himself in a manner fitting an Alpine lord. He sat stiffly, avoiding his father's gaze.

"My lords," continued Erthoron, "it is paramount that something be conceded by this Alpine council. These are Silvan lands with Silvan people. You push too hard and too far, and my people are digging their heels in the ground. Our culture is being lost, our languages ignored, our music and our writings are not heard or read here, but even more than this, you are not defending us against the *enemy*. Tell me, then, why the Silvan people *need* the Alpines? What is in this unspoken pact for the Forest? What is in it for us? Will you continue to take and take and *take* and give nothing back?"

There were murmurs of agreement from the Silvans and silence from the Alpine public areas.

"Lord Draugole!"

"Lord Erthoron, I can tell you many reasons why the Silvans need the Alpines. For one, you have no central government. You have scattered leaders in scattered villages and therefore do not gather taxes. You have no money for provisions for an army. Where are your barracks, your swords? Where is the iron you need, the raw materials for your blades? You need money for these things. You must trade with Pelagia and Tar'eastór. How do you propose to do that without collecting taxes? Without appointing administrators? You can't fuel an army to face Sand Lords and Deviants, and you know it. You *need* this government, our army to defend yourselves, to pay your warriors and protect these lands."

"Lord Erthoron!"

"I do not deny these things, Councillor, but I must draw attention to your wording. *Our* fortress, you say; *our* army . . . you do not even realise that with every word you are claiming these lands and everything in it for yourselves. Or perhaps you *do* realise. Is that it, my lords? Is this talk, this apparently random choice of words in fact a slow but brutal indoctrination to reduce my people to nothing but a quaint nuisance so that you can claim our lands?"

The murmurs were back, Silvans nodding their heads in agreement with what Erthoron said. "I will tell you what we *don't* need, Lord Draugole. We don't need commanders who care nothing for the well-being of the Silvan people. We don't need strategists who make spurious decisions regarding patrol routes, outposts, and defences. We don't need Alpine commanders who send the Silvan troops to the front lines to be killed while the sons of their lords are made *captains*.

We don't need poor leaders who couldn't care less when they make mistakes that lead to the destruction of our villages and then tell us it is *our* fault, that we must leave in order to be defended. We don't need Alpines who come seeking the bounties of this land even while claiming their superiority over its native people. You say we need you, but it is *you* that need the Silvan people more," continued Erthoron, his robes swishing around his calves as he paced before the onlooking councillors. "Timber for your fires, crops for your fine tables, honey, resins, medicinal plants and furs, *troops*, my lords. What does it matter if you can pay an army if you don't *have* an army? Do not presume to sway the council with false presumptions, Lord Draugole. The balance is tipped against you. Should you force us away with your unjust laws, *we* will survive, but *you* will be isolated in your stone fortress, forced to trade with Pelagia and Tar'eastór for the goods you need, for the soldiers you will need. And how they will *leech* you, knowing that you have no choice but to barter."

The Silvan crowd was increasingly noisy in its support of its leader's words, and Erthoron took a moment to watch those indecisive councillors, the ones who remained silent, the ones whose eyes did not seem to focus on anyone at all. And then he turned to the merchants who sat, opposite the Silvans, looking on, equally silent, expectant.

He felt sick to his stomach.

"All this can be avoided, my lords. We *can* live together if we so wish it. The Silvan people once had requests—requests that were never granted. Now, it falls to me to inform you of our *demands*."

The Silvans had fallen utterly silent while the eyes of the councillors darted here and there. The king sat forward on his throne, and Aradan and Turion shared a look of increasing alarm. What was it that Erthoron had not told them? What were these *demands* that had never been a part of their plan?

"What we want is fair representation on this council and at the Inner Circle. We want *all* our own noble houses to be represented on this council so that votes are balanced, a *true* representation of the people of these lands. We want our warlord of old, our *native* warlord, our best warrior and strategist, so that my people will have equal say at least in the battle against the enemy, which I may add is fought in *our* forest, amongst *our* trees. Our warlord needs to represent the Silvan people at the Inner Circle, and for this task we propose Fel'annár Ar Thargodén."

The only sound in the hall was the click of Lord Barathon's boots over the polished stone, and upon his face was a disbelieving smile, the kind of smile given by a father to his naïve child.

"Lord Barathon!"

"Surely you *jest*, my Lord Erthoron. Tell me, you would assign such a task to a *child*? He does not have the training, the experience, the *command*. He is a base warrior barely past his majority."

"Lord Erthoron!"

"You find this amusing, *Captain* Barathon?" asked Erthoron. "You, a captain at barely one hundred. Tell me, *Captain*, how many battles have you commanded in the Forest? How many friends and brothers have you lost in the fight? How many hearts have you broken with news of some dreadful loss, or perhaps, perhaps you have lost a new-born daughter to Sand Lords, watched your home village razed to the ground so tell me—*Captain*—do *you* have the training? The experience? The *command*?" Erthoron smiled, but it was twisted and angry, and he sneered at Barathon's red face and turned to the king, waiting for the jeers from the Silvans to die down.

"These are our demands, my king, and we ask they be put to the vote."

The murmuring was back, but it soon became a surging tide of voices and exclamations. The Silvans shouted out how right they were, and the Alpines from the other side waved their hands at them and shouted their outrage.

Aradan spared a glance at the king and Rinon at his side, their angular features sharp and harshly schooled. But from the corner of his eye, a chestnut-haired elf drew his attention.

"May I speak?" he called loudly.

Aradan turned to the Silvan, a forester if he was not mistaken.

"May I speak?" he asked, louder this time.

He was not a councillor—he had no rights to speak, but this meeting was fast becoming a diatribe on Alpine superiority. He could not stand by passively and allow Band'orán to continue rallying the indecisive Alpines.

"He is not a councillor!" shouted Draugole from the circle, but Der'hán held up one hand while he banged his staff repeatedly upon the ground.

"Order! *Order!*"

Aradan stood, holding his arms up for silence, but the Silvans were too enflamed. They were angry, unwilling to hold their silence, and the Alpines were outraged at the breech of their solemn protocol.

"Silence!" he shouted, but to no avail.

Moments later, the entire hall fell mute, their angry shouts still ringing off the walls as King Thargodén stood, and he waited. Once satisfied that no one would interrupt him, he spoke to the forester.

"On what grounds would you take the floor, Forester?"

"There are no councillors here who can speak for Fel'annár, Sire. Only Lord Erthoron and Lord Lorthil. But the Silvan *people* can speak for him. You cannot vote if you do not have the necessary information. You cannot make a decision if you do not understand why we ask this of you—that Fel'annár be named Warlord."

"You have not earned the right to speak at this summit!" shouted Lord Barathon and then Lord Cal'hedin.

"And what of the right of the *Silvans* to participate in this council?" thundered Erthoron. "Where *are* they? I see twenty councillors and three of them—*three*—are Silvan. What is this travesty?"

The chaos was back, and King Thargodén rose his voice, anger dripping from every sound, an innate ability to command projected into the only word he said.

"Silence!"

He was immediately obeyed.

"What is your name, Forester?"

"Sarodén of Sen'oléi, my king."

"Sarodén, you have my permission to speak," he said, eyes travelling from Band'orán to Barathon, Draugole and Cal'hedin before turning back to Sarodén, nodding, and sitting on his throne once more. Rinon straightened his stance, head tipping upwards.

Sarodén stepped forwards until he was at the front line of the public area, all the Silvan spectators behind him.

"I am Sarodén, Chief Forester of Sen'oléi. My lords," he said, and then cleared his throat and spoke a little louder. He was nervous, unused to speaking in public. He was a humble Silvan elf from the Deep Forest. "I have a story to tell; it is the story of a Silvan elf, a warrior still in novice training. He travelled on his first mission to the village of Sen'oléi, where he and his patrol stayed for three days, under the command of Captain Turion here." He gestured to where the captain stood and Turion nodded at him. "The young warrior worked hard to fulfil his captain's orders. Humble and servile, he toiled along with the rest of us. He was witty and kind, unassuming and quick to help, and the source of much giggling from our younger lads and maidens." He smiled as he remembered, garnering a few soft chuckles from the crowd that had now settled in to listen to Sarodén's story.

"It was on the second day that a cry went up from our brothers in the distant fields. 'Fire!' they cried, 'Fire in the woods!'. The patrol organised itself, leaving two behind at the pumps, for should the wind change, the flames would surely engulf our village. And so they worked, one Alpine and one Silvan. They worked and they worked until their hands shook, but still, our people came for water. It was then that the Silvan warrior turned to his Alpine brother in arms.

"'*I must go,*' he said, and so, securing a villager to take his place at the pump, he ran into the village. Alféna's children were trapped in the woods, but to go after them would mean sure death. The flames were too near, the smoke too thick."

"What has this got to do . . ." came a sudden protest.

"Sshshshshshs," a chorus of whispered voices answered back.

"He ran, nevertheless, into the forest, away from safety and was lost. Later, his patrol returned, wounded and exhausted, barely having made it out alive, but there was no sign of the Silvan warrior or Alféna's children."

Aradan's eyes fell upon Turion, who turned to meet his gaze, and then he momentarily glanced at the king, but his eyes were trained on Sarodén, silently willing him to continue with his tale. This was the first time he was hearing about his son, about his deeds.

"The next day, though, we all lived the most extraordinary of events, a moment that I will cherish always. The birds . . . the *birds* sang a herald, and we, the Silvan people, sang with them. It was sacred thing, a fanfare of nature, and it was beautiful, and as we wound our strange choir to a soft end, the Silvan warrior stepped from the ruined trees, and upon his back were two children, another at his side."

The Silvans murmured solemnly, nodding their heads as they remembered. Some of them had lived through those events while others had heard the story many times over. The Alpines, too, sat on the edge of their chairs, and even the king was leaning forwards. Sarodén, though, was so engrossed in the story he did not see the expectation he had created.

"The Silvan warrior had known he was needed, for the *trees* told him it was so. He rescued the children from a situation that was almost impossible, stepping upon a branch that would not hold his weight, escaping the burning tree against all the odds."

The Silvans gasped, as if they had forgotten where they sat and had suddenly been transported into the forests, into the burning glade.

Sarodén paused and took a deep breath, a breath that echoed around the utterly silent hall.

"This is the story of a Silvan elf, a warrior still in novice training. This is the story of The Silvan, of Hwind'atór, the one we have always known resided amongst us, have *always* known would one day step into the light and stand for his people. That day has come, for this is the story of Fel'annár Ar Thargodén, son of Lássira, Lord of Ea Uaré."

The echo of a chair leg scraping over stone, the clank of a sword against a belt, the ruffle of a standard swaying high above their heads.

"Lord Erthoron," called Der'hán quietly.

Erthoron nodded at Sarodén from across the room, and the forester bowed in respect to the Silvan leader. "You asked, my lords, why we would choose a child as our warlord—what we *see* in him. This is our answer. We see an elf who stands before a mountain of flame to save a child's life; we see a warrior with the skill of an Alpine blade master; we see a Listener, the youngest ever Master Archer. We see an elf with the face of an Alpine king and the heart of a Silvan forester. He carries the blood of kings and commanders, should have been a prince but would have none of that for himself. And above all these wonderful things, we see his wish, his need to serve, not for the promise of personal gain or renown—but for the simple *joy* of it. We see these things in no other save for Fel'annár Ar Thargodén. You need to understand how much this means to us so that you can understand the consequences should you vote against our petition. You will it or not, these are the wishes of the Silvan people. These are our *demands*."

And there it was. The Silvans were forcing the king's hand. In that final sentence was a warning, and his eyes caught those of Turion once more. This was what Erthoron had kept from them. This was why they had sheltered Fel'annár all of his life, why they had hidden him away. The Alpines had not allowed Lássira to sit upon the throne, had denied Fel'annár his right as a prince. But they would not deny the Silvan people their warlord.

"Lord Draugole."

"*You will it or not,* you say? That sounds very much like a threat, so tell us, Lord Erthoron, are the Silvan people, indeed, threatening their king? Would you now sway the vote of the council with your Silvan tales, spoken by a *forester*?"

Aradan closed his eyes while Erthoron stood in a flurry of robes.

"*You!*" he thundered, "you make an insult out of our most noble occupation? You laugh because he is a *forester?*" he shouted. "Let me explain our position, Draugole, in such a way that even *you* will understand. We have made our demands, and should you refuse them," he pointed with his finger at the Alpine councillors, "should you continue to hold your silence despite your obvious dissent with this elf, then you may as well join him in his absurd claims—you would be just as responsible as he is for the result of your *disdain!*" he proclaimed.

"What result, Erthoron?" said Draugole dismissively, sitting imperiously upon his padded chair.

"If you refuse, I and every one of us in this hall will turn our backs on you—on *all* of you."

There were gasps and urgent murmurings as reality seemed to sink in, a reality that spoke of rupture, of confrontation, and perhaps rebellion.

The king stood and strode towards his Alpine councillors, sparing a cutting, icy glare at Band'orán, Draugole and Barathon.

"There are but two points on your agenda, my lords. Two questions that you will vote upon in seven days. I urge you to think deeply on the things that have been said, and I urge you to be fair and selfless, to understand the consequences of your vote." He walked around the circle, looking at every one of his councillors, Alpines for the most part.

"*My* vote is that we agree to Lord Erthoron's requests, with some minor amendments, and I urge you all to see the wisdom in this. However, you must seek counsel, be just in your deliberations. Think of the collective good, Councillors, and be *brave*. Know, though, that I will not allow an *unfair* vote to be passed. Whatever the result, if your reasoning is not sound, I *will* veto it."

There was a challenge in Thargodén's eyes, trained now on his uncle's glacial gaze. Band'orán had not expected him to speak in those terms and was hard-pressed to hide his anger.

"This session is adjourned until next week. I urge our Silvan compatriots to enjoy our hospitality at the feast this evening. I would be honoured by your presence, my lords," he said.

He was pleased, though surprised, when an Alpine councillor stood and, in a clear voice, spoke. "I, too, would be honoured by the presence of our forest kin!" he said bravely, courageously, to which Erthoron bowed in satisfaction and Thargodén smiled a genuine smile of pride. Only then, did another Alpine rise, and then another, and when they had finished, Erthoron stood once more.

"It brings joy to my heart that not all the Alpines have been turned against us. "Personally, I must decline your offer, my king. We have said all we can for today. We will speak once more in seven days."

Seven days, mused the king. They would be long, hard days of ferocious debate and dispute, of political wrangling and negotiation. He knew that Band'orán would make his final move while Aradan and Rinon would rally those who had embraced Silvan culture, endeavouring to persuade the indecisive. As king, Thargodén could veto laws he deemed detrimental to the land, but he knew that that was precisely what Band'orán would want—so that he could justify his move on the throne, claim Thargodén was a dictator.

Thargodén would watch, pull out every resource he had to grant the Silvan people their wishes. He would do everything in his power to pull this nation back from the brink of revolt, from the horrific yet looming threat of civil war.

Fel'annár. Hwind'atór, The Silvan. His son was becoming a legend to the Silvan people, and pride swelled in his heart for a child he had yet to meet.

~

Commander Hobin's journey from Araria had been eventful, and Commander Gor'sadén's claims of increased Deviant activity had been confirmed time and again.

Hobin now sat bent over a bubbling pot of water, preparing tea for the patrol. There were fifteen others who could have brewed it, but Hobin always insisted he take his turn. It was just one more reason why the Ari'atór revered him as they did.

High above them, the land sloped upwards. There was a forest up there that almost obscured the plateau from sight. Still, he knew they would arrive tomorrow evening, and the day after that, he would seek out Commander Gor'sadén, tell him what they knew and in turn, he would hear what it was that had the commander as worried as he had seemed in his missive. After that, Hobin could seek out the Ber'anor, tell him of Lainon's return, understand, if he could, the nature of the Silvan's duty.

They would not be expecting him to have answered Gor'sadén's call personally, and that suited him well. If they *had* known, they would have prepared lavish rooms, organised a feast, and other such extravagant events. He wanted none of that. He had a duty to perform, one that called strongly to him. The Silvan Ber'anor had lost his Ber'ator, at a time when perhaps the boy had needed him most. Hobin had seen his grief, his disorientation, just as he had seen the power that lay behind his eyes. That, too, was a mystery to Hobin.

He wondered, then, if Fel'annár knew the truth. Did the boy know his own nature? Did he know what Aria asked of him? Tensári didn't—it was why he had sent her away, so that she could think upon what Aria had shown her and that which she had yet to understand. And when the time came, when she finally *did* understand and could forgive, only then would he send her out to confirm it for herself, to step upon her own path.

It was not his place to tell her.

NINE
ATONEMENT

"We cannot undo the past, but we can reshape the future, and in doing so, create a different past. But to perceive fault, accept its nature, and rid oneself of the ensuing sense of failure is no easy task. Only through atonement can it be achieved—through the daunting task of begging forgiveness."
On Elven Nature. Calro.

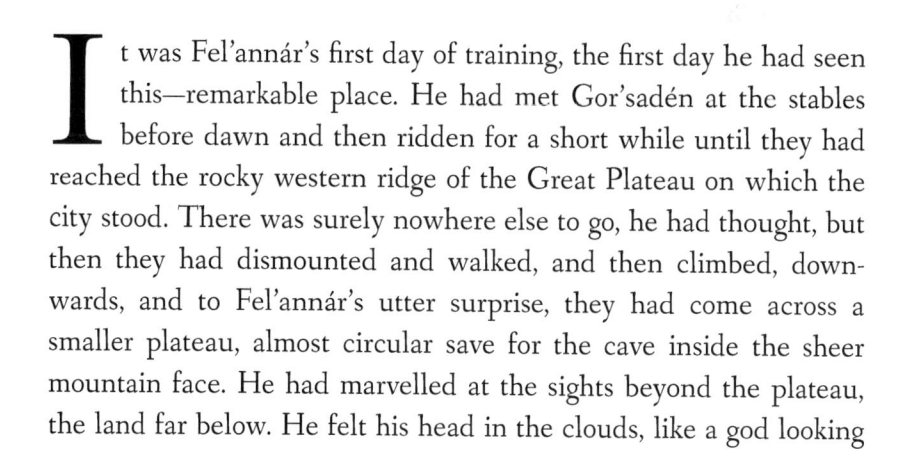

∼

It was Fel'annár's first day of training, the first day he had seen this—remarkable place. He had met Gor'sadén at the stables before dawn and then ridden for a short while until they had reached the rocky western ridge of the Great Plateau on which the city stood. There was surely nowhere else to go, he had thought, but then they had dismounted and walked, and then climbed, downwards, and to Fel'annár's utter surprise, they had come across a smaller plateau, almost circular save for the cave inside the sheer mountain face. He had marvelled at the sights beyond the plateau, the land far below. He felt his head in the clouds, like a god looking down upon his creation. This truly was a secret place, for no one could ever get close enough to watch the Kah Masters and their apprentice, not without discovery. He had then turned and spotted Pan'assár, sitting in simple garb upon the ground, caring for his weapons like any other warrior. Looking up, he simply nodded and returned to his work, apparently unconcerned with the day's events.

"Strip to your breeches. No boots," said Gor'sadén, himself standing naked save for his own leggings and his purple sash.

Complying, Fel'annár stood still and waited, wondering what Gor'sadén would show him first. He watched as the commander came to stand beside him, a strip of sumptuous grey cloth in his hand.

"Here. Watch and learn."

Gor'sadén's deft hands wove the material around his waist and then tied a knot on one side and then smoothed down the ends which tapered to his knee.

The material lay heavily around his waist, an intimate reminder of what he was, who he would become should Gor'sadén allow it.

"Now. Watch, and when you are able, follow, and once you are following, listen and rectify. No questions until the exercise is finished."

Aligning himself due east, he brought his arms up and before him, so slowly that Fel'annár was reminded of a water weed swaying in a soft current.

"Slowly. Feel your hand as it pushes through air, *feel* its resistance. The energy within your flesh and bone slices through it, even before your fingers do. They tingle with the energy you conjure."

Fel'annár mimicked his movements, eyes trained on Gor'sadén's arms and hands. One leg slid backwards, equally slow, utterly precise, movement so controlled. He understood this principle, had read about it and adopted it in his own training exercises, and he found it strangely satisfying to be able to put a name to it.

Dohai.

He copied, and he listened, and before long, the sun was peeking over the horizon and he was falling into the routine, feeling everything the commander was murmuring. He felt heat at the centre of his chest, energy he imagined was concentrating there, ready for him to use at will.

"Slowly, feel the power as it suffuses your muscles, moves them in tempered strength. The Dohai centres your power, allows you to *control* it."

Arms to the sky, palms up, slowly dropping to his sides, palms down, back straight. Only his waist moved now, from side to side as arms moved in cyclic swirls, moving the energy around him, the grey sash of a Kal'hamén'Ar apprentice swaying softly against his thigh.

"Feel the earth beneath you; that hums, too, the same energy that warms you pulses beneath us. Draw it, allow its tendrils to climb, up legs, around your waist, let it in."

Fel'annár did, and as he moved in continuous, languid strokes and swirls, his belly and chest pulsed with energy from the earth, the sun-bathed stars, the trees around him. His eyes burned, and he wondered if that, too, was part of the ritual. He faltered.

"What is it?" asked Gor'sadén.

"My eyes..."

Gor'sadén's face was before him as he cracked his eyes open. He knew it was him, logically it had to be, but the commander was immersed in blue, green, and purple light. Gor'sadén scowled. "Is there danger? Is something happening?"

"No. I don't understand..." He had lost his concentration. "I'm sorry," he said, but Gor'sadén was not interested in Fel'annár's apology but in the sparking lights in his eyes. They weren't blazing as they had done in the king's gardens; they were twinkling, like stars on a frigid night.

"Try to work as you are, tell me what you see."

Fel'annár started the Dohai once more, eyes open, and the lights were still there, around the stone of the cave beside him, around Gor'sadén and Pan'assár, who sat further away, apparently unconcerned with his training. But it didn't frighten him, he realised.

Nothing was happening except that he could physically feel everything Gor'sadén said he should.

"The sequence concludes and the warrior is ready," murmured the commander. "You must do this every day at sunrise, wherever you are. You will perfect the technique, your strength better channelled by your mind, body more efficient for battle. Kah masters will perform the *Dohai* before practice, or before the Dance. It is not forbidden to do so in public; only the Dance."

Fel'annár turned to his master. "Why would I transform if there is no danger, no message?"

"It is encouraging, I think," said Gor'sadén. "Perhaps it is the imagery, the conjuring of one's own inner strength that may help you with this gift of yours, to control it, even."

Fel'annár nodded slowly. It made sense, and he was encouraged. The Dohai was one important concept of the Kal'hamén'Ar, just as important as *projection*, as Gor'sadén had called it. Gor'sadén had set Fel'annár to striking a wooden plank with the heel of his hand and then had explained the relationship between the intention of the mind and the execution of the body. This combination would give added strength and precision to every move. When Fel'annár applied the technique, he had been in awe of the results, had even broken the wood without the slightest twinge of pain.

"You must practise projection, apply it to everything, even the Dohai," said Gor'sadén as they sat closer to where Pan'assár had set up his own personal camp. It was lunchtime, and Fel'annár was ravenous.

Gor'sadén held out a flask of water. He took it and drank. Fel'annár rummaged through his own bag and pulled out a tied napkin. Opening it, he held out the cloth, upon which sat a pile of nutty biscuits. Blue eyes lit up as Gor'sadén's fingers plucked one. Fel'annár held it out to Pan'assár, who simply shook his head.

"Where did you get these?" asked Gor'sadén, wiping the crumbs from his lips, his eyes already fixed pointedly on the rest of the biscuits.

Fel'annár chuckled and pushed them over, watching Gor'sadén pick another one and stuff it whole into his mouth. He couldn't help turning his eyes to Pan'assár as he ate his own lunch, body half-turned away from them. He wasn't interested, thought Fel'annár, unaware of the memories in Pan'assár's eyes—of this place and of another elf who had been so much like this one.

∼

It had been a long day, but Fel'annár was ecstatic and the weather agreed with him, for in spite of the cold, a radiant sun beamed its late afternoon warmth down on the three elves as they made their way back to the fortress.

The song of the Nim'uán had dimmed to a nagging echo, and he had learned so much of the Kal'hamén'Ar he had not wanted to stop. He had begun to understand the Dohai, had grasped the concept of projection, had even seen the lights and controlled his gift. That was progress, and he could not wipe away the smile that had taken up residence on his face. Gor'sadén had praised him—and Pan'assár had ignored him, but at least he had been there.

They climbed the rest of the way up until they were back on the main plateau. Retrieving their horses, they mounted and started the upward trek towards the city. The land here was mainly open, with the occasional group of large boulders and the odd copse of fir or spruce trees. The city gates were less than half an hour away, and the further they progressed, the busier the main road would become. For now, though, there was nobody here off the beaten track.

It started as would a discordant choir, voices steadily rising until it was a shrill scream that sent a lance of pain through Fel'annár's temples. His smile faltered, and he stiffened in the saddle. A frown and he turned towards the copse of trees in the distance.

His horse shrieked and then reared, so suddenly he slipped in the saddle. He clung desperately to it, and when all four hooves were back on the ground, Fel'annár found himself hanging from one side.

Gor'sadén and Pan'assár's mounts were bucking, panicked by some unseen terror, and Fel'annár struggled to understand what had frightened them. His horse reeled sideways, and he thudded hard onto the ground, instinctively rolling away from the stomping legs. He sat up, dazed and winded.

Their horses had scattered, and Fel'annár had seen Gor'sadén land some ten paces away from him, on his feet, while Pan'assár was further away, holding himself up on all fours, stunned no doubt from the unexpected fall.

Fel'annár barely had time to take in the commanders' positions before a wave of dread washed over him. They were being attacked.

"*Incoming arrows!*" He threw himself to the floor, lying flat. Four arrows thudded around him, one of them pinning his cloak beneath him. He pulled hard on it, desperately trying to rip it free but it wouldn't budge. He yanked on it again and again, head whipping sideways and to Gor'sadén, who sprinted to a nearby boulder and then tucked himself behind the stone.

The commander's eyes were wide, fixed on Fel'annár for a moment before turning further afield—to Pan'assár, who was trying to sit up. He must have hit his head, he realised, for he seemed unaware of the danger he was in.

Sitting targets.

Gor'sadén gestured desperately to a stone further behind Fel'annár. It would hardly shield him, but at least he could protect his head and chest. Reaching into his harness, he pulled out his bow and notched an arrow, searching for a target in the trees. The enemy was well-concealed, but still, he fired in the hope of throwing their attackers' aims off balance.

"*Move!*" yelled Gor'sadén, a note of panic in his voice that Fel'annár had never thought to hear, but there was no time to think, for another warning washed over him with startling clarity, even as he finally managed to rip his cloak free.

"*Arrows!*" yelled Fel'annár with one last, desperate look at Gor'sadén, at a struggling Pan'assár, and then at the rock he was to take shelter behind. Making his decision, he rolled to his feet and sprinted towards Pan'assár, who had managed to stand, albeit he swayed on shaky legs.

Fel'annár skidded to a halt just before the commander, sending a veil of dust over him just as the trees screamed at him to move away. Grabbing the back of Pan'assár's cloak, he dragged the sluggish commander towards him and then took one of Pan'assár's arms and slung it over his shoulders. Fel'annár's other arm supported him around the waist and together, they stumbled as best they could towards the nearest boulder. Arrows thudded around them, skittering off the stone, and Pan'assár felt Fel'annár turning him, angling to the left so that his back was against Fel'annár's chest. He felt him jerk forward, almost losing his footing before regaining his balance and covering the last few steps to safety. Both collapsed breathless behind the stone.

Pan'assár looked up at him through blurry eyes. "There's an arrow sticking out of your shoulder blade," he murmured.

Fel'annár smiled grimly, raised one hand over his shoulder, and tugged on the loosely embedded shaft. He grunted as it came away and then slid it into his quiver.

"Not anymore." Another volley of arrows whooshed over the top of the boulder and they ducked.

There was silence then, save for the wild neighing of their horses and their own harsh breaths.

"Fel'annár! Pan'assár!" came a shout from Gor'sadén.

"Here!" Fel'annár shouted as he stood.

"Get down, you *fool!*" hissed Pan'assár, tugging on his cloak.

"They have gone," said Fel'annár coolly and then walked towards a frantic Gor'sadén, who emerged from behind his boulder, replacing his bow as he strode, thunderous, towards his apprentice.

"What in Aria's name did you think you were *doing!*" he boomed, eyes roving over Fel'annár's form for any sign of injury. But Fel'annár looked back at him calmly.

"Saving my commander's life," he said, turning and walking back to Pan'assár, wisely giving the commander no time to reply.

Pan'assár was on his unsteady feet, and Fel'annár turned to Gor'sadén. "He has a head injury."

"And *he* has a hole in his shoulder," said Pan'assár. Gor'sadén startled. "What hole?" he asked, looking at Fel'annár.

"He was hit dragging me to safety. The half-wit pulled it out himself," Pan'assár said, collecting his weapons as they walked back to the open clearing and their three, still skittish mounts.

"It's just a scratch; my weapons harness protected me well enough. Are the horses able to carry us back?" Fel'annár asked, concealing the discomfort he felt from the shallow wound that stung nonetheless.

"They will have to," said Gor'sadén, eyes travelling from Fel'annár to Pan'assár. "Whatever frightened them, it has gone. I have only ever seen horses startle like this with tone flutes," he mused. "Come, we move now lest those snipers come back for another try."

Fel'annár was not going to argue with that, and after a few moments spent calming their mounts, all three were back in the saddle and galloping towards the citadel. He'd read about tone flutes in a book on northern warfare. Sand Lords used them to dismount their charging enemies. But there were no Sand Lords in Tar'eastór, were there?

"No mention of the nature of this attack. This was a training accident. Once you have both received attention, we will meet in Fel'annár's rooms and discuss what must be done. For now, you go nowhere alone, Fel'annár. That is an order you *will obey*," commanded Gor'sadén.

Fel'annár nodded that he understood, although how he was going to hide this from The Company was quite another matter.

Gor'sadén's gaze lingered for a while on his apprentice, watching even as they arrived, dismounted, and handed their dishevelled mounts to the stable hands.

They walked three-abreast across the courtyard and nodded at all who bowed as they passed, and once they were inside the Halls of Healing, Gor'sadén turned to them. "I will go first to arrange for a more private healer's examination room for you. Even though this is to be the result of a training accident, it would be prudent to keep Fel'annár away from prying eyes. I want to make sure both of you are well before I go to inform the king and Captain Comon about what truly happened. Wait here."

They nodded, watching as Gor'sadén strode away. Pan'assár studied Fel'annár, who was leaning against a pillar. This boy, this Silvan half-blood whom he had mocked, scorned, and mistrusted, even to the point of demanding an insulting oath from him to not harm his king, his *own father,* had consciously jumped into the path of danger, exposed himself unnecessarily to archers who were trying to kill him in order to save his prejudiced commander-general from harm. Never in all the cycles of the world had Pan'assár thought Fel'annár would put his life at risk for him. He knew Gor'sadén would snort at this notion, would remind him that Fel'annár had done so before, on their way to Tar'eastór when Galadan and The Company had rallied together and miraculously saved the survivors from sure death out in the wilds. He had shamefully ignored that sacrifice, pushed it away as if it meant nothing at all.

There was still a question in his mind, though, something about those hazy moments when Fel'annár had dragged him to safety that Pan'assár still did not quite understand, and his eyes focussed once more on Fel'annár, himself deep in his own thoughts. A cloud of brilliant blue light crossed over the green irises, and Pan'assár started. He had seen this before during the test he had subjected Fel'annár to in order to train in the ways of the Kal'hamén'Ar. It was what had triggered his own loss of control, when he had finally *looked* at Fel'annár and had nearly killed him. If the Silvan had not been as skilled as he was, he *would* have.

He was jolted from that moment as Gor'sadén returned and beckoned to them to follow him.

They walked together towards the first aid area under the curious stares of injured warriors and healers. Gor'sadén led them to a private treatment room near the end of the long aisle where a healer stood waiting for them. He gestured to a wooden chair.

"Which of you has the arrow wound?"

"Him," replied Pan'assár, jabbing his finger at Fel'annár. Fel'annár sat and unbuckled his jerkin while Pan'assár stood cross-armed to one side and Gor'sadén looked on.

The healer pulled away the leather and then ripped the already torn shirt below, revealing a shallow wound on the shoulder blade, just as Gor'sadén had told him he'd find. It wasn't serious, and before long, the wound was cleansed and bandaged and the healer stepped back.

"Free to go," he smiled, holding out a jar of cream. "Use this once a day for a week and come back if you feel any discomfort."

Fel'annár nodded his thanks and then stood, making way for Pan'assár to sit. He froze, legs tingling. He sat back down. How did the healer suddenly appear so close to him? he wondered.

"Warrior?"

"Yes," he answered, frowning at the oddness of the moment.

"What is it? What's wrong?"

Wrong? thought Fel'annár. Nothing was wrong, and yet it *was*, because the healer's voice was too far away, his face too close to his own. He didn't answer, and then he felt hands on him, under his arms. He thought he heard Gor'sadén's voice calling him, but nothing registered clearly in his mind. His boots dragged over the floor and then the side of his face met with soft linen. Was he lying down?

There were frantic voices around him, scuffling feet, and then a hand upon his head, a hand he thought he recognised. He smiled into the pillow beneath him.

"Llyniel?"

The hand faltered for a moment, and then he felt himself being turned onto his back. He stared up at the blurring ceiling, only vaguely aware of what was happening around him. There were voices and strange lights, sounds he had never heard before. He felt fine, he mused. He felt more than fine. He was floating on a soft summer cloud, his mind wandering deliciously. He thought he would use his hand to touch some of the strange lights but found he couldn't move, not any part of his body. He decided it didn't matter.

"We need Master Arané here, now," ordered Gor'sadén.

"He is busy, Commander. He will come shortly. Calm yourself and tell me exactly what happened," she said, the other healer standing at her shoulder in alarm.

"He took an arrow in the shoulder. It was shallow, and he pulled it out himself," replied Gor'sadén.

Llyniel turned to him. "Do you have the arrow?"

"It's in his quiver," gestured Pan'assár to the door. Gor'sadén was gone and was soon back, just as Arané was arriving, standing over Llyniel's other shoulder and peering down at Fel'annár, who lay placidly, unmoving and unresponsive, staring at the ceiling.

Gor'sadén gave the singular arrow to Arané who took it and sniffed the tip. He blinked rapidly. "Red leaf or . . . or . . . it smells fruity, like binny pod. No, wait. This is black berry—*canimbula* poisoning."

Llyniel whirled around, heart racing. "Tell me you have *spade root*, Master Arané."

Arané frowned, eyes darting to one side, remembering. Mestahé had made a list of the missing stock that had been taken from their supply rooms just the other day.

"Sweet Aria, this was *planned*," he muttered. The commanders shared a meaningful glance at each other and then turned on Arané.

"Explain," ordered Gor'sadén.

"Someone broke into our store rooms two days ago. We made a list of the items taken. The spade root, the *key ingredient* to the antidote for canimbula, was missing."

Pan'assár closed his eyes in anger, and Gor'sadén looked to the ceiling, quelling his rising panic. "Tell me you have an alternative to spade root, Healer," he said carefully.

But Arané was shaking his head, even as his mind worked to provide an alternative.

"Master Arané, do we have black bark?" Llyniel's urgent voice from beside him.

"Black bark, black bark . . ."

"You call it *charflake*, perhaps?" she insisted, eyes wide.

"Charflake. Yes, but surely . . ."

"Where is it?"

"Aisle five, section four . . . Llyniel?"

"Give me two minutes!" she called over her shoulder and then darted from the room, and Pan'assár turned to Arané.

"Do you know what this charflake is?" asked Pan'assár.

"I know what it is, but I have never heard it used to counteract canimbula poisoning. We must pray she is right, though; black berry poisoning is fatal within one hour," he said grimly, and the commanders' expressions darkened. "How long since he was shot?"

"Around thirty minutes," said Pan'assár before adding, "Do you *trust* her?"

Arané frowned. "From what I have seen so far, she is an able Head Healer, Commander, an expert in deciduous tree bark. And, quite frankly, she is our only hope."

Pan'assár nodded. Aradan's daughter was a fiery half-blood who had always looked upon him with disdain, and he knew why. Just months ago, he would have ordered her away with the flick of the wrist, would have been unconcerned with her aversion to him, and yet now, it stung. It made him angry.

"Where in Aria's name *is* she?" He stood and began to pace despite his thumping head, and Gor'sadén watched his friend carefully. Fel'annár had risked his life to save Pan'assár, had been hit in his endeavour, and that fact had affected his friend deeply. It had somehow unbalanced him, thought Gor'sadén.

"I am here," came Llyniel's curt voice, cutting eyes boring into Pan'assár as she passed him and sat at Fel'annár's side, a vial of green liquid in her hand. In spite of the tense situation, Gor'sadén felt like rolling his eyes at the open antagonism between the Silvan healer and Pan'assár. They obviously knew each other well, too well, he decided.

"What is *that*? An antidote I hope." Pan'assár's voice was rude and demanding, but Llyniel's voice was sharp.

"This, yes. Canimbula is quick to act and kill but equally easy to counteract—for a *Silvan* at least." She turned and smiled grimly at the commander. "Black berry has been used by Sand Lords extensively these last few decades in the far north of Ea Uaré. I see it has been a while since you last visited," she said, even as she held Fel'annár's head and fed him the potion, her face changing from anger at Pan'assár to tempered concern for her patient. She was confident in what she fed Fel'annár, even though there was always an element of danger where poison was concerned.

"Note—day one, fifteenth hour. One third charflake, one third loár, one third white root," she said over her shoulder to Arané, who scribbled on a parchment. Pan'assár watched her, reluctantly acknowledging Aradan's daughter as a resolute and effective healer. She would be an excellent battlefield physician, he thought.

"With a few days of rest, he should be fine," said Llyniel, gazing down thoughtfully at Fel'annár. "May I stay and administer the antidote, Master Arané?"

"Of course," said the master healer. "I would speak with you later, though. You have much to tell me of this *charflake*," he said carefully, eyes moving from Fel'annár to Llyniel and then to the commanders.

Gor'sadén blew out a breath. "All right. As you have already deduced, this was a planned assassination attempt. Our attackers are still at large; he is still in danger, and I want him moved to the safest place you have," he said meaningfully. "Whoever did this has already broken into your store rooms."

Arané nodded and then gestured to the still mortified healer. "Help me move him, Mestahé," he ordered, moving to lift Fel'annár's other side. But Pan'assár stepped in to replace him, his chin lifted high. Arané frowned at him, intelligent enough to know it would get him nowhere to argue with the mule-headed commander.

"Once you are done, Pan'assár, you will sit down and allow us to see to that knock on the head."

Pan'assár nodded, and before long, Fel'annár was lying in a very different bed, a light sheen of sweat on his brow, staring blankly at the ceiling. Gor'sadén sat on one side while Pan'assár stared down at Fel'annár from his other side. A bandage had been woven around his head, one Gor'sadén knew he would rip off no sooner he stepped out of the Halls.

Arané had left and Llyniel stood beside the roaring hearth. With the next dose of charflake already prepared, she set to crushing herbs in a bowl, but her eyes were almost always on Fel'annár.

"Now that the immediate danger has passed, I need to speak with the king," began Gor'sadén. "You will watch over him until I return?" He watched his friend closely for a while, for although he understood that Pan'assár was grateful to Fel'annár for getting him to cover and safety, for taking an arrow for his efforts, there was something more about his friend that he could not quite fathom.

"My oath," nodded Pan'assár, sitting in his chair at last, a frown on his face.

"What is it, Pan?" murmured Gor'sadén, stepping closer so that Llyniel would not hear.

"I—I didn't understand. When he grabbed me and we ran, well, *he* ran and I staggered—I didn't understand why he turned me around..."

"What do you mean? I don't understand you," said Gor'sadén, frowning, but he was leaning forwards, searching his friend's eyes.

"You *heard* him during the attack, Gorsa, heard how he sensed every single volley. The arrow that hit him—he *knew* it was coming, and he did not duck. He spun me out of the way, turned his back to it so that it would not hit *me*."

Gor'sadén was quick to understand, and he leaned backwards. Pan'assár had been labouring all this time to understand what

Fel'annár had done, and perhaps more importantly, *why* he had done it.

Gor'sadén smiled softy. "I am not surprised, Pan'assár," he whispered. Placing one hand on his friend's shoulder, he murmured, "Watch over him."

Pan'assár nodded, not turning to look at Gor'sadén, listening as his friend began to leave. But before he stepped out of the room, he turned to the Silvan healer further away.

"You have my thanks and my gratitude, Lady Llyniel," said Gor'sadén, bowing.

Llyniel inclined her head respectfully and then smiled, watching the commander leave. She respected him, understood where his reputation as a warrior came from, could see his command, his leadership. So different to Pan'assár—and yet so close they were, she mused.

"Healer Llyniel," called Pan'assár, startling her from her thoughts.

"What is it?" she murmured, moving towards the bed and fiddling with the bedclothes.

"My thanks, too, for your intervention."

She turned, cool honey eyes staring back at him. "I did *my* duty, Commander."

He knew what she meant but hadn't said, and he wasn't inclined to argue with her. His head was thumping—and she was right.

She nodded at his silence and then walked back to the hearth, setting water to boil while her mind begged for answers. If she wanted them, she would have to speak civilly to Pan'assár, and that would not be easy. Still, she was Silvan and she was curious.

"What happened? How did he get shot?"

"Archers ambushed us on the way back from training."

"Do you have any idea who it may have been?" she tried, pouring the hot water over a brew.

"Not yet. But when we find out, I will be there to ensure justice is done."

She scowled, words leaving her mouth unchecked. "Why do you

care?" She turned to him in confusion. In all the years she had known Pan'assár, he had never once shown concern for any Silvan.

Pan'assár held her icy stare, and when he answered, it was flat and curt.

"Because he saved my life. Saved *me*."

She had not expected that and turned back to the steeping herbs. This was a side of Pan'assár she had never thought to see. She took the hot mug and walked to the still-sitting commander.

"Here. Drink this. It will help with that headache you think to hide from me."

Pan'assár's eyes dropped to the cup she held out to him.

She smirked. "It's not poisoned, Commander."

He surprised her again as he mimicked her grim smile.

Turning away, she sat on the other side of Fel'annár's bed and looked down at him in concern. He was finally stirring, coming out of the unresponsive state he had been in. Pan'assár breathed a sigh of relief and leaned forward, but Llyniel was already speaking.

"Fel'annár. Do you know who I am?"

"Llyniel," he managed, blinking his eyes. Looking around blearily, he saw Pan'assár.

"Commander."

"Welcome back, boy," was all Pan'assár managed, but there was no malice in his voice any more.

"Do you need anything, Fel'annár?" she asked, masking her own feelings as best she could. There would be time enough to address them later, when she was free of her duties.

"Just a kiss," he murmured under his breath, and Llyniel glanced at Pan'assár, who was studiously observing the fibres of the bedspread.

"Later," she murmured just as quietly, knowing his brashness was due to the effects of the toxin.

"How are you feeling?" asked Pan'assár after a while, reminding Fel'annár that he was sitting right beside him.

"Strangely . . . serene. Where am I?" he asked in confusion.

"You are in the royal infirmary. The arrow that hit you was poisoned and you became unresponsive. We moved you here for your safety and gave you the antidote," explained Pan'assár.

"Thank you," he said, eyes latching onto Llyniel who stood over him. She smiled back at him, confident and sure in spite of the whirlwind of unfamiliar emotions she hid from him with practised ease. He shifted his position and grimaced as his wound pulled, and once Llyniel had helped him to get comfortable, she held the second dose of the antidote to his lips. He drank and then laid his head back with a sigh.

"I suppose I should sleep, but I have no inclination to do so."

"You will, Fel'annár. Just give the herbs time to act. I will be here," Llyniel assured him from the other side of the bed.

"I know," he smiled.

All three slipped into silence until Pan'assár broke it somewhat hesitantly, his voice uncharacteristically soft and far away.

"I suppose I should thank you . . . for what you did."

"There is no need, Commander," murmured Fel'annár. "It was a lucky shot I should have dodged."

Pan'assár closed his eyes, emotions threatening to spill out, for Fel'annár was lying so that Pan'assár would not thank him, so that he could minimise what he had done. It was the last straw, and Pan'assár's bright eyes landed on Llyniel. He needed to speak, purge his guilt, but Aradan's hostile daughter sat just across from him. Yet however much he disliked the idea of her hearing what he had to say, the urge to say it was too strong. He should have done this before, when he had accepted to himself his faults. He had thought it enough to be conscious of them, but he had been wrong. He needed to atone for what he had done. He needed to ask forgiveness.

He had seen the questions in Fel'annár's eyes, the sincerity, the desire to understand him in his simple offering of sweet biscuits. And then he had seen the sacrifice Fel'annár had been willing to make so that Pan'assár would not be harmed. Shame, deep and nauseating pushed him relentlessly to speak. He would no longer hold back for pride. His eyes begged for her discretion, for her silence and her comprehension. She held his gaze boldly, as only a Silvan could do, he mused. There was a warning in her eyes, protection burning in them . . . and something else. He wondered if she realised what he could see there; he wondered if *Fel'annár* knew.

"I know you have questions about what happened during the test."

"Will you tell me? Will you tell me why you lost control?" asked Fel'annár quietly, aware that he had blurted exactly what he had thought. The herbs were loosening his tongue, and although Fel'annár was aware of it, he could not stop it.

"You deserve that much at least."

Silence followed those words. Llyniel stared at the far wall, suddenly feeling like an intruder while Fel'annár lay in his bed, his sluggish mind working as fast as it could to comprehend what was about to happen. For the first time, Pan'assár would speak to him of that moment, of why it had happened, and ultimately, about what had driven Pan'assár to hate him, hate all the Silvans.

"A long time ago, three elves made history," came the quiet voice, deep and mellow. "Of a similar age, they shared a dream, a dream to be the best warriors Tar'eastór had ever seen. Masters in three weapons, soon, all three became Grand Masters and were allowed access to the teachings of the Kal'hamén'Ar."

"The Three," said Fel'annár with a smile.

"We danced the Kah before the court of King Cal'asté, to the awe of all. It was the culmination of our achievements, and we did indeed become known as The Three: Gor'sadén, Pan'assár, Or'Talán . . ."

Fel'annár had known The Three had been close, but he had never heard the tale, never truly understood the depth of their union. And he never thought to hear it from Pan'assár's lips.

"Gorsa, Pan, and Orta," smiled Pan'assár, and his face seemed to utterly change. Gone were the lines between his brows, at the corner of his mouth. His skin seemed smoother, more luminescent; he seemed younger and unburdened, and Fel'annár marvelled at the transformation.

"We were the heroes, Fel'annár. We were the keepers of the Warrior Code, of the ethics of the true warrior. We instilled in our army such loyalty and sacrifice as has never been seen. They were the glory days, child. Gorsa was the strength, the determination, the sacred sacrifice, they said. Pan was the scheme, the strategist, the shrewd mind of a great warrior, and Orta . . ." Pan'assár faltered and then looked away for a moment before his heavy gaze landed squarely on Fel'annár.

"Orta was the *soul*, Fel'annár. He was the love and the passion, the fire and ice—he was the *shining house* we two stood in the shadow of, the one that united, that created a kingdom in foreign lands and was *loved* for it."

Silence stretched long and thin, Fel'annár and Llyniel not daring to move lest the moment be lost and Pan'assár speak no more. "He died upon the barren lands of the Xeric Woods and with him, our brotherhood was dissolved. My life was taken from me the day he fell. I still feel his last breath as it grew and then dwindled, my own life as it followed that last breath, and I was left a shell. Cold and angry, I could do nothing but find blame—in *anyone* but in him."

Fel'annár saw it all as Pan'assár painted that tragic picture, thinking that perhaps he, too, would have reacted in the same way should Idernon or Ramien die.

"I had pledged my fealty to the line of Or'Talán. I could not leave for Tar'eastór. Thargodén was now king and my place was at his side, as I had promised. He was a good king; strong and determined, with many of the qualities his father had boasted. He needed me to guide him but I—Pan'assár—had dwindled. I moved in a half-world, where my devotion was confronted by my grief, my purpose dulled by my anger. And then, when the queen left and Thargodén began to fade, my anger soared. The Silvans had been incapable of defending their great King Or'Talán, and now, they had corrupted his son, Thargodén. They had killed their king with their incompetence and then all but done the same to his son, for they encouraged the love Thargodén shared with Lássira, your mother. I told myself they were the ruin of Or'Talán's line, and my hatred for the Silvans grew, proportionally to my devotion to his memory. And then Band'orán came with his talk of Alpine superiority. It was all too easy for me to embrace that idea."

Fel'annár dared not speak, but questions were bubbling up into the back of his throat and he fidgeted.

"I did nothing; indeed, I was seduced by his talk of a return to the splendorous days. But then, something changed. *You* came, and with you my fall was complete, so complete I hit the ground so hard it jolted me. I nearly killed you."

"But you didn't," whispered Fel'annár.

"No. You were right, you know. After the test, when I told you that I did not trust you. You said something then that stuck in my mind, even though I did not realise it at the time. You said I would never trust you if I cannot *look* at you. But you see I *did*. As we fought and you finally found the rhythm of the Kah, I looked at you and I was taken away, to another time and place—centuries past and to the Battle Under the Sun. That was the last time I would fight with Or'Talán, the last time I would serve honourably.

"My foe was before me, a Sand Lord who stood between me and the one I had followed for many, many years. They were slowly, brutally cutting him down, but I could not reach him. And then a flash of blue came to your eyes, and the Sand Lord was Or'Talán. I was fighting my brother, but before I could stop myself it was me—I was fighting *myself*—and so you see, all that time, since my king died and I was left behind . . . all that time I have carried this frustration, this guilt, this self-denial, and my own pride, which would not allow me to forgive myself."

Pan'assár fell silent for a moment as he slowly brought himself back to the present. "I looked at you, and I was forced to take stock of myself and I saw—I finally *saw*—what I had become, what Gor'sadén told me I had become. Complacent, indifferent, unjust: an abominable *racist*. Or'Talán had loved the Silvan people, and I . . . I beat them into the ground with everything I had, just as I did with you that day you passed the test."

Pan'assár looked away in misery while Fel'annár tried to process the story, tried to understand its protagonists. But his mind was slow. All he knew was that Pan'assár had told his sad story in the presence of Llyniel. He had humbled himself for the first time, and a wave of sympathy slammed into him. He had lost Lainon, still mourned for him, but Pan'assár had known Or'Talán for centuries. He turned his head and peered blearily at the commander.

"What are you thinking?" asked Pan'assár softly.

"Many things," murmured Fel'annár. "I have so many questions, but tell me," he said, his voice becoming softer as sleep beckoned. "Why? Why tell me this?"

"Because . . . I needed to free myself from the prison of my own blind stupidity. I needed to purge the guilt, lift the undeserved blame I had misplaced on the Silvans. I never hated you, Fel'annár. I hated *what* you were and *why* you were—but not *you*."

Fel'annár's consciousness was slowly slipping, but he was aware enough to feel the weight lift from his chest, aware enough to feel Pan'assár's suffering, to understand this humble act of atonement. He embraced it and reached with his hand. Pan'assár looked down at it, as if he could not fathom what it was, but Fel'annár, with his last vestiges of strength, lifted his arm and splayed his fingers and the commander slowly offered his own arm, fingers wrapping around the offered forearm. A warrior's clasp, a new beginning: forgiveness. Pan'assár understood and he squeezed, almost as hard as he squeezed his own eyes closed. But Fel'annár didn't see it, for his eyes had slid closed, head falling to one side in slumber.

Llyniel was staring openly at Pan'assár. He turned to her, unsurprised that she would do so. She had lived through his worst years, had seen the arrogance and the hatred, the injustice and the complacency—she was half-Silvan. When she had looked upon him before he had seen judgement, disgust even. Yet now all he could see was open curiosity and the stirrings of respect.

She stood and bent over her patient, who now slept peacefully. She placed a soft kiss to his brow and then turned to Pan'assár again—and then she smiled at the soft smile that graced his lips. She nodded slowly. She would never speak of what she had heard to any other than Fel'annár. Such was the oath of a healer inside this room . . . and also the one in her heart. But Commander Pan'assár was reborn, she thought. A mighty warrior had returned from the depths of despair, and for all that she had hated him for his treatment of her people, now she finally understood why he had once been revered.

A while later, Sontúr entered the room, eyes already fixed on Fel'annár, who had shifted to one side in his sleep. He nodded at Llyniel and then stared at Pan'assár who sat sipping tea at the bedside. He arched a brow at the unlikely scene and then turned to Llyniel.

"The Company are outside," he murmured. "See if you can calm them down." He smirked. There was no mention of the angry words they had shared in the glade some days ago, but there *was* acceptance in his eyes, and so she stood, placing one friendly hand on his shoulder. "He will be well," she said and turned to leave, but she hesitated, turning back to Pan'assár. "And so will he," she said thoughtfully and then left the room.

TEN
REVELATION

"It was a time of uncertainty for Fel'annár. He knew the voices of the trees, understood their ways, heeded their warnings, and smiled at their chatter. But he had always known there was more. There was no sense of finality, he once said. There was something teetering on the borders of his knowledge, like a name long unused but never forgotten."
The Silvan Chronicles. Marhené.

∽

Fel'annár woke to the sound of hushed voices. His back was stiff and painful, and he felt light-headed. Turning, he sat up and waited for the dizziness to pass. Llyniel and Sontúr were beside him in a moment, and he nodded at them both, accepting the vial of disgusting green liquid that they had been feeding him every few hours.

He'd slept deeply, and he wondered if Sontúr, or even Llyniel, had laced his tea with something. But whatever it had been, it wasn't enough for him to forget Llyniel's concerned eyes in the night—or Pan'assár's story of his fall . . . and his *return*.

"I'm hungry." That should encourage his over-zealous healers that he was fine and that he could return to his own rooms. Sontúr didn't disappoint. He nodded at him and then left him alone with Llyniel.

"I . . . may have asked you for a kiss . . ." he said ruefully, but there was a saucy twinkle in his eyes.

Llyniel cocked a brow and then leaned over him. "Fool warrior," she tutted and shook her head. "The poison has melted your mind and loosened that tongue of yours."

"Did I worry you?" he smiled.

"You did," she said, turning away from him so that he would not see just *how much* he had worried her. It was something she had yet to ponder—those strong feelings she had experienced when they had discovered the canimbula—and then Arané had announced that the key ingredient to the antidote had previously been stolen. It wasn't until her mind recalled the black bark and Arané had told her only thirty minutes had passed that her heart had stopped its irregular thumping and the weight upon her chest had lifted.

She fancied Fel'annár, had all but accepted a Silvan fling in the trees with him. But her reactions were not those of a casual friend. She frowned inwardly, because the thought was disturbing. Unwanted.

"Shall we get you dressed?" she asked, turning back to him only to roll her eyes at his lopsided grin, knowing exactly what he was thinking and unable to hide her own mirth. "Get up, you Silvan oaf, and do it slowly. The herbs in the antidote will linger in your system for a while. You will be unsteady on your feet."

Tossing the bedcover to one side, he swung his feet over the edge and sat up. She was right, and he closed his eyes for a moment.

"Slowly," she warned.

By the time Sontúr was back, Fel'annár was walking slowly to the chairs before the fire and then sinking into one of them, careful not to sit back and jostle his wound.

Fel'annár knew what was coming, and Sontúr smirked as he took the lid off the dish.

"Damn it. No sausages."

"No sausages," repeated Sontúr. "The sooner you eat this nutritious gruel, the sooner we can get back to your private sanctuary. The Company are waiting outside. They're *peeved* that I have not allowed them to visit you." Fel'annár nodded, knowing he had some explaining to do.

Fel'annár did as he was told and when he had finished, he changed into simple clothes and allowed Sontúr and Llyniel to poke and prod him once more. Satisfied, they left the royal infirmary and The Company surrounded Fel'annár with smiles and nods, even though their hands rested upon the pommels of their blades. Once back in his rooms, Fel'annár was suddenly grateful that Damiel had insisted he live here in the palace and not at the barracks. Before long he was sitting on his princely bed and Idernon was standing before him.

"We leave you to your rest, Fel'annár. Ramien and I will guard the door and later, we will *speak*, yes?"

It was a question, but Fel'annár heard the warning in the Wise Warrior's tone. They wanted answers and would not be fobbed off. He arched a brow at his friend and then nodded, watching as he left the room and closed the door.

He slept for a while, but then the smell of dried flowers, resins, and herbs brought him gently from sleep, and he inhaled deeply. Head turning to the hearth, he saw Llyniel working quietly before the fire, muttering under her breath, and Fel'annár smiled fondly at her back.

"You're angry," he said.

Her head whipped over her shoulder. "Well, yes, as a matter of fact. It is too early for you to be answering questions and receiving a roomful of commanders and warriors."

"What's going on?" he asked sleepily, smoothing a hand over his hair as he sat up.

"The commanders are coming . . . to *take collective counsel* they say."

"I'm all right, Llyn. And I understand the need for haste. The commanders need information. We need to decide on a plan of action; our attackers are still out there."

"Yes, well, *I* am not leaving," she said with a pinch of her jaw, and Fel'annár admired her bravery.

Rising from his bed, he walked to the sitting room and chose a comfortable chair by the hearth and Llyniel followed him.

After a curt rap on the main door, it clicked open, and to Fel'annár's surprise, Lord Damiel glided into the rooms, Prince Handir at his side, and behind them, both commanders. Moments later, The Company walked in, eyes glittering defiantly.

"Stay outside, warriors," ordered Councillor Damiel, but Prince Handir placed a calming hand on his forearm.

"I vouch for these warriors, my lords. Fel'annár will need protection in the days to come, and I can think of no better solution than *The Company* here. If they are to guard him, they need to understand the situation."

The Company stared at Handir, not having expected his words at all. They hardly knew the prince and he certainly didn't know them. Still he would have seen them together on many occasions, but it was Sontúr who was, perhaps, the most surprised. He had seen the cold, calculating prince that hadn't bothered to think of Fel'annár's feelings at all. They almost seemed to be two, separate people and his curiosity was piqued. He joined The Company as they moved to the window and stood by silently.

Gor'sadén's eyes searched Fel'annár, who in turn nodded at him in what he hoped was a reassuring way, while Pan'assár's hand rested momentarily on Fel'annár's shoulder as he passed by. The Company watched their interaction, eyes darting between themselves. The questions were mounting, and Idernon was surely keeping track of them.

"The king has been briefed on yesterday's attack," began

Gor'sadén. "An inquiry is ongoing as we speak, and both Commander Pan'assár and Prince Handir have asked to collaborate. As such, it is my job to inform you of what we know so far and what we suspect. But have a care; you are all under oath to not speak of this. My king requires it, and it is common sense, of course." Gor'sadén's eyes travelled over them all, reinforcing what was, in fact, a direct order.

"Commander Pan'assár?" prompted Gor'sadén, stepping to one side. While Fel'annár had rested, the Forest commander had taken his lieutenant back to the site of the attack, in search of clues that may lead them to identify the would-be assassins. What happened during their field investigation, Gor'sadén couldn't say, but Pan'assár had returned in a fine mood, despite the circumstances. Galadan too, had seemed less stiff, his brow smooth and he couldn't help but wonder if they had spoken of *other* things beside the attack. Of all the people in this room, beside himself, it was Galadan who would have seen the darker side of Pan'assár. He glanced briefly at The Company, noticing their keen eyes, their expectation of what their commander would say, and perhaps more importantly, *how* he would say it. Fel'annár, though, did not seem surprised at all.

Pan'assár truly was on a mission to atone for his years of hatred.

The Forest commander nodded and stepped into the centre of the room with natural confidence. "Lieutenant Galadan and I personally scoured the area of the attack, and concluded that there were four archers, three of which used standard longbows. One of those shooters, though, used a different bow, the arrows expertly crafted and laced with canimbula poison. Coincidentally, all those special arrows fell in the same place, namely, wherever Fel'annár moved. Whoever wielded that bow and those arrows was skilled and was specifically targeting Fel'annár. Luckily, only one of them hit its mark.

"Notably, there were few tracks to mention, but we did find a hidden door just over the lip of the north-eastern overhang. We believe this was the route the assassins used to escape. We will know where it leads once our preliminary search is concluded. Commander Gor'sadén will, of course, be conducting a closer inspection into other possible passageways that are not recorded on the city maps.

"However, evidence seems to suggest that this attack was carried out by highly-skilled soldiers, mercenaries perhaps. Whoever the mastermind was, he or she was a master archer and tracker. The use of these specially-crafted arrows shows expertise, and the choice of poison is significant. Canimbula is deadly within the hour, should the antidote not be administered. It is not a coincidence that the entire stock of spade root, the key ingredient for the antidote, was stolen from the supply halls just days past. Should their arrows fail to kill Fel'annár, the poison would certainly have finished the job, had it not been for Healer Llyniel here," said Pan'assár.

Startled at the mention of her name, Llyniel's face shot up, wide eyes landing on the commander. He smiled wickedly at her shocked expression, and she felt her own mouth turn upwards, but then her gaze crossed Handir's and the smile was gone. They had not spoken since the incident in the corridor, but there was no missing the regret in the prince's eyes—not perhaps for *what* he had said, but for the simple fact that they had argued.

"I would also suggest that it was a tone flute that panicked our horses, used so that we would be thrown and then prevent us from fleeing. These instruments are not easy to come by and if we consider the nature of the canimbula poisoning, also difficult to locate in these parts, our conclusion, so far, is that at least one of these attackers is a Shadow, possibly a renegade. Their skills are certainly compatible with the training we provide our loyal secret warriors."

"If this *is* the work of a renegade Shadow, Commander, such a service would come at a high price," said Idernon, stepping forward.

"That is exactly what I think, Warrior," said Pan'assár. "The question, of course, is who—and what it is they have to gain."

Handir couldn't be sure if Pan'assár's question was rhetorical, but as far as *he* was concerned, there was no reason to hide his own suspicions, not after an attempt to kill one of the king's recognised sons. He stepped into the centre of the room with a nod at the commanders.

"I suggest we may be dealing with King Thargodén's detractors," he stated boldly. "With the Forest Summit, presumably still in progress, and the proclamation of Fel'annár here as a son of Thargodén, the radical Alpine Purists will not be pleased he has been named 'lord'. I believe they will see him as a threat."

"Who, exactly, do you believe we are dealing with, Prince? If what you say is true, treason runs deep in your realm. Someone schemes, to an end I do not wish to contemplate," said Gor'sadén gravely.

Handir turned to the commander and nodded. "I believe we must concentrate our investigations on the House of Sulén. They have *everything* to gain, Commander; that is, if my uncle, *Band'orán*, has his way and overthrows my *father*."

The Company gasped, Gor'sadén stepped backwards, and Pan'assár lifted his chin.

"Over my dead *body!*" he hissed.

Handir held the commander's furious gaze, glad at his passionate reaction albeit a little surprised. He nodded in satisfaction and then continued.

"As you may know, my king has family here, distant cousins whose forefathers rode with King Or'Talán in the days of the colonisation. I have heard their hushed talk of Alpine superiority, heard their veiled insults at court. It is likely they are sympathetic to the beliefs of Lord Band'orán. In answer to what they have to gain with Fel'annár's demise, I would say it is *favour*—favour from a would-be-king, one who may grant land, power . . . "

Damiel stared back at his pupil in respect. He had spoken boldly and clearly, no hint of hesitation or insecurity. He was proud, he realised, because in spite of his pupil's conflict over his half-brother, he had put that aside and done his job admirably.

"And so you see, I cannot claim this to be true, but my suspicions are well-founded. I have watched my cousins for months now and have curbed my tongue before their derogatory comments against the Silvans of Ea Uaré, and I have done so for the sole purpose of observing, of inviting them to perhaps reveal something which may be of use to us. They speak highly of Lord Band'orán and I have led him to believe I am neutral in the matter."

"And *are* you, Prince?" asked Galdith, boldly stepping forwards, ignoring Carodel's hand on his forearm. "We Silvans do not rightly know *what* our rulers think. You have not *told* us. All we see are your rulings, which favour the Alpines in commerce, in the military, in education, in anything and everything that is important to us."

All heads turned in disbelief to Galdith, but he simply stood there, stubbornly waiting for an answer.

Pan'assár stepped forward, but Handir held out an imperious hand to stop him and then turned to face Galdith, cloak fanning around him, jaw clenched and eyes glittering. "I am averse to the suffering of my people. I am averse to injustice and intolerance. I am averse to arrogance and the lust for absolute power, but above all I am averse to *vermin* who would use good people, crush them underfoot, and spit on them for the sole purpose of gaining land and coin and renown. It disgusts me, gnaws on my very soul, burns my blood, and so help me, Warrior, *yes*, I am averse to those beliefs. I have *nothing* to gain with the death of this warrior," he said, pointing at his half-brother even though his eyes remained on Galdith.

To Fel'annár, a king stood before him. This was a side to his half-brother he had never seen. Handir's words had stirred him, and he knew he was not alone. Galdith stepped forwards, and where before there had been suspicion and challenge in his eyes, now there was only curiosity—and dawning respect.

"Then you will forgive my impertinence," he said softly. "But when you have lost everything, your soulmate, your infant child because our Alpine rulers did nothing to defend their people, perhaps you can understand that it is hard to stand by and continue watching the same injustice being committed, time and time again. It is *enough*, surely, that we die."

Handir's anger was gone, and in its wake, Fel'annár saw his conviction strengthen in the prince's eyes.

"It is *too much*, Warrior," he said, walking towards Galdith and placing a hand upon his shoulder. "And it is time to stop it."

Galdith lowered his head in thanks, and Handir turned back to the respectful gazes of them all. Llyniel smiled at him in pride, her lingering anger forgotten, while Pan'assár was looking at him as if it were the first time he was seeing him.

"To conclude," continued Handir after a while, "I suggest we set a watch on Lords Ras'dan and Sulén, and his son, Lord Silor, with whom some of you are familiar."

A snort echoed in the ensuing silence, and Fel'annár looked over at The Company . . . and to Ramien who was studying the cuff of his tunic.

"None of you may discuss this with anyone," continued Handir. "The commanders will, of course, keep us all informed should any further information be uncovered. For now, we must assume that the danger may come from the palace *and* the barracks. As such, I am placing Fel'annár under *your* protection," he stressed, his eyes travelling over the warriors he knew were called The Company. "You are to stay with him at all times, except when he is training with the commanders." He found Gor'sadén's gaze and nodded. "Furthermore, Fel'annár will take all meals here in his rooms. In case of injury he is to be treated here, with healing supplies that can be trusted and only by Prince Sontúr or Lady Llyniel. Also, I or the commanders must be notified of any further break-ins at the Healing Halls. Fel'annár, you understand the safety measures that have been set in place?"

"I do, Prince," he said as he made to stand. Handir held out his hand for him to stop.

"See that you heed them," he said. He nodded at the commanders and then made to leave, but he stopped on his way out and turned once more to The Company.

"Guard him well, Warriors. I am counting on your loyalty to him . . . and your discretion in this matter."

"You have it, my prince," said Idernon. Handir nodded curtly and then strode away, Chief Councillor Damiel just behind him.

"Was that a royal prince I just saw . . . or a protective *brother*?" murmured Carodel under his breath.

"It was both," said Idernon thoughtfully.

∽

After a restful sleep, Fel'annár sat pondering the meeting that had only recently ended. The Company, charged with his safety by Handir himself, had left him alone with Llyniel when they had seen his pale face and drooping eyelids. The healer had gestured to the door and they had obeyed her silent command, albeit reluctantly, resuming their diligent guard outside. They would surely be back soon to discuss the surprising council, in which Pan'assár had seemed utterly changed, and Handir had become a true prince in the eyes of The Company.

Llyniel sat behind him, cleaning and rebandaging his wound, wading through her own thoughts and impressions. Handir had shone so very brightly, had publicly announced his mission to stop Band'orán's plans to take the throne from Thargodén. She smiled as she worked, and then a question popped into her head.

"What happened with Silor?" she asked suddenly.

"He was a trainee lieutenant. Let's just say that he *dislikes* Silvans."

"You said *was*. He is no longer training?"

"He committed acts of misconduct and was temporarily relieved of his duty by Commander Pan'assár, even though it was *he* who gave him the honour of training as lieutenant in the first place."

"Of course. Alpine lords must have their sons in the Inner Circle while we Silvans fight on the front lines," she said sourly. "Mind you, our commander seems changed of late. He's hardly recognisable as the racist bigot I have come to know. *Galdith*, now, spoke well before Handir."

"Yes. And Handir answered him well."

"He *did*."

She smiled as she tied off the bandage. Shuffling sideways, she sat beside Fel'annár on the padded bench. "He makes me proud," she said, eyes slipping to Fel'annár, but he did not return her gaze. "I wonder if things will ever be the same as they were before. If Handir really can restore our forests to what they once were."

"Before the Alpines came?" asked Fel'annár.

"No. To what it was under Or'Talán's rule . . . and Thargodén's rule, before the queen left."

"I don't remember those days, Llyniel. I am not even fifty-two years old, I am a base warrior with a thousand things to learn. I have only ever known the Forest as it is now."

"And have you given any thought to what you might do, Fel'annár? After this, you *know* who is responsible as well as Handir does. You will never be free while Band'orán is left to his own devices."

"Somebody has to do something, Llyniel. I understand that much. *Handir* is the statesman—and a good one from what I can see, and your father is the chief councillor. *They* are the ones who can change things."

"Handir is an able statesman, yet to prove himself at his father's court, but he *will*, just as he did today. He is good and with Lord Damiel's help, he will be exceptional. He is sharp, with a gifted mind, and he is well-loved by our people. But he will not move the Silvan people as *you* will. He knows this. He needs *you* to do it. You *are* a key player, you will it or not."

Fel'annár turned, pulling his undershirt on. "I *do* see the merit, Llyniel. Handir claims I can move the Silvan people, and I know you trust his assessment, but that, to me, sounds wrong. Why would they listen to a fifty-two-year-old warrior? The plight of the Silvan people requires experience, wisdom—I have none of those qualities."

Llyniel smiled and nodded. "I can see that it would look that way to you. And I know you do not yet trust Handir when he says that they *will* look to you. So who *will* you listen to?"

"Lainon. But he's not here. And then perhaps I need to see it for myself, once we are home."

"Well, I can't say I blame you. It does sound strange that you would hold sway over the Silvan leaders. But then, as you said, I *do* trust Handir. I know that if he says it is so, it is truth. But I cannot *will* you to see him as I do."

"However," added Fel'annár softly, "the fact that someone saw fit to kill me ... if this *is* related to who I am, then someone else, at least, agrees with Handir."

"You have a point, yes," said Llyniel, "and that does seem likely, Fel'annár."

He shifted, taking one hand to his chin. "You believe strongly in this cause, even though you come from a privileged background. Your parents are lords, you were raised at court, where your own father is chief councillor," he said, observing her features as they hardened at the mention of Aradan.

"What is it? I've never heard you mention your parents ..."

"That is a long story."

"Longer than mine?"

"No," she chuckled. "I would have preferred a childhood such as yours, in the Silvan villages. I have always felt my forest blood strongly. I could not stand the scheming, the absurd rhetoric, and the spreading racism that few seem concerned with. But I saw it so clearly, saw how my mother looked away and held her tongue despite her distress, and saw how my father assured me it would end. And yet he did *nothing* to change it, even as the chief councillor to the king. I could not respect that, and so I travelled, in search of a fairer place to live."

Fel'annár's head tipped sideways as he tried to read her, understand her. She had a family and had left them. "Your convictions are stronger than the love you hold for your family?"

She started, for a moment unsure of how she felt about Fel'annár's comment. But all she saw in his eyes was confusion. "Not stronger. But my parents will always be there, enjoying their life of privilege while others are stepped upon, scorned, and belittled. I cannot stand by and watch that, Fel'annár. It is beyond my Silvan blood, in spite of my own feelings for my parents."

"They may not always be there, Llyniel. True, we have endless years, but they can be sundered. You see this every day in your duties as a healer, and although they are not warriors, still immortality is not guaranteed. Do things change, now that your father is involved in this plan? Can you respect him for the risks he takes?"

"I'm shocked that he would do such a thing. I had not thought him brave enough, Fel'annár. Perhaps I just never understood his position; perhaps I had assumed it was *easy* to speak out, to risk it all for a dream."

"*You* are brave," said Fel'annár with a soft smile. "Perhaps it was your idealism that drove you to see only one side of his dilemma. Perhaps now you can return, try to see the other side, understand why he waited for so long, to the point that you thought he did not care."

She had already decided to go back, but it was for *Handir*, not for her father. But she stopped herself from saying so, because in Fel'annár's eyes she saw the unequivocal spark of hope that she would be reconciled with her father. He had never had his true parents as a child, could not understand that she would willingly walk away from them. She smiled, but her wilful eyes latched onto his. She had never seen eyes like his, and she watched as specks of light danced in a sea of green. There was something there, behind Fel'annár's emotions, behind his defences, his hopes and his dreams, something she could not fathom.

And then her own uncomfortable questions were back, the ones that incessantly asked about her emotional reaction to Fel'annár's poisoning, reactions she had ruthlessly hidden at the time. She had tried to convince herself that her feelings for Fel'annár were passing, an entertainment for the present, but when she had looked down on him, poisoned and shot, she had thought of the future, of a future without him, and her heart had squeezed her lungs, deprived them of air.

She allowed her eyes to focus on him, watched as he smiled at her, and something shifted in her chest, pulled uncomfortably.

Fel'annár was struggling with his shirt, and she moved to help him, fastening the clasps up his chest and all the while he watched her, so close he could kiss her.

"Perhaps we will do this together, then, once you have worked it out for yourself, Fel'annár. It is enough that you are willing to consider helping us, that you have not closed your mind to it. This *is* right, Fel'annár, and I know you know that," she murmured, hot breath ghosting over his lips.

"Yes, this is right," he whispered, moving closer until their noses touched. She didn't move back, so he leaned further forwards, and still she did not move. He would not deny himself this moment of pleasure, this inexplicable need to press his lips against hers.

Llyniel closed her eyes in unbearable anticipation. The future be damned and she opened her mouth to welcome his soft, warm lips. Then her eyes flew open, and she snapped back, startled by the familiar knock on the door. Sontúr poked his head inside the room, and Fel'annár and Llyniel stood abruptly, smoothing down their clothes. The prince watched as he opened the door fully and then arched his princely brow.

"Are you administering the *treatment*, Healer?" he drawled.

Fel'annár smirked, and Llyniel turned to face him. "Of course. And you have interrupted the procedure."

Sontúr barked in laughter, and Fel'annár snorted at her Silvan wit.

"Shame you won't get much privacy in the time left to you here in Tar'eastór," said Sontúr as he strolled into the room, the entire Company right behind him.

"Thank you for that," scowled Fel'annár.

"My pleasure, Lord Fel'annár." He bowed with a flourish.

"Lackwit," muttered Fel'annár, watching as Llyniel smiled as she passed him and then left.

~

Pan'assár had found the tunnel before Macurian could destroy it, but that was not what concerned him.

It was the fact that he had failed to kill his objective.

He had hired three expert archers to accompany him, had chosen an opening with nothing but a handful of low-lying boulders for cover, had found the tone flute deep in the treacherous areas of the city, knew it would panic their horses, throw them so that escape was not an option. And then, just in case something failed, he had used canimbula, for which they had no antidote—Macurian had made sure of that.

How the hell had he failed?

He remembered the first time he had thought to strike. He had not even been able to make the shot because the boy had seemed to sense him, had been alerted in some way to his presence. Macurian had sought answers and found them in the form of an overly exuberant warrior who had spoken of the boy's ability to sense the trees. He had told the story of how The Silvan had warned of danger by simply placing his hand on the bark of a tree.

Sceptical though he was, Macurian had made sure to strike where the boy had no trees to touch. Now he understood that the warrior had been wrong. The Silvan had not needed to touch the tree to be warned of the danger. He had simply sensed it.

Since his failed attack, The Silvan had disappeared into the palace and had not shown himself at all. And yet even if he did, Macurian would not strike again until he found a failsafe way to finish the job.

What he needed was a weakness. Everyone had them, and he wondered now . . . what was The Silvan's weakness? And how could Macurian use that against him?

By now, Silor would have realised he had failed, would have seen The Silvan or at least had word of him. And if Silor knew, then so did Lord Sulén. It stung to have failed, and the completion of this job was now a matter of personal pride.

He had people to speak to, plans to make, but above all, he needed to watch from the shadows—discover The Silvan's weakness.

Sulén wanted the boy dead because he was a threat to whatever plans the lord had, and Macurian had always wondered why such a powerful lord feared one lone warrior.

Now, though, he thought Sulén was right to fear him.

～

The Ari'atór had arrived, but Commander Gor'sadén had never expected Supreme Commander Hobin to answer his call personally. The stunned guards had informed him not an hour past and Gor'sadén had sent a runner to inform the king of Hobin's unlikely presence in Tar'eastór. It had been decades since he had last seen the leader of the Ari'atór and his reasons for coming now were surely not good. He bore ill news and Gor'sadén's mind was already preparing itself for almost every eventuality.

He had called Pan'assár away from his investigations into the assassination attempt and the three other captains on the Strategy Council had arrived just minutes ago. They stood now, murmuring quietly amongst themselves, until the doors to the map room opened, and the imposing figure of Hobin strode towards them.

"Commander Hobin, you are most welcome in Tar'eastór, although I confess I had not thought you would personally honour us with your presence." It *was* a question, and Hobin nodded that he understood.

"It has been many years since I visited the Motherland, Commander, and I confess to being intrigued by the current turn of events," said Hobin, stepping forward. He had not answered

Gor'sadén's question, not that it surprised the commander. There *was* a reason for it, though.

Hobin climbed the steps, eyes travelling downwards and to the features of the land.

"You asked if we have experienced an increase in the number of humans crossing the Last Markers. We have, and yet the number of Deviant killings has *not* increased. There is a discrepancy, Commander. The Deviants would appear to be hiding themselves away."

"Then how are they escaping our notice?" asked one captain.

Gor'sadén turned to him, nodded, and then faced Hobin. "We may have a problem, Commander. Come." He gestured to the walkways around the map and explained as they walked.

"Here, at Queen's Fall, is where the fighting is taking place. We have been familiar with these caves for many years. They are deep but narrow, insufficient to house a large number of Deviants. However, this new threat that we have detected is coming from *here*, Crag's Nest, precisely where the fighting is *not* taking place."

"That is unusual, yes," said Hobin, the first hint of emotion on his dark face—confusion.

"And this brings me to the other reason I called upon the Ari'atór," said Gor'sadén. "We have reason to believe that there is a new threat, some creature that may be organising the Deviants."

Hobin scowled back at Gor'sadén. "What creature?" he asked carefully.

"We don't know, Commander. A Listener has sensed a presence through the trees. They speak of a creature that is not so rotten. They call it *Beautiful Monster*." Gor'sadén waited for Hobin to process the information. He would be sceptical, critical, perhaps, that he should have given credence to such a ridiculous claim.

"Nim'uán . . . " repeated Hobin, brows drawn together in thought.

"When I asked the Listener to tell us where he had sensed this creature, he said it came from here, around Crag's Nest. I was surprised he did not say it came from Queen's Fall, where Deviant activity is at its highest. So you see, we have the fighting *here*, but the Nim'uán *here*. Two separate areas."

"They may be separate events," said a captain. "On the one hand, we have increased Deviant activity around Queen's Fall, and on the other, we have the arrival of some new beast. They don't have to be connected."

"No," agreed Hobin, "but that would be highly unlikely, Captain. The key is in their unusual behaviour. Deviants are not engineers, they do not build homes, they do not plan in such a way. They do not care for their own comfort. So why adapt those caves and take shelter inside them? Incipients would, perhaps, do that, but not fully-turned Deviants. If they are adapting those caves, something drives them. And at the same time, we have a *Nim'uán*. It cannot be coincidence."

The captain remained silent, and Pan'assár nodded at Hobin.

"This is likely a diversion," said the Forest commander. "Whatever this thing is, it thinks—is strategic. If it is purposefully drawing our attention to Queen's Fall, we must be ready for the danger to come from elsewhere."

"I concur," said Gor'sadén. "Our scouts should be back within two days. We will meet again to discuss their findings. Meanwhile, I am reinforcing our defences beyond the Downlands. Extra patrols must be deployed here, here, and here." He pointed on the map. "Are there any further suggestions?"

No one answered, so Gor'sadén turned to Hobin. "It is clear that you had no knowledge of this thing, Commander. I would have you attend our Strategy Councils while you are here. You will stay until the question is resolved?"

"Of course. It is the Ari'atór's duty to find out what this thing is, and then destroy it. You may certainly count on my presence," he said with a nod.

"King Vorn'asté would be honoured by your presence at his table this evening," said Gor'sadén. "And both I and Pan'assár would relish the opportunity to speak with you."

"The honour is mine, Commander. Until later then." He bowed, first to Gor'sadén, then to Pan'assár, and then he turned to leave, but he stopped himself, one final question rolling from his tongue.

"Commander Gor'sadén, the Listener *is* Fel'annár, correct?"

"Yes," he replied, repressing his urge to frown. He remembered Comon's report of the battle in which Lainon had been killed. The Ari'atór had come, led by Hobin himself, but Gor'sadén had not realised he had met Fel'annár, that he knew of his gift.

Hobin nodded. "Then we must be ready to face a new creature, a new Deviant, perhaps. Something we have not yet encountered."

"You *know* Warrior Fel'annár?" asked Gor'sadén evenly.

"I met him—at a time of great personal duress. An extraordinary warrior, as I am sure you already know."

Gor'sadén nodded, his suspicions confirmed. Hobin had a hidden agenda, one that included Fel'annár, and Fel'annár was *his* apprentice. He considered it his solemn duty to find out what it was—why Hobin, Supreme Commander of Araria, had come to Tar'eastór himself.

∽

It was late evening, and Fel'annár sat on the window seat in his rooms, his journal open in his lap and a stick of charcoal in his hand. Behind him sat The Company, mostly quiet except for Carodel's incessant murmuring—some new song he was inventing lyrics to.

His hand moved over the blank page, short lines and then longer, a finger smoothing over them and smudging, shaping, creating a face his mind remembered so well. That haze was suddenly back, flitting over his vision, and he wondered again, if he should speak to Sontúr about it. It might one day hinder his aim.

The simple line drawing was gaining depth. Long, twisted locks, skin darker than any Alpine, any Silvan, eyes brighter, deeper, more expressive. His charcoal moved over the line of lips he had first drawn as straight, but then he turned one corner upwards, as if he smiled, and Fel'annár mirrored it, even though there was deep sadness in his eyes.

Lainon had rarely smiled.

A deep breath and he turned to the window, to the deep blue sky and the black shadow of the citadel before him. Windows glowed with candle light that would soon be doused, and stars began to twinkle more clearly in the darkening sky. There was a soft melancholy in his heart and time seemed to pass strangely, too slowly, he thought as his eyes travelled over the high roof-tops and domes, the spires that sat at the four corners of the citadel and the ramparts not too far away. And then his eyes fixed on a figure that stood high on the walls, cloak swaying softly in the breeze. It was nothing more than a silhouette, and yet it was a familiar one. It could have been Lainon standing there, in spirit form, watching over him. His eyes welled with tears.

But no, it was not Lainon. This figure was too tall, too strong. But he *was* Ari'atór.

Fel'annár cocked his head to one side in thought. The figure reminded him of a great black bird poised for flight, or perhaps some dark god contemplating the lands he ruled over. He shook his head, mentally smirking at his fanciful thoughts. It would be one of the Ari patrol Galadan had told him arrived just that day to discuss the Nim'uán. It was a simple Ari soldier taking an innocent evening stroll.

Idernon's voice made him jump, and he closed his eyes to steady his thumping heart.

"Can I see?" asked the Wise Warrior, peering over his shoulder at the sketch of Lainon. Fel'annár held it out to him.

"You're getting better at it," he said quietly.

"It's been so long since I opened this journal. Perhaps because it's so full of the past," said Fel'annár thoughtfully.

"The past is what makes us who we are, Fel'annár. It is what makes us *how* we are. You cannot separate the past from the present."

Fel'annár's brows rose, not quite sure he understood his friend, and so he shrugged his shoulders. He couldn't be bothered with philosophy right now.

"Has the song of the Nim'uán stopped? Can you still hear it?"

"It is soft and distant, almost gone but not quite," he said, turning his eyes back down to the drawing of Lainon. He smiled softly and closed his journal reverently, buckling the leather straps that wound around it.

Idernon nodded, returning to his chair and his book. Fel'annár didn't seem to want to talk any time soon. He was lost in his thoughts, pondering on the loss of Lainon, but he couldn't help but wonder if it was also about the Silvan healer. Fel'annár wasn't the romantic kind, not that he didn't enjoy himself from time to time—he *did*, but he wasn't Carodel. In fact, he had never seen his friend overly interested in any lover he had ever had, not even Dalia back home. Still he was not sure of the nature of Llyniel's relationship with Fel'annár, not sure how he would feel if Fel'annár *did* harbour feelings for her that went beyond those of a simple distraction.

He wondered if he should just ask, but Sontúr beat him to it. "And where is Lady Llyniel?" he asked lightly from the other side of the room, conspiring eyes briefly catching those of Idernon. Carodel's eyes snapped to the prince while the rest of The Company stared at Fel'annár. He smiled but didn't look at any of them.

"With Prince Handir . . . or at the Halls."

"She'll be back later then?" asked Sontúr with a sly smile. "Perhaps for a Silvan *nightcap*?"

Fel'annár did look up then and at his impertinent friend. "A warrior can hope." He grinned and then shrugged, and Galdith let out a long, high-pitched howl and Ramien yipped along with him. Fel'annár chuckled at their antics, shaking his head fondly and then not quite managing to stifle a yawn. This lingering tiredness would surely be gone with a good night's rest and so he turned, bid them all goodnight and disappeared into his bedroom.

And so, The Company left amidst quiet murmuring, except for Galadan and Idernon who were on duty that night. Alone now, they sat in two identical armchairs before the roaring fire, the flickering orange light dancing over their faces. It reminded Idernon of the late-night celebrations in the Forest, when too much dance and drink turned one thoughtful and nostalgic.

Galadan's voice, although soft, seemed overly loud to him.

"They tried to kill him".

"Yes. Fel'annár's intuition was right, *again*." Idernon smiled. "He leaves none indifferent, does he?"

"He does *not*. You have grown beside him, but those of us who have met him in adulthood . . . I don't think you quite understand who he is, *what* he is," said Galadan almost absently.

Idernon scowled and turned to study Galadan's glowing profile. "Explain."

"Do I *need* to? You who are wise despite your years?"

"Still I would hear it from your lips."

Galadan peered at Idernon with eyes that seemed aflame, and the Wise Warrior suddenly realised what it was Fel'annár had seen in Galadan to baptize him as Fire Warrior. He visibly started when the lieutenant spoke.

"We skirt around the question, Idernon, but it must be answered. *Ber'anor*," said Galadan. "Commander Hobin called him that—you heard."

"I did. I even investigated its meaning with Sontúr one strange evening in the library. *You* already knew what it meant, though, didn't you, Galadan?"

"I did. You forget your youth sometimes, Idernon. I know you are sceptical, just as Sontúr is. I, though, am an elf of faith. I know that Fel'annár is charged by Aria to fulfil a purpose."

The sudden claim took Idernon by surprise, and he took a moment to steady himself. "Ari lore, Galadan. A belief system based on faith."

The fire was still in the lieutenant's eyes, but he smiled all the same, and a chill ran down Idernon's spine.

"You have seen the lights in his eyes, have seen the trees move on his account. You have witnessed the knowledge he gleans from the land, and still you doubt?"

"I must, Galadan. It is the only road to the truth."

The fiery eyes lingered for a while before Galadan nodded. "You see it from the inside, Idernon. I see it from without. I see his skill with nature, I see his ability to command. I see a great warrior who still does not understand who he will become, *what* he will become. I wonder what it will take for him to accept it."

"Accept what?" whispered Idernon, thinking perhaps he knew what Galadan would say.

"His destiny, Idernon. His destiny as Aria's Ber'anor . . . for a purpose yet to be revealed."

Whether Galadan was right or not, Hobin too believed this, had called Lainon "Ber'ator", Divine Protector, and then he had called Fel'annár "Ber'anor", Divine Servant. The possibility that Aria had charged Fel'annár with some purpose was becoming uncomfortably plausible, strangely possible, and yet Idernon did not believe in gods.

Aria was a symbol of goodness . . . and Idernon was fine with that.

ELEVEN
SHORES OF COMPREHENSION

"Fel'annár had changed in many ways since his arrival in Tar'eastór. But that one morning marked the biggest change of all, for he went from ignorance to understanding. From doubt to faith. From warrior to Ber'anor."
The Silvan Chronicles, Book IV. Marhené.

～

Fel'annár shifted onto his side and closed his eyes, the now familiar list of recent events lining up in his mind, begging to be remembered. He had begun to harness his gift on some elementary level through *projection*. He had become a Kah Warrior, had become close with Gor'sadén, and Pan'assár had finally begun to accept him. And then he had met Llyniel. He remembered the kiss they had almost shared. And then he remembered the dark god that had stood upon the city walls, poised for flight.

His eyes felt heavy, his mind slowly emptying of its many voices even as his body grew heavier and he seemed to sink deeper into his bed.

He saw himself performing the Dohai, encased in streaks of coloured light as he moved his arms and legs, and he smiled because the trees copied his movements, moving backwards and forwards as if they danced, or perhaps they were mimicking him. It was a dream, but it was entertaining to watch. He smiled as he passed them by, making for the thicker parts of the forest until he was before the mighty Sentinel in Ea Uaré, the one he had always seen in his dreams. He knew this place, had visited it a thousand times in his mind, and perhaps he would find it in the *real world,* one day in the future.

The lady in the tree looked down on him in love as she always had. He was a babe once more, chubby arms and legs paddling in clumsy glee. He knew how it played out. He would smile up at her. She would say his name, tell him he would shine for them all.

But then something changed.

His mind blinked, familiar images disappearing only to return—but they were altered. He saw himself before the same tree, somewhere within the Deep Forest. He saw his own hand, almost touching the bark, not with the hands of a babe but those of an adult, a master archer. But fingers did not dare touch though. He somehow knew that if he did, things would never be the same again. But then things never are, he mused, for with every second of life, the future is changed in some way. He needed to embrace it, not fear it.

Fel'annár stepped closer. His entire body tingled and then seemed to move forward even though his legs did not. Something popped at the back of his neck, and then she was back, not up in the boughs of the Sentinel as he had always seen her but standing before it, upon the dry land, and yet she seemed to float under water, hair dancing around her inexplicably beautiful face, eyes like blue fire through water. She smiled.

"Aria..."

He felt so cold; his stomach clenched, and yet hot tears swam in his eyes. He heaved another breath, and then he saw himself surrounded by shimmering lights of green, purple, and blue, his features almost impossible to see behind the sparking energy that he knew connected everything. He stood staring for a moment. He had only ever seen this a handful of times: once when he had first come to understand he had a gift, again during the fire of Sen'olei and then when Lainon had died. Just recently, he had seen it when Gor'sadén had taught him the Dohai. Now, though, he could see himself as his own light danced with the shimmering, pulsing power around him. It was beautiful.

"Aria."

Had *he* said that? The sound had seemed whispered into his own ear.

Fel'annár, Green Sun you are named, for you shall shine for us all, Ber'anor.

Ber'anor—the word he had turned his back on. His knees felt weak, but he knew that he stood now upon the shores of comprehension. He'd had this feeling before, in the waking world, the surety that something was coming, that something transcendental would change everything.

He remembered the dark god upon the walls, saw him turn and stare back at him over his shoulder, strange paintings upon his face.

Fel'annár looked up, into the watery pools of Aria's eyes. She knew the answers to his questions, and only then did Fel'annár realise that perhaps he too had always known them. He straightened, eyes widening. This was about Lainon's plan—his own part in it.

She smiled, sensing, perhaps, the moment he had understood.

Ber'anor, she had said, *Divine Servant*, and suddenly, his own light became blinding. He felt his body suspended, held rigid even though his own knees would have failed him. Aria, still before him, slowly held out both hands, palm upwards. In one was a single acorn, and in the other a broken emerald. She smiled wider and then brought her hands together until there was nothing but blinding light and he could no longer see her.

The power was suddenly gone, and he felt himself crumple to the ground, chest heaving wildly as he struggled to accept what now seemed inevitable. Lainon had masterminded a plan to restore the king, Handir had embraced it, had asked Fel'annár to help him.

Aria *demanded* it of him.

The emerald, symbol of the Alpines of Ea Uaré—the acorn, symbol of the Silvan people. He was *both*.

"Wake up!"

With a long, involuntary cry, consciousness slammed back into him, and he opened his eyes wide and sat up, only to come nose-to-nose with Idernon, who jerked backwards just in time to avoid Fel'annár's head.

Idernon lay sprawled upon the floor, the anxious eyes of Galadan fixed upon him, helping him up, but Idernon was too distracted by Fel'annár.

"What happened? asked the stunned Wise Warrior.

"A dream."

"But no ordinary dream, your *eyes* are . . ."

"It cannot be," said Fel'annár, shaking his head slowly.

"What, Fel'annár? What cannot be?" asked the Wise Warrior, slowly rising and then sitting on Fel'annár's bed and placing one hand on his friend's heaving shoulder. It shook beneath him.

There was no easy way to say it. His own mind was in a mess, incapable of engineering a coherent sentence. The woman in the tree was Aria—this he already knew, just as he knew the Sentinel he saw her in was in Ea Uaré, somewhere in the Deep Forest.

"Aria has answered my questions," he blurted out, breathless. He didn't want to talk, but he needed to say it so that he could truly believe it.

"What—what questions?"

"Who am I . . ."

"Who?" Idernon shared a worried glance with Galadan and momentarily startled when he caught the lieutenant's intense stare.

"She's always known, tried to make me understand . . ." He was speaking to himself, remotely aware that he didn't want to explain, but the words slipped from his slack mouth just as his tears streaked unchecked down his face. The words sounded stupid, infantile, naïve, and yet his brain would not cooperate.

"Aria has spoken to you?" repeated Idernon, frantically searching for Galadan's eyes. A sinking feeling was replaced by a slowly rising panic he struggled to quash. He frowned deeply, eyes stinging.

"What did she say, Fel'annár?"

Fel'annár shook his head again, but his eyes were wide in shock. He looked around himself, as if he searched for something.

"Ber'anor."

Idernon blinked. "You know its meaning?" he murmured, eyes searching those of his friend, whose gaze turned away from infinity to meet his own.

"Yes . . . yes, I know."

Idernon raised his chin as the cogs of his rational mind began to turn. He startled when Fel'annár took his forearm in a steely grip.

"Don't tell anyone, Idernon, Galadan."

"Why not?" asked the Wise Warrior.

"Because—it is not the time. There is important work to be done and I would not have it jeopardised by questions of faith." He ran a shaking hand through his loose hair. "It's hard to believe, Idernon. Yet still, I don't understand why I do not doubt."

"Fel'annár, you are making no sense."

The dream and its implications were playing havoc with Fel'annár's capacity to speak . . . and to react. His problem, now, was that Aria's message proclaimed him Ber'anor, Divine Servant, to carry out a destiny he now understood: Lainon's plan, the unification of Ea Uaré, the union of emerald and acorn—the restoration of the Silvan people.

But how could that be? he asked himself. Aria was nature, existence, the physical power of the world. How can it choose an elf and give him a purpose? He had never believed Aria was a conscious entity as the Ari'atór did, but that belief had slipped further and further as his powers had unravelled. He had once chosen to see the lady in the tree as his own portrayal of nature, not as a real, living entity and yet now...

It was preposterous.

It was the truth.

~

Idernon and Galadan had finally left him alone but Fel'annár had found no rest, in spite of his assurances that he would and as the darkness of night began to lighten, Fel'annár took stock of himself.

His eyes burned and there was a heavy weight in the pit of his stomach. He felt ill, exhausted, his own internal battle playing havoc with him. He was charged by Aria, and he knew why. He finally had the answer to the question of whether he could help Handir—because he knew *what* he needed to do, even though he couldn't imagine the *how* of it.

She had shown him the two sides of himself, the emerald of the Alpines of Ea Uaré, the acorn of the Silvans; the two sides of himself must bring together the people of Ea Uaré.

But how could such a thing be achieved? What exactly did Handir plan to do?

His stomach lurched. He had been chosen by a deity, one he had never really understood to be a physical being. He had always understood Aria to be the force of nature, to be respected and revered but not a *person*. He had always thought the lady in the tree was his own representation of that force that unified everything, a face he chose randomly to make it more understandable. He had been wrong, and it frightened him.

He sat up in his bed and raked a hand through his locks. Tiny speckles of light sparkled here and there, over a wall, off the pommel of his blades. They were everywhere, like fireflies under the light of day. He needed to see himself. Rising, he padded into his bathing area and looked into the mirror. He forced himself to watch as his eyes shimmered blue, green, and purple, and all the while, his stomach hurt, as if he had been punched.

He threw on his undershirt and breeches and then picked up his cloak. Throwing it over his shoulders, he pulled the hood up. Taking a deep breath, he stepped out and into the living area where he knew Idernon and Galadan would be.

"Here, Ramien has brought us tea," said Idernon, turning to greet Fel'annár and then stopping dead in his tracks. "Why are you wearing your hood?"

Fel'annár stepped closer to the fire, knowing Galadan watched him from the corner. He sank down onto the floor before the hearth, crossing his legs and enjoying, for a moment, the warmth. But it did nothing to quell his anxiety. He just didn't know what to say. Aria was a goddess, existed as a living, conscious entity, and she required him to restore harmony to her land of trees. What was he *saying*?

He was sinking, drowning in the enormity of it.

"Talk to us," said Idernon as he knelt beside Fel'annár.

"I can't," he murmured and then turned his head a little, enough for Idernon to see the lights. The Wise Warrior was on his feet in seconds.

"What is it? What's happening?" Galadan tensed beside him.

"I am changing. I am changed..."

Idernon frowned and shared a concerned glance with Galadan.

"I need a Spirit Herder..."

"I'll go," said Galadan.

"Galadan, don't let anyone else in," said Fel'annár.

The lieutenant nodded and was away, not before first issuing explicit orders to Ramien who stood guard outside the door. The Wall of Stone had frowned but nodded, knowing Idernon would tell him what was going on as soon as he could. The rest of The Company had arrived, but Ramien would not let them pass into Fel'annár's chambers, so they sat and talked quietly of what may have happened and why they were being excluded.

Sometime later, their conversation ceased abruptly and they

stood, bowing reverently from the waist in spite of the chills that ran down their spines. Supreme Commander Hobin was a force of nature, as imposing as Fel'annár in his altered state. Galadan shot them an apologetic gaze and then knocked on the door. Idernon opened it and then swayed backwards, questioning eyes turning to Galadan. But then he, too, bowed low and then opened the door for Hobin. He stood indecisive for a moment, unwilling to leave Fel'annár alone with the Supreme Commander, but logic told him there was no threat, so he turned and left the room, closing the door softly behind him.

Idernon turned to Galadan. *"Hobin?"* asked Idernon in confusion.

"I found him simply sitting cross-legged on a bench outside." A shiver ran down Idernon's spine. "He called out to me as I passed, must have recognised me from the battle when we lost Lainon. It was *he* who insisted on seeing Fel'annár."

"What is going on?" asked Carodel with a deep scowl.

Idernon breathed deeply and then met the gazes. "It is a question of the soul, brothers. Something only a Spirit Herder can handle. We must wait, and then, perhaps, Fel'annár will tell us."

~

Hobin stood quietly on the other side of the door, his eyes fixed on the cloaked figure sitting cross-legged before the newly-stoked hearth. He saw the hunched shoulders, the head that was fractionally turned to one side.

"You seek guidance, child?"

That voice, deep and beguiling. It reminded Fel'annár of Golloron and Narosén. It was a voice he had heard before. It was the voice of the one he had thought a dark god.

"Commander Hobin?"

There was wonder in his voice, for this was the Holy Commander, leader of Araria. He wanted to stand, uncloak himself, and bow low. But he couldn't, because his eyes were blazing. All he could do was listen as Hobin drew closer—until he was standing beside him. Fel'annár's eyes focussed on the Ari'atór's boots. He saw runes that ran their way around the upper rim, runes he did not understand. Further up his black leather tunic, more runes could be seen along his belt, his vambraces, Ararian script he suddenly wished he could understand.

The silence stretched on, but strangely, Fel'annár did not feel uncomfortable; indeed, he realised that he could speak to this stranger, that he trusted him, because however strange his own words would sound to anyone else, this supreme Ari'atór would not judge him as a freak of nature. He breathed deeply. It was time to reveal himself.

He stood, turned to the commander, and then slowly, he slid back his hood.

Hobin's face was before him, painted with some black pigment, only slightly darker than his own skin. Three half circles down his forehead, three wavy lines from the middle of his nose to the middle of one cheek and down his chin, a line from his bottom lip and on either side, three circles. His eyes, though, were blazing pools of liquid azure, and Fel'annár wondered how much of that light was his own, reflecting in the Ari's eyes. Hobin hid his surprise well, but Fel'annár saw the subtle widening of his slanted eyes, the momentary slackness to his jaw.

"What am I?" asked Fel'annár softly.

Hobin's face was rigid, as it almost always was, but his eyes were open gateways to the Ari's soul, a swirling cauldron of emotion and thoughts. Everything he thought and felt seemed to be reflected there. It had been that way with Lainon, too.

"You are Ber'anor, Divine Servant."

"Yes. She has shown me at last. She has shown me for years, as many as I can remember, but I never understood."

"It is her way. She knows the weight of her existence; she understands the implications. For an Ari'atór it is natural to believe, but for others, it is a question of choice, a choice she does not judge—none of us do. It is logical not to believe, just as it is logical to feel the existence of divinity."

"Did she . . . did she *create* this world?"

"We do not think so. We believe she guards it, guides it. She is Divine Guardian."

"How can you *know* that?"

"Because she is good. She is the heart, Ber'anor. And yet bad things exist in this world, things she did not wish for, things she exists to defend us from. That is the job of the Ari'atór. We are her soldiers, Spirit Warriors, upholders of her will."

"And how do you know her will, Hobin?"

"She tells us, Fel'annár. As clearly as you and I speak now. I feel her; I envy *you*," he said suddenly.

Fel'annár frowned. "You shouldn't."

But Hobin smiled softly. "Fel'annár, *I* feel her, but *you see* her, her light, the energy . . ."

"That is what the *trees* see, Hobin. It is their world I see," he said, shaking his head.

"Yes. And are they not blessed, Fel'annár? To see the light of Aria every day? To see the energy that pulses through this world? That light is everything good—it *is* Aria."

"And why should I be able to see this? Why is it necessary for me to see it in order to embrace her dictates?"

"In what other way would you have understood, Fel'annár? How else was she to make you see what she requires of you?"

He didn't answer immediately. "But why take so long, why be so *cryptic* about it? I have had this dream since I can remember: a blue-eyed lady in the trees who looks down upon me as a babe. I used to think she was my mother, but then I saw her, too; darker hair, *green* eyes."

"Did she speak to you?" asked Hobin.

"Eventually. She said I would shine for us all." He said it so softly it was almost a whisper.

"You are frightened. And I understand you."

"How can you, Hobin?" he asked, desperation shining in his still scintillating eyes.

"Because I, too, have had that dream, Fel'annár."

Fel'annár stepped backwards, utter shock on his face. "What?"

Hobin's unnerving face was right before his own, eyes searching him. "Because I, too, am Ber'anor."

A wave of frigid cold rolled painfully through his body, and he stepped backwards again. "You had dreams, of Aria in a tree?"

"For me, she sat upon the mountainside, but yes, for many years I dreamed of her until one day, she revealed the nature of my service."

"But you are Ari'atór . . ."

"Yes," he nodded and then stepped forward, peering closely into Fel'annár's eyes. "And so are *you*."

Fel'annár stared back at Hobin, confusion warring with realisation. "No." He shook his head, took another step backwards, even though he knew it was true.

"You *are* Ari'atór, in all but the colour of your skin, Fel'annár. Had Lainon not died performing his duty, he would be the one to tell you now."

"He knew this?"

"He would certainly have suspected, but he would never have told you until the revelation of your purpose had taken place. Aria reveals her plans slowly so as not to cause pain or confusion, so that the journey from ignorance to knowledge is taken willingly. But there is no mistake, Fel'annár. Only Ari'atór are Ber'ator, Ber'anor."

"But all Ari'atór are dark-skinned. Why . . . why is my skin pale?"

"That is a good question. It is one I cannot answer, Fel'annár."

Ari children were born to any race; Silvan, Alpine, occasionally even Pelagian. It was impossible to know which parents would be graced with a Spirit Warrior, or perhaps Herder, but it was always counted a blessing, even though they knew their child would be taken at an early age, to Araria and training. Most parents would follow, stay until they were adults at least. But these children were always born with dark skin and slanted blue eyes and Fel'annár wondered if his mother had known. If Amareth had known.

"Then I have no choice in this? If I *am* Ari'atór, then I am bound to her will."

"You *do* have a choice. Your destiny is not written. You can reject it, turn your back on all this. You will not be judged for it, because Aria is heart. It is for you to choose, Fel'annár. But you *are* Ari'atór."

His mind was in disarray, thoughts scattered, bouncing here and there. He was Ari'ator, just like his grandfather, Zendár. Fel'annár had always been a warrior, even when he was a child, and now, he finally understood why. It was in his blood, in his *Ari* blood. A shaky smile pulled at his lips despite his confusion, and he turned, walking to the full-length windows, eyes gazing past the glass and to infinity. He felt Hobin move beside him.

"I thought myself strange, Hobin. So different from everyone around me. Always thinking of warfare and training, of being a captain. I was *obsessed*, they said."

"And now you understand, finally. You are not strange, Fel'annár; you are Ari'atór. This is in your blood, despite the colour of your skin."

Fel'annár nodded, a sense of finality settling on him—not heavily though. It was more like a soft, warm blanket that soothed his soul, and he smiled timidly. The heat in his eyes had cooled, and he turned to Hobin, nodding his thanks. But then a thought popped into his mind.

"Commander..."

"Hobin," corrected the Ari.

"Hobin. How did you come to understand the nature of your duty, as Ber'anor?"

Hobin stared back at him while he considered how to tell Fel'annár how it had happened. "I had a dream, a dream I could not fathom. I was lucky to have a friend to help me work through its implications."

"Will you . . . can you tell me what it is?" asked Fel'annár hesitantly.

Hobin nodded slowly. "I can, although it is something I do not readily reveal."

"Because you wouldn't be believed?"

"Yes, for the most part, but also for the unwanted attention it can garner."

How Fel'annár understood that! Still, Hobin had not told him, and he stared back expectantly at the commander.

"It is my duty to guide others. Guide those chosen by Aria to understand their path and accept it, should they so choose to."

Fel'annár's eyes widened. It *was* Hobin who had stood upon the walls, the catalyst of his final dream. Hobin had come to the Motherland purposefully, so that he could guide Fel'annár on his path as Ber'anor. He felt overwhelmed, but through the mists of his thoughts and his slowly collecting mind, another question begged to be answered.

"Hobin, what happened . . . when Lainon died? What was that blue light that lingered between us?"

Hobin considered the young Silvan before him. He was the most powerful of all the Ber'anor he had met, but he was so young. He wondered if the boy would understand, but a question had been asked and Hobin would not leave him in the dark. Fel'annár had loved Lainon—this he could see, and Lainon had loved the boy just as fiercely—Hobin had known that from the moment he saw the Giving.

"There are three of many things in this world, Fel'annár. There is the spirit, the material, and the guide."

Fel'annár's eyes roved over Hobin's face, over the decorations, and Hobin nodded.

"This here." He pointed to the three half circles on his forehead. "This represents the spirit while this, here . . . " He pointed to the wavy lines across one cheek. "This is the material." He concluded by jutting his chin skywards, decorated with a single line and three spots on either side. "And here, this is the guiding hand—or light as some call it. The *blue* light that you saw, which left Lainon and entered you, that was his guiding light, the light every Ber'ator possesses which makes them Divine Protector, a small part of Aria, of the energy that guides them on their path. Lainon was your Ber'ator. His guiding light was yours to keep."

"But he's dead, and yet that light stirs in my mind . . ."

"He is *not* dead."

Fel'annár's wide, disbelieving eyes snapped to Hobin beside him. He briefly wondered if the Ari'atór spoke figuratively, but no, he spoke literally—the rare smile on his face told Fel'annár it was so, and his eyes filled with tears that fell over his bottom lids and down his face unchecked. He turned back to the window, nostrils flaring.

"You loved him well, and that is as it should be. The bond between Ber'anor and Ber'ator is never broken; the guiding light is eternal, just as soulmates are eternally one. The greatest Ber'ator stand upon the borders of Valley, and I wonder if perhaps Lainon will take his place there one day."

"The Last Markers? They are Ber'ator?"

"Yes. Perhaps you will see them one day. I would show you, tell you their stories."

"I would like that," said Fel'annár, still struggling to control his emotions. All his questions had been answered. He understood Lainon's death at last, understood that he had returned, *alive*. He breathed deeply, a calm sort of peace descending over him—despite the enormity of it all, despite what still lay before him. Hobin's sudden question brought him back to the present.

"Do you know what it is that you are charged with?"

"I do," said Fel'annár after a while, turning to face Hobin. "Although those it affects have no idea . . . and even if I told them they would not believe me. I am to restore the forests of Ea Uaré. Bring her people together, restore harmony where now there is nothing but discrimination and injustice. I pray you will not ask me *how*."

Hobin didn't. "That is a mighty task, Fel'annár. You will need help, you will need to recruit the collaboration of others."

"Yes. Prince Handir and perhaps Commander Pan'assár."

"Do they know what you are?"

"No. They know only that I am a Listener, and the commanders know I have a gift. That is the short of it."

"You will not tell them?"

"No. It seems unnecessary at this point, yet I *will* tell my brothers of The Company. They need to know if they are to follow me in this. And then perhaps I will tell Gor'sadén . . ."

Hobin nodded, satisfied it seemed. Tensári was not ready, and Fel'annár needed protection . . . every Ber'anor did. He did not expect Fel'annár's next question.

"What of Tensári? Now that Lainon is restored?"

"Tensári is . . . was . . . angry for a while, resentful. She is not yet ready to leave Araria, but I wager you will see her again, sometime soon."

"She blames me."

"In a way, and yet she knows the truth, Fel'annár. She knew Lainon was your Ber'ator. For now, though, she must learn to connect with her Connate, just as Lainon must learn from the other side. This is one of the boons of being Ari'atór, Fel'annár. Should a Connate die, the one that is left behind is broken, half-dead, just as with any other elf, but all Ari'atór find themselves, sooner or later, and when they do, that grief is gone as the Connates learn to feel each other across the divide. We are blessed in that our grief will end, be it tomorrow or a thousand years from now. For others, though, that grief may even be eternal."

Fel'annár considered Hobin's words and could not help but think of his own father and mother. They were not Ari, not Connates but *soulmates*. Lássira had died, and the king's grief might well be infinite.

"Hobin. Did you . . . did you know my grandfather, Zendár?"

Long moments of silence followed Fel'annár's question, and

Hobin's face seemed to momentarily crack, stony features becoming as expressive as his eyes for just an instant, long enough for Fel'annár to wonder what he had said to upset the commander. There were deep emotions hidden under layers of responsibility and command.

"Yes," he said quietly, a stiff smile glancing over his lips. "Yes, I knew Zendár. I did not know he was your grandfather. I will tell you about him one day."

Fel'annár watched him. He wanted to ask, wanted to know everything that Hobin did about his mother's father, the other Ari'atór in his line, but Hobin's reaction had been strange. He opened his mouth slowly. "Is he dead?"

"*No*." The word had been loosed no sooner Fel'annár had finished his sentence.

"Not any more. He is beyond the Source. Alive."

"Did he have family, apart from his daughters? Do they still live?" asked Fel'annár, head only half turned to Hobin as both stood before the full-length windows that looked out over the dramatic landscape beyond.

"Yes, he had family. As far as I know they are still in Bel'arán. A wife, a son, and two daughters."

"One died," said Fel'annár before Hobin could continue. "My mother died."

The commander breathed deeply. "When Zendár took the Short Road, I believe they returned to the forests of their birth. I pray you will be reunited with them, one day. You have a grandmother, an uncle and an aunt."

Fel'annár's eyes were wide, his mind rushing far forwards, wondering when he would be free to find them, the uncle and grandmother he had never met. But then what would he say? Would they know about him? They must surely, he mused. But then why had they not come? Why had he never met them? Why had Amareth hidden him away as she had? Turned her back on her own family?

He turned his head fully to Hobin, studied his severe profile, the rigid expression on his face and the broiling, swirling emotions in his eyes. There was much suffering there, thought Fel'annár.

"I will need your guidance, Hobin."

"And you will always have it, Fel'annár Aren'Zendár."

∼

That evening, Fel'annár sat in his rooms with The Company, knowing that he could put it off no longer. Their conversation was quiet, muted almost, their usual banter absent, but still they did not press him and for that he was grateful. He had needed time to allow his mind to temper itself—for his new knowledge to find its place. And yet in spite of the gravity of what he would reveal, his joy at Lainon's return could not be hidden, and so Fel'annár sat in some strange place between joy and apprehension. He had thought one and a thousand times of how he would tell The Company of his nature and duty . . . so that it would be *believable*. But he had failed to find that formula. He knew he was asking of them a leap of faith and both Idernon and Sontúr would not be able to jump it. He had hardly been able to jump it himself.

"The woods call to me. Shall we heed these poor Alpine trees and lend them some *company*, so to speak?" His tone was light, but his idea to tell them in the trees was not random. He needed to *show* them, needed them to see—help them to believe, just as Aria had done for him. He just hoped he wouldn't frighten them in the process . . . or himself!

"You want to sit in the trees outside the gates—at sundown in the frigid cold? Are you *mad*, Silvan?" asked Sontúr.

Fel'annár smirked. "You Alpines and your roaring hearths. Have you no coat?"

"Of course I have a *coat*, but what is the point of sitting in the cold? Oh, and did I mention there is an assassin after your hide?"

"Stay if you wish," he said with a smile. "But I have something I must tell you all, and there is no other place I would rather be."

They all stood then and Sontúr dashed from the room. "Wait for me!" he called over his shoulder. Minutes later they were striding through the main gates and into the surrounding woods. They were silent, but Fel'annár felt strangely confident, eyes moving from one tree to another as they passed until they came upon a sprawling oak. Hauling himself upwards with one arm, he watched as the other Silvans and Galadan followed with practised ease. Sontúr though, remained on the ground, looking up at them in annoyance.

Finally, he tutted. "Help me up, you Silvan *tree hamsters.*"

There was a giggle and then two strong arms reached down and hoisted the Alpine prince aloft. Before long, they were navigating their way up the central trunk until they found an expanse of thick branches upon which they could all comfortably sit—albeit Sontúr sat somewhat stiffly, back firmly pressed against the bark behind him. Galdith patted the Alpine reassuringly on the thigh, but the sour look on the prince's face did not ease.

Fel'annár settled back, bending his legs and resting his wrists on his knees. He sniffled in the silence. It *was* cold, but he wasn't going to admit to that. He breathed deeply, still unsure of how he would tell them, how he would *show* them. He said the first thing that came to him.

"Lainon is ever-present in my mind, but recently I have felt that presence more acutely. I thought it was simply a part of what it means to grieve for someone, the onset of acceptance that he had gone. I was *wrong.*"

He could feel their eyes on him, silent and impatient, and he pressed on. "Commander Hobin put me right. He said . . . he said Lainon has found himself, that he is *alive* in Valley."

A gasp, a strangled exclamation, a triumphant shout and meaningful silence but his own joy was contagious, and he felt their hands on his arms, on his head. They all knew how important Lainon had been to Fel'annár—indeed he had been important to them all, but none had shared that bond of brotherhood that Fel'annár had with the Ari'atór.

"So *that's* what all the mystery was about!" said Carodel. "Why didn't you just tell us!"

"Because that's *not* what all the mystery was about," he said, and The Company shared a perplexed look with each other—all of them except for Galadan and Idernon.

"I've had a dream since as long as I can remember. Idernon and Ramien have always known. It is a dream of a lady in a tree. I used to think she was my mother, but I was wrong. This woman would smile down at me, a babe who wiggled and gurgled up at her. For years I saw the same tree, the same lady, the same baby. Until last year."

"You saw your mother." Idernon nodded. "I remember."

"Yes. I saw her dark hair and green eyes, and I knew she was not the blue-eyed lady in the tree. After that, again and again I would see her smiling eyes, but she never spoke . . . until just a few months ago."

"You never told us about that," said Ramien, leaning forward as if his physical closeness would make Fel'annár speak quicker.

"I couldn't. Because I didn't understand, not entirely. All I knew for sure was that the lady in the tree . . . was Aria."

Stunned silence followed Fel'annár's unlikely claim. Carodel broke it.

"So, you've been dreaming of Aria your entire life?"

Fel'annár nodded. "I convinced myself that she was simply my way of visualising nature, the way I see the life-force of the land—embodied in a woman. A symbol if you will. I thought perhaps that I saw her because I have this ability with the trees, that it was part of my trying to convince *myself* that my ability is natural, that it's good. My way of dealing with the fear I felt for what I'm capable of.

"Again, I was wrong."

He had expected questions, quick and fast, but there were none, and he thought perhaps he had shocked them into silence. And so he pressed forwards. "Just last night, that dream changed once more, and this time, the lady came down from the tree and stood before me. In one hand she held a roughly-cut emerald, symbol of the Alpines of Ea Uaré, and in the other, the acorn, symbol of our Silvan kin. Her light was blinding, but before it hid her from me, she brought her hands together. The acorn and the emerald merged. And then she called me *Ber'anor*."

"Ber'anor. What's Ber'anor?" asked Carodel, desperately seeking Idernon's attention.

"Ber'anor is a Divine Servant, an elf chosen by Aria to carry out some duty," answered the Wise Warrior, but his eyes were locked on Fel'annár. "That is what the Ari claim."

"The question must be asked," continued Fel'annár. "I had always believed that Aria was life, nature, not a person with a conscience—with a will to decide. I could not bring myself to believe this, and so I asked Commander Hobin. I'm glad that I did."

"Wait, Hobin called you Ber'anor when, when Lainon . . ." said Galdith.

"He did," said Sontúr. "Idernon and I investigated later. We read the Book of Initiates, Ari lore for trainee Ari'atór. You see, Hobin also called Lainon Ber'ator—Divine Protector. If we are to believe the divine nature of this puzzle, then Lainon was charged by Aria to protect Fel'annár, who is charged with some duty he must carry out in her name. Am I right?" asked the prince.

"You are right, Sontúr. You will have to tell me about that trip to the library sometime." He arched an eyebrow at his princely friend.

"We will, but not now. Go on."

"I struggled with the concept of a god and yet, after all that has happened . . . I needed to ask questions of someone who had the answers, and Hobin has taken away my doubts—at least most of them. You see he, too, is Ber'anor. He had the same dream his entire life until his destiny was finally revealed to him. His story is mine."

"But Lainon was . . . is . . . Ari'atór, *Hobin* is Ari'atór," said Galdith. Fel'annár turned slowly to face him, and his eyes flashed wide in dawning realisation.

"And so, too, am I—Ari'atór."

"What? No, you *can't* be!" exclaimed Carodel, standing now on his branch. Galadan though, was staring coolly back at Idernon, who returned it with a deep frown.

"Only Ari'atór can be Ber'anor, brothers. If I accept one thing, I must accept the other. Hobin recognised me no sooner he saw me, and he says Lainon too, would surely have known. There must be a reason for my pale skin. Perhaps I was meant to grow in the forests and not in Araria, as I would have done had I been dark."

"I can't grasp it, Fel'annár. You are an *Ari'atór*? You laugh, you joke . . ." This from Idernon, whose legendary control was slipping visibly.

"And I have always been obsessed with fighting, with warfare, with serving . . ."

"Yes. Yes, you have," conceded Idernon.

"So, if I am not mistaken," began Galadan, shifting forwards until he was kneeling, "Aria has charged you, a pale Ari'atór, with a purpose and sent Lainon to protect you. But what, then, is this purpose?"

Fel'annár smiled, and for a moment he allowed his eyes to travel over them all.

"You remember the day Prince Handir called for me, gave me the missive from my father?"

"We *knew* you held something back," said Idernon, eyes searching and finding confirmation.

"He spoke to me of a plan, a plan to restore Ea Uaré to what it once was, to rid it of the taint of the powerful Alpine lords who seek to perpetuate discrimination and racism to their own gain. He spoke to me of Lord Band'orán and his desire to take the throne from King Thargodén. Lainon had this dream, one Handir shares together with Captain Turion and Councillor Aradan. They four devised a plan to bring the Silvan people back onto the side of King Thargodén and thus confront Band'orán. They think I can help them do this. But I couldn't see it. I told him that I needed time, to understand what a young and inexperienced warrior could do in such a lofty plan. And then last night, I dreamed of Aria. I saw the emerald and acorn come together in her hands—Silvan and Alpine living as one people, in harmony."

Silence followed, and Fel'annár's hand smoothed over the branch below him. He felt the torrent of energy, allowed his mind access to it so that he could show them his gift was no longer uncontrolled—did not always set his eyes to glowing like some demon, did not always evoke the wrath of the trees. He felt that energy and then projected it into the twilight. He had not been sure what they would see, and he smiled because fireflies blinked into existence, glowing a soft orange, flitting here and there and leaving tiny trails of light behind them. They seemed to chase each other around the gaping elves who watched in wonder, open-mouthed and shocked to silence—except for Carodel.

"Fel'annár?" asked Carodel softly, watching the lights as they reflected in his friend's eyes.

"Peace, Bard Warrior. 'Tis a game we play."

"Can we *all* play?" asked Sontúr with a curve of his brow.

Fel'annár glanced at him. Could they? he wondered. He opened his mind a little more, and Ramien gasped and then chuckled, holding out his massive hand to a spark of light as it flitted past his face. Galdith's eyes crossed as another light hovered a little too close to his nose, and Idernon stared on in awe, waving his hands softly before him, wondering if they would follow it.

"It's beautiful," he whispered.

"It's magical," added Galdith, his fingers following the frolicking lights.

"It's not magic, Galdith. It's a part of nature, the life-force that we take for granted every day—only that today you can see it. It is always there, though. It joins us all together, joins the land with the sky and the sun, binds us to everything . . . even those that have taken the road. They are in that light somewhere, far away though they may be."

Fel'annár thought of Lainon and Lássira, Galdith remembered

his soulmate and his infant daughter and Sontúr saw his mother's brave face.

Utter silence. Even the fireflies stopped their incessant zigzagging, hovering now before them, around them, poised on the boundary between the visible world and the natural world that Fel'annár had conjured to show them it *did* exist, even though they could not see it without his help.

Idernon's breath was loud, and the lights blinked out, simply gone.

"Fel'annár," began the Wise Warrior, "if you accept this duty, you walk into even more danger than you were already in. It is clear to me that Band'orán sees you as a danger, seeks to eliminate you because you are a threat to his plans. This shows us it is not only Prince Handir who believes there is something you can do." Idernon turned to the others. "Fel'annár is Silvan—he is *their* prince, Lássira's child. He can rally them, should he choose to, and Band'orán cannot rule if the Silvans will not subject themselves. He knows this and so do his allies here in Tar'eastór."

"And there you have it, brothers," said Fel'annár. "I am already a threat. By undertaking this task, I am stepping into the light of an already existing danger."

"And making yourself visible to all that seek to harm you," said Galdith.

"Someone has to do it, brother, and the gods know I have no idea *how* to do it. But Aria has placed this before me, and I have chosen to accept. Besides, I won't be alone in this, will I?"

The question was now before them, spoken plainly. It was Idernon who answered first.

"This goal that Prince Handir speaks of—we *all* want that, even the Alpines, the *good* people," said Idernon. "As a warrior I say there is no better cause. I have always followed you, Fel'annár, even when I had no teeth."

Ramien and the rest chuckled, but the laughter soon died and

Ramien spoke. "Aria has chosen Fel'annár, has shown him his path, and I will walk it with him . . . to whatever end."

Fel'annár startled for a moment, for the simple explanation that Ramien offered was one based on faith alone. Fel'annár's tense face slowly relaxed into a smile, and he nodded.

"And I will follow you—if your path leads to the freedom of my people, if it will rid my forest of the enemy amongst us," said Carodel. "If it will bring back our songs and our dances, our stories and our myths, if Silvan music will be played at court once more, I will be there to play it."

"And I am with Ramien," said Galdith. "I believe in Aria, believe she has chosen you, Fel'annár. It's too late for my village, for my soul mate and my child, but I can stop it from happening to others. I need no other motivation than this."

Fel'annár nodded in respect, and then his eyes slipped to Galadan. "And you, Lieutenant? What would you say?"

Galadan smiled, and Galdith mirrored it, so rare a treat it was. "I am old, as you know. Perhaps my turn has finally come to shine," he shrugged. "I will follow you, Forest Lord."

Fel'annár struggled to contain his emotions, for they said things to him that he had never dreamed of hearing. He had always been so occupied with defending himself, proving himself, hiding and then accepting the truth of his lineage. He had never stopped to think what others thought of him—other than the friendship they bestowed upon him. He was seeing himself in a totally different light, and for all that he tried, he did not recognise himself at all.

"And you, Sontúr. Will your father agree to free you of your duties here?"

"I cannot say. I must speak with him. Crown Prince Torhén should be home soon enough . . . I will find a way, Fel'annár. You are not doing this without me."

He smiled then. Each of them had their own reasons for following him on this dangerous path. For some it was faith, for others it was brotherhood, or remembrance of those beyond the Veil. But there was one thing that bound them, a unifying factor that defined The Company, that would keep them together, to whatever end.

It was love.

"Then from now on, brothers—now that I know you are all with me—I will tell you everything. I will need you all in this endeavour to remind me that I am a soldier first and foremost. I am not a politician or a diplomat, and I will not be made one. I do this as a warrior."

"What of our prince, Fel'annár? Can you trust his intentions? What of his animosity towards you for your mother's part in all this?" asked the Wise Warrior.

"He is genuine in his beliefs, Idernon, you heard him the other day. But I don't think we should reveal the divine nature of our duty. The prince may see that as a threat of some kind. He may think I have designs beyond that of a warrior."

"I agree," said Sontúr. "We follow his dictates for now, Fel'annár. I am not sure how you think this thing can be achieved, but perhaps *he* does."

"I don't know either," said Fel'annár. "We do as he says for now, as you say, but if there ever comes a time when I think he is wrong, I will not hold back. I think perhaps we need to return to Ea Uaré and once we are there, the path forwards will become clearer. For now, we have much to learn: *I* have much to learn of lordship and courtly manners." He smiled ruefully at Sontúr. "And if we do this thing, brothers, if our land is restored and the Silvan people given back their place, perhaps Galadan here will become captain and I may become lieutenant."

"Ahh!" roared Carodel. "A song is coming to me, the words appearing before my very eyes . . . Captains Galadan and Fel'annár and their loyal warriors of The Company!"

The others laughed and batted at Carodel's loose auburn hair, and Fel'annár watched them, eyes momentarily catching those of Idernon. The Wise Warrior smiled and nodded, and that was all Fel'annár needed.

All that was left to do now was to speak with Handir, accept his part in the plan, and then ask him what he intended to tell Pan'assár. The commander would surely need to know, would surely play some pivotal part in the Restoration, as Fel'annár had come to think of it.

Lainon's presence swelled in his mind, and he smiled through the warm haze of love and unconditional support from his Ber'ator, and for a moment, his vision blurred. He knew what it was now. It was Lainon's guiding light, his presence across the Veil manifesting itself in his eyes.

Lifting his head, he listened to the growing chorus of leafy voices. They sung a herald to the forest lord, and of a sudden, that feeling of impending doom lifted. This was what he had sensed, this moment in which he came to know himself, just as Golloron said that he would on the eve of his departure from Lan Taria. The Ari Spirit Herder had referred to this moment in which Fel'annár finally understood he was Ari'atór, Ber'anor. Golloron had known.

He was Lord of Aria's Forests.

TWELVE
REVOLT

"A king returns, a councillor stands, a prince emerges."
The Silvan Chronicles book IV. Marhené.

∽

The two Kah Masters and one disciple wound the Dohai to an end as the sun bathed them in a light that was slightly warmer than it had been just weeks ago. It reminded Fel'annár of the turning season—and that it would soon be time to return to the Forest. His stomach lurched at the thought.

He was back to training after the assassination attempt, and it was his first day as Ber'anor, albeit only The Company and Hobin knew. He needed to speak with Handir about Lainon's plan; he needed to ask if the prince would speak with Pan'assár on the matter, recruit his help if they could. And then there was Gor'sadén, Llyniel . . .

Yesterday he had felt stiff, but today, his wound hardly pained him at all, and he had trained well—even Pan'assár had joined them in the Dohai. But the streaks of light were always there, wispy and dim, a reminder of what lay dormant inside him, of the power he could not entirely control. Fear of the limits of his ability was holding him back, because he could feel it, coiling and writhing beneath the surface as soon as he projected his energy into his moves, as Gor'sadén had explained. It was like some caged beast, frantically struggling to bend its bars and escape.

His mind was a half-open door, and he stood in the middle of it, not sure whether he should open it completely. Fel'annár knew that Gor'sadén could see his hesitance, that he suspected the reason behind it.

"A Kah master is proficient in three weapons, Fel'annár. What will your third be?" asked Gor'sadén from where he sat, taking a long swig of water from his flask. Fel'annár had no doubts about his answer.

"A double-edged spear."

Pan'assár froze where he sat, just beside Gor'sadén, their shoulders almost touching.

"Nobody wields that weapon any more, not that I am aware of," said Gor'sadén carefully. "Why not the scimitar or daggers?"

"The spear has range. It can be used over a certain distance or in close quarters. It requires the skill of a sword and the agility of hand-to-hand. It's versatile . . . and it fascinates me."

"Your grandfather had a measure of skill with the spear." Fel'annár turned to Pan'assár and held his gaze for a moment.

Nodding thoughtfully, he turned back to Gor'sadén. "Are there any spear masters left?"

"There are, although admittedly not many. But come, we must press on. Your projection skills are progressing well in hand-to-hand but not so with the swords: why do you think you fail?" asked Gor'sadén, and Pan'assár's eyes narrowed as he turned to listen.

Fel'annár knew why, but could he admit it?

"Well?" prompted Pan'assár.

"I'll try harder."

Gor'sadén glanced at Pan'assár, and both commanders stood, walking towards the centre of their training area.

"I want the ten blade stances and I want projection. See the move in your mind, apply the power you have built up with the Dohai, project it into your blades as you perform the moves."

Fel'annár breathed deeply. Perhaps if he allowed just a little of his energy to filter through to his hands, then nothing would happen. And so he began, under the watchful gazes of the two commanders. Lifting his two blades, he saw the faint wisps of light that chased after them as he performed the stances, and when he had finished the first set, Gor'sadén was shouting his orders.

"Again!"

Fel'annár initiated the sequence once more, opening his mind just a little. The wisps were back, stronger, and he closed his mind to them.

"Again!!" shouted Gor'sadén, louder this time, his irritation finally seeping into his words.

He performed the sequence again, and then again, and every time the light began, he would stop it—he *had* to. He let out a long, sonorous rush of air, frustration because Gor'sadén would not let it go.

"Do it again. *Don't* hold back." Gor'sadén was circling him, and even Pan'assár was watching closely, following after his friend.

Fel'annár wanted to scream. He *couldn't* open his mind entirely because he knew that whatever happened, he would not be able to control it. And yet he could feel it, all the pent-up energy pooling in his gut, setting his fingers to tingling, his scalp prickling.

"Do it again and *don't* stop until I tell you to."

Damn it, he spat to himself, but he started again, his mind frantic to hold on to the door so that it would not fly open and let everything out.

Pan'assár scowled and elbowed Gor'sadén.

"What *is* that?" he murmured.

"When I spoke to him about it, just after the first Dohai, his eyes were scintillating. There is something about the Kah that is activating his ability. I saw this during the Kah test, although you would not have noticed."

"Is it purposeful?" asked Pan'assár as he continued to watch the strange wisps of light.

"No. It frightens him because he cannot control it. He will not admit to that, though. He is holding back."

Gor'sadén walked towards Fel'annár, Pan'assár right behind him.

"Your gift likes the Dohai," he said softly as he watched Fel'annár work. He could see the worry in his disciple's eyes as he swung his blades this way and that. "You hold back. You are breaking your word to me."

Fel'annár faltered and Gor'sadén shouted. "I did not tell you to *stop*!"

Fel'annár resumed the sequence, but he was frowning deeply, concentrating on limiting the energy he channelled to his limbs.

"Why do you do it? Why do you train half-heartedly? You promised me your *all*," said Gor'sadén, eyes blazing, goading his disciple because he knew it was the only way for Fel'annár to let go of his fear and allow his worst dream to come true: to lose control.

"Your projection is half-hearted. This is what I would expect from any other warrior. *Mediocre! Anyone* can do that, Fel'annár, but you are a *Kah Warrior!*"

The trailing lights pulsed, and then they were colourful ribbons dancing in the spring breeze. Pan'assár stepped back, but Gor'sadén continued his onslaught, eyes wide and body tense.

"Show me you are *worth* it! That I am not wasting my time. *Unleash* this thing, Fel'annár."

"I can't," he said unsteadily as he continued to work, his control beginning to slip.

"I told you I wanted everything, in exchange for teaching you the Kal'hamén'Ar. You gave your word—you *lied*!"

"I did *not*."

"Then show me, *damn* it!"

The few trees to be had upon the small plateau groaned and creaked, and leaves swayed in a non-existent breeze. Low rumbling boomed in their ears, and a grating, high-pitched metallic sound broke through the droning.

Fel'annár's eyes flared into blazing green pools of pure energy, hair snaking around his head far too slowly to be natural, and still he did not stop the sequence.

He had *not* lied. He *was* worthy.

"Don't stop!" shouted Gor'sadén over the noise, the groaning wind, the frantic thudding of his own heart in his mouth.

Fel'annár's movements were precise, fast yet elegant, infused with a power neither master had seen before.

"Fel'annár, can you fight? As you are?" shouted Pan'assár urgently over the din, unsheathing his own blades.

"I don't know."

"Try. *Fight* us!"

"I cannot trust . . ."

"*Do* it!" thundered Gor'sadén, taking his own swords and striking a ready stance, Pan'assár at his side.

Fel'annár brought both swords before him, facing the commanders who stood in a haze of green. The lights were everywhere, but Fel'annár struggled to ignore them, to concentrate on the warriors before him. It worked, and all Gor'sadén's training came to him with startling clarity.

Initiate, side and feign, back, then swivel left, flip sword right, then circle left. He was moving, fast and furious; he was projecting without reserve, and around him, blond hair fanned this way and that. Blue and grey eyes danced before him, around him, blue-white steel seeking to strike a blow and failing every time.

The screech of sword against sword faded to the background, and his heartbeat was deafening, breathing fast but even, ears roaring with the rush of blood through his veins—or was it sap through roots?

He saw it all, countered it all, avoided their blows and countered with his own. The world tilted to one side as he side-twisted, the flashing metal arcing below him, meeting nothing but air ... until his feet hit the ground and the same blade whooshed over his head.

"Fel'annár. Try to stop it now. Slowly, try to regain control," shouted Gor'sadén as he fought.

The words were muted, like a distant call from an eternal corridor.

"Fel'annár. *Control* it."

The voice seemed a little closer now, yet still his body moved, eyes registered everything, swords stabbed and arced and swivelled in his hands.

"Come back."

He startled, for the words had been said by someone standing close by. He *wanted* to come back but *how*? It had all started by outwardly projecting the energy he had generated with the Dohai; perhaps the key was to take it back, draw it in, but how could he contain such power?

He imagined those traces of light as extensions of himself, reaching out to the trees around him, and then he imagined pulling them back, coiling them in his chest. Too fast and he gasped at the sudden white-hot heat that slammed into his chest. He staggered backwards, stumbled and then held one arm out to brace his clumsy fall. Every nerve was alight with raw energy, his chest too tight, he couldn't breathe. He cried out, and then his eyes focussed, enough to see the treetops as they swayed left and right, the dry leaves as they spiralled in the wind, still strong as it whipped around him.

Too fast; he had pulled it back with a simple thought and he tried again. This time he imagined himself holding out one hand, calling the energy back, channelling it slowly into himself. Green, blue, and purple mist slowly dissipated, and his muscles regained their weight. He sat, starved lungs filling with air, deep breaths echoing in his ears. He closed his eyes, feeling his own hair fall heavily on his shoulders.

Silence.

"Fel'annár."

Breathe, just breathe and do not think, not yet.

"Fel'annár."

"Yes."

"Open your eyes." Gor'sadén's voice.

Slowly, he cracked them open to the bright light of day. Emotion came back to him, and he remembered Gor'sadén's harsh words, Pan'assár's intervention. He had stirred the world with his gift ... and all that had happened was good. He had fought well.

He had *controlled* it.

The two commanders knelt beside their student, gaping in open fascination as his green eyes slowly lost the scintillating lights, and when they had completely dissipated, Pan'assár quite unexpectedly smiled a *wicked* smile.

"Show off."

Fel'annár barked in laughter, his mirth mixed with disbelief for what had just happened. It was a small victory, one he could thank Gor'sadén for—he had purposefully goaded him so that he would not hold back, so that his *fear* would not hold him back.

Only later, when the commanders were alone, did they speak of what had happened, of their shock and then of the nature of Fel'annár's strange gift.

"What are the limits of it, do you think?" asked Pan'assár, bracing his arm against the mantle in Gor'sadén's rooms that evening.

"Who can say? *He* doesn't know; it is why he holds back, and I don't blame him."

"Strange times," murmured Pan'assár. "You know I sometimes wondered if my time in Bel'arán had concluded—that perhaps I had become a thing of the past, left behind by everyone I ever loved."

"You have much to do yet, Pan. This boy has much to achieve, and you can help him. He will need you before it is done."

Pan'assár scowled as he turned to his friend. "Before *what* is done?"

Gor'sadén's brow twitched, and he shook his head. "Before he becomes a master . . ." he lied. However much he tried, Gor'sadén could not shake the feeling of some impending event, that something important was to take place and that he would be a part of it. He had thought it the Kal'hamén'Ar and the birth of an extraordinary warrior, just as he had told Pan'assár, but the feeling persisted.

There was more to it than that.

Pan'assár's softly-spoken words startled him. "We are in this together, Gorsa. Don't think to deceive me. He will need us *both*. The question is . . . what *for?*"

~

For seven days, the court of King Thargodén was a broiling, simmering cauldron of passionate discourse and intrigue in the Forest. Aradan had known this would happen, had warned the king—still, it was far worse than even *he* had imagined.

Debate raged in every corner and at every table, sometimes loud and uncouth while at other times it was subtle and manipulative, and when the king happened upon one such session, sometimes the speakers would turn and bow low while others would gaze speculatively and offer only curt, stilted nods. The councillors pulled out every weapon they had. Rhetoric, fallacy, logic, faulty reasoning—it was a study in statesmanship, and Thargodén watched, listened, and soon, he came to understand who was loyal to him . . . and who was *not*.

Every one of those seven days drew him further and further away from his old life, further away from the passive, symbolic king who had haunted the palace for the last fifty years. In seven days, his transformation was almost complete, and he took it upon himself now to mend the damage that had been done, that *he* had done, if that was at all possible.

Just as the king observed the machinations of his councillors, so too did Aradan observe his friend. What he saw was both encouraging and profoundly disturbing. Now, more than ever, Thargodén needed his legendary measure, his composure so that he could think clearly, and yet with every day that passed, Thargodén drew quieter and quieter, and in his eyes, the glittering lights of his emotions grew brighter and brighter. It was times like these when Thargodén was capable of the most volatile of deeds. Aradan still remembered the days when Lássira had been forbidden to him, his silence, the inner turmoil that had then led to the unlikely day in which he had confronted King Or'Talán himself.

But just as the king was returning, so was Aradan changing. He had always been the measured voice of caution and yet now, he wondered if it was, perhaps, time for him to show his colours, show his loyalty, and cease trying to pull people together, stop trying to negotiate and start *imposing* order rather than *asking* for it. Surely *measure* was no longer possible while Band'orán was still in the picture.

But Aradan wasn't like that. He never had been. He was a negotiator, a believer in a society that was diverse in its beliefs, in faith or in the lack of it. He had always believed that respect for others was the key to harmony. He had never doubted that—until now.

The day had come to vote and still, there was no consensus at all.

As Thargodén sat on his throne, head bent towards his crown prince as they spoke quietly, Aradan turned his head and watched the councillors in the semi-circle before them. They were already arguing, even before the session had begun. The two Silvans and half of the Alpine councillors were immersed in debate, while those Alpine councillors who either followed Band'orán or had yet to decide, listened, almost impassively. It was these councillors that Aradan watched the closest.

Band'orán had surely lavished promises upon them in exchange for their negative votes, and Barathon and Draugole had undoubtedly reminded them of Band'orán's determination to bring back the glory days of Tar'eastór. Rinon had remained neutral to the public eye, but every one of the last seven evenings, he had reported what he had seen, what he had heard, and then king, prince, and advisor would analyse and plan their tactics for the following day.

For today.

Now, there was no more time for persuasion: the day of voting was upon them. The council chambers were ringing with raised voices, not only from the semi-circle of finely-decked councillors but also from the public areas to each side of the room. Elves shouted and argued, waved their hands about, and Aradan thought General Huren wise to have set extra guards around the chamber.

Hopes were high, tempers were high. Even Aradan's.

"Order, *order!*" shouted Den'har, banging his staff repeatedly against the stone floors, face red and veins bulging in his neck. "*Order in the King's halls!*"

The noise began to die down, and the master of ceremonies wasted no time.

"To the proposal of an equitable council, in which the current number of Alpine councillors will be complemented by an equal number of Silvan councillors, state your vote '*aye*' or '*nay*' after your name."

The silence was absolute now. From one side of the hall, the Alpines watched their rulers with keen interest while on the other, the Silvans looked on with barely-contained hope. Aradan watched them, saw Erthoron and Lorthil stand with their people and behind them, two Ari'atór.

And then the voting started and what Aradan had first seen in Erthoron's wise eyes began to change. The hope dulled, and for a moment he thought he saw grief. It was fleeting, and his endearing face seemed to sharpen.

Hurt, rejection; despair, anger.

Aradan closed his eyes, because his worst fears had been confirmed. The royal council had voted against equality. They would not allow any more Silvans amongst them, and all he could hear now was the beat of his own distressed heart.

Den'har, master of ceremonies, wisely pushed forward and to the second vote, and while a decent number of councillors agreed to the return of the warlord, the rest refused to vote, stating that it was a military decision and, as such, should be voted by the captains, by the Inner Circle. It was utter cynicism, because the outcome of such a vote was clear. The Inner Circle was Alpine. They would never allow the return of the warlord and the Silvans knew this all too well.

Aradan spared a momentary glance at his king's profile. Something had changed in that stony countenance, and he wondered if Rinon on his other side had noticed. There was feeling in the normally blank stare the king wore on occasions such as these, and the colour of his face was not so pale and frosty. His features were not slack and placid but pulled tight, ready to snap.

Chaos erupted in the hall.

"*Order! Order!*"

But Den'har's pleas for silence were drowned beneath seething words of anger and equally heated words that called for dignity and acceptance. Guards tightened their fingers around their spears, eyes darting around for some sign that perhaps they should intervene. Most were Silvan, struggling to ignore the plight of their people and yet keep them from invading the semi-circle. They wanted to stand with them, shout out their own indignation, but their sense of duty and honour would not allow it.

One Silvan jumped over the wooden railings that separated the public from the council, waving his arms and shouting madly.

"Have you all lost your *minds*! We are not your *slaves*!"

Laughter from some of the younger Alpine spectators far on the other side of the hall followed the impassioned words, while the councillors stood in alarm at the breech. Soon, more Silvans were jumping the railings and converging on the council, and guards ran to block them, holding their spears out to stop them. Civilians crashed with the guard and clamoured for a way past them, but they were held at bay while the councillors made to flee, eyes wide and disbelieving. Only three stood their ground, one with a smile of disgust, one with distant, cool interest and the other in growing trepidation for what his father had unleashed.

But some Alpines bowed their heads in shame, even as others

shouted and gestured for the Silvans to get back, to behave themselves like elves and not animals.

One Silvan managed to worm his way through the barricade but was caught by the gloved hand of an Alpine guard and thrown to the ground. He stood defiantly, only to be viciously backhanded, but the shouting did not stop—and now, it was accompanied by screams from both sides, and even from the semi-circle itself. Vardú held her arms out to her compatriots, a desperate plea for calm while others looked wildly around them.

Another Silvan ran through the struggling line of guards and made it to the semi-circle. Standing in fury before an Alpine councillor who had given a negative, had sneered at his people, his fist reached out to grab the fine cloth of his tunic and then he shook hard while most of the remaining council scattered in alarm, scrolls left abandoned upon the now almost empty benches.

"Why? *Why?* Have you no *shame?!*"

The councillor was jostled wildly, blond hair flying around him, panicked eyes and hands held up in surrender. The Silvan was pulled back by another guard and pushed away, back to the Silvan enclosure and timidly, the councillors crept back to their places, albeit their eyes did not leave the angry Silvan mob that was now being successfully contained as more guards ran in to reinforce the barricade.

Aradan stood, almost as if he had been pulled up by some invisible entity. He strode up to the front benches of the semi-circle and then filled his lungs with air with a sonorous rush. He bellowed long and hoarse into the air, all the frustrations of the past days rushing from him violently, all the years of measured patience suddenly gone. It was not only the king who had changed. It was *him*.

Aradan had snapped and one word rolled from his mouth.

"*Silence!*"

An echo—and then another.

The councillors turned shocked eyes away from the Silvans and to the king's chief councillor. Aradan had never shouted, not once . . .

and *never* like that, not that hoarse, pent-up roar of anger. Soon enough, even the public areas had fallen silent, their curious eyes upon Aradan, even those of his Silvan wife who stood at the very back, anonymous in her long cloak and hood—but she did not stand with the Alpines. She stood on the Silvan side.

Aradan had things to say—things that would no longer be contained behind his steel doors of temperance and measure.

"I am so very *ashamed*," he hissed. "So very humiliated to be a part of this mockery of a royal council!" he thundered. "Where is your dignity? Your pride? Where is your loyalty to your king and your vocation to service—unto *others*? Where are your scruples and your common sense? Where are your hearts? By Aria, *have* you none?

"You all took an oath, an oath to uphold the law, to serve our people – our *people* – Alpine and Silvan alike and yet you will not allow them to have a say in the rulings of these lands? None of you, not one, can convince me that this comes from your common sense or even your hearts. This vote is a consequence of your *pride* and your *pockets*. It is a grotesque manifestation of the *rot* that has taken hold of you, twisted you into servers unto yourselves. Greedy, power-frenzied elves, seduced by an elf who pursues but one thing. To take the throne from its rightful owner, take it *all* for *himself*."

He paused, eyes turning away from the councillors and landing squarely on Band'orán. "You couldn't take it from your brother and now, you try to take it from your *nephew*."

The council was utterly silent, incredulous eyes turning from Aradan to Band'orán, watching as he stood, his black robes of velvet and silk falling gracefully around him but his face – his face was a twisted and warped version of the mask of indifference he had always maintained in public. Until now.

Aradan suddenly realised what he had done, what he had *said*. He faltered, stunned that he had let go of his measure, of his control. Band'orán would use it against him now, call him weak and frightened, rally the Alpine councillors he had fought so hard to win over, use Aradan's outburst as proof that Thargodén was ill-counselled. He had failed his king and he opened his mouth to speak. But no words would come, even though his mind screamed at him to stop Band'orán from speaking, for he would bend those words, warp them out of all recognition and strengthen his sway over the indecisive.

What have I done?

The dangerous hiss of one long sword sliding free of its scabbard jolted him and Aradan spun around to the source, to a king who stood tall, powerful, commanding and wrathful, the legendary sword of Or'Talán glinting before him—and he was thunderous: *fearsome*. Aradan's eyes slipped to Rinon, just behind the king, his hand upon his own sword hilt, following his father as he strode towards the council.

Aradan turned back to Band'orán, his eyes no longer slits of unsuppressed ire but wide and surprised, words frozen on his poisonous tongue. His mask slowly slipped back into place and Aradan stepped sideways as the king approached, but instead of continuing to the semi-circle, Thargodén turned towards the Alpine guard with a Silvan civilian lying bleeding at his feet. The guard turned, dropped his spear, had every intention of falling to his knees, but there was no time before the back of a jewelled hand impacted with the side of his face, sending him reeling to one side, his helm skittering across the floor.

"Your oath is returned to you. I do not want it. You are not *fit* to serve in my army."

"My king," pleaded the guard, kneeling before him with a split lip and messy hair.

"You *disgust* me. Out of my *sight*," he growled.

The guard's eyes widened, and then he seemed lost, did not even straighten himself, and the king turned to the Silvan on the ground, who looked up at him with wide eyes. Thargodén's imposing ire seemed to simply disappear, one strange moment in which his face was soft and kind and love, not wrath, shone in his eyes. He held his hand out, watching as it was taken, tentatively, and he pulled the elf to his feet. He nodded, and then whirled on his heels and strode towards the semi-circle, eyes blazing a burning trail across his councillors. Some knelt, heads bowed while others stood wide-eyed, disbelieving, for before them was a version of their vanquished king which they had never seen. It was as if some more primal version stood before them, all atavistic power, as if he had surged from the depths of the earth to wreak terror upon them, and Aradan watched, wide-eyed, a surge of almost painful pride stealing his breath, and as Thargodén came to stand beside him before the council, for the first time in decades, Aradan stood tall, unfettered, *unleashed*, just like his king.

Band'orán, though, stood watching, eyes apparently curious but Aradan knew better. For one, odd moment, the eyes of an uncle locked with those of his nephew. Thargodén's eyes blazed in unchecked anger, unwavering, so intense that Band'orán felt his own resolve falter. He almost looked away, had almost been defeated, but the king's eyes lifted from him.

Thargodén had come to know who paid genuine obeisance to him, just as he knew the identity of those who had been swayed. They bowed, too, but the treachery in their eyes was so clear to Thargodén that he almost laughed at their pantomime. He could see it as plainly as he could see his father's sword in his own hands.

"Seven of you have failed to offer satisfactory reasoning as to your votes. Seven of you offer no reasons as to your unwillingness to accept Silvan councillors amongst you. Racism is not a reason, it is a fundamental fault in your characters. But then, some of you have done nothing but remain silent. Not one word. Tell me, how can you vote – in all conscience – if you have no opinion? And tell me, how can you have an opinion, if you do not listen? Are these the acts of a worthy councillor?

"They are *not*. It is unworthy. You are not fit to serve on this council, and I have lost all faith in you. You can redeem yourselves though, if you can prove that you are willing to serve my people, *all* of them, and that you are loyal to this crown.

"Hear me, all of you," said Thargodén, his voice ringing with inherent power, inborn command. "Your king vetoes the decision of this council until such time that each and every one of those seven *unlikely* votes can be duly documented, and their casters deemed loyal. To this end I will speak to each and every one of you. With due consideration, your vote may be considered valid . . . should your reasoning be sound, and should your *loyalty* be deemed genuine. If, at any time thereafter, your treachery is revealed, I will cast you from these lands in public shame, never to return.

"This shameful council session will be repeated two months hence. Time enough to reconsider. Time enough to prove your loyalty. Time enough for Commander General Pan'assár to return home and oversee the vote regarding the return of the warlord. When these conditions are in place, we will pass judgement once more and my right to veto will be void—the future of these lands and its people will be in *your* hands."

The king breathed deeply, spared one, last, searing gaze at his councillors and then turned to Aradan beside him. The chief councillor bowed low to his king and Thargodén returned it, the deep friendship they shared flaring to life, and from the depths of the Silvan side, at the very back of the stunned crowd, a cloaked lady wept silently, for joy and for pride, and the yearning of a mother who wished with all her heart that her daughter could see her father now.

Back on his throne of dark, carved wood, Thargodén schooled his features but not so his voice. "Heed me, Councillors—Alpine and Silvan people of Ea Uaré. I will not tolerate treachery. I will not tolerate violence. I will not tolerate discrimination, and I will be *implacable* in my punishment. This kingdom was built upon the noble premises my father held in his heart his entire life. *Service* to others, not to himself. *Love* for others, not for himself. *Bravery* when honour is called to question. These three things I bid you hold in your own hearts so that you may *shine* as he once did.

"In two months' time I will know where your hearts lie. This mockery of a royal council is dismissed."

Thargodén turned to face Rinon, who bowed from the waist for long moments, and Thargodén watched his eyes, saw the fire and the conviction, a captain poised for the final charge. His throne suddenly felt comfortable, for the first time in years—just as Or'Talán's sword no longer felt frigid, cold in his lax hands. It was a burning lance, a beacon that had somehow shown him the way back to kingship. He had hated his father for tearing Lássira away from him, but so too had he loved him. It was why his father's treachery had broken him. It was why Rinon hated him so much—because he loved him.

The three elves cast their eyes over the now softly murmuring hall. Erthoron caught Thargodén's eyes, and when he did, he bowed slowly, purposefully, giving his people time to notice what he did, copy him if they would, but they didn't. He straightened, nodded, and then turned to the semi-circle of councillors. He took a moment to watch as they murmured quietly, and then he turned his back on them, waiting for the rest of his people to do likewise. They *all* did, and soon, the entire Silvan side stood with their backs to the council hall, and the quiet murmuring turned to shocked silence.

Aradan closed his eyes and then watched as the Silvan leaders and their people left in silence, watched as Band'orán's eyes twinkled and glinted oddly.

Outside, Erthoron turned to his people, his eyes dull, the spark of hope gone and, in its place, the blank stare of one defeated. With his next words, the first Forest Summit ended, as surely as their faith in their Alpine rulers had shattered, as surely as the forest would now be tossed into a heaving mass of indignant and embittered Silvans Erthoron knew he would be hard-pressed to control.

"We have failed."

∼

Later, Aradan, Rinon, and Thargodén sat in the king's chambers in silence, a glass of wine in their numb hands and a far-away look in their eyes.

"We have two months," said the king. "Two months to wrench

an oath of fealty from those councillors—under pain of exile should they break it. That may be enough to dissuade them from openly supporting Band'orán in his endeavour to take this throne from me."

"Dire measures," murmured Aradan.

"Dire *stakes*, Councillor," replied Rinon, and Thargodén turned to his crown prince in approval.

"Some will call you dictator, Thargodén," warned Aradan, but there was no disapproval in his voice.

"Only by those Alpine councillors who cleave to Band'orán. That will be *his* game now, calling me a tyrant for overruling the vote of the council. I am conducting an *investigation* into the finances and movements of those councillors who sided with him. I would compare the *before* and the *after*, what they have *now* and what they end up having after the vote. I can hopefully discredit them with proof of their treachery, at least."

"It may not matter. By then you may no longer be king," said Rinon.

"That will not happen, Rinon," said Aradan, his jaw clenched, and Rinon stared back at him thoughtfully. "We obtain the oath of fealty as the king says, we make those councillors see that they are under our scrutiny, and we should make that a *public* fact. It is entirely possible that they will change their vote for fear of public humiliation."

"If that happens, Band'orán will be stretched to breaking. He will be desperate," said Rinon.

"Yes. Yes, he will," murmured the king. "But years of hatred and scheming, years of treachery and careful planning—it must all come to a head, one way or the other. I believe that time has come."

"It has," confirmed Aradan. "And that end will be defined in two months. Pan'assár will be back by then. He will help us obtain a favourable vote for the reinstatement of the warlord."

"Will he?" asked Rinon with a scowl. "You are far more optimistic than I. It is *he* who has filled the Inner Circle with mewling lordlings who know nothing of warfare. Any soldier knows of his aversion to the Silvans."

"He will do it because I will *ask* it of him," said Thargodén, and Rinon turned to his father.

"You would coerce him then? Order him to act against his own beliefs?"

"Yes. The consequences of a second negative vote will bring war to these lands, Prince. This Alpine army would force the Silvans into submission and a monster would ascend to the throne of the House of Or'Talán. I will do everything, *anything*, to stop that from happening."

Aradan breathed deeply. "I believe you, my friend; indeed I second your words. However, we must be prepared, for two months is a long time to wait and to think, especially when there is no hope. The Silvan people believe they already know the outcome of the vote of the Inner Circle, and they have lost faith that you will be able to change the vote of the council, in spite of what they saw today. They see Band'orán as a powerful, influential elf that others listen to."

"But so too did they see their king, Aradan. Thargodén Ar Or'Talán is back, and that must surely give them a glimmer of hope at least."

Aradan turned to the crown prince, eyes roving over his glacial form as if he were seeing him again after a long sojourn. "It will be enough for some, sufficient perhaps for Erthoron to try and convince his people that not all is lost. However, we all saw how they left. We all saw their resolve. This land is fractured." He sighed deeply. "I wish Handir were here, I wish Pan'assár were here, and believe me, I never thought to say *those* words of late."

"The situation is volatile at best," murmured the king as he sipped absently on his wine. "I am so deeply disappointed in my people, Aradan. So ashamed . . . just as they have been of me."

"They have been poisoned, turned slowly and deftly," said Aradan. "Band'orán is skilled and he is patient. His plan is unfolding, and it is a brilliant one, but heed me, Thargodén. Your years of absence are not the main cause of this. I had your back."

Thargodén smiled sadly. He was grateful for what Aradan tried to do—exonerate him from the guilt of having led his nation to the cusp of civil war. But he couldn't. No one could rid him of the facts, however one wished to justify his motives. But that did not mean that the fight had gone from Or'Talán's son.

He *had* been the cause of Band'orán's dangerous rise in power, but so too would he be the one to wrench it away from his greedy, grasping hands.

Rinon watched his father closely, and all the while his mind was working through Band'orán's plan, even as Aradan spoke.

"You know, for the last few months I have been pondering Band'orán's strategy, striving to understand him so that I can anticipate his next moves. And then I noticed a strange pattern I did not think important at the time. Now, though, I begin to realise." He turned to face the others. "Petitions from lords to acquire land in the Forest, and I do not speak of land surrounding the fortress. I speak of land in the deeper areas of the forest. Tell me now, why would they wish to set up residence there, where they say the Silvans should leave in order for us to protect it? Why would they venture into lands they say cannot be protected in the presence of civilians? Lands they *vote* not to protect until they are emptied?"

Rinon's eyes widened, but Thargodén's expression was one of tired realisation.

"They are colonising."

"Yes. That is what I believe. And if this is true, then we must also accept that our military reports—are *spurious*."

"No, Huren and Pan'assár are loyal, I am sure of that," said Thargodén, shaking his head.

"They may be, but what of the other generals? Maybe they, too, are being played," mused Aradan. "And if this is the case, the Inner Circle will clearly vote against the return of the Warlord, with or without Pan'assár. The Silvans already believe that—they have been on the receiving end of our Alpine commanders for too long without justice."

Silence settled upon the three elves until Rinon's uncharacteristically soft voice broke it.

"I wonder if this is not the first time Band'orán has targeted you, Father."

King and advisor turned to the crown prince in curiosity. "What do you mean?" asked Aradan.

"Or'Talán was a warrior king. He led our troops into battle. It was surely a question of time before he fell to the enemy. But of course the king had an heir, one that would take the throne after his demise . . . or *not*."

After a while, the king spoke quietly and thoughtfully. "That is an interesting theory, Prince."

"There are many ways to destroy one's enemies," added Aradan, eyes moving from one side of the rug to the other. "There are many *weapons* with which to clear the path to the throne . . ."

"I wonder," said Rinon, "I wonder what it was that Band'orán used against Or'Talán in order to separate you from Lássira."

"That is, perhaps, the last part in the puzzle, is it not?" asked Aradan. "If you are right, Rinon, and the gods forgive me but I believe you may be, then Band'orán had something to bargain with, some asset, some knowledge that was more important to Or'Talán that the heart of his own son."

Thargodén considered their words and he could not help but think his uncle was capable of this and much more. "There is a spark of strangeness about him. I have always felt it, writhing beneath the surface."

"And I," said Rinon. "Handir, Maeneth, and I discussed it often. We were frightened of him when we were younger."

"So was I," admitted Thargodén. "Now, though, all he provokes in me is disgust . . . and pity. If he did have something to do with why my father broke me, my hand will not be stayed. I will strike him down, so help me Aria. There will be no exile for him."

Aradan looked to Rinon in alarm, but the crown prince was watching his father and in his eyes was something new, something that Aradan, in spite of the dangerous spiral of events, could not help but rejoice at. Upon the crown prince's face, he saw respect—and he saw pride.

As for Thargodén, he marvelled at his faithful councillor, his friend of many centuries. Would that his wife, Miren, had seen him standing for the Silvans as he had never done in public before; would that his daughter, Llyniel, returned and mend his heart—see just how brave her father was.

∼

"Cousin!"

Rinon turned, watching as Barathon walked towards him and then clapped him on the forearm. "Barathon." The crown prince smiled stiffly. The meeting he had just left with Aradan and the king had left him in deep thought; the last thing he wanted was to have to deal with his fool *cousin*.

"Come, I have human brandy and some time to spare before the evening meal. Drink with me."

Rinon considered his offer. He had just left his father's rooms and he needed to think, but he also knew that human brandy was Barathon's attempt at gleaning information, at gauging his own reaction to the king's veto, to the Silvans' gesture of rejection and the upcoming inquiries the king would conduct. But Rinon had his own information to glean, so he nodded and followed Barathon to his nearby suite of rooms.

They were opulent, fit for a crown prince. Rinon smirked to himself. Perhaps he thought to prepare, for should Barathon's father succeed and take the throne from Thargodén, surely that was what Barathon would be. The mental smirk turned into a snarl he was hard-pressed to hide.

"Here, try this!"

Rinon reached for the goblet and allowed his eyes to fix on the thick amber liquid. He swirled it once and took it to his nose, inhaling the heavy aroma of wood and spice. His eyes watched Barathon as he drank with a scandalous gulp and a roar of delight.

"So strong." Barathon wheezed and then smiled, watching as Rinon took a sip of his own brandy and swallowed it down, his face as frigid as it almost always was in public. Barathon's smile slipped a little as he gestured to the sofa before the hearth.

"I wonder, Cousin, what your thoughts are with respect to The Silvan boy."

Rinon turned to Barathon, who sat beside him, staring into the flames.

"My thoughts do not matter, Barathon. It is the king's thoughts that matter."

"Rinon, I know you are loyal, but I ask as your cousin—he is, after all, your half-brother."

"I have one brother, Barathon, and that is Handir."

"Ah. Well, I cannot blame you for feeling that way. I certainly would." There was silence for a while, until Barathon spoke once more. "You heard that forester, saw the reaction of the Silvan people to his tale. It worries me, Rinon, for they make of him a hero."

It was true; Rinon could not refute Barathon's words. The Silvan people were desperately seeking a way to escape their submission, a way to make their voice heard, and The Silvan was the only claim they had.

"I will give you that, Barathon. They have made of him a legend it seems."

"And legends are dangerous, Rinon. We cannot allow the Silvan people to rebel, to claim their own lord, their own *prince*. If we allow this, we hand them the power to overthrow our king."

Rinon's eyes were back on Barathon, but he did not show his rising temper at being played for a fool. "Well, the boy is not here—and still they have turned their backs on us. I do not think they need *him* to rebel. They are already doing that."

"Yes. But Erthoron is not the one to move them, Rinon. They will be back. They need us to survive."

It was Rinon's turn to smile, but it was not kind. "You underestimate them. We would do well not to push too hard lest they push back."

"Then we let them push. With no leader, no organised army of their own I see no need to tremble in our boots, Prince. This *will* end peacefully. The Silvans will not raise weapons against us. They may be many things, but they are not *stupid*."

"There was nothing peaceful about how the Silvans left the talks, Barathon." Rinon watched his cousin from the corner of his eyes, observed the soft smile he tried to hide.

"No. But we will not be goaded into a war, Rinon. We can temper their anger. What is important now, perhaps, is that they do not close off the Forest, impede our passage and thus grow strong, rebuild their army and stand against us."

"Speak clearly, Barathon. You are skirting the question with subtleties."

Barathon smirked. "There will be an important decision to take at the Inner Circle, one I believe will solve that problem. We must not allow them their warlord, especially not the one they propose. The vote must be negative, and many of our captains will look to you for guidance."

Rinon held his tongue for a moment so that Barathon would think he was considering it. "I will listen to that proposal and vote accordingly, of course."

"Of course. You are Crown Prince; you have a duty to be objective. I expected no less of you."

Rinon nodded and took a gulp of his brandy. It momentarily distracted him from Barathon's oily presence, his naïve attempts at sounding him out, his failure to understand that Rinon had done exactly that. He would leave him guessing as to where Rinon's loyalties lay, and then, he would report directly to his father and Aradan.

Erthoron, Lorthil, and Sarodén sat together with Amareth at the evening fire. The Silvan camp was slowly being dismantled. They were in no rush to leave. Two months stood before them, two months of doubts and fierce discussion. Erthoron knew he would be hard pressed to keep the Silvan people united.

"We need information," began Erthoron. "We need to know that he is safe, that he knows who he is. We need to know that he will *help* us."

"We don't even know if he's *alive*," said Lorthil. "The fact that we have received nothing from Tar'eastór suggests that communication is being intercepted, hindered at the very least. Lainon would not have left us guessing like this purposefully."

"No, he would not," said Erthoron. "We are alone for now, as we have always been. We had one hope, and that hope is dwindling."

Amareth's eyes caught Sarodén's gaze from across the fire. If Fel'annár *was* dead, then her own isolated life of constant vigilance and censored words would have been for nothing. But something told her he was alive. Her question was whether he would accept this duty his own people laid upon him, which they all but demanded of him. But then, had the Alpines not just taken away his right to represent the Silvan people at court? Had they not just flung the decision regarding the warlord to the Inner Circle so that it could be summarily cast out?

They had placed their hopes in Fel'annár, but of all of those present, Amareth knew Fel'annár the best. He would not be manipulated. He would not accept an imposition unless he saw the benefits, *believed* in them. She couldn't blame them, though, because they could not feel what lay beneath the extraordinary face, could not feel his power, that unnamed element she had always known resided in her son's soul.

Lássira, too, had felt it.

Clinking glass and then silence. Band'orán sipped his wine, and Draugole watched him while Barathon stared at the floor. The fourth elf in the room sat silently, nursing his goblet.

"That was—*unexpected*," said Draugole, breaking the charged silence in the room.

"Yes. And we must now ask ourselves why we had not expected it. Thargodén was broken . . . until the Silvan *bastard* made himself known," droned Band'orán.

Draugole frowned. That note of anger was not characteristic of Band'orán's day-to-day demeanour. He had seen it before, though, and his body tensed. "My lord, the king has vetoed his own council. We can exploit that, show Thargodén unfit for the throne."

"Yes. But what of those councillors? They cost us a great deal in time, money and promises and now, we have two months to stop them from changing their minds. The king will wrench from them an oath of fealty . . . under threat of exile should they break it. We *will* lose some of those votes."

"They may fear Thargodén, but they will fear *you* more, my lord. We can show them the consequences of a *change of heart*."

"But who will they fear more, Draugole? Me or the king we saw today?" The lord's glacial eyes skewered Draugole, and the councillor hesitated to answer for a moment, because somehow, he knew that a wrong word would tip the precarious balance in Band'orán's mind.

"They will fear you more, my lord. We must assure them that those consequences are heftier than any punishment the king may impose upon them."

"Yes," said Band'orán, temporarily placated, and then he turned to his son. "And you, Barathon? Who will they fear more?"

Draugole resisted the urge to close his eyes, and Barathon stood frozen. "You, of course, Father," he murmured, but the young lord's face was petrified and Band'orán saw it. It satisfied him, and it disgusted him.

"My lord," called Draugole. "I will speak with our new councillors immediately, before the king's summons. I feel confident I can make it clear to them the better option—the stronger king."

Band'orán's head snapped to him as if he had been jolted from deep thought. Draugole knew that he had, just as he could feel the almost tangible relief from Barathon at his intervention.

"Very well. Report to me as soon as it is done. The next time this vote is taken, our path will be clear at last."

"Very well, my lord," said Draugole. "Lord Barathon, a word if you will," he said, cocking his head to the door.

Barathon nodded and, with a bow to his father, strode for the door. Once on the other side, the young lord kept his eyes to the ground, unwilling to acknowledge that Draugole had rescued him from his father's wrath, yet again. He was a loyal son, and it was times like these when Draugole rued the day he had been caught in Band'orán's web. It was not too late for Barathon, but it was for him.

He had seen too much, done too much, *changed* too much.

THIRTEEN
LET GO

"To dive blindfolded over the edge of a cliff... close your eyes and fall backwards into the arms of a stranger. It takes faith and no small amount of temerity. Fel'annár knew this, just as he knew he could no longer avoid it. Perhaps there was water beyond that cliff, perhaps the stranger behind him was a brother—or a lover. And so he jumped and he fell, for this was the only way to understand what lay beyond."
The Silvan Chronicles book V. Marhené.

˜

Captain Dagarí and his reconnaissance team had returned, and he stood now before the three commanders in the map room. Dagarí had positioned himself upon the carved cliff face of Queen's Fall, and Gor'sadén followed as the captain slowly circled the area, Pan'assár and Hobin close behind.

"Commander, we have observed multiple signs of old Deviant activity here." He pointed to the entrance of a system of caves on the opposite ridge—Crag's Nest. "While the tracks lead inside, there is nothing to suggest the Deviants left. We ventured inside, as far as we dared, but the truth is that those tunnels are narrow. I cannot understand what they are doing down there in the dark."

Gor'sadén's boots clicked over the carved wood, hands behind his back.

"Any engagement . . . anywhere?"

"None, Sir. The only *unusual* Deviant activity is that there now seems to be none at all, not even at Queen's Fall. However irrational this may seem, it looks as if they have all come together at this one point, inside these caves, and have just—disappeared."

"Is there any indication of their numbers, Captain?" asked Hobin.

"Sir, our best estimate is a thousand at least. There could be more, though, for the tracks were multiple and sometimes three and four-fold. They are difficult to quantify."

"This is highly uncommon, Gor'sadén," began Hobin. "Deviants band together for protection, but I have never seen groups of more than seventy or eighty."

"Sir, there is something else," said Dagarí, his eyes darting from Gor'sadén to Pan'assár and then Hobin. "We found other tracks, not Deviant, and they also lead inside the caves. I have only ever seen such markings in the War Tomes."

"Show me," ordered Gor'sadén.

"Sir, we drew these," he said, pulling parchment from one of the pockets in his tunic and showing it to the commander.

Gor'sadén scowled while Pan'assár peered over his shoulder. Hobin stepped closer and took the parchment from Gor'sadén. He straightened almost imperceptibly. Turning, he stepped off the map and walked to a long table upon which a large, leather-bound tome stood open upon a frame, two candles flickering beside it. The War Tomes were always open, ready to be referenced at any moment the commanders might need information. Hobin flipped through the heavy pages until he found what he was looking for. He tapped the page three times and then turned to his companions.

"They have a Gas Lizard."

"That's not possible. They are extinct," said Pan'assár.

"We *thought* them extinct, Commander. It seems we were wrong," said Gor'sadén.

Gas Lizards had not been sighted for centuries. They were thought to have originated on the shores of the Pelagian Sea. The caves around those bays and inlets were once treacherous. Nobody ventured there save for the poor souls who had been shipwrecked and then left to the mercy of Lizards. The creatures were large, twice the height of an elf, with gills on either side of their heads. Dangerous in themselves, but it was what lay *inside* those gills that struck fear in the hearts of any unlucky enough to stand before the beast—bright orange gas, a toxic haze that rendered any who stood before it unconscious. It was a small mercy for its victims, as it would then rip apart their bodies and feed to its heart's delight.

"This is perplexing," murmured Hobin, walking back onto the map and rounding on Queen's Fall and then Crag's Nest. "A fully-grown Gas Lizard is large, and Captain Dagarí has reported only narrow passes towards the back of these caves. How has it navigated those? Where has it *gone*?"

Hobin's strange blue eyes sparkled in the orange light, and Gor'sadén stared back at the Ari Supreme Commander, unable to answer the question they had all been asking themselves.

"These caves must be deeper and larger than we suspected," began Hobin. "There must be sufficient space, water, and food for them to remain inside. This is abnormal in itself, just as the company of a Gas Lizard and Deviants is unnatural. Why have they not killed each other?"

"Sir, we know *where* they are. Surely that is all we need. We can wait for the thaw and then destroy the entrances. This may be a blessing in disguise. We could kill perhaps thousands of Deviants without engaging them in battle."

"Perhaps, Captain. But I do not think that is the case at all. We cannot ignore these strange movements, this strange alliance of

Deviant and Gas Lizard," said Gor'sadén. "Your thoughts, Commanders?"

"This Gas Lizard could be what Fel'annár's trees were referring to," mused Pan'assár. "The creature has the most colourful patches of skin around those fiery gills, and while it is vile in every other aspect, that collar is quite spectacular, lovely from what I have seen in books."

"Then it may make sense that this thing, the *Nim'uán*, is the Gas Lizard. Still, it does not answer the questions of where the Deviants are, why they are converging, and why a Gas Lizard is with them."

Pan'assár nodded. "Still, we *can* try to seal those entrances, bury them. The thaws are upon us—by the time we arrive at Crag's Nest, the risk of avalanche will be over."

"I don't like this," said Gor'sadén, shaking his head. "There are too many unanswered questions, too many unlikely events. I am calling a General Alert. Dagarí, I want all our captains in the briefing hall tomorrow at the ninth hour. Anyone on leave is to return immediately, effective as of tomorrow. I want Master Healer Arané to join us for the briefing tomorrow morning—if we are to face a Gas Lizard, I would have our warriors understand the risks and how to avoid the fumes. I need our engineers to take us through the details of how to seal those caves, and I want the weapons masters to prepare spears and shields; we may need long-range weapons, heavier than arrows.

"We ride in two days, Commanders, and we will be ready for every possible outcome—even full-out war. Commander Hobin, are you with us?"

"I am with you. Araria will see this done."

Gor'sadén's stern gaze lingered on Hobin, who returned it steadily. Pan'assár passed his friend, eyes moving from him and to the Ari'atór and then leaving, sensing Gor'sadén's need to speak with the commander, thinking perhaps he had an inkling as to why.

Alone in the map room, the doors banged shut and Gor'sadén turned to Hobin.

"Will you tell me now, why you are here?" His voice was slow, soft, not that of a commander.

Hobin raised his head and then turned slowly, towards the table where the War Tomes stood open. Gor'sadén followed.

"Ari'atór do not lie, Gor'sadén. I am here at your behest, although admittedly, there is a second reason."

"You are here for Fel'annár."

Hobin turned, and then nodded. "Yes. He was close to Lainon; I thought to tell him personally, that he has found himself, alive once more in Valley."

Gor'sadén scowled. "So fast? Surely that is not normal."

Hobin stared back at the commander, unwilling to disclose Lainon's status as Ber'ator, because Gor'sadén would guess the rest and it was not for Hobin to tell him. Only Fel'annár could do that, if he saw fit to.

"It is not unheard of, commander. Lieutenant Tensári was shown his return, by the grace of Aria," he murmured and turned to the War Tomes, one finger tracing over the ancient parchment.

"However," continued Gor'sadén, "you met Fel'annár but once, you do not know him at all. Why did you feel the need to tell him personally of Lainon's return? Surely Tensári was the obvious choice. Hobin. I know you do not lie, but neither do you offer me the truth. I have taken Fel'annár as my apprentice in the Kal'hamén'Ar. As such, he is my responsibility. If there is something I should know …"

"Gor'sadén. I cannot tell you what you want to know." He walked towards the commander, head cocked to one side, as if he was reading into his mind. It took a lot to unnerve Gor'sadén, but Hobin did just that, even though he would never allow him to see it. "I understand that you are close to him, that your concern is genuine, and I am thankful that he has you to guide him. He will need you, but as to why; only he can tell you that."

"Then answer this one thing, Hobin. All Ari'atór find themselves, yes. But there is only one reason I can think of, as to why Lainon has returned so fast. It is in your books of lore. I am sure you understand my meaning ..." Gor'sadén's eyes were bright in the half light of the map room but Hobin's shone from the inside and he was reminded for a moment, of Fel'annár.

"Hobin. Was Lainon Ber'anor? Did he have some purpose to fulfil?"

Hobin's head rose but his eyes remained on Gor'sadén. After a while, he answered. "Lainon was special, but he was not Ber'anor."

Gor'sadén nodded slowly. He knew Hobin would speak no more but at least now he had something to go on, something he could ask Fel'annár. What was the significance of Lainon's death, that the Supreme Commander felt he needed to tell Fel'annár personally?

"I will see you later, Gor'sadén," said Hobin, bowing, and then leaving, and the commander watched him. He was a powerful elf, wise and thoughtful, humble yet strangely unfathomable. Indeed he had not lied, but neither had he told Gor'sadén what he wanted to know.

Hobin had some interest in Fel'annár he did not wish to discuss and that did not sit well with him. He would ask his apprentice, as soon as he could find time.

〜

Later that day, Fel'annár sat at the window seat in his rooms. Winter was ending and the thaw was beginning—not quite the end of nature's slumber, not quite the onset of its renewal. This was what Commander Gor'sadén had been waiting for.

A General Alert had been called, and Tar'eastór would ride out in two days to Crag's Nest to deal with the Deviant threat. Fel'annár would ride to battle with Commanders Gor'sadén, Pan'assár, and Hobin. The thought of such an honour sent a thrill down his spine. Tomorrow they would be briefed, and preparations would begin. So little time to address so many issues, he mused.

He needed to speak with Handir, tell him he was with him and then ask him whether he would involve Commander Pan'assár. He had questions for Commander Hobin about his grandfather.

And then he wanted to see Llyniel.

Ever since his talk with Hobin, he had begun to question himself, ask himself incessantly whether he was being selfish, reckless even to pursue her, to act on his growing feelings for her. There were dangerous times ahead for Fel'annár and he would not expose her to them. Would not endanger her because of what he was, of *who* he was. She had her own dreams to fulfil, her own family to mend. Yet still, he would sit before her the next time he asked himself these questions, see for himself whether he could resist the strong tide that was pushing him towards her.

And then he wondered if it was already too late.

Dressing in the simplest clothes that Handir had brought for him, he strapped his weapons onto his back and left his rooms, clapping Galdith and Idernon on the shoulders as he passed. Together, they made for the king's gardens and the Sentinel. If there was one place where he could, perhaps, straighten things in his own mind it was there, where his connection to Aria was strongest. After he had ordered things in his mind, he would find Handir—and then Llyniel.

With a nod at his friends, he climbed the tree and settled upon a branch high in the boughs of the Winter Sentinel.

Lord.

Sentinel. Fel'annár smiled softly. Spring was coming, he could feel it . . . and so could the tree. He couldn't rightly say whose feelings were in his mind right now, and then he wondered if it really even mattered. Funny, he mused, that he had come so far with his skill in so short a time, and although it still unnerved him at times, he was beginning to enjoy it with every successful attempt at harnessing it.

He pulled out his journal and opened it. Lainon stared back at him, an unlikely smile on his face, and then he turned the page and studied the sketch of the lady in the trees, only he had drawn her standing on the forest floor, an acorn in one hand and an emerald in the other, and beside her . . .

"Am I intruding?"

He jumped at the familiar voice that called up to him from far below. Fel'annár turned and looked down, his hair falling over his shoulder as he caught sight of Llyniel. His heart fluttered in his chest, and he smiled.

"It's not my tree. Come up, Silvan."

She climbed and then settled on the same branch and took a moment to observe him. She'd never seen him in civilian clothes, save for when he had been proclaimed a lord, and she could not stop her eyes from travelling down his chin and neck to the open expanse of what she knew was a beautifully sculpted chest. Damn that dark green tunic he wore, she smirked to herself. And then she caught sight of the weapons on his back. Did he ever rest? she wondered. But the thought had spoiled her enjoyment, because she was reminded that he was a warrior, one who would one day ride out to battle and perhaps never return.

Her eyes returned to his, and she cocked her head to one side in thought.

"You are brooding," she murmured.

Fel'annár shook his head. "No. Just thinking."

"About what?" she asked, head tilting to the other side.

"Well. About Handir, about home, and other . . . things."

"Don't you want to talk about it?" she invited.

"I do. But I wouldn't bore you with that. It is a beautiful morning —almost spring."

"It is, but still, I would not be bored, Fel'annár. I am a healer, and being a healer is as much about healing the body as it is about understanding the mind of others. I know you worry about our return. About meeting your father and about what will happen."

He *was* worried about those things, but they were not the ones at the forefront of his mind. "Yes. Still there are more immediate concerns . . . things I don't think you are aware of."

"Then tell me. I won't share them with anyone, not even Handir."

Fel'annár heaved a breath, and she knew he was debating whether or not to speak with her. She couldn't blame him; they were almost strangers, and yet in their short time together, they had spoken of intimate things, things no strangers would ever dream of disclosing. They had almost kissed—both had wanted it, and both had stopped themselves.

"You know that I am a Listener, I suppose."

"Oh yes. I did hear about that, even before Handir told me. You can hear the voice of the trees and that is a fascinating thing, Fel'annár. I would know what it is like; I mean, even now, can you hear *this* tree? What it says? Does it use *language* like ours or is it some form of *mind* speak? What . . ." Her enthusiasm was running away with her, and she stopped when Fel'annár began to snicker.

"I can hear it, yes." He smiled fondly.

"Well? What does it *say*?"

His smile was gone, and in its place was doubt.

"I won't laugh," she assured him.

"No. No, you won't," he murmured, and she briefly wondered at his comment.

"I wonder—what it feels like to understand it," she said, softer now, and Fel'annár reached out, an invitation for her to take his hand. It was large, well-used and calloused, but it was warm and she wondered if, later, she would be able to let go.

He leaned forward, as if ordering his thoughts, and she thought she saw liquid swirl in his irises. She frowned.

"It calls me *lord*, sings to me of the coming of spring. The earth beneath its roots is warming, twigs are tightening, the pressure inside is growing. It is warmer, and the leaves stir, still inside their protective skins. It is not yet time . . ."

All mirth was gone, wiped from her face as she listened to the far-away words that Fel'annár muttered, almost as if he were seeing what he described. She didn't laugh, just as Fel'annár had said. His eyes fascinated her, and at times she thought she could see stars, tiny pricks of golden light.

"How can you know all that?" she asked, eyes drawn to Fel'annár's other hand and his fingers as they stroked over the rough bark beneath. She'd seen him do this before, she realised.

"Because I can *feel* it, Llyniel."

She frowned, even as her hands held tighter onto his, as if she braced herself because there was something in his voice that was not him, a tone she had never heard. Her blood tingled in her veins.

"There are snowdrops and buttercups in the Downlands, and in the Forests, wild daffodils peek through the ground in search of light. There is a musky aroma of wood anemone—it reminds me of home." He smiled and cocked his head backwards, as if he could smell them here in the towering heights of Tar'eastór. A flash of blue light flitted across his eyes, and Llyniel blinked in confusion. She had indeed heard that he was a Listener, but what was this strange play of light in his eyes? This deep stroke of something unknown, impassioned words spoken by a warrior. She was an experienced healer, but she had never seen the likes. Had never felt this way.

Her eyes were suddenly attracted by movement over Fel'annár's sleeve. The hand that stroked the branch was partially covered by a thin green shoot that protruded from a spindly branch. She could not stop the sudden intake of breath as she flinched backwards.

"Don't be frightened, Llyniel."

She could hardly breathe, couldn't even move her own body. She wanted to speak, but her tongue was numb, eyes fixed on the shoot. Fel'annár brushed it softly with his other hand and it danced away, back into the twig, and Fel'annár leaned forwards, his eyes a little too bright.

"Don't be frightened, Llyniel. It is playful, 'tis all," he said as he took both of her hands in his.

She was frightened because she could not explain what she had just seen, just as she could not fathom why his words had touched her so deeply. He painted a picture of Silvan wonder at the coming of renewal and she saw it all, smelled the flowers and felt the warming sun on her own skin, or was that *his* touch?

She leaned forward, watching the spectacle of light. One hand came up to touch the side of his face, tentative, searching. She had told herself her attraction to Fel'annár was physical, and it *was*. But just this simple touch of her skin against his told her there was more, just as she had always known but never acknowledged. She was falling into a place of warmth and comfort, to an end she could not foresee. Her own ambitions, her own fears that Fel'annár would be killed in battle . . . they were fading away, and her eyes lowered to his mouth. She leaned forwards until she could feel his lips upon hers. She pressed harder, inviting, and he accepted. She felt his strong, calloused hand against the side of her throat, fingertips ghosting over her skin. They felt too cold—or perhaps it was her flesh that was too warm.

Llyniel had only ever fallen twice. Once when she was a young child, she had fallen from a tree. It had hurt, and now, she was falling into an unknown place of wonder and heartache. She was plummeting forwards, upwards, but she did not hold her hands out to brace the fall. Handir had asked her to step away from Fel'annár, told her only pain would come from loving this warrior. She had not heeded him—because she had told herself she *didn't* love him. But then Fel'annár's hand moved to the back of her head and his body leaned forwards, strong, powerful muscles wrapping around her, pulling her closer. She wanted to fall into him, and she opened her mouth as he deepened their kiss. Her heart seemed to stretch and something jolted in her chest: surely *she* would not be the one to end it. Her body felt too light, her heart too heavy, but all she wanted was to melt into him, transcend his skin and see what lay beneath.

She didn't love him, did she?

She leaned back, watching Fel'annár's eyes looking back at her in wonder, like an astounded child contemplating the first snows. Slowly, his lips stretched wide until his teeth sat on display.

"What have you done to me, Healer," he murmured, and Llyniel could not help the hand that came up to cup his cheek—and then the traitorous thumb as it brushed over his lips.

"I don't know," she whispered truthfully, shaking her head. She had broken their kiss, and she suddenly wished that she hadn't.

"We will ride out soon," said Fel'annár, playing with her hands as he spoke. "Tomorrow, or perhaps the following day. After that there will surely be little time left to enjoy the spring, for Prince Handir will call for our return." He sat a little straighter, and his eyebrows rose. "Shall we go into the forests, Llyniel? Shall we be Silvan just for today?"

She arched a brow, wondering what part of being *Silvan* he was referring to *this* time, and he laughed. "The Company won't leave me alone, Healer. Besides, it's high time you got to know my brothers properly. Let's just enjoy this day together, all of us. We may not have another chance for a while. There will be time enough for us—to talk of what the future may hold."

The joy and anticipation on his face was addictive, and she nodded, feeling like a child once more when her own mother announced they would visit the Deep Forest. It hadn't happened often, but when it had, she had stored up the best memories of her life. There would be time enough to talk, just as Fel'annár had said, but he had shown her the coming of spring, and she was Silvan. Her smile widened.

They were soon scurrying down the bark, and Idernon and Galdith turned. The Wise Warrior arched a brow, and Galdith grinned like a ten-year-old imp.

"*What?*" asked Fel'annár in mock anger.

"Nothing," said Galdith, his voice a little too high-pitched, and Llyniel snorted in mirth.

"We are spending the day in the forests. I don't suppose you'll want to come?" asked Fel'annár with a lop-sided smile.

"Of course we do, you *fool*," said Idernon, and Llyniel smirked.

"Galdith, find the rest of The Company. We meet at the gates in thirty minutes. And take this to my rooms, will you?" he asked, handing his friend his leather-bound journal.

Galdith took it and was away at a brisk trot.

Llyniel had seen The Company together on many occasions by now, had seen their steadfast protection of Fel'annár—indeed he called them his brothers. Theirs was a special bond she wanted to understand, because by understanding them, she would, perhaps, learn what it was that made this elf so special . . . learn what it was that her heart had recognised but that her mind had yet to grasp.

∼

Lord Councillor Sulén turned from the hearth in his personal suite of rooms, hands clasped at the wrists, expression trained on his only son, who stood rigid, blue eyes trained on the plush carpet beneath his supple, gold-trimmed boots.

"I have spent countless coins on your education, sat you at my knee as I worked, taught you everything I know, and yet everything you do is a *failure*. Tell me, Silor. What have I done to deserve such a weakling son?"

"Father, Macurian is a legend at what he does—there are no others better suited for the job."

"Then what is going *wrong*, Silor? Are you not explaining yourself sufficiently clearly? Is that why this legendary *Shadow* fails time and again?"

"He is good at his job, Father. He has been studying the Silvan, watching his movements, speaking to others. The bastard's powers with the trees are stronger than we thought—Macurian knows this now. I have doubled his sum, and he will strike today. He and his men wait only for an opportunity to arise."

"A simple arrow will not do it, Silor, we know that much. What is his plan this time?"

"He does not say. All I know is that he has many at his service and that he promises me it will be done today."

"Lord Band'orán is relying on us. The Forest Summit will soon end, if it has not already done so; this is the last stretch of our lord's plan, and you know what this means. Our departure will be imminent, before even Prince Handir returns, but that unnatural abomination must be put down before then. We cannot let our lord down, Silor. Do whatever you must, and do it now."

"I won't fail you, Father, I swear."

"See that you don't," said Sulén bluntly and then left, closing the door quietly behind him.

~

Macurian was no lover boy, but he recognised the attraction between the two Silvans.

He watched from afar, careful not to touch the trees. He'd seen the Silvan's powers of perception, had heard the rumours, and he was taking no more chances. Sulén was a generous patron, and Macurian would oblige him. He'd promised the lord's son he would complete his task today, and the perfect opportunity may just have arisen.

He followed the three Silvans, watching as they met Prince Sontúr and the rest of what he now knew was The Company at the city gates. They laughed and joked as they prepared to head out of the citadel, and Macurian knew that now was the perfect moment to put his plan into action. Turning, he raised his hand and executed a flurry of hand signals. Pulling the cloak over his head, he walked to the stables.

He had done as he'd said. He had watched and waited, and soon enough, he had found The Silvan's weakness. The healer would serve his purposes well, for if his plan failed, *she* would be his solution. All that was left to do now, this very day, was use that weakness against the boy and claim his recompense—and his lost pride.

FOURTEEN
SILVAN INTERLUDE

"Fel'annár was a lord of Ea Uaré, but so too was he a lord to the trees and an apprentice of the Kal'hamén'Ar. Soon he would ride with the greatest warriors of their time, back to the mountain and perhaps to battle. But Fel'annár was young and he was Silvan, and the gentle breeze of love danced playfully, just beyond the limits of his consciousness."
The Silvan Chronicles, Book V. Marhené.

∼

The entire Company stood talking animatedly at the open gates of the citadel as they waited for Fel'annár, Idernon and the healer to arrive. The Bard Warrior stood with his lyre slung over one shoulder while Ramien carried a heavy sack on his back, filled to brimming with delights Sontúr had procured from the kitchens. It smelled of all things wholesome, and the Silvan giant was hard-pressed to stop himself from ripping into the cloth and gorging himself on the hot pies he knew were nestled in there somewhere.

Fel'annár could see them talking, excited at the day of rest and relaxation they had hastily organised. As he approached them, Llyniel at his side, his hand itched to take hers, but that would have been a statement he had yet to decide he should make. He wanted to though. Their kiss lingered in his mind, like balmy haze in the summer, yet more than that it had changed him. Something had nudged him, moved him in a way he had yet to understand. Still, she had broken off their kiss—she still had reservations.

The Company's playful banter fell away, and they turned to stare at Fel'annár and Llyniel as they approached. All they knew about her was that she was a healer and that she was Silvan . . . that and the fact that it had been *her* to come up with an alternative antidote to the canimbula poisoning. Still, they had only exchanged cursory niceties with her, all of them except for Sontúr and Galadan, who had seen her before at Thargodén's court. It was Galadan who broke the awkward silence.

"Lady Llyniel," he nodded.

"Lieutenant Galadan," she smiled.

"Llyniel: Lake Girl, Lady of the Lake, Lake-like . . ." began Carodel.

"Would you like me to get you a *thesaurus*, Carodel?" asked Idernon.

"I don't need one. Words spring to my mind like mushrooms in winter."

Ramien guffawed, and Sontúr grimaced at the simile, but Llyniel laughed scandalously. They hadn't expected it, had never seen the mischievous, Silvan side of the healer she had just shown them. Galdith grinned while Ramien peered at Llyniel and then at Fel'annár.

"I assume you are all aware of this one's *dubious reputation* back in Sen Garay?" she asked rhetorically, poking her finger at Carodel with a good-natured smile. It could have been misconstrued, but the smile on her face and the twinkle in her eyes told them all it was good-natured; indeed Idernon and Ramien snorted.

"We have been told," said Ramien, and the Bard Warrior shrugged his shoulders—there was no point in denying the obvious.

"I live life to the fullest, pluck fruit when it is ripe lest it shrivel and fall," he said defensively, but there was a false innocence about him and the others jeered as they checked their weapons and started towards the gates. Carodel expounded on the virtues of his many Silvan lovers while the others only half-listened, furtive eyes darting from Llyniel to Fel'annár. She could feel their gazes on her, and Fel'annár smiled at her grace—for remaining silent and allowing them their curiosity about what she meant to him.

And what *did* she mean to him? He had told himself he would be a distraction to her on her road to the status of master healer, and then he had tried to convince himself that she would remain in Tar'eastór while he was bound to return to the Forest. He had stepped away from her kiss days ago because he had felt himself losing control.

But then she had kissed him in the tree...

They strolled down the main path that led from the citadel gates and downwards. It was barren here save for the many rocks and boulders that were strewn about the place. He turned to Sontúr. "These boulders seem to have fallen," he mused. "They are all over the descent, even inside the forest down there."

"Caves used to litter the sides of the plateau. Gor'sadén ordered them sealed off many years ago. Too many hiding places for thieves and smugglers, he said."

Fel'annár nodded, his eyes drifting to a lone tree which stood a little further down. How it had grown here with no others to keep it company, Fel'annár couldn't say, and a thought occurred to him. "Did the forest once extend to up here? Was it felled for some purpose?"

Sontúr's brows rose to his hairline, and he shrugged. "I don't know. I'll ask my father."

Fel'annár reached out and stroked the bark of the lonely tree as they passed, felt its noble heart, its brave existence.

It took them half an hour to finally stand upon the onset of the forest that surrounded the citadel. It was still somewhat sparse here, although further down, Fel'annár knew it was thicker, shadier, more reminiscent of the forests of the flatlands of Ea Uaré.

There were scattered groups of elves, some sitting in shady spots, talking and eating, while others laughed and played games. Two elves stood leaning against a silver birch. They smiled indulgently and then pulled each other close, lips coming together for a succulent kiss, and Fel'annár's eyes searched for Llyniel. She was chatting and waving her arms in the air while Carodel smirked and Galdith chuckled.

She almost seemed to have fallen into them, melded naturally without the slightest bit of awkwardness save for the wary glances that Idernon cast her way. Fel'annár would speak to his brother, understand where his reservations came from. Sontúr had not taken kindly to her the day they had met, after his investment as a lord, but Fel'annár knew that was because he had thought she was defending Handir's careless deeds. But then Fel'annár had been poisoned and they had worked together to save him. Since then, a special bond seemed to have formed between the two healers, even though Sontúr was not at all fond of Handir, her self-proclaimed brother.

They soon found themselves in the more secluded areas. The forest was thicker here, but still there were rocks and boulders scattered everywhere. They made for excellent places to stop and eat, and so, choosing a delightful spot in the sun, Ramien unravelled the contents of his cloth sack.

"Now the merit is not mine," he began. "Sontúr got this for us and then used me as his mule."

"A logical move," said Idernon, and Galadan rolled his eyes to the heavens as he laid back against the boulder behind him, watching as the pastries, bread, cheeses, and wine were unravelled.

"Oh, *cake!*" shouted Sontúr, although the others might say that he squeaked, for the prince loved his cakes and buns, *sticky* buns, and he reached out to poke his finger at the spongy, toasted crust.

"Don't be a *pig*, Sontúr," said Carodel, crossing his legs and retrieving his lyre from where it sat on his back. He strummed and then twisted the pegs until he was satisfied with the tuning.

Llyniel smiled at them and then turned to Fel'annár, who was helping Ramien to organise their feast. She watched as his heavy Ari locks danced around his shoulders, the tips reaching almost to the ground. She watched his hands as they arranged the food and then watched his mouth as he spoke and laughed. He was as beautiful as the day, she mused. But it wouldn't last—he was a warrior and Tar'eastór was on General Alert. He would soon ride out, perhaps to battle, and she would be left to wonder if he would ever return. The thought squeezed her gut, and for a moment she could not eat. There was a choice before her, one she needed to make soon, because somehow, she knew that after today, that choice would be taken away from her, that it would be too late to turn away.

Ramien and the rest had no such hefty thoughts to spoil their appetite, and before long, little else but crumbs were left, some of which decorated their tunics, but they didn't care at all, and they chatted while Carodel strummed his soft melodies. There was no mention of their upcoming patrol, of the Deviants they said were massing at Crag's Nest. Today was for enjoying, and Llyniel would do no less. She fell into their brotherhood, observed them, came to understand that the one, unifying factor amongst them—was Fel'annár.

There was a mystery about him, she thought. Something they all seemed to understand but did not give voice to. She had had a taste of that something earlier, when she had seen the swirling lights in his eyes.

"Who's that?" asked Ramien, watching as a group of mounted soldiers approached. Sontúr slowly stood, observing as they dismounted and strode forwards. He nodded at them as they bowed.

"What has happened?" he asked. They all stood now, thinking that the moment to ride out was finally upon them and these soldiers had been sent to inform their prince. Carodel slung his lyre over his shoulder, arranging it beside his weapons harness.

Fel'annár stood rigid, a discordant note in his mind, but these were fellow warriors, weren't they? Something was wrong, though, and his eyes fell to their hands.

Too tense.

The leader of the group stepped forward.

"Galadan?" murmured Fel'annár, hand straying to the dagger at his belt without turning to look at the lieutenant.

But there was no time to answer. The leader was crouching low, one arm stretched out as if he had thrown something, but they had not seen anything move. Fel'annár, though, was sailing through the air, landing on two feet even as three small blades thunked into a tree trunk behind him.

"*Ambush!*" cried Galadan, and The Company drew their swords.

Fel'annár drew both his blades and faced his first opponent, parried his attack and then slashed one blade along the back of his knee. He fell with a scream, but three more were running at him. Fel'annár sprinted towards them, and then jumped, and with both feet before him, he projected all his energy into a flying kick that sent all three swordsmen crashing to the ground. He turned, searching frantically for Llyniel only to realise that the *soldiers* had split into two groups. One had been keeping them busy while the other was circling Llyniel. Tree branch in hand, she brandished it before her in sweeping arcs, eyes wide. She was scared, but she was not going meekly. Fel'annár wanted to run to her, but the trees screamed a warning and he leaned backwards, spine stretching almost painfully as the tip of a blade hummed past his cheek.

He parried a skilful attack on his right flank and then whirled away and sent his long sword through one soldier's leg while the other attacked from the left. Not fast enough, and Fel'annár parried, sending his opponent's sword flying into the air. In three strides he was before the wide-eyed soldier and then smashed the hilt of his short sword into his temple.

Turning to Llyniel once more, his heart sank, for she had obviously been subdued, her hands tied behind her back. She'd been wrestled into the saddle before a burly, armoured guard, yet still she struggled, legs thrashing about the horse's shoulder, but not enough to keep the soldier from wheeling his horse around and galloping away.

"Fel'annár!" she screamed, but all he could do was watch as the rider disappeared into the trees. The other group of soldiers had disengaged and vaulted into their own saddles, leaving their fallen companions and following after their leader at a thundering gallop, and Fel'annár was loping over the ground, deaf to Galadan's calls for him to come back. The Company sprinted after him, barely able to keep him within their sight.

Fel'annár could no longer see the horses, but he didn't need to—the trees guided him, but there was a warning in their voice. He leapt over roots and logs, skirted bushes and fallen branches, but then a thick branch dropped into his path and he dug his heels into the loamy earth and skidded to a halt, just inside the tree line.

Before him was an open glade, and as he caught his breath his eyes focussed on three figures in the distance, standing out in the open. His eyes scanned the trees off to the left, searching for the remaining group. He couldn't see them, but he knew where they were, crouched behind a low ridge of stone, close to the tree line. He calculated his own distance from them, their distance from the tree line and then the distance from the three who stood in the open. A crashing sound behind him alerted him to the arrival of The Company. He turned and gestured for them to stop.

"It's a trap," he whispered. "Two are holding Llyniel out in the open where we can see them, using her as bait to lure me into the clearing and then shoot me down. There are six archers behind that ridge there." He pointed.

Galadan peered over Fel'annár's shoulder, the rest behind him.

"I need to get over there," said Fel'annár.

"And what are you going to do? Step into range and allow them to shoot you down? And even if you did somehow manage to avoid their arrows, what are you going to do when you find yourself alone before two foes with Llyniel tied and vulnerable?" asked Idernon.

"If we stand here and do nothing, they will *kill* her."

"You take that for granted?" asked Galadan.

"You saw them, Galadan. They are warriors, better than most. They are hired hands, sent to kill *me*. Llyniel was their fall-back plan. If we ignore her plight it is nothing to them to kill her. And still they will come for *me*."

"And if you go, they will kill you. It is not your responsibility, Fel'annár," said Galadan. "Let *us* handle it."

"It is *my* responsibility," hissed Fel'annár, eyes blazing, and Galadan swayed backwards. "She is in danger because of *me*, because of who I *am*."

"So you will just barge in there and get her, is that your plan?" asked Idernon, angry now.

Fel'annár closed his eyes. He needed to calm his rising anger. It was not characteristic of him to allow his emotions to interfere with his duty as a warrior, but they had tied her, held her before them, seeing her as nothing more than prize bait. He was outraged, *enraged*. He breathed deeply, but his eyes remained stubbornly on Llyniel.

"No. That is not my plan. All of you skirt around, behind the archers that lie in wait behind those boulders. We have an advantage —we know where they are, and they have foolishly turned their backs on the forest. You can neutralise them as I stand before the ones that hold Llyniel. We must time this to perfection, but we *can* do this."

"And even should we kill those snipers before they shoot you, what will you do when you stand alone before two skilled swordsmen holding Llyniel at knifepoint?"

"I won't be alone, Idernon."

"No. But trees don't fight, Fel'annár."

"No. But they can help, Brother."

"You are asking me to have faith, and you know my answer to that."

"I do. But I also know you know we have no other choice."

Idernon stared back at Fel'annár, but he didn't answer.

"You must be silent, and you must do this simultaneously. They will be distracted, trying to shoot me down. You must take advantage of that."

Galadan, too, was scowling, but Fel'annár was right. The only alternative was to walk away, and none of them were capable of doing such a thing.

"This plan is held together by ribbons, Fel'annár. If one of us fails to kill a sniper, the rest will realise what is happening, and we will be engaged in battle while you confront *them*. Then what?" asked Sontúr.

"I won't fail. I am not alone."

"Yes, I can see one spindly tree—a *formidable* warrior," said the prince with a clenched jaw.

But Fel'annár ignored Sontúr's familiar sarcasm and placed a hand on Idernon and Galadan's shoulders. The others gathered close. "You stalk them from the trees, and I wait until you are in position. Once I leave my cover, do not be distracted. Wait for Llyniel to be set free. Once she is out of their range and I am within their sights, they will be shooting, and you must take them unawares lest they turn their bows on you. Neutralise them and find me but stay behind me. Questions?"

"Are you *mad*?" asked Ramien.

Fel'annár's nostrils flared. "No."

The Company watched the rocky expanse before them, six of them imagining where their prey lay in wait while Fel'annár watched the two that held Llyniel, one hand resting on the birch at his side.

Save her.

"Are you ready, Brothers?"

"We will have *words* when this day is done," said Sontúr.

Fel'annár nodded. There was no more time for discussion. The Company left, silent and stealthy, and Fel'annár waited for a sign that they were ready. Minutes passed and still he could not see them, could not sense them.

Llyniel's captors had been waiting for him to arrive, but time had passed and they had surely guessed he waited inside the woods. Any moment now, they would make their demands, and Llyniel prayed Fel'annár would not simply walk up to them and give himself up. He was young—perhaps impetuous, what did *she* know. Handir had hinted at it, and then his feelings for her, however deep they ran, might lead him to place himself in danger. These mercenaries were out to kill him, but Fel'annár needed to *live* so that he could help Handir, so that he could help her Silvan kin.

But he wouldn't walk away. Somehow she knew that. All she could do was pray he had a plan that did not include senseless sacrifice.

A soft brush in his mind and Fel'annár's eyes strained harder. Minute movement over to his left told him at least one of The Company was in position. He needed to wait, just a little longer. He had to be sure.

"Come out, Silvan. Your lady friend is anxious. It is *you* that we want, not her. Show yourself and we'll release her!"

"If I show myself, you'll kill me!"

"If you don't, we will kill *her*!"

"You give me no guarantee of her safety in any case. Send her to me. I will meet her half-way."

There was a moment of hesitancy that Fel'annár used to think, just as he knew his enemy would be calculating distances. The half-way mark was where he knew he would become a target, and Llyniel *would* be caught in the cross-fire, but to confront his two opponents while one held her at knifepoint was equally risky— if not more so.

"All right. Come out!"

One more glance at the tree line behind the snipers and a sharp whisper in his mind told Fel'annár they were ready. He took a deep breath and then another . . . and then he stepped out into the sun.

Nothing happened, as he knew it wouldn't. He was out of range for now, but with every step he took, he walked further and further into the trap they had set for him. Llyniel's bonds were cut, and she was pushed forward, almost stumbled to the ground but broke her fall with her hand. Straightening, she walked slowly towards him. He could see her stiff gait, her fear, her bravery.

Llyniel kept her eyes on Fel'annár, saw his wary confidence, his overly-bright eyes trained on the enemy behind her.

They were closer now, and Fel'annár allowed his eyes to fall on hers for just a moment. There was something in them, something that threatened to shake his concentration.

Closer still so that she could hear him, just as through the trees, Fel'annár could hear the creak of bows being drawn, trained on him, ready to fire no sooner he stepped into range. He wouldn't let them hit her.

"When you pass me, drop to the ground. Lie flat, face down, and don't look. When the arrows stop, run to the tree line."

"Fel'annár . . . don't. Not for *me* . . ."

"*Trust* me."

And she did. With all her heart she trusted him, but her tongue was tied. She should have told him when she had the chance—should never have pulled away from their kiss.

They drew together and his hand brushed hers. Her fingers entwined with his for a brief second, even though the sight of him struck fear in her heart. Was this the same elf she had kissed in the tree? Her gaze briefly crossed with his strangely glowing eyes, his hair that seemed to move too slowly for the lunging strides he took. This was no longer Fel'annár, The Silvan. This was a force of *nature*.

"Down."

Fel'annár's muscles bunched and he surged forwards, powerful legs propelling him onto his hands, and he flipped forwards, feeling the rush of air just past his cheek as an arrow flew close by. A whispered warning, a streak of purple as if it traced the direction he should follow. Another arrow grazed the sole of his boot just as he landed, running with the momentum. Another thwack he knew he should not be able to hear, and he cartwheeled and then side-twisted, an arrow glancing over his thigh, ripping the material. A green wisp, like a gauzy green banner, and he followed it, summersaulting forwards as yet more arrows rained down on him, but they missed and he was sprinting towards two open-mouthed assassins who held their swords out before them—as if they stood alone before a charging host of Deviants.

The arrows had stopped and Fel'annár could only pray to Aria that Llyniel had scurried away, that she had not been shot and that the trees would protect her.

He jumped, one last time, both legs out before him, booted feet smashing into the elf that had been holding Llyniel. He crashed to the ground like falling timber, unmoving, and Fel'annár whirled around to face the second assailant, both blades before him.

He lunged forwards, a probing move to test his opponent's skill. The blades were parried, and this enemy countered. Fast enough, skilled enough, but Fel'annár easily blocked the move and stepped forwards again. He attacked, and his foe was hard-pressed to defend himself. He stepped backwards and then again. A crafty lunge to one side and then the other, meant to confuse, but Fel'annár had foreseen it, countered it, and then, with a flick of his wrist, his opponent's sword flew from his hands and Fel'annár kicked out.

The elf stumbled backwards, drawing a small dagger from his belt as he backed further towards the spindly birch tree. Using the trunk as leverage, he lunged forwards—and then seemed to stop mid-air, eyes bulging wide as he looked down to the source of his problem. A tree root had wrapped itself around his boot and would not let go. He shrieked and threw himself upon the ground, desperately trying to free himself.

Fel'annár kicked the dagger from his hand and then turned with just enough time to duck and keep his head on his shoulders. Manoeuvring under the blade, he cursed his inattention, for the other soldier had not been knocked out. He had only fallen and then cunningly played dead. With one, perfectly executed frontal attack, Fel'annár disarmed him . . . just as a cloud of stones and dirt flew into his face. He was momentarily blinded, and it was all his attacker needed to move in. Before Fel'annár knew what was happening, he felt a body behind his own and his throat begin to tighten, rope burning into his flesh, squeezing. He was choking, and he instinctively dropped his blades, grappling with the rope that was throttling him. He felt himself tugged sideways, turned about, and then his attacker was shouting at his companion.

"Shoot him, *shoot* him!"

Fel'annár found himself face-to-face with a loaded bow even as he was being strangled from behind. The kneeling elf drew—a sure target, impossible to miss, and then an arrow came sailing through the air, hitting him in the temple. The arrow pointing at Fel'annár flew wide, and the body of his would-be shooter crumpled to the ground, tree root still coiled around his boot. There was another thud, and Fel'annár's attacker momentarily loosened his hold on the rope around his neck. Fel'annár pulled hard and then drove his elbow into his opponent's stomach. Kicking backwards, he sent the elf flying away until he fell, quickly rolling onto all fours, an arrow sticking out of his shoulder. Fel'annár was free and he crashed to his knees, struggling for breath, just as his attacker made to escape; but Carodel and Idernon were running towards him, bows trained on Macurian, who raised his hands in surrender, even as his eyes darted around, searching for a means to escape. It was Ramien who fisted the neck of his cloak and shook him like a dusty blanket until he stilled.

The rest of The Company and Llyniel soon joined them, breath short and eyes wide.

"You foolish *idiot!* I swear I could beat you to a *pulp* for what you just did," roared Galadan in wrath, while Galdith pulled Fel'annár to his feet and then hugged him so tight it hurt, and when he let go, Fel'annár sucked in a much-needed breath of air. The others laughed, but Idernon was shaking his head, eyes a little too bright.

"That was a mighty shot," rasped Fel'annár as he clapped Idernon on the shoulder before nodding at Carodel. "Two mighty shots."

Carodel blushed. "I was aiming for the back of his neck..."

Idernon's eyes rose to the heavens but Fel'annár snickered and then coughed. "Good enough," he rasped.

"All the better for you, *lackwit*," muttered the Wise Warrior, his fear slowly abating.

Llyniel stepped forward, and Galdith moved to one side for her. Fel'annár's eyes roved over her face, her body. She seemed mostly unhurt save for a bruise on her cheek and her messy hair. She wanted to speak, but she wasn't capable of it. Too many questions, too many things she wanted to say, but her body moved of its own accord and she walked into his arms, relishing the strength and warmth of his chest—and the heart that miraculously still beat below, against all the odds.

This was what Handir had warned her of, and she had foolishly discarded it, telling herself it was pleasure she sought . . . but Handir had always seen through her, seen what she herself had not wanted to admit.

"Let's get this one back for questioning," said Idernon, gesturing to a still struggling Macurian. "I am sure he has a fascinating story to tell."

Fel'annár held Llyniel at arm's length with a sigh of relief, before turning and nodding at Idernon and then bending to pick up his discarded blades. His eyes strayed to the dead attacker and then to the root that was still wrapped around his boot. He smirked, bent down, and brushed his fingers over it, watching as it loosened and then disappeared into the earth.

Control. He smiled.

Standing, he turned to Sontúr, who was striding towards the elf Fel'annár somehow knew had been stalking him all this time.

"So *you* are the renegade Shadow . . ." said Sontúr, voice low and dangerous.

"It is not personal, my prince."

"It is to *me!*"

Macurian stared back at the furious prince, but he said no more—and then he startled when Llyniel gasped and then staggered backwards. All conversation stopped, and they turned to Fel'annár. A soft breeze lifted his hair behind him, and his eyes seemed overly bright—until they flared and Llyniel stepped backwards again, and then again, bumping into Galadan's chest while Macurian struggled in Ramien's grip, eyes wide in terror.

"Don't be afraid, lass," said Galadan quietly.

Everything was shaking. The ground beneath his feet was vibrating, something was surging from the depths, but he knew the others couldn't feel it, just as they couldn't hear the trumpet calls of the Sentinels as they echoed over the land. From far below and the Downlands to the tallest Sentinel upon the High Plains. They bellowed their warnings across the land—and to Fel'annár. His soul lurched, and deep dread weighed in his heart.

"Company." His voice sounded weak, but he could hardly hear himself over the din he knew the others could not hear.

"Fel'annár?" called Ramien.

"The Nim'uán. I didn't understand."

"Nim'uán?" asked Llyniel, but Fel'annár was lost in some vision. He saw a tall, powerful being, sitting atop what he knew was a Gas Lizard, and in the creature's keen, intelligent eyes was the light of curiosity. He was beautiful to behold in his fine armour, but then he smiled and the beauty was gone, and in its wake were the jowls of a predator. He seemed paler then, almost dead. This *was* a monster—and yet he *was* an elf.

This was the Nim'uán, not *beautiful* monster but *elven* Monster.

"Fel'annár?" insisted Idernon in growing anxiety.

"The trees call Deviants *monsters*. I did not understand why they would say '*beautiful* monster.' *Beautiful* is their word for *elf*."

Galdith hissed, and Sontúr strode forward. "What is happening? Is there movement? We should inform Gor'sadén and . . ."

"Too late. They are *here*," he murmured.

"Who are here?" asked Macurian, still struggling before Ramien, his relentless fist bunching his collar.

"The Nim'uán and his army. He rides atop a Gas Lizard as his Deviant army comes through tunnels deep in the mountain."

"What in hell is a *Nim'uán?*" asked the assassin in rising panic. He couldn't see this army Fel'annár spoke of, yet still, the others did not question the veracity of his claims, for they stood wide-eyed and pale, and for the first time he wondered just who it was that Silor had ordered him to kill. For the first time he questioned *himself.*

The ground lurched, and rocks and boulders began to fall around them. Ramien jumped sideways, losing his grip on Macurian. A large rock caught the Shadow in the side of the head, and he fell away, rolling with the boulders until he was lost to their sight.

The rock slide was the first evidence that something was happening, and Fel'annár turned urgent eyes to them.

"Listen to me, Sontúr. They are too close to the citadel. Your army will not be able to march out in time before they are breeching the walls. We can't allow that to happen."

Sontúr visibly paled, eyes wide. "What are you saying? Breech the walls? You speak of an *army!*"

"They come by the *thousands*, Sontúr."

He had not understood the magnitude of Fel'annár's claims. None of them had.

"But what is it you think you can do? Charge them all by yourself? What will that gain us? We all run back now, raise the alarm, and then we march out with the army."

"*Listen* to me, Sontúr," hissed Fel'annár, taking his friend by the shoulders, his grip bruising. "By the time Gor'sadén organises our ranks, they will be upon the gates. He needs time, time we do not have. You are a lieutenant—you know I am right. He needs to gather our warriors, archers, captains, and lieutenants. He needs to stock the ramparts with arrows, prepare the defences on the high walls. Warriors need their armour, shields, and pikes. The Halls need to prepare. If they are not ready when the Deviants charge, the war will be fought *inside* your city. I must make sure that does not happen.

That Gor'sadén can meet them *outside* the wall, away from the citizens. *Heed* me, Prince."

Sontúr released a shaky breath and half-turned away from Fel'annár.

"I can't leave you here to die..."

"You *must*. You are their prince. They will heed you."

The prince closed his eyes, and when he opened them once more, he looked at Fel'annár and The Company, eyes pleading with them to gainsay Fel'annár's words.

But they didn't.

"What are you going to do, Fel'annár?" he asked.

"I must try to use this gift I have. It may not work, and yes, I *will* die. But there is a chance that it *will* work, enough at least to give Gor'sadén the time he will need to march out with the army."

"And if your gift is not powerful enough and you die, I must live with the knowledge that you died for *nothing*."

"No. You will live with the knowledge that I died for *love*. That is the warrior's pledge."

Sontúr's eyes filled with tears and he stepped back, but his eyes stubbornly refused to leave those of his friend, this brother he had found just months ago. He knew this was the last time he would look upon that extraordinary face, one he would never forget. Fel'annár's eyes were glowing bright, but there was no mistaking the farewell in them. Sontúr wanted to scream, he wanted to stay, but his duty was to his people, to his city, and his king. Drawing his sword, he saluted with the pommel of his blade, fighting back the tears. "I will march out and avenge you, *all* of you. This is my promise." With a nod and a watery smile, he turned to Llyniel.

"Come, Healer. There is much to do," he said. She returned his gaze of water and steel and then turned to Fel'annár. Panic threatened to loosen her tongue, but she stilled it. She did not know what Fel'annár planned, and there was no time for explanations. Still, his eyes shone unnaturally, his gift with the trees bared to them all. But what good would that do him before a host of thousands of Deviants, as he claimed were coming?

She was angry, told herself she was confused, but she wasn't. She was denying her heart like a fool, and her legs ran to him and embraced him hard, as if he were dangling from the edge of a cliff—as if she thought perhaps that she could save him from inevitable death. He pushed her back by the shoulders and then bent his head and kissed her so hard she grabbed hold of his sleeves lest she crash to her knees. She felt him then, his passion and his love—she felt his soul as it blazed its last, felt it sinking into her, joining with her own, simple Silvan heart, as if he gave a little of himself to her . . . for her to keep safe when he was gone. It flared: something new, something that would last precious little, but still she would have lived for millennia for this one moment of realisation.

There was no doubt left in her mind, because the choice had been taken away from her. He *was* a warrior, he *would* surely die and she—she had always *loved* him.

He pulled away and then pushed her toward Sontúr.

"Go," he said with difficulty and then watched as they both sprinted away. Llyniel felt a part of him inside her and she knew that a part of her had gone with him, for it pulled tight as she ran away from him, so tight that it hurt.

"I can do this alone, Brothers," said Fel'annár, turning back to The Company.

"You can, but you won't. Whether this works or not, I will stay to find out. You will not do this alone," said Idernon.

"It is suicide," said Ramien even as he stepped beside him.

"I know," said Fel'annár with a smile.

"I will either die with you or live to write the greatest panegyric of all times," said Carodel with a crooked smile, and Galdith nodded, resolute.

"You stood by my people at Sen'uár when they were cut down. I will do no less for you."

"Dear gods," murmured Galadan, eyes fixed on the thicker part of forest in the distance below them. It was darkening before their eyes, as if ink had bled from the stars and was slowly staining the forest floor. It was then that they truly began to understand.

"What *is* that?" asked Carodel, even though he thought he knew.

"Deviants, Carodel. An army of them, under the command of the Nim'uán, for a purpose we have yet to understand."

"Holy Aria," exclaimed Galdith quietly. "How did we miss this?"

But Fel'annár did not answer. Instead, he began to climb the path back towards the citadel, to higher ground, and as they navigated the thinning wood, they shouted warnings to the already retreating civilians who ran upwards, towards the gates, their belongings left behind in their panic to retreat, to reach safety behind the mighty gates of Tar'eastór.

They were back at the lonely tree they had passed on their way down. Beyond it, a fifteen-minute walk through open, rocky terrain led to the citadel, but Fel'annár turned his eyes back to the slopes and the gradually thickening forest beyond.

"They must not pass this point," he said, knowing The Company stood behind him, watching the slowly spreading stain of Deviants. "There is still time for you to get back, Brothers."

"We'll all die," said Galadan, drawing his blades.

"Yes. Soon, The Company will be reunited," whispered Fel'annár. He had come this far. He had learned of the family he never thought to have, had excelled as a warrior, found friendship and love, even though he had still to confess it. All this would end today, and he would make it a mighty ending. He would make Gor'sadén proud, make Lainon proud—and then join his brothers in Valley.

The darkness was moving faster now, no longer liquid but reminiscent of a swarm of insects spreading over the horizon.

The mighty blast of the trumpets of Tar'eastór sounded behind them, shaking the ground beneath their feet, and then a deep rumble and a resounding boom as the gates to the citadel closed. Sontúr and Llyniel had given the warning, and even now, Gor'sadén would be organising the army, readying them to march out. Sontúr would have told him what came, of the Nim'uán and his Gas Lizard, and then he would tell the commander what Fel'annár would try to do. Gor'sadén would think it madness, and perhaps it *was*. But madness was the only chance they had to keep the battle away from the people, away from their very homes and their children.

∽

"*Move!!* Comon, to the gates, *Dagarí!* Spears, shields, *Polán!* Archers on the battlements. *Barhai*, I want every warrior in armour here in ten minutes."

"*Sir!*"

Gor'sadén's voice yelled out orders hard and fast. He was in control—and he was frantic. Fel'annár was out there, standing before the enemy, waiting for him to organise his warriors and march out to meet them . . . away from the city gates. He was a whirlwind, desperate but controlled—*precise*. Pan'assár had sprinted to the barracks and even now was organising the captains and lieutenants while Commander Hobin helped with the provisions, as if he were a base warrior and not the Supreme Ari Commander.

Just minutes ago, Sontúr had come with Fel'annár's outlandish claims on his lips—thousands of Deviants would march upon them and the Nim'uán was an elven Deviant who had a Gas Lizard and was commanding them. Gor'sadén had not doubted his words, however incredible they had sounded, and that had given him precious time to initiate the city's defence plan. But an army cannot be organised in minutes. Deviants *would* walk in their city this day, he did not doubt it. The tower guard had sighted the enemy spreading over the horizon; they were already inside the forests below them. It would take them less than an hour to reach the gates, and only The Company stood between them.

They would not be ready in time to march out. Gor'sadén knew this, as surely as he knew Fel'annár would die trying.

Captains yelled their frantic orders, their powerful, urgent voices carrying over the courtyard, across the battlements, and still the trumpets called. Citizens ran into the palace or towards the town proper and their homes, children clutched to their breasts. Windows needed sealing, doors barricading. They needed provisions and weapons to defend themselves. All they knew was that the Deviants were coming and that they should defend themselves and their families.

In a mansion, not far from the fortress, Sulén dismissed his staff and ushered his son into a trap door under the floor of his study, sealing it from the inside, where they would be safe to hide . . . or to flee to the other side, into the lower caves and away from the city. This one, at least, had not been destroyed; years ago, Sulén had made sure it had not been detected by the city engineers, keeping it for just such a need.

In the courtyard and just before the now closed gates, the lines of warriors began to form, still buckling their armour and checking their weapons. Recruits ran down the ranks with stacks of arrows while others ran onto the battlements and filled the holders for the archers who would soon stand upon the walls.

Husbands and wives kissed desperately with hurried warnings about how to defend their houses—what to do should a Deviant come knocking. There were desperate assurances that they would see each other again, but they had never thought to live this day, the day the Motherland was attacked by Deviants.

As the trumpets continued to blast out their message, Commanders Gor'sadén, Pan'assár, and Hobin met at the front of the still forming lines of warriors. They peered through the small door in the gates. In the distance they could see the seven warriors who stood defiant, dressed in nothing but their simple civilian garb. But then the land sloped downwards and all they could see beyond were the very tops of the first line of trees. The watch upon the ramparts, though, had confirmed that the forest had turned black, and every minute they called out the enemy's distance from the walls as they drew closer and closer.

Fel'annár and The Company could still make it back to the citadel. But they didn't.

"What do they think they can *do*?" murmured Pan'assár, shaking his head.

"He means to give us time. You know him, Pan. You know he is unsure of this gift he has. This is a gamble—and he knows it. But even if by some miracle he should give us some more time, this is a *suicide* plan." Gor'sadén could not stop the wave of grief that rolled over him. Pan'assár's strong hand squeezed his shoulder.

"I cannot say what he is thinking. But whatever it is, he will have a victorious end, Gorsa. He dies a legend," said Pan'assár, and Hobin nodded slowly, blue eyes shining brighter than was normal. Zendár's grandson would fall before he could even begin to carry out Aria's will.

But Gor'sadén could not speak. All he could do was watch as the grandson of Or'Talán, his own chosen son, waited for death to take him.

~

"The brave warriors of Tar'eastór need us, and we will not fail them!" said Master Arané. "Stay focussed. Emotion has no place in war. Stay calm, be efficient, compassionate. Make this city and our king proud," he finished, his head healers before him, the juniors and apprentices behind.

"*Arún! Mestahé! Ruaní! Nernan! Llyniel!* With me here in the Halls. All apprentices and juniors to the barracks. Organise yourselves as you have been taught. Mestahé—triage. I want only the critical cases in here. The rest to the barracks. If any can be given over to the care of our citizens, you will allow it. We will need the space."

The healers strode away, dark robes billowing around them even as the convalescing warriors already in the Halls rose and left for the barracks. Some limped, others swayed unsteadily on their feet, but they had heard the healer's words. Even those abed were leaving with the help of their companions, and still, the mighty trumpets of Tar'eastór rattled the ground, shaking the ancient stone around them, drowning out the sounds of rising panic.

"Llyniel."

"Arané."

"Is it true? Is young Fel'annár out there, standing before those demons?"

Llyniel turned to the master healer, and when she spoke, it was soft and defeated.

"Yes. And I pray I will see that face again in life."

She turned away, blind to Arané's lingering stare only to come face-to-face with Sontúr. He was not wearing the robes of a healer.

"You are marching out," she said.

"I belong with The Company, Llyniel. Serve well, Healer," he said curtly, but there was a softness in his eyes that warred with steely determination. A true warrior prince and Llyniel felt proud to serve this land, this *Alpine* land.

"Stay safe, Prince. Bring them all home if you can," she said, stepping forward and placing a reverent kiss on his brow. Sontúr startled and then smiled softly. He bowed, and then he was gone.

~

Inside the palace, Prince Handir was being fitted with armour for the first time in his life. They had given him a sword, which hung useless by his side. It felt wrong, but it was for his protection, they said. He was then led to the ramparts by two guards who left no sooner they had met with King Vorn'asté and Lord Damiel, both in their own armour and weapons.

"King Vorn'asté. What news?"

"Join us, Prince," said the king as he looked out over the walls and to the small group of warriors who stood before the slowly spreading stain of Deviants. Handir stepped up to the king's side and looked down: six warriors and in their midst, the silver locks of Fel'annár.

He froze.

Damiel half turned his head to Handir. "Your brother is *brave*, Prince."

Brother. Your *brother*. He couldn't understand why Fel'annár simply stood there, and he turned questioning eyes to Damiel.

"We do not know what he intends, Prince. All we know for sure is that *they* will not make it."

"We can ride out and bring them back."

"The army is not ready," explained Damiel. "Look down, Handir. See our commanders, our captains as they still organise our ranks? There are warriors still arriving, shields and pikes to be distributed, arrows to be hoisted up onto the walls, fires to be lit. You will learn these things in time."

Handir saw the pity in his tutor's eyes, and he rebelled against it. He looked back down and allowed his eyes to register what his mentor had said. The troops stood waiting, armour glinting in the afternoon sun, but they were not yet ready to face the enemy, just as Damiel had said.

Movement from the corner of his eye and Sontúr was striding past him, clad a warrior, buckles and blades glinting in the afternoon sun, his grey hair braided intricately into patterns he had never seen. He was reminded of Rinon, but where Sontúr was grey, black, and silver, Rinon was blond, green, and blue.

He watched as the prince knelt before his father, his king. Vorn'asté bid him stand and placed both hands upon his son's armoured shoulders. He could not hear the words the king spoke, but he knew they would be of love, honour, and duty. A sense of sadness rolled over him, for even though there had never been friendship between them, Handir respected the prince for what he did now. He may die this day, and he realised that he cared, just as he wondered if his own father would ever look upon *him* the way Vorn'asté did at Sontúr—with pride in his eyes.

Handir was jolted back to the present by a distant spectacle that approached from the skies beyond the walls. A chorus of squawks and screeches exploded above them, and all heads turned skywards, watching in awe and dread as every bird in the Median Mountains seemed to pass overhead, fleeing the onslaught of imminent battle, leaving only the carrion birds behind.

The world had gone mad, thought Handir. This could not happen. Fel'annár could not die now. Handir didn't understand why he simply stood there when he could flee to safety. Fel'annár was destined to return to the Forest and help bring the Silvan people back to their king—he could not die before justice was returned to the Forest people—he could not die without meeting his father, his sister. Handir realised, then, that he would never be able to call Fel'annár his brother.

Anger, as strong as he had ever felt it, stiffened his body and hardened his features until they were ridges of pure, unyielding ice. *Hatred* for the Deviants that would kill Fel'annár. *Hatred* for Or'Talán and how it had all begun. *Hatred* for Band'orán and what he had made of his forest home.

Hatred for *himself* and his own blind selfishness.

He had doubted Fel'annár's heart, his devotion to his people. He had withheld his father's message, not bothered to tell him of his unknown family in the Forest, and he had blamed Fel'annár for his mother's departure. And then he had dissuaded Llyniel from loving him, even though he had seen the depth of feelings in her eyes, seen the spark of love in Fel'annár's own gaze. He would have *cleaved them apart*, just as Or'Talán had done with Thargodén, his own son.

So many crimes. So many reasons to beg forgiveness.

I'm sorry, Brother.

I am so very sorry.

FIFTEEN
PRAYER FROM THE MAELSTROM

"Aria, lady of light and air, earth and water,
Lend us strength at the time of our sacrifice.
With our end we serve you unto death and beyond.
For duty and honour—for justice and for love."
Book of Initiates, Chapter III. Hulan.

∽

The trumpets of Tar'eastór sounded once more, and Fel'annár took one last, deep breath. The enemy was thick in the forest. It was time. The trees had named him *lord*, and he would call upon them now, in Tar'eastór's hour of direst need.

Holes were breaking open in the rocky ground, and from them, Deviants began to ooze, spreading like a black velvet cloak billowing in the breeze. It seemed to Fel'annár that the rock had turned liquid, running not *down* the slopes as it should but *up*, through the forests and beyond, to the six warriors who barred their path towards the citadel. They could no longer see the trees for the Deviants, and everywhere they looked, the ground was splitting open.

A mighty crash sounded further down the slopes, and then another, like lightening striking a tree. The explosions came faster and then another, closer by, and they watched as debris shot into the air.

"Don't be afraid, Brothers."

"We're not. Death is our destiny as warriors. We face it at your side," said Galadan.

"Don't be afraid of the *trees*," he whispered, turning his head to them. His eyes changed from green to blue to purple, until they were all three and the light flared so that his face could no longer be seen.

"Aria..." whispered Galdith.

A pungent smell of onion and rotting vegetation prickled Fel'annár's nose, setting his eyes to watering. He wondered if the others could smell it or whether it was the trees that told him of it.

It didn't matter anymore, because the clacking of rusty armour and the wails of thousands of Deviants could finally be heard. They were climbing up the slopes, and Fel'annár could feel the trees recoil in disgust, their outrage for the unholy violation of the earth in which they lived.

But they could not *move*.

Fel'annár sensed their frustration. They wanted to *fight*, he realised, but they had not been born to move. Why, then, were they screaming at him? Why were they beckoning to him to *touch* them?

A lone wail resounded over the rest, and The Company stood taller. The Deviant commander was surely just beyond their sight, urging on his troops, but then a shrill scream joined the macabre choir, sending a stab of pure fear down their spines. The sound was unfamiliar, but it reminded Fel'annár of the Deviant that had screamed in his face the day they had been ambushed on the way to Tar'eastór. He knew what it was, though. It was the shriek of the Gas Lizard—the trees had shown him.

Fel'annár thought that he finally understood what it was he had to do. He would unleash the power without restraint, even though he did not know the limits of it, even though it terrified him to think of it.

That pulsating source of power he had felt the other day as it struggled to break past his control . . . he had quashed it then, but now, he opened his mind, projected as Gor'sadén had taught him, and then he held out a hand to touch the tree beside him. But just before his fingertips reached the bark, he stopped and turned to Idernon and Ramien, to Galdith and Galadan, to Carodel. He smiled at each of them and then turned back to the oncoming tide of rotting humans.

His hand touched the bark.

A light breeze, a silent farewell to the world, but then a deep, pulsing hum grew around them, the droning of some arcane magic and the breeze became a wind which whipped around their braids and buckles and Fel'annár's Heliaré. He could feel the rest of his hair rise around his head, but it did not whip around his face—rather, it floated around him, just as it had around Aria in his dream.

And then the lights came, first green then blue and purple, playful wisps chasing each other, darting around The Company like dancing sprites, and Galadan murmured a prayer from the maelstrom that was engulfing them.

Galdith, Galadan, Carodel, and Ramien lifted their swords in salute while Idernon's hand tightened around his pommel and Fel'annár raised his free hand outwards.

The wind grew and expanded, travelling towards the Deviant-filled forest like a devil bent on destruction, and the boughs thrashed and twisted. The Company stood before it, amidst it, feet firmly entrenched, yet still their bodies swayed with the force of it. Deviants shrieked and moaned, and the noise became deafening. But when they looked closer, through narrowed eyes, they realised that it was not only the wind that moved the trees; it was the trees themselves that began to move their branches, thick trunks swaying from side to side. Although still deeply rooted, even their thickest branches bent alarmingly, coming down upon the Deviants in a creaking whoosh or sometimes swiping them into the air by the scores.

And still The Company stood firm, praying that the trees would not stop their dance of death, counting every second that was afforded them, time for Gor'sadén to ready his army, protect his people.

Through Fel'annár, Aria had conjured an army of wood and leaves for as long as they could withstand—to whatever end.

∼

"The trees boughs are *moving!*" called the tower guard, unable to hide the rising panic in his voice. The wave of disbelief that followed was almost tangible, and Gor'sadén damned the steep incline which hampered his own vision. All he could see through the small hatch in the gates were the backs of the warriors and a haze of light just over where the forest would be. It was enclosing the trees, like a shimmering dome of translucent gossamer, and a strange rhythmic rumble was shaking the ground beneath his boots. He had heard that sound before, softer.

"The trees have turned on the Deviants! They are *killing* them!"

"He has conjured the trees," said Gor'sadén to the commanders and captain beside him, all four peering out of the small door in the gates.

"That's impossible," whispered Captain Comon at his side.

"It is *not*," said Hobin, but he stopped himself from explaining, and he sought Gor'sadén's eyes, seeking confirmation that the commander had understood. This was the perfect time to march out —while the enemy was trapped in the woods. There was no guarantee that Fel'annár could keep up with what he was doing, and they were as ready as they were ever going to be.

Whirling around to face the troop, Gor'sadén bellowed.

"*Steady!*"

There was a loud clap of metal as the troops saluted and hoisted aloft their shields and spears, yet still, warriors were joining the ranks, more archers running up the stairways as the recruits scurried away to join the rear guard. The commander waited for them to take up their places.

"*Ready!*" A practised voice of command.

Weapons masters distributed their last batches of spears and then sprinted to their own units, still pulling on their helms.

"For Tar'eastór! For the *Motherland!*"

"*Aye!*" thundered the troops, all black and silver.

"*Open the gates!*" shouted Captain Comon from the other flank.

"Commanders from abroad, you bring honour to Tar'eastór."

"Wherever you fight," said Pan'assár, stepping forward, and Hobin nodded. Standing before the troops, the three commanders stood defiant before the emerging slopes and the haze of coloured lights that awaited. The wind howled and the Deviants screamed and wailed, and the earth rumbled and hummed. When they charged, it would be blindly—until the path bent downwards and they would face their enemy.

Gor'sadén reached backwards and curled his fingers slowly around both blades. Pulling, he brought them over his shoulder and then held them out before him.

With one final gaze, Gor'sadén and Pan'assár said goodbye to each other, not for the first time, and then turned to the fore.

∼

The Company watched as the boughs thrashed to and fro, so violently they wondered how their trunks did not snap. Live wood raked the ground, tufts of leaves and branches were thrown into the air . . . and other things they could not make out but well guess at. Coloured lights flashed over the forest, and the deep droning was accompanied by the trumpeting of trees that continued to decimate the ranks of Deviants.

Fel'annár watched, unable to reconcile the actions of the trees with what he was doing. All it had taken was one simple touch and a mind open to the natural world: no filters. No fear. The question was—how long would it last? His hand gripped the tree bark tighter, eyes burning and scalp prickling so hard it hurt, but he dared not let go.

The odds were being evened, but more than this, they were gaining the precious time they needed for the army to meet the enemy here, on the slopes and not upon the very walls. But he wondered if it would be enough for Tar'eastór. It wouldn't be for him or The Company; they were all now past the point of safe return.

And then something changed. He wavered where he stood, holding on to the tree like a drowning man clutching to an offered hand. Deviant shrieks mixed with the same high-pitched scream they had all heard previously. The Gas Lizard was coming closer, and Fel'annár resisted the urge to cover his ears. The scream inside his head was deafening, and in his mind he saw the creature as it swayed left and right, imperious in its colourful beauty and its terror, and upon its back rode what must surely be the Nim'uán.

He saw the elven beast step down from his mount and then gesture to the trees. Turning, the dark commander chose his vantage point upon a boulder, eyes scanning the Deviants as they were slaughtered by the trees. He drew his sword and raised it high in a gesture the Lizard seemed to understand, and it scurried to the trees to do its master's bidding.

Boughs descended, sweeping down violently upon this new adversary, but the beast caught them in its razor-sharp teeth and pulled and then ripped, head thrashing from side to side as it snagged entire branches as if they were nothing but petals on a daisy.

Fel'annár closed his eyes, as if by doing so he could block out the images, but he couldn't. The thick tail smashed into trunks with such force that some were snapped in half while others cracked and groaned. Fel'annár could feel it—crashing timber, cracking wood, and leaking sap. The voice of the forest changed from wrath and destruction to pain and desperation. They called for aid, but Fel'annár could not give it.

Where before no Deviants had managed to escape the thick of the trees, now, they began to emerge from the slowly dying forest. Scimitars raised high, they ran towards the six warriors that stood beyond the treeline.

"Shall we make our final charge, Brothers?" asked Fel'annár softly.

"*Aye!*" they shouted. Fel'annár held his sword up, knowing it would be for the last time. It had been a short life, but he had burned brightly and there was comfort in that thought. When he ran, he would run to his mother, into the arms of Aria herself, and when he uttered his last word, it would be for *love*.

"*Charge!*"

His battle cry was long and furious, and no sooner had it finished than a whispering rumble of thunder took over and the sky behind them grew dark, as if a giant had passed before the sun. But it wasn't until they heard the heavy thunk of arrows hitting rotten flesh that they realised the archers of Tar'eastór had moved into range. The first line of Deviants fell, but more came, jumping over the dead as they wailed their own battle cries, and The Company continued to run. Another volley slammed into the oncoming Deviants, and they too fell, but another wave was soon approaching. The sky darkened once more, and this time they *did* see it, for the swarm of arrows came from the Deviants. The Company braced themselves as they ran, but the piercing agony they had expected never came—in its place, the thud of arrowheads hitting wood. From the corner of his eyes, Fel'annár saw the gleaming armour of the Tar'eastór warriors as they sailed past them, a mighty leap, their shields held out before them, protecting them from the oncoming arrows. Pride surged through Fel'annár, so powerful he joined them as they roared, like wild bears after their prey, sprinting down the slopes and into the trees that twisted and thrashed and trumpeted as they skewered the Deviants that passed too close.

Gor'sadén's army had arrived. Fel'annár had not failed them.

With a mighty clash and the clatter of pikes and armour, they came together, and for a moment, they could hardly move—a sea of elves and rotting Deviants, of rusted scimitars and gleaming silver.

Slowly, each warrior made for themselves some space, and soon, the real fighting began. Pangs of metal, grunts of pain and effort, shrieks of horror as limbs were severed, and Fel'annár struggled for space, trying and failing to swing his long sword around, but only his short sword was practical, that and his fists and elbows, knees and feet. It was brutal and vicious hand-to-hand and with no armour to protect his body.

As more Deviants fell around him, Fel'annár could finally use both his blades in tandem without endangering the lives of his fellow warriors. A towering Mountain Deviant was hurtling towards him, purple tongue hanging out of its slack mouth, yellow eyes wide and deranged. He ducked under the wild swipe of a scimitar and stabbed it in the back. Whirling around, he plunged into his next foe, his mind on one thing only: the whereabouts of The Company. He cut and sliced, whirled and parried, dodged and kicked, but still they came by the twos and threes. He tried to find his brothers as he fought, knowing that logically they must be close by, but it was too close quarters. All he could see were Deviants.

Another terrible screech and Fel'annár struggled not to lose focus. The Gas Lizard was approaching the side lines, where the trees still fought bravely. He had already seen the beast in his mind, but in the flesh, it stole his breath. It was twice his height, much bigger than he had imagined, and he realised that he had seen it from the perspective of the trees. Its reptilian jowls were full of razor-sharp teeth designed for ripping and shredding. Around its neck was a beautifully coloured ruff of red, purple, and vibrant greens, and just behind, on either flank, were three gaping gills. Inside, a luminescent haze coiled, and the stench of it was eye-watering. Fel'annár wanted to gag.

The enemy shrieks and wails were drowned out by the screams of the wood inside Fel'annár's head. The Deviants were turning on the trees, empowered by the killing frenzy of the Lizard. They were weakening under the relentless onslaught, ripped apart, dismembered and hacked into pieces, and Fel'annár cried in frustration and angry grief as he fought the front lines, furious at his inability to help them. They were dying and his anger—turned into *wrath*.

A Deviant barrelled into him from the side. He fell, immediately sweeping out with his legs and bringing his opponent crashing to the bloody ground. He plunged into it with both blades and stood with a grimace.

Whirling his blades around, he came face-to-face with Ramien, who smiled back at him, blood covering his front teeth, but he was alive with the fight.

"Brother."

He sounded weak, tired, but he turned and blocked another attack and Fel'annár watched, red hair dancing in the corner of his eyes. Idernon's auburn head bobbed into sight, stained though it was by blood. And then he saw Galadan, Galdith, and Carodel.

Relief flooded him. They were still alive, still on their feet, and Fel'annár was fuelled into action once more.

The Lizard shrieked, throwing its head back and showing its enemies its three rows of jagged teeth as it scurried from the ruin of trees. He heard a rush of air, and the putrid smell was bitter in his mouth. Elves and Deviants fell senseless to the ground, and Fel'annár and The Company rolled away.

"*Fire!*" came a yell from behind him, a captain and his archers, and Deviants fell not far before him, but the arrows clattered off the thick hide of the Lizard.

A flash of gold and Gor'sadén was beside him, formidable in his sweeping fury, his purple sash sailing around him as he fought—and on his other side, Pan'assár, just as imposing as his brother in arms, his own sash around his waist, where it should always have been. The Ari commander, Hobin, was there, too, their gazes briefly crossing. This was the front line, and the mightiest warriors of Tar'eastór and Araria had come. Fel'annár stood amongst legends, and as he fought, he could feel the rhythm growing in his mind, the beat of four, and he fell into it, projected without reserve, just as Gor'sadén had taught him, and all around him, tentacles of green and blue and purple snaked here and there. Gor'sadén and Pan'assár danced with it, with *him*, and for a while, at least, they were unbeatable, unstoppable.

More arrows sailed overhead, not seven paces away from their position, and an answering volley whispered over them. Pan'assár faltered but soon rid himself of the arrow in his calf and continued his forward inertia. Slowly, they were gaining ground towards where they knew they needed to be—before the Gas Lizard.

The beast had turned its attention away from the dying trees and to the front lines of elves. The Deviants made way for it and then watched as it hissed a spray of orange fumes at the elven warriors. They dropped like falling timber, and their fellow warriors dragged them away as best they could. The Lizard turned, ready to spit again, but the troop ducked and rolled, the fumes setting their eyes to watering, the enemy blurring before them.

Fel'annár blinked to clear the fog and spared a glance at the imposing figure of the Nim'uán, who stood upon his boulder, looking out over the battle, watching proudly as his Gas Lizard took down warrior after warrior. Then he tipped his head to one side. Fel'annár followed the Nim'uán's line of sight to Pan'assár, who was striding towards the Lizard, slightly to one side of the creature's jowls. Fel'annár didn't think the commander had ever fought a Gas Lizard—surely none of them had, but still, other warriors came to stand tall beside him, long pikes stretched out before them. They jabbed at the Lizard, dancing backwards as it snapped and bit off the metal tips and then lashed out with its thick tail, sending three warriors sailing through the air. It turned back to the shining warrior, and Pan'assár moved with it. With a mighty yell he attacked, but his blade glanced off a spiny horn along its flank. He spun out of the way of the giant tail, feeling a rush of air as it passed inches over his head, and he lashed out again, managing to land a cut to its side. The blow had been hard, and yet the beast did not falter. Pan'assár, though, was undeterred, and once more he danced sideways and drove his sword into the beast's leg. It screamed, and with its other leg, it swiped out and hit the commander with a thud, sending him flying backwards. Even before he landed, a hissed breath and a rush of toxic fumes streamed from the Lizard's mouth.

Pan'assár twisted as he fell and then rolled out of the way of the vaporous trail.

"*Pan'assár!!*" Gor'sadén was running forwards, ready to take his brother's place before the monster, but Pan'assár was already on his feet, shaking his head and rolling his shoulders, eyes narrowing into slits of pure steel as he strode forward and then brushed Gor'sadén's shoulder, a brotherly gesture of thanks.

He ran and then jumped into the air, one boot landing on the beast's upper leg. Propelling himself upwards, he clung to the spines on its back with one hand and hoisted himself into the ornate chair which sat close to the base of its thick neck. It screamed and writhed, and Pan'assár held on, hair flying left and then right, knees squeezing hard. Letting go with one hand, Pan'assár held his sword aloft and then plunged downwards with all his strength, his second hand joining the first and pushing harder with a roar of sheer effort. Metal pierced skin and muscle and then sunk through bone and when his blade could go no further, he twisted. The beast lost control of its body and fell forwards, sending Pan'assár flying over its head.

Landing with a dull thud, Pan'assár only had time to stand and turn, finding himself directly in front of the gaping jowls. Grabbing the pommel of his short sword with both hands, he sent a prayer to Aria and then plunged his blade into the Lizard's bloody mouth. A rush of yellow mist hit him in the face, as he knew it would. He stood rigid, his breath seizing in his chest as his eyes rolled back in his head —and he fell backwards, face purple.

"*No!!!*" screamed Gor'sadén, even as the other elven warriors roared in victory as the beast ceased its mad thrashing and stilled. Dead.

Grabbing Pan'assár's harness in one hand, Gor'sadén dragged him away from the Lizard, as far as he could from the fighting, where Pan'assár would at least have a chance of survival. Turning back to fight, his eyes latched onto the Deviant commander, who stood staring at the inert body of his Gas Lizard. The stony, somewhat unconcerned air about the Nim'uán had gone—and in its place was seething ire.

Gor'sadén advanced on him, cutting down a Deviant that charged at him with ease and then another that thought to surprise him. Gor'sadén all but flung it to one side, and still, he advanced on the dark-haired commander. This *was* an elf, realised the commander, tall and imperious in black velvet and shining silver armour. It was not the uniform of the warriors of Tar'eastór, but he was not wrong. Fel'annár had been right: this *was* an elf—only he was too large, too pale.

The Nim'uán ripped his angry eyes from his dead Lizard and turned his gaze on Gor'sadén, first on the insignia on his breast plate and then up to his face.

"Commander," it called, voice smooth and melodious. Gor'sadén couldn't have heard the voice, for he was still too far away, but he could read its lips, imagine the sound of it. His confusion must have shown, and the odd elf smiled. But Gor'sadén detected a note of strangeness in it, and he repressed a shudder of horror as the elf opened his mouth and all its pale beauty leeched away in the wake of razor-sharp teeth, incisors curving downwards past his bottom lip. It reminded Gor'sadén of a snake's jowls. He was beautiful, but he *was* a monster. The trees had named him well.

The largest sword Gor'sadén had ever seen sat at his waist, only the pommel visible, but it twinkled and glittered with the promise of pain and death, jewel-encrusted hilt a mass of exquisitely-carved swirls and symbols. Here was a vicious enemy, a powerful foe that would not be easily vanquished.

Gor'sadén steeled himself for the fight of his life.

The creature stepped gracefully from his vantage point and walked towards the one he had chosen to fight. Only now did Gor'sadén realise just how large this creature was. It stood two heads taller than himself, limbs thick with worked muscle. Closer now and the Nim'uán spoke.

"You have questions, yes. I can see your confusion."

"Why are you doing this. You are *elven*, in some way . . ."

"I am elven, yes. And I am *Deviant*," it hissed, leaning forward a little. Still too far away to engage but his hands flexed, not quite touching the monumental sword.

The commander's eyes were wide, horrified at the dark beauty and the sickening cruelty, struggling to reconcile one with the other. He shook his head in denial.

"It *is* possible, Commander. And now—I have come to take your *city*."

"Why?"

"Everyone needs a home, *Gor'ssssadén*," it whispered.

All his shock and denial fell away, and he stood tall and proud. "You can't *have* it." He lifted his sword and readied himself.

"We shall see." It smiled and then finally wrapped its strong hand around the jewels and the carvings. Pulling, the blade hissed, reminiscent of the beast's snake-like voice, and then he struck his stance, liquid blue eyes glittering in anticipation. No fear, no apprehension at all.

Gor'sadén had known he would be a formidable foe, and he braced himself as the creature roared and then swung his sword around and towards his neck. Gor'sadén met it with his own blade, shock waves reverberating up his arm and through his entire body. They pushed away and the duel began, even as the fighting continued around them.

Fel'annár and The Company saw the commander as he faced the strange being, but a desperate call from Galdith and they turned away. Galadan staggered to one side, but he did not fall, and The Company rallied around him. Fel'annár swivelled around and slashed over the back of a Deviant that was battling with Carodel. A warning shout and he shot around . . . only to see a shocked Deviant, sword raised to kill him, frozen in the air. It slumped to the ground, and a warrior prince emerged, his swords dripping. Sontúr's eyes shone with pride, and Fel'annár had just enough time to bow his head in thanks, heart swelling at the presence of his royal friend. He had come back for them, just as he had promised.

Then they were assailed on all sides, and the Deviants, in spite of the loss of their Lizard, seemed driven by their commander's fight with Gor'sadén, as if they were *proud*, mused Fel'annár. He was knocked to the ground, and all he could do was roll and then flip upwards. He almost slammed into a Deviant, narrowly avoiding a slashing dagger before slicing through its forearm and then kicking into its grotesque face.

"*Valour!*" he yelled to The Company, but others around them heard and they pushed on, pushed forwards, themselves empowered by the mighty spectacle of their commander general fighting as they had never seen before, a true master of the Kal'hamén'Ar.

Black and grey cloaks fanned around and around as they fought. Gor'sadén was speed and precision but what the Nim'uán lacked in skill, it made up for with the sheer power of its strokes. The sound of their blades clashing together was shocking and grating, and Gor'sadén called upon every ounce of his strength, summoned the energy inside himself and projected it into his blades. The Nim'uán stepped backwards, and Gor'sadén bore down on him again and again, searching for the slightest opening in its defences, but his arms were burning and his heart frantically trying to keep up with the vicious strokes of power from the Nim'uán. It was a fierce fight, a long fight, and the commander endured, and with the last of his reserves he attacked with all that he had. But he was tired, movements slower than they had been. All it took was a minute gap between his blade and his leg. The Nim'uán saw it, lunged forwards and then fell to one side, thrusting its sword straight through Gor'sadén's thigh.

A strangled cry of pain and his leg buckled, sending him to his knees in utter agony, blood pouring down his leg. He braced himself for a killing blow, but it did not come, and through pain-clouded eyes he looked down at the heavy sword that pierced him from front to back. Raising his head, he watched as the Nim'uán rose from the ground, breathless but jubilant.

He had to get up.

He flexed his muscles but his leg would not respond, blood flowing freely. He stuck his own long sword into the ground beside him and pushed down until his good leg could gather beneath him and he rose, a mass of quivering limbs, teeth gritted in pain, glittering eyes defiant.

He would not face death on his knees.

The Nim'uán bent down and picked up a heavy, fallen log as if it were nothing but balsa wood, and then walked towards Gor'sadén, a smile on its face, eyes fixed on the commander's sword that shook under his weight.

The twisted smile widened and then he tossed the log at Gor'sadén. Letting go of his sword, he only had time to bring his arms over his face. He fell backwards, the log landing on his chest and pinning him to the floor while the rest of the Nim'uán's sword buried itself to the hilt in his leg. His scream was strangled, almost whispered, for all the air had left his lungs, but his eyes searched desperately for his short sword, for anything to protect himself, but the beast was closing on him.

Bending down, the Nim'uán reached out, grasped the pommel of his sword, and pulled hard.

Gor'sadén screamed, and Fel'annár turned in horror. All other sounds muted, and he was immersed, under water on dry land. A chorus of distant voices approached until it was a climactic herald in his ears and everything moved too slowly. He turned, as if he were stuck in mud, hair too light, eyes turning to the elven Deviant and then his fallen mentor. Sounds welled from the depth of his soul, of panic and pain, of grief and fury, collecting at the back of his throat and then choking him. He filled his lungs and screamed from the heart.

"Nooooooo!!!"

The Nim'uán turned his head and looked right at him, even as he raised his bloody sword over his head. It meant to butcher the commander, make of him a macabre standard for the Deviants to behold. Was this what Pan'assár had felt—forced to watch the brother of his heart ripped and hacked to pieces before his very eyes?

Streaks of light jetted this way and that across Fel'annár's vision, even as his feet began to move, and he was hurtling over the ground. The world tilted as he jumped and twisted, the whizz of an arrow streaking through the air, just past his head. Running, he was running, and yet he could not feel the thump of his feet over the ground, could not hear his own frantic breaths. His swords were in his hands, and with a roar he threw the shorter blade at the Nim'uán. The beast turned, startled, and tried to swipe at the sword that was hurling towards him.

Reaching up to touch the cut on its once flawless cheek, the beast hissed and turned to his new opponent, who had come to stand in front of his fallen mentor in nothing but plain civilian clothing, an equally plain sword in his hand. He was not deceived, though. He had seen the magic this one had unleashed, had chosen him from afar, just as he had done with Gor'sadén.

Fel'annár heard Idernon's voice from far, far away, heard Ramien roaring something closer by and then a string of almost unintelligible curses from Sontúr. But his mind was tunnelling, focussing on the Nim'uán, and whatever the others were doing, they faded away, the silent world broken only by the now steady beat of his heart and the streaking lights around him. Fel'annár edged towards where his short sword had fallen, careful not to take his eyes away from his enemy.

The two warriors stared at each other in fascination. And then the Nim'uán smiled, sharp incisors slowly emerging and then retracting. He was an illusion. An elf turned monster, some hideous mutation that turned beauty into a thing of dread, an immortal soul turned from love to hatred. But *how?*

"You are beautiful, like me—only *I* am surrounded by rot and decay." A silky-smooth voice, like that of a poet or a bard expounding on the tragedy of love. Fel'annár's blood froze. He had never heard a Deviant talk.

"You have magic. They fear you, just as the Deviants fear me.

Tell me, did you suffer, I wonder, as a child? Were you mocked for your skill, for your beauty? Mocked for being *different*? For being *better*?" he asked as he closed the distance between them. Fel'annár watched his every move, for when the Nim'uán attacked, it would be quick, in spite of its size. He needed his short sword.

"I wonder what your mother thought of you. Did she love you as mine did me? Did she sacrifice herself for you as mine did for *us*?" The voice was wistful, its eyes momentarily lost to memories Fel'annár did not want to imagine.

He stood now, beside his fallen sword. Manoeuvring the tip of his boot under the hilt, he brought his leg up and grasped the pommel tightly in his left hand.

"What are you? How did you turn Deviant?" asked Fel'annár cautiously.

"Indeed, that is the question." It glanced down at the blade in his right hand and then brought it up before his face, pale skin reflecting off the bloody, silvery surface. "This blade was given to me by my father. It has served me well, as it will serve me now—to kill you."

"Why are you doing this? What do you hope to achieve?" asked Fel'annár as he edged sideways, closer to Gor'sadén, who was struggling weakly with the log that was surely crushing him.

"This," said the monster as it struck a ready stance, eyes glittering in thrilled anticipation. "This . . . is a *mother's* revenge."

There was a whirl of metal rushing through air, and Fel'annár brought his long sword up to meet the admittedly beautiful blade the Nim'uán wielded. Sparks flew with the ferocity of the blow, and a painful vibration rattled his bones. His foe was far stronger than he was, skilled enough to have found an opening in Gor'sadén's defences. Fel'annár knew he had to steer the beast away from the fallen commander lest it use him to his advantage, as leverage—Fel'annár had shown his desperation, shown the Nim'uán how important Gor'sadén was to him.

Fel'annár whirled sideways, attacking the Nim'uán´s right flank, but it turned, surprisingly fast, and blocked him, so hard that Fel'annár's muscles bunched painfully and he was driven backwards. Bringing his blades back to the fore, he feigned left, then moved into the right flank and slashed before the Nim'uán's perfect armour. One step back, and then two—not enough to steer the Nim'uán away, and Gor'sadén was before his mind's eye and then Pan'assár, their words of wisdom echoing in his mind, reminding him of their lessons, of the Kal'hamén'Ar, and his feet moved of their own accord. He was dancing amidst colourful streaks of vaporous light, and the Nim'uán's strikes were no longer so close, so dangerous.

Colour was everywhere. One, two, three, *strike*. Now, the battle was not forwards and backwards but circular, yet still, the Nim'uán blocked Fel'annár's strikes and did not step backwards. The enemy sword flashed in the corner of his eye, and Fel'annár jumped backwards, somersaulting just high enough to feel the blade as it cut through the air below his head. He landed squarely upon the ground and attacked once more, but their swords clashed so violently that Fel'annár's shorter blade was knocked from his hand. Somebody shouted a warning, and he jumped and then flipped backwards, his foot landing on something hard—a broken pike. Placing the tip of his boot under the strong wood, he kicked upwards and then grabbed the weapon in his left hand. He held it out towards the Nim'uán, but it whirled around and then sliced through the wood, cutting off the steel tip. Fel'annár's jaw clenched, but the Nim'uán simply smiled, pity warring with humour.

Still there was a long, thick shaft of hard wood in his hand that would still serve a purpose. He stepped forward, jabbing at the Nim'uán with the pike, hand tightening around the wood as he once again remembered Gor'sadén and Pan'assár—willing tutor and reluctant ally. Those legends might now be dead, Gor'sadén crushed and bleeding, Pan'assár unable to breathe from the toxic fumes. His blazing anger was back, stronger than ever, and he was moving forwards as one hand whirled the pike over his head while the other slashed this way and that. His sharp eyes saw pupils closing and the beast stepped backwards for the first time. The Nim'uán met his furious strikes, only this time he no longer smiled as he fought. Fel'annár ducked and rolled under the strange blade only to flip back up and strike the beast across the head. Blood oozed from a cut at the creature's temple, but there was no sign of pain. He lunged forward with blade and pike and then swivelled sideways, scoring a blow to the Nim'uán's forearm, kicking out and striking the side of its already battered head. Blood gushed into one eye, and it stumbled back but was soon rushing forwards once more, snarling now as anger replaced arrogance, fuelled his enemy's violence.

One, two and then three heavy strikes and Fel'annár was staggering backwards under the sheer power of the Nim'uán. A blade sliced over his hand. He kicked out, eyes catching the movement of his enemy's blade as it arched towards his neck. He jumped sideways, body twisting in the same direction as the metal, pain lancing up his arm. On the ground once more, he swayed away from a boot that threatened to smash into his nose. He couldn't remember the moment he had lost his blade, and he flipped the pike from his left hand and into his right. Deflecting a punch with his own forearm, he felt steel slice over his shoulder. He gritted his teeth and pressed forwards, kicking and punching—and then he felt the frigid bite of metal sliding into his side. His boot landed on a rock and his ankle twisted, sending him crashing to the ground, too close to Gor'sadén.

The Nim'uán was running towards him, and he rolled out of the way of the blade that sliced into the ground and then stuck there. The Deviant pulled desperately on the pommel. Fel'annár watched from where he lay as it finally slid out, and he breathed in, closed his eyes, and then projected all the energy he had left into his right leg, kicking with all his might. He was rewarded by the sickening crunch of bone, and the Nim'uán toppled to the ground, its blade flying sideways, out of reach.

Fel'annár made to stand, but burning agony ripped down one side of his body and he felt his blood pouring free from the stab wound in his side. He crashed to the ground, helpless on his back, and the world blurred for a moment.

He couldn't get up, and even before he could ponder the implications, the Nim'uán was crawling towards him, its broken shin bone bent unnaturally to one side. It stopped, perched on one elbow. There were no weapons in his hands as it gazed down at him in fascination, respect even. Its mouth gaped then, throat working strangely, as if it was fighting to swallow something, and a trickle of saliva ran from the corner of its mouth. Fel'annár stared in horror, wondering if perhaps the beast thought to eat him.

When the Nim'uán moved, it was so fast, all Fel'annár could do was hold out both arms over his chest and turn his head away. A heavy weight was on top of him, and then pain exploded in his side.

He screamed, but the agony did not stop, and he turned his head back to the monster that had bitten into his flesh—beautiful blue eyes gazed back at him blankly, impossibly wide jaws clenching around his chest and side, razor-sharp teeth embedded, unmoving in his flesh, a defiant kiss of death that burned strangely in his veins.

It wasn't eating him—it was *biting* him.

A deep creak of wood, like a moan of grief, and then the whoosh of a heavy branch moving through air and on, through flesh and innards. The Nim'uán shrieked, jaw releasing its victim, its movements ripping away a part of Fel'annár's flesh, blood dripping hideously from its jowls. The killing branch drove further in, through half-rotten innards, emerging from the centre of the Nim'uán's stomach, and Fel'annár strangled another scream even as his hand came around and thrust what remained of his pike into the monster's gaping mouth, sending it through the back of his neck. The wail of an elven Deviant turned into a wet gurgle, and then the weight was inexplicably gone from Fel'annár. Through the patches of green, blue, and purple clouds that hovered above him, he saw the ruined body of the Nim'uán as it was hoisted aloft, far into the air, impaled upon a tree branch, limbs hanging loosely and feet twitching over the bloodied ground of a once vibrant woodland.

An elf screamed, long and desperate from somewhere close by, but even that began to fade away.

He lay flat upon the ground and turned his head, in search of anything to replace the horrific sight of the impaled Nim'uán. Fel'annár felt himself slipping away, dying, and he sought comfort in those final moments. He saw a hand, fingers reaching out, clawing at the ground. He lifted his own hand, as far as he could, the effort leeched his remaining strength.

Gor'sadén.

His mentor wasn't dead. The legend who had taught him, listened to him, guided him and understood him. This was the father he had chosen for himself, and he lay beside him now, in his moment of passing.

Turning his head to the trapped commander, they locked gazes. Gor'sadén stared back at him, despair and grief and *love* in his eyes.

Fel'annár smiled, even though his lips trembled with pain. He whispered, unsure of whether Gor'sadén could hear him.

"If a . . . son could . . . choose . . . a father, I—choose *you*."

The light in Fel'annár's eyes began to dim, images fading slowly, colours paling to every shade of grey. The screams and shrieks fell away. All his childhood dreams, all his Silvan memories dissolved. Everyone he had ever loved sung a sweet farewell, and Fel'annár felt himself sail away, hand-in-hand with the only father he would ever know.

SIXTEEN

JUNÁR

"We don't speak of the days that followed the Battle of Tar'eastór. But we don't forget. We'll never forget."
The Alpine Chronicles. Cor'hidén.

∼

The battle had turned in their favour the moment the Nim'uán had been vanquished and hoisted aloft by the trees, as a warning to any remaining Deviants. It was a trophy the decimated forest kept for itself: behold the fate of the Nim'uán, dark bane—*kinslayer*.

Small pockets of fighting still broke out further down the slopes as the uninjured warriors pursued the remaining Deviants, who were hiding amongst the boulders, thinking to flee the battlefield as soon as the elves had gone. But that would not be soon. There were injured to rescue and take to the Halls. There were bodies to honour and others to burn. The people of Tar'eastór swarmed the battlefield from the front line and backwards, knowing that it was *there* where the critically injured would be.

Captain Comon had taken control of the field, shouting his orders here and there, clapping his warriors upon their weary shoulders even as he demanded of them that they continue, despite their wounds and fatigue. They were needed; it was not yet time for rest.

Prince Sontúr directed the warriors assigned to getting the wounded back to the citadel, even as part of him constantly searched for Fel'annár, and when he found him, lying side-by-side with Gor'sadén, his eyes fell to the clasped hands. Tears welled in his eyes, not for the first time that day and certainly not for the last.

And right there, Sontúr fought his second battle that day—the fight to save Fel'annár from death even before they could get him back to the Halls. Blood poured from a blade wound on his right side and from some horrific bite that had mangled his left side.

Gor'sadén, too, was bleeding out, and the heavy log that sat over his chest had been carefully removed. Still he was black and blue, breath shallow, almost gone.

Some distance away they had found an unconscious Pan'assár, blue lips a tell-tale sign that he had been gassed by the Lizard, and as for Hobin, his leg was barely intact, the pain almost unbearable.

The prince sent a runner to Arané's Halls as he worked so that the master healer would be prepared. Indeed, Arané blessed his royal boots for it and sent the junior healers to the supply rooms to retrieve the things he knew they would need. Meanwhile, the runner, a young recruit, star-struck, awe-inspired, and breathless from his run and the news he had gleaned, had gushed it all to Arané and Llyniel, and the din of ailing warriors and healers waned as the boy told the story and the healers worked.

He told the tale of Commander Pan'assár and how he had defeated the Gas Lizard. Commander Gor'sadén had confronted the elven Deviant and almost vanquished it, and then Commander Hobin had razed the ranks of Deviants with a ferocity seldom seen. As for Warrior Fel'annár, he had stood together with The Company, alone before the oncoming hoards, and had conjured the trees. The *trees* had fought for *Tar'eastór!* Then, later, Fel'annár had saved

Gor'sadén himself, had fought the Nim'uán—and then helped the *trees* to kill it.

Oh, but they had danced the *Kal'hamén'Ar,* he said, and their enemy had fallen by the scores! The Three had returned and Tar'eastór was invincible!

They should have been rejoicing, should have been celebrating their victory—but the fate of their bravest lay in the balance and all was muted and expectant. The glory days *had* returned, but they would not celebrate that return until their saviours' fates were known.

When Prince Sontúr finally arrived with the stretchers, the crowded Halls had parted before them, silent as they watched, and when they passed and then fell beyond sight, they thought that tonight, Tar'eastór would surely lose at least one of its glorious sons.

Outside, captains were shouting orders while soldiers and civilians alike were cooking food at makeshift fire pits for the many elves who toiled through the night. Soft melodies floated on the air, songs of healing and heroism . . . songs of hope and in praise of Aria. Songs of farewell to the glorious dead.

But Fel'annár heard none of it.

∽

Llyniel looked down upon the body that lay on the stone table before her, watched as Arané performed his preliminary diagnosis, and all the time a mantra played in her mind, telling her not to think of that morning, of how her life had changed, how she had fallen into that strange place without ever meaning to. A moment of weakness and she had leaned forward—for a taste of a warrior's lips. She had not expected the world to tilt. Had never imagined herself thrust to the brink of the highest cliff edge, left to dangle there, her heart over a land at war. She should have leaned back, should never have longed to feel his lips against hers. She should never have felt that irresistible thing that had moved her forwards—

to his mouth and her present despair. She should never have kissed this warrior.

She should have listened to Handir.

She heaved a mighty breath and stepped forward, stroking loose strands of hair from his bruised and bloodied face. There was no going back, no "should haves." Even if she wanted to, she could not undo the consequences of her actions.

A roar of pain from Commander Hobin jolted her back to the present, to the royal infirmary and the aftermath of battle. The three commanders lay in beds behind her, receiving treatment from the head healers while Fel'annár lay inert upon a stone table before the fire, still dressed. There had been no time to make him comfortable. All they could think about was stopping the blood that oozed from the blade wound at his side and from the bite of the Nim'uán.

But it wouldn't stop.

Arané was shouting orders to his team, and even now, Sontúr frantically unbuckled his own armour with a grimace of pain, watching as the master healer pressed down on the blade wound on Fel'annár's side while Llyniel inspected the horrific bite mark. It spanned half of his lower chest and back. They said it had been an elven Deviant who did it, but Llyniel thought this surely the jowl of some larger beast. The teeth marks were clearly visible, but the flesh seemed half ripped away. A shiver ran up Llyniel's spine, and her eyes slipped to Sontúr, who was walking towards them, wiping his hands on a cloth and then flinging it into the fire.

"What manner of beast did this to him?"

Sontúr turned to her, and in his eyes, she thought she saw fear.

"The Nim'uán. Elven Deviant, a mutant creature that hangs dead from the branches. No one will touch it."

She shook her head and then moved in to inspect the wound, a bowl of herbal water at her side. "It still bleeds, although slowly. Arané?"

"The blood is not clotting as it should. We have a problem."

"Poison?" she asked.

"Perhaps," he murmured. Llyniel was wracking her brains for an answer, for any other cases of bites she had treated that could bear some relevance. She checked for fever and found none. There was no laboured breathing, no twitching or abnormal bruising. It didn't look like poisoning. If only he would wake, but the blood loss had been great. He had already been unconscious when they had brought him in.

"Whatever this is, we need to replenish his blood or he is going to die on this very bench. I need surat and henum bulb, pettyhead and straw cane—quickly now."

"I'll go," said Llyniel, moving to the door but she turned, despair clawing just behind her eyes. "Don't let him go, Arané, Sontúr."

"We will see him through this or hold his hand in death," said Arané as he worked. "This warrior saved my city."

Llyniel nodded and then sprinted from the room, her mind retrieving the names of the herbs and roots she needed, swiping angrily at the tears that ran down her cheeks, oblivious to the pity in the eyes of those she passed.

While Llyniel collected the supplies she would need, The Company made their slow and painful way to the Halls. They had not been quick enough to follow the stretcher bearers who had taken Fel'annár away, for they were all wounded and exhausted. Others supported them the entire way back, proud of the service they paid to Fel'annár's brethren.

This was The Company, they said, defenders of Tar'eastór.

It had taken far too long, and by the time they entered the Halls, the need to know if Fel'annár still lived was urgent.

"Where is he? Is he still *alive*?" Idernon groaned as the arrow in his leg moved.

"With the master healers, Warrior. Hold still."

"Where?" ground out Ramien, gritting his teeth as his own wounds were cleaned.

"Somewhere you cannot go. You would be in the way."

"I will go there, you will it or *not*," spat Idernon and then moaned again as the healer braced his leg.

"Peace, brave one. Let the masters work."

"Get this *thing* out of me, and then we shall see."

Galadan's steady hand was on his forearm. "Idernon. Still yourself, Brother, otherwise that is going to hu . . ."

Idernon screamed as the arrow was pushed through the other side of his leg, and Galdith held him down.

"Hurt," finished Galadan.

None of them were seriously wounded, but the healers had not seen fit to send them to the barracks and the junior healers. These warriors had faced certain death with the Forest Lord . . . and they'd had enough dealings with warriors to know it would have been futile to separate them. And so, they allowed The Company to sit in the antechamber to the royal infirmary. There was a fire and clean water there, and they sat now, filthy in their ripped and torn clothes, wounds bandaged and smarting. The fire was gloriously warm, yet still they sat hunched and stiff.

"They won't let anyone near Fel'annár nor the commanders," said Galadan, eyes fixed on the door he knew led to the royal infirmary.

"You tried?"

"Oh, yes. Sontúr is in there, knows we are here anxious for news. He won't leave us second-guessing for longer than necessary."

"No," said Idernon softly.

It had now been hours since Fel'annár had been brought in. The implications were not good, and they waited, drooping eyelids stubbornly held open in spite of their bodies' demands for sleep.

A healer did finally come, but it was not Sontúr—it was Llyniel, and The Company sat straighter, watching her face closely for signs of what had happened, but all they could see was her exhaustion and an uncharacteristic coldness in her expression, as if she were not there at all.

"I won't lie. Not to you," she said as she wandered over to the fire.

"He was stabbed in the right side and arm, bitten on the left side and chest by that . . . that *monster*. His wounds won't stop bleeding, and we are working hard to keep him with us. Those fangs held some substance we are trying to understand, but it seems to be hindering the blood from clotting. His heart is compromised, and the bite itself is swollen and bruised. Had he not lost so much blood his chances would be better. If only we could make it stop, regenerate what has been lost, then he may have a chance."

"You must find a way," said Galdith.

"We are missing something, Galdith. If I could identify it—or administer something that will counteract it . . ."

"But surely if you treat the symptoms . . ." said Carodel.

"Then whatever is inhibiting his blood from clotting will continue to work until he bleeds to death. There is something we are *missing* . . ." She shook her head, eyes turned inwards, to her books, to all the things she had learned as a healer.

"We want to see him, Llyniel," said Idernon.

"You can't."

"If he's going to die, we'll be with him when he does."

"Even as the healers work to save him? You would push your way through so that you can hold his *hand*?" She stood wide-eyed and rigid, anger glittering in her tired eyes.

Galadan placed a hand on the Wise Warrior's rigid shoulder. He shook it off.

"If he dies without his brothers at his side, you will answer to *me*."

"I know," she murmured, the anger leeched from her. With a last glance at them all, she visibly calmed herself and left.

"That was not necessary," said Galadan. "Not hours past she was snatched away and held hostage. She has been working for hours to save Hwindo, left his side only to tell us how he fares. I wager she has not seen to her own comfort at all."

"I need to see him, Galadan."

"We *all* do. But not now. Trust her. She is a head healer, Idernon

—yet more than this, can you not see that she *loves* him? That she will do the best for him? Isn't that what you want?"

Idernon looked down, and when he caught Galadan's gaze once more, his eyes were filled with acceptance and apology.

∼

The frantic work of the healers did not stop, even when King Vorn'asté strode purposefully down the main aisle and towards the royal infirmary. Handir was beside him, his eyes taking in the scenes of war, scenes he had never before lived through. His father would have, though, for Ea Uaré had lived through a battle such as this one —the Battle Under the Sun, when Or'Talán had died and Thargodén had become king.

On the outside, Handir was a cool, determined leader, but on the inside, his heart leapt about in his chest and his soul cried for the suffering of the injured warriors. Llyniel herself was somewhere here, easing their pain . . . easing their passing. He felt such respect for her, for being able to help where he himself could not. Handir's job was to *avoid* war, not *wage* it—not clear up the mess it left behind.

He wondered if the rumours were true, that perhaps they had exaggerated when they said that Fel'annár would die. He needed to see for himself, and yet with every step they took towards the infirmary, the slower they seemed to be moving and the faster his heart hammered in his chest.

They passed through the open doorway, watched as healers came and went, some walking, others running. There was no time for protocol save for the odd bow, and soon enough, king and prince stood to one side of Gor'sadén's bed, far enough away to allow the healers to tend to him. Vorn'asté looked down on him, but Handir's eyes travelled over to the next bed and Pan'assár, and then to Hobin, and finally, to the inert body of Fel'annár on the far side.

Then Vorn'asté's hand was on his forearm, bringing him back. Handir was accompanying Vorn'asté on an official duty and he would have the prince's full attention. It was a lesson in kingship, and Handir nodded a subtle apology.

"Commander," said the king, eyes roving over the heavily-bandaged leg, the mountain of cushions behind the commander's back, the tightly bound chest and the ashen hue of Gor'sadén's skin.

"M'king."

"We will not tax you with questions. Know only that Tar'eastór is so very grateful for your service, brave commander, and when you are well enough, our people will show you."

The king's eyes came to rest on the commander's leg. "How bad is it, old friend?" he whispered.

"I will—live," came the laboured reply.

"And your leg?" he insisted.

After a moment, Gor'sadén answered, his voice almost inaudible, and Vorn'asté had to bend down to hear him.

"I will live."

The king stood straighter, his singular face turning almost to stone at the implications. Should Gor'sadén lose his leg, he would not be able to teach Fel'annár, would never dance the Kal'hamén'Ar again. Fel'annár would be devastated—if he lived. Yet more than this his friend of old would surely take the Long Road. Vorn'asté couldn't imagine this life without Gor'sadén in it.

The king's hand rested on the commander's forearm for a moment, and then he moved on, to Pan'assár's bed, but he was hacking so badly they walked on and to Hobin. But he, too, was suffering as his leg was rebandaged. Agony would not allow him to speak or even to concentrate on who was standing before him.

They were finally at the bed at the end. Llyniel and Sontúr were there, working together in silence. It was then that Handir realised that they had not exaggerated at all. His eyes stared down at the horrific bite—and for all that he tried he could not rip them away. Llyniel caught his gaze, stared back at him in silence. He willed her to speak to him, tell him it was not as dire as it looked . . . that Fel'annár would live. He willed her to admonish him for rejecting his own brother, for blaming him for the bitter moments of his own life—and he willed her to remind him that he had tried to dissuade her from loving Fel'annár. But she said nothing. She didn't need to.

It was all true.

Vorn'asté was talking quietly with Arané, and Handir listened as he spoke. When the master healer explained Fel'annár's condition in somewhat technical terms, Handir all but blurted out his question.

"Will my brother live?"

Vorn'asté's brow arched acutely, but Handir didn't see it—for his eyes were boring into Arané's.

"There is a . . . slim chance . . . that something may be done for him." Arané's bright eyes were filled with compassion for a fleeting moment before he schooled them and turned back to the king, even though Handir's eyes lingered on the healer, as if he had not quite understood what Arané had just said.

The master healer thought Fel'annár would die.

Handir spared one last look at his half-Silvan brother from where he stood. He tried to school his features, quell his mounting desperation. He needed Fel'annár—for the Forest and his father's continuity on the throne, but he also needed him as a brother. He had realised that upon the ramparts, just before the battle had begun. He had stopped fooling himself, forced himself to watch and to finally understand his own path forwards.

He needed to show Fel'annár that he cared.

Vorn'asté's hand was on his shoulder. Time to leave but Handir would be back, not as a prince but as a brother. He paused upon the threshold of the room, and Vorn'asté allowed it. Handir watched as Fel'annár was rolled to one side, arm falling limply over the side of the bed, unaware that Gor'sadén also watched, his pained blue eyes fixed on Fel'annár's lax hand—the same hand he had held upon the battlefield when the Nim'uán had been skewered and Fel'annár lay dying. Fel'annár had called him father, and the memory of it brought tears to his tired eyes. But he couldn't move, couldn't reach out and take that hand once more . . . not as he had before as an offering of comfort before death, but to feed him with strength, tell him he was not alone— to will him back to life.

But he couldn't. All he could do was lie there and watch as Fel'annár's life slowly slipped away.

～

That night, Arané sat by the fire, his head half inside a large tome. Llyniel sat opposite him, eyes moving from the title of his book to his bent head. Arané lowered the book and stared back at her blankly . . . and then he shook his head.

Arané had found nothing.

Her heart plummeted to her boots. The problem was clear to her. *Excessive bleeding leads to slow circulation, which compromises the heart.* Replenish the blood and treat the heart but stop the bleeding— find something they had not already used.

She turned her head, eyes on Fel'annár's bed. He did not move at all: so still, so pale. She was reminded of Rovad, a rather handsome human warrior she had treated after a skirmish with bandits during her early years in Pelagia. He had almost bled out.

Rovad, yes, that was his name. He'd been married to Mavey, a plump lass who showed promise in the healing arts. She would visit the Halls frequently, and Llyniel had tried not to become too friendly with her. She was mortal—she would die. Still, Llyniel was Silvan, and she had failed to purposefully distance herself. They had been friends until the couple had moved on.

Rovad had lived even though she remembered thinking that he wouldn't. Her skin began to tingle, an image popping into her head of a day she had ventured out to the high hills on the island of Dan'bar. Gurgling streams and wide, shallow rivers graced the land, and along their banks had been a tree she had never seen before. Triangular leaves and a flaky, silvery bark had captured her attention. She had carefully harvested the bark . . .

She stood from her chair opposite Arané. "I will be back in a moment," she murmured, turning from the room and walking slowly to her quarters. Arané nodded into his book.

Another specimen for your collection?

Yes. I have never seen this tree before.

Her skin prickled and she walked faster. She needed to remember...

Light grey bark sitting in the sun, inquisitive fingers prodding it, then grinding it, using it on herself...

She pushed her door open so hard it banged against the back wall, and she was striding to her book, the one that always sat open on her table. She picked it up reverently and shuffled through the pages, backwards in time until her fingers froze, eyes landing upon the sketch of a tall, spindly bark and sprawling branches. She scanned her own scribbled words and doodles, and her heart raced.

Junár. *Junár* bark...

She turned, walking briskly from the room. She had found it in Pelagia, on the Island of Dan'bar. *Dan'bar*—a wave of dread hit her. They surely wouldn't have it.

The paintings upon the corridors she had first admired on her arrival in Tar'eastór flew past her in colourful streaks, but all she could see was the silvery bark of the Junár tree and a fatally-injured warrior.

Rovad had *lived*... but he was human. It may not work for an *elf*.

She ran through the waiting area, past The Company who were on their feet, watching as she dashed past them and then entered the room, a startled guard closing the door behind her. She stood breathing hard, book clutched to her chest, eyes wide, mind only now emerging from the mists of her memories. Arané stood slowly, his own book forgotten on the side table.

"What is it? What have you found?"

"Tell me you have it, Arané. Tell me you have *Junár* bark..."

"*Junár?*" he scoffed. "Why? Someone got an upset stomach somewhere?"

"Upset... you *have* it?" Her eyes bulged wide.

"I keep some for upset stomachs, yes. One of many remedies for that ailment. We don't use it much and . . . " His voice trailed off. "Mestahé," he called, gesturing with his hand, but his eyes were trained on Llyniel.

The healer left Fel'annár's side and walked to his colleagues, looking between one and the other.

"What do you need, Llyniel?"

She turned to Mestahé. "One part Junár bark, one part star blade and echin—a milk decoction. Five measures."

"One part Junár bark, one part star blade and echin . . ." He scowled and shook his head.

"Mestahé, *trust* me. One part Junár . . . "

"Yes, yes. I have it."

He ran from the room, and Arané turned to Llyniel.

"Tell me what you think you have."

"I can't be sure, but I think we may have a chance."

"Let's hope it's not too late," murmured Arané as they both sat and Llyniel reverently laid her journal in the master healer's hands.

SEVENTEEN
THROUGH THE EYES OF ARIA

> "*A dawn can herald many things. A new day in peace, the first day of a life—or perhaps the last. It can be dramatic, or it can be shrouded in cloud, visible only to the gods. But there is one dawn that we all remember, a dawn that heralded a day we would never forget.*"
> The Alpine Chronicles. Cor'hidén.

~

The dry hacking would not stop, and tears streamed from Pan'assár's eyes. Two healers placed a bowl of steaming water before him, infused with ginger and tulsi. The commander did as he was told and inhaled the vapours. But still he coughed and then retched . . . and then inhaled again.

Sontúr winced. Pan'assár had suffered with these coughing attacks for the last two days, and when he was not hacking, his breath was laboured and he could not speak. And so he whispered—to Gor'sadén or Hobin in the beds beside him or to the healers who were always close by. But when it was time for the decoction to be fed to Fel'annár, it was almost always quiet, the air rife with stubborn hope and then utter disappointment when still he did not wake.

Sontúr approached Gor'sadén, who lay awake, lying with a mountain of cushions behind his back and under his leg. His face was pasty white and he sat as if petrified, and Sontúr couldn't blame him. His leg had been skewered, and his chest had been crushed. The slightest of movements would cause excruciating pain, and so he lay there, murmuring words so that only those close enough to him could hear—not that they needed to. His question was always the same.

"Fel'annár?"

And then the healers would avoid his gaze and fuss with the bedclothes. Today, though, Sontúr met his worried eyes and sat in a chair beside his bed.

"You seem a little better, Gorsa."

"Perhaps. Fel'annár?"

"There is no change, Gorsa. He just lies there and does not stir. We are feeding him the mixture Llyniel has created, but after two days... we must face reality."

"He can't die, Sontúr."

"He *can*, Gorsa. He may very well die."

Gor'sadén closed his eyes and steadied himself. He had known it was bad, had held Fel'annár's hand when he had fallen, had thought that he had died until the healers had come.

"Did you see him, Sontúr? Did you see him *dance*?" The whisper waned and Gor'sadén's eyes closed in misery.

"I saw him," replied Sontúr, standing and busying himself with the herbs that had been left for use on a small table. "How is the pain?"

Gor'sadén exhaled noisily, the only answer Sontúr got, and he mixed another potion of poppy. In the background, Pan'assár's hacking continued.

"At least I know *he* will be well."

"Yes. But he may have lasting damage to his throat, to his voice."

"He is a commander."

"Yes. I know," said Sontúr carefully. "We will do what we can."

"And what of Hobin?"

"He is doing well. However, it will be years before that leg of his is back to normal. He was lucky not to lose it."

After a while, Gor'sadén managed to ask the question that had haunted his fevered dreams for the last few days.

"And mine? Will I lose my leg?"

Sontúr stopped his work and looked down at the commander. "I don't think so, Gor'sadén. The damage was extensive, but Arané is a true master: we believe we have fixed it enough for you to begin recuperating your mobility, once the wound heals."

The commander closed his eyes and allowed himself a deeper breath, wincing as he opened them and allowed his gaze to stray to the ceiling he now knew so well. For the first time in his life he prayed, the words just behind his thready breath. He prayed for Fel'annár's return; he prayed that his own, new-found hope would not be snatched away from him. He prayed that Llyniel's potion would work, but above all he prayed that he would not be left alone to mourn the son his heart had chosen.

~

Arané administered the tonic himself for the third time that day, and still, there had been no change. Fel'annár lay upon the bed, his breathing shallow and his skin pale and clammy. The master healer breathed deeply, his hope now tempered by the passage of time. The concoction had not killed the boy, but neither had it done anything for him. He ran his hand down his face and turned back to his patient, studiously ignoring the gazes of the commanders.

Lifting the bandages covering the horrific bite, his eyes travelled over the mangled flesh, wondering if it would ever fully regenerate—should he live, of course. It was red and angry . . . and then he swayed back with a frown. Bending further down, his eyes moved from side to side. There was no blood, only a thick clot over the deepest puncture. A *clot*.

He stood straight, so suddenly his hair flew about him, and then he walked stiffly to where Llyniel stood grinding herbs, gaze lost to infinity.

"Llyniel."

Foggy eyes blinked slowly, and Arané's figure sharpened before her.

"It's working."

"What's working," she murmured and then started. "The Junár?"

"There is a clot. He no longer bleeds. The unknown element has been counteracted. The echin, the star blade, the *Junár* bark . . . we have a *chance*."

Llyniel couldn't speak. She needed to see it for herself, and she walked stiltedly to Fel'annár's bed, eyes peering down at him, Healer Mestahé at her shoulder.

"Thank the gods," she whispered. *Thank you, Rovad, wherever you are*, she said to herself. But Llyniel knew as well as the rest of them that it was not yet time to celebrate. Although the decoction was working, the blood loss had been so great that Fel'annár might not be able to wake. They had solved the problem, but the damage it had wrought might prove too much for Fel'annár to fight.

~

For two more days they had fed an unconscious Fel'annár with Llyniel's Junár bark mixture, and although his blood had clotted, he remained a prisoner in a place he could not escape from.

Gor'sadén had grown stronger, albeit he could still hardly move at all, and although Pan'assár still coughed and rasped, the irritation had calmed. Both he and Hobin had been released to their own rooms, but while the Ari commander was confined to his bed, not so Pan'assár, who spent his days sitting in an over-stuffed chair beside his friend's bed.

Prince Handir was a regular visitor. He would talk with Llyniel or sit beside Fel'annár's bed and endure the puzzled stares he received from Sontúr and Llyniel herself.

As the light of day faded, the people of Tar'eastór sung once more in soft, melodious voices. Their placid harmonies were meant to ease the mounting despair that was setting in. There were songs of comfort, prayers to Aria, muted thanks for the victory they had yet to proclaim. But at times it seemed to Gor'sadén that Bel'arán sang Fel'annár away, a herald to those in Valley to welcome him in honour.

Arané, in a last-ditched attempt to garner a reaction from Fel'annár, had finally allowed The Company to enter the infirmary—under the command that they were to bathe and change first and then stay out of his healers' way. He bid them talk to him, call to him. If he had lost his way, perhaps the sound of familiar voices would show him the path back.

"I still remember that day we met you," said Idernon, his voice soft yet loud enough for the rest to hear. "You were fighting, fists flying about even as the other boys gave you a pounding. I remember your face—feral, angry. An Alpine child in the heart of the Forest. You didn't cry, even though I knew you wanted to."

Healer Mestahé stepped closer as he rolled bandages, and Arané lifted his head from where he sat reading Llyniel's book in his chair.

"I took hold of them," continued Ramien. "I bashed them together and knocked the wind out of them," he said, showing them how he had done it with his hands. "They ran home wheezing to their mothers," he explained, his mind reliving the scene, forty-five years into the past in Lan Taria.

Llyniel stood preparing the Junár decoction, listening to childhood stories meant to wake Fel'annár up. But she didn't want to *hear* them, didn't *want* to feel the crushing pity that was weighing her down. This was *Fel'annár*. This was the *warrior*, the elf she had loved almost from the moment she had cast eyes on him. She had never admitted that to herself, not until she had kissed him in the trees, but even then, she had not said it . . . and neither had he.

She needed to tell him before he left without her—before he took her heart with him to Valley.

"We walked to the nearby river to hide the evidence of your fight, but your nose had grown fat and puffy and so we devised an excuse, elaborate and so plausible to the mind of a seven-year-old. We told Amareth we had been taunting the chickens in the baker's garden, but that one of them had turned on us and chased us, its feathers all puffed up, wings flapping as it gaggled like some forest banshee. It was *really* angry, we said, and Fel'annár, in his terror, tripped and fell over, bashing his nose on a stone. But Amareth had somehow seen through the subterfuge and you were punished—*again*," said Idernon with a soft smile. "No chicken for a whole cycle of the moon."

Mestahé was quietly snorting in one corner, but his eyes were overly bright, and even Arané's jaw clenched with repressed emotions despite the countless times he had seen himself in similar situations.

"Ramien and I sat under the tree in your garden the following day, waiting for you to go to the school house. I remember you stopped short, suspicion shining in your eyes. You couldn't believe we were there to help you, but we *were*," said Ramien.

Idernon smiled, eyes momentarily glancing over the rest of The Company, who stared back at him in expectation.

"On that day, at that very moment, The Company was born. It was the moment we learned to fight—not with our fists, for we already excelled at that. Nay, we learned to fight for what we wanted, for what was right. There were no more cruel words, no more loose fists or pilfered lunches. We were The Company: we stood up for ourselves and we have never stepped backwards. *You*—must not step away, Fel'annár. You must stay and fight as you always have. You must come back to us so that we can fulfil this purpose we have." He bent low, next words whispered into Fel'annár's ear.

"*Wake up, Hwind'atór.*"

Idernon turned away, catching Galadan's intense gaze as he did so.

A cleared throat—Mestahé.

A long, tired breath from Ramien. "I'm going for a walk. I won't be long," he said, and Idernon watched him as he left, knowing the memories that would be playing havoc with his friend's emotions.

They slipped into silence once more until it was time for the next dose of Junár, and before long, Ramien returned with a potted plant in his arms.

"Here. He'll be horrified when he wakes up to find himself in this place with no plants."

They watched as he placed the pot on the bedside table. He leaned back, tilted his head, and then reached out to place it a little closer to Fel'annár's head.

"Better," he nodded in satisfaction.

Those of The Company looked away while Mestahé sniffled from where he stood in one corner. Nobody spoke until the evening had slipped away and the dark of night was upon them.

Galadan dreamed of their near-fatal journey to Tar'eastór, of that strange moment in which he had called Fel'annár *"my prince."* Galdith remembered the tiny face of his infant daughter, before she had been slaughtered by Sand Lords at the Battle of Sen'uár—and how he had thought Fel'annár an Alpine. Carodel remembered Fel'annár's flushed face singing along to one of his tunes while Sontúr remembered his own sarcastic humour and how it made Fel'annár laugh, and all the while, the deep dark of night stretched on in silence.

Pan'assár's heart was heavy in his chest, though he had returned a Kah Warrior, worthy of its symbols at last—had purged his guilt and atoned for his sins. He had become fond of Or'Talán's grandchild, but more than this, he knew what the boy meant to Gor'sadén, what it would do to him should Fel'annár succumb. His eyes turned to the healer in the corner, the one he knew loved Fel'annár. He had hated her, too, until he had seen her, understood her, and finally came to respect her. What would become of her if Fel'annár died, he wondered. His own king's face came to his mind and then the green eyes of the woman he had loved—the woman his own heart brother had inexplicably forbidden his son to marry.

A cry of shock jolted them all, and Arané clambered to his feet, heart beating wildly.

"What is it?" He looked around for the source of the disturbance. Mestahé stood frozen, eyes on Fel'annár's bed, and the master healer slowly turned. Ramien's potted plant had grown three times its size, had burst its clay pot and toppled onto the bed beside Fel'annár, and around his inert fingers, tiny roots had coiled.

Arané walked stiltedly towards the bed, the rustle of cloth around him.

"By all that is holy . . ." he muttered.

"Sweet Aria," exclaimed Carodel.

Llyniel's eyes travelled from the coiled roots and up the limp arm to Fel'annár's face. She felt his brow and leaned down to feel his breath.

"His breathing is steadier; he feels warmer."

Galdith's eyes moved between the singular spectacle of roots that had entangled in Fel'annár's fingers and the healer who assured them Fel'annár was better.

"The Sentinel," murmured Galdith.

"What about it?" asked Sontúr.

"We take him to the Sentinel."

"He's going *nowhere*," said Arané.

"Brothers," pleaded the Silvan. "If one plant can bring an improvement, imagine what the Sentinel may do for him. We have to *try*."

"I won't allow it."

"He's right, Arané. You have nothing else to try. We do. What is the worst that can happen by taking him into the night?" asked Idernon.

The healer stared back at him, unable to refute the argument. Fel'annár would die one way or the other—he had convinced himself of that already. "I'll come with you. Mestahé, warn the guard outside. Clear the way. We don't want to draw attention to him."

The healer nodded and then left the room, whispering quietly with the guard. Moments later, Ramien, Galadan, Carodel, and Galdith bore the stretcher that carried Fel'annár out of the room, his body bundled in woollen blankets. Arané, Llyniel, and the rest of The Company followed, while inside the infirmary, all Gor'sadén could do was watch in frustration as they left to attempt their one last chance to bring Fel'annár back to life . . . or give up the fight and let him slip away. Pan'assár could sense his helplessness, knew he wanted to be there, to whatever end, but that was still not within Gor'sadén's capacity, and so he stayed beside his friend. They would wait together, deal with whatever happened together.

And so they waited, useless words held at bay until troubled sleep took them both.

∼

Fel'annár lay on his stretcher, a mountain of pillows behind him, which in turn lay against the impressive trunk of the Sentinel in the king's gardens. Idernon had placed one of Fel'annár's hands over the roots, a gesture Fel'annár often adopted absently.

Llyniel watched The Company from where she, Arané, and Mestahé sat a little further away. This was a moment for these warriors to share, she realised. She would be intruding if she were to lie down beside him as she so desperately wanted to do, but Idernon turned to her then, eyes searching hers, as if he pondered something important. She watched him patiently. Idernon was much younger than Galadan, a warrior, not a lieutenant, and yet he had always been Fel'annár's second in command. The others understood this as clearly as she did, as clearly as she had seen his disapproval of their relationship—even though the Wise Warrior thought she had not seen it. But looking at him now she wondered if he *had* realised. He slowly held out one hand, a gesture for her to join them, and her heart jolted. Rising to her feet, she walked the few paces that separated them and sat beside Idernon, giving him a grateful nod and then turning back to Fel'annár.

Perhaps some had thought the tree would move, that branches would gently brush his cheek and bring him back to life. Perhaps they thought the tree would glow—or that roots would emerge from the depths and spiral around his body, infuse him with some magic.

But nothing happened, and so they sat, and they waited, and then they dozed. They didn't see the hazy tendrils of light that floated lazily around them, sailing over them and then converging upon Fel'annár. The colourful ribbons played with his hair and circled his limbs, as if they would pick him up with their translucent arms and fly him away . . .

∼

He knew he existed, yet he couldn't remember his name, wondered where he was and whether this was Valley, for he could not feel his body, could not feel the hard ground beneath him. Perhaps this was his spirit form. Perhaps he had died and was waiting to find himself.

Energy passed through flesh, into his blood, into his very essence. It surged through his veins, pulsed inside his body, and he remembered. He was Fel'annár; he was Hwind'atór, brother of The Company.

But then a crack of tenuous light appeared before him, his eyelids opening to the twilight canvas that was slowly lightening to soothing lavender. He could almost smell it as the deep purple leeched to rosy grey and then a blush of shocking scarlet streaked through it, and it was powerful, bold, *invincible*.

He had never seen a dawn such as this one.

Those shocking colours seemed to ignite his soul, and his breath paused in his lungs as the first slither of sun broke the horizon, rising a master, absolute commander of the day. He tilted his head towards it, felt his open eyes smile, an oaken embrace behind him, holding him with tender care. He could feel every leaf upon every twig upon every branch, shimmering cobwebs dripping with dew. They told their story to the wind and the sun—to him.

Were these the dawns of Valley?

As the sun continued to break over the lightening firmament, the shadow of a lady stood before him, hardly visible, but in just that moment, under just that light and on just this day, he could almost see her, and even though her face was steeped in shadow, he knew those eyes: they had been the first eyes he had ever seen. He reached out with one hand, fingers tingling in anticipation, for before him was the incomprehensible beauty of life.

Radiating light replaced the lonely darkness.

Comforting warmth banished the numbing cold.

She dissipated, merged with the colours and the sun and the warmth, even though he knew she was still there . . . and always would be.

Aria.

His heavy hand dropped to his lap, so tired. He would sleep here, under the protective sky, but there were sounds around him, a dawn chorus of birds, someone shuffling beside him. He was too tired to turn his head and look away from the blossoming sky, but he felt the world around him, beckoning to him from wherever he had lingered.

He was not dead; this was not Valley. He was *alive,* and he wondered how many dawns like this he would see. But then what did it matter? He had seen *this* one, a dawn that would stay with him always.

Dawn through the eyes of Aria.

"Fel'annár?" A soft, tentative call.

He felt the pillows behind his back and the roots beneath his hand, and then there was searing-hot agony in his side, but someone was gasping, someone was crying, someone was stroking his hand, and someone was giving thanks to Aria. He could feel others, too, their souls, their love, even though he hurt, eyes slowly closing to the world after their feast of nature.

He was alive and he was safe, and he slipped willingly into the healing arms of Aria.

～

Gor'sadén stirred, Pan'assár's hand squeezing his shoulder. He could hear muffled voices, shuffling boots. His eyes opened, and he turned to the door. They were back, Fel'annár just as still as he had been when they had left. But something about their countenance gave him pause, for their eyes were overly bright and puffy, like lost children, he mused.

Panic surged through his body, but Mestahé broke from the main group and came to stand over Gor'sadén, watery eyes too wide for one that grieved. His tears were not for the fallen but for the returned.

"I have seen a *miracle*," he whispered through his smile. "He has woken."

Pan'assár stared dumbly back at the healer while Gor'sadén's eyes slipped shut in utter relief, and when he opened them once more, his eyes searched and found the confirmation he needed.

"Thank you, Mestahé," he whispered.

The healer smiled, nodded, and then scurried away.

～

Later that morning, when Arané had finished tending to Fel'annár, he turned to The Company.

"Go and get some rest. I don't want to see you again until after lunch."

They complied reluctantly, filing out of the room, but Idernon stopped and turned, eyes latching on to Llyniel, who stood grinding bark. She caught his gaze, cocking her head to one side in curiosity. She watched as he limped towards her, and she placed her bowl on the table beside her.

"Llyniel. I have not always been civil with you."

"You were worried. We all were."

"You have my eternal gratitude, Healer, for saving him. You will always have me as a brother, if you so wish."

She smiled at the Wise Warrior, but before she could say anything, Idernon had wrapped her in a tight hug. She smiled wider and then patted him on the shoulder. He stepped away from her and walked back to the departing Company. They stared back at her—and as one they nodded slowly and then left the room.

Arané's hand was on her shoulder and Mestahé smiled back at her. A sense of achievement such as she had never felt settled upon her. She had saved the elf she loved, with Aria's help, the elf who might bring change to her forest home, and she had done it with Junár, because she had invested her entire adult life to studying tree barks so that one day, she could make a difference such as this one. And this was her reward. She had found a family in The Company, for they were bound in heart-break and love, in their desire for a better forest for the Silvan people . . . and by their love of Fel'annár.

She snapped back to the present as Gor'sadén groaned while Pan'assár and Mestahé lifted him from his bed. Arané would not allow him to walk, and so he endured as he was carried to a chair at Fel'annár's bedside and the healer arranged his damaged leg on a stool. All Gor'sadén wanted was to hear Fel'annár's voice.

Reaching for a limp hand, the commander called to him.

"Fel'annár. Fel'annár . . ."

~

His name was Fel'annár, Green Sun. He was a brother of The Company . . .

His eyes opened. He wished he could focus, but that was not meant to be. He could see dark bulks moving around his bed, could hear voices as if he stood in an empty tunnel.

There had been a battle. They must have won because he was

alive, however strange this place was. But where were his brothers? Had *they* survived? Was Gor'sadén dead?

His head was pounding, and he grimaced as his leg muscles stiffened painfully. Somebody's hands were on him, flexing his ankle and pulling on the twinging muscle. He scrunched his eyes closed, felt tears rolling down his temples. A damp cloth wiping over his face.

"Fel'annár."

Someone was peering down at him, and he blinked to clear the haze that would not lift. Grey hair and blue eyes, an acutely arched eyebrow—Sontúr. He wanted to say it, but all that came out was a long "sssss."

The face smiled and then was gone, and in its place was another. Auburn hair and honey-coloured eyes.

"Lly..."

He couldn't get his body to move, not even his tongue, and his brain was playing games, he knew. Someone was lifting his head and then water trickled into his mouth. He swallowed, and the hand disappeared.

They were moving him, touching him. He could hear clinking glass and smell burning wood, but a soothing calm descended on him and the pain was receding. His eyelids felt heavy, but he couldn't sleep, not until he knew the fate of his brothers.

"Fel'annár?"

"Gorss...?" he whispered.

"I'm here, sitting beside you."

Fel'annár slowly turned his head, feeling the hand that held his, and for a moment he was back on the battlefield, lying hand-in-hand with Gor'sadén. He had thought he was dying, had chosen the commander as his father; he'd said goodbye to him.

"B—brothers?"

"They are well. They never left your side."

"And Panss?"

"Is coughing his guts up thanks to that unholy beast he fought. But he will be well."

A heavy breath, a slow blink, utter relief washing over Fel'annár.

"I thought you had died." Gor'sadén's voice wavered, and he cleared his throat, embarrassed at how his tongue had taken over his mind and blurted the words.

"So—did I," said Fel'annár, the ghost of a smile on his lips, and Gor'sadén laughed. He took a deep breath before speaking again.

"When they told me you were still alive, I thought it a gift—from Aria herself."

Fel'annár didn't answer, couldn't, for his throat felt too tight and so he listened.

"I was so proud of you, standing there with your brothers, giving me the time I needed to prepare my army and march, face the Deviants on the slopes and not on our very doorstep. And then we danced . . . and you saved my life. Teaching you will be an intriguing and exhilarating ride, a duty I am honoured to undertake." A pang of fear rolled through him, for although it was true, Gor'sadén did not know if he would ever be able to dance the Kal'hamén'Ar again. But it was not the time to disclose that. Only time would tell whether he would make a full recovery.

A tear slipped from the corner of Fel'annár's eye. He wanted to lift his hand and swipe it away, but he couldn't, and so he lay there, incapable of uttering a single word.

"Once you—we, are on our feet and strong enough, we will speak publicly of everything that has transpired these last few days. The king wishes to hear it from your lips, and there are questions that must be asked. After that, I don't think it will be long before Prince Handir calls for your return to the Forest. It has been long since last I travelled those lands."

Fel'annár had listened quietly, emotions rolling off him like mist over the highest ridges of the Median Mountains, and his grip on Gor'sadén's hand tightened, even though it was still weak, as if he were holding on to him from below.

Gor'sadén felt his own eyes fill, and he squeezed the hand of his son, the one he had thought lost, the one they said Aria had brought back to life through the hands of a Silvan healer, through the loving embrace of a Sentinel.

~

Hours later, Llyniel bowed low and whispered in Fel'annár's ear. "Handir is here to see you." Practised eyes roved over his face before she turned, nodded at the prince, and then walked back to her mixing table by the fire.

"You slept a long while, *Brother*," murmured Handir, standing over Fel'annár.

Fel'annár was struck silent, not that he was capable of speaking much. His tongue was sluggish, and he wondered if his mind was, too—whether he had misunderstood. But the misty eyes of a royal prince looked down on him with nothing but pride. No judgement, no resentment. No censure. It *was* Handir who stood over him.

"Brother," repeated Fel'annár blearily. His weakened state loosened his tongue.

Handir smiled down at him and then placed a hand on Fel'annár's shoulder. It was warm and firm, and Fel'annár's heart soared in his chest. He had been touched with affection by a brother he never thought to have.

From afar, Llyniel watched with tears in her eyes, for a bond between brothers had been formed, a bond between an Alpine prince and a Silvan lord. It went against the odds, but the hope of a brighter, more just Forest flared to life in her soul.

There was only one thing left for Handir to accept.

She walked to the other side of the bed, watery eyes fixed on her heart brother. And then she smiled, bent, and kissed Fel'annár on the lips. It was chaste and tender, so very eloquent to the eyes of a trained statesman. Cool eyes wrinkled at the corners, and a subtle smile graced his countenance.

He nodded, and Llyniel understood him perfectly. Turning her eyes back down to Fel'annár, he smiled as she smoothed a hand down his face. "There are things I would say," she whispered, and Fel'annár's smile did not wane as he nodded that he understood.

The door clicked open, and Llyniel and Handir turned. The Company filed in, saluting to Gor'sadén and Pan'assár as they passed and then converging on Fel'annár's bed. Their clothes were clean, hair shining and freshly-braided, and they smiled as they greeted their brother, careful not to jostle the bed.

Fel'annár watched them fondly, proudly. They had accepted their own deaths to stay with him, had refused to leave him and save themselves, knowing they could have died, *would* have, had Gor'sadén not arrived when he had.

He loved these warriors with all that he was.

That night, the people of Tar'eastór flooded the streets. The soft singing had gone and in its wake were the beats of drums and clapping elves, hails for their brave dead, chants of victory to the glorious warriors that had beaten back the hordes of terror.

The Nim'uán had come for their homes and Gor'sadén and Fel'annár had vanquished it. The Gas Lizard had wreaked havoc and had paid the price . . . Pan'assár's legendary sword through its mouth. They spoke of the Kal'hamén'Ar and of The Company, of how they had stood before the Deviants, offering their young lives so that others would live.

But most of all they sang of the trees, of their battle, of the Forest Lord who had commanded them and then had been brought back from death itself by the Winter Sentinel.

The city hummed with excitement, with pride for their people, for their commanders, and their king. It was the beginning of a new era, a second coming of the glory days of the Motherland.

∼

Days later, Arané informed Fel'annár that he was allowing him to return to his own rooms—under strict instructions not to leave them and, of course, to do as he was damn-well told. It had taken a miracle to bring him back, and the master healer was taking no chances. First, he would eat and then allow Arané to perform his final examination. Then, Arané would explain to Fel'annár how he should use his crutch. Fel'annár had balked at the thought of hobbling around on a stick, but Arané had explained what might happen should he decide *not* to use it. Fel'annár had promptly agreed that he would.

Just after the lunch hour, Hobin and Gor'sadén hobbled into the room, Pan'assár hovering around them. Fel'annár comforted himself in the knowledge that *they* had to use *two* crutches where he only had to use one. A small mercy, for it was almost painful to watch them. He was relieved when they fell into chairs beside his bed and Pan'assár sat at the end of it.

"You are finally free," began Gor'sadén with a smirk that was also a grimace of pain as he settled himself.

"Almost. I am minutes away, although I fear Arané's long list of conditions—and that bloody crutch he wants me to use."

Pan'assár snorted in a most undignified manner while Hobin raised his dark brows. "It could have been worse," he said, and Fel'annár nodded thoughtfully.

"How was the strategy meeting?" asked Fel'annár, watching his mentor closely.

"It went well," began Gor'sadén carefully. "All cautionary measures have been approved, the city's defences reinforced. We have patrols scheduled to explore and exterminate and, of course, to map those tunnels. Once we have a clear picture of them and have gleaned as much information as we can, they will be destroyed."

"The captains had questions, I assume," asked Fel'annár with a lingering gaze.

"Oh, they had *questions*," said Pan'assár somewhat hoarsely. He cleared his throat. "But they must wait for another day. When you are better able to deal with those questions, we will hold a hearing at the Inner Circle. For now, you must regain your strength. I wager Prince Handir will soon be calling for your return—for *our* return."

"It's safe then, for you to leave the city's defences in Captain Comon's hands?" Fel'annár asked, turning back to Gor'sadén.

"As safe as it can be, Fel'annár," said Gor'sadén. "Comon has been fully informed of everything. Commander Hobin will return to Araria in a few weeks, after the hearing and as soon as he is able to ride," he added, turning to the Ari leader, who spoke next.

"We need to understand how an Elven Deviant came into being —where he came from. I suspect he was not fully Elven, perhaps with a human mother or father. I will search our records for any cases of half-elven children passing the Last Markers. I will send missives to Tar'eastór and to Northern Ea Uaré with anything we can uncover. We have close ties with the village of Abiren'á. It is a common route for messengers from Araria on their way to King Thargodén. Commander Gor'sadén will be close enough to respond should there be an emergency."

Fel'annár nodded again, but their stares lingered, and he knew they had their own questions. Gor'sadén had been careful not to overtax him until now, and Fel'annár was grateful for that.

"You have questions," he began.

"We do," confirmed Gor'sadén. "About the Nim'uán, about the trees and—about what happened at the *Sentinel*."

Fel'annár stared back at Gor'sadén, and then his eyes slipped to Hobin, who was staring back at him unwaveringly. Fel'annár nodded that he understood, but before he could even try to get his mind around where to begin, Pan'assár was speaking.

"It can wait, Fel'annár. We didn't come here to interrogate you but to accompany you away from this infirmary, from where we did not think you would ever leave, at least not on your own two feet. And... we also came to *commend* you."

Fel'annár had not expected that, and he frowned, but again, Pan'assár was speaking.

"This has been in my mind for some time, but today, as we spoke of the battle during the strategy council, it seemed so utterly out of place, for every time I referred to you, I said *Warrior Fel'annár*. I found myself explaining that this *warrior* had stood beside a lone tree, had conjured some power, stood in the company of only five other warriors and watched an army of thousands swarm the land. I told them that I knew you expected to die and that you accepted that, because you are a *warrior*. It sounded wrong."

Fel'annár's frown deepened, but his eyes were riveted on Pan'assár.

"Silor never deserved it, but you . . ." He reached into his tunic pocket, then pulled his hand out and held it before Fel'annár. He looked down, to the outstretched palm, and upon it, a simple line of silver—to be pinned onto the collar of his uniform.

Fel'annár's eyes stared at the object he had seen before, eyes burning and heart hammering. And then he tore his gaze from it and looked at Pan'assár. A smile slowly blossomed on the commander's face, one Fel'annár had never seen, and it moved him.

"Trainee lieutenant?"

Pan'assár nodded. "I have commissioned your pauldon. The next time you don your uniform, be it Alpine or Silvan, you will do so as a trainee lieutenant. I have already spoken to Galadan. He will teach you all he can. In one year, you and I will speak again."

Fel'annár breathed deeply, closed his eyes and turned his head downwards, and the three commanders watched him fondly. When Fel'annár opened them once more they were bright and intense, full of wonder and pride. They drifted to Gor'sadén, in search of complicity. The commander nodded.

"I am proud of you, Trainee Lieutenant Fel'annár. May you serve your king well."

"May you serve *Aria* well," added Hobin, and both commanders glanced sideways at him, wondering if he would elaborate. But he didn't.

Fel'annár couldn't speak, his throat too tight, and so he smiled, turning the silver insignia in his hand. It symbolised the earth. When he was no longer a trainee, it would be replaced in gold, but Fel'annár would not stop, not until he bore the golden sun of a captain. That dream had once been a distant fantasy, one he had come to doubt would ever come to pass. Now, though, that dream was a step closer, no longer wishful thinking but a reachable goal, for Pan'assár the legend was back and the Silvan fighters of Ea Uaré could, perhaps, serve with dignity once more.

Movement behind the commanders and Prince Handir came through the doors, closely followed by The Company. The prince nodded at the commanders and then placed clothing he had brought for Fel'annár at the foot of the bed, and upon his face was a knowing smile—but to what, Fel'annár could not say. The Company came to stand on the other side of the bed, and to Fel'annár's dismay, they wore the same smile. Something was going on.

Before long, Fel'annár changed into the simple clothing and then turned to The Company. Opening his hand, he revealed the silver insignia of a trainee lieutenant, and the brothers fell together amongst cries of joy and celebration, but Galadan stepped up to him and placed a hand on his shoulder.

"Justice has been done at last. It is my very great honour to train you in the ways of a lieutenant, Warrior."

"And I am so very grateful that *you* will be my guide," he smiled and then hugged Galadan, for the first time since he had known him. And while Idernon's eyes strayed to Pan'assár in utter surprise at what he had done, Handir and the commanders watched The Company with soft smiles. Handir too could not help but catch Pan'assár's eyes and nod softly at him. He had missed something important, missed Pan'assár's transformation, and he wondered. Blue eyes strayed to the purple sash and then to Gor'sadén, but he was watching Fel'annár and in his eyes was the unmistakable pride he had always missed in his own father's eyes.

Pan'assár reached into his pocket once more, *this* time pulling out a golden clip he held out towards Gor'sadén. He took the delicate object from his brother's hand, stared at it and then looked up at Pan'assár, gaze intense even though he smiled. Pan'assár's unspoken question was answered with a tip of the commander's head, and

Pan'assár sat on the side of the now empty bed. Gor'sadén weaved the Heliaré back into Pan'assár's hair for the first time since The Three had been sundered, and while the others looked on, Pan'assár's gaze turned inwards and to the image of Or'Talán's face, smiling back at him in joy and pride.

At last it was time to leave, and Fel'annár stood with The Company at his back, his crutch tucked under his arm. He gestured for the commanders to precede them, but Gor'sadén was shaking his head even as the commanders pulled themselves to their feet. Gor'sadén's head gestured to the door. Neither he nor anyone else would step out before Fel'annár. It was *his* moment to shine.

Llyniel, too, took leave of Arané and Mestahé and stepped outside the infirmary, behind the commanders, a heavy book in her hands, and at her side was Handir.

Inside the public areas of the Healing Halls themselves, every bed had been vacated, every injured warrior standing, alone or with the help of loved ones or healers, and as Fel'annár and the others passed, they bowed low as they would to their king. Healers, too, stopped to pay deference to the warriors that had saved their city.

Fel'annár didn't know where to look, wanted to acknowledge them all but that was not possible, and so he walked, slowly and with a heavy limp, head moving from one side to the other. His entire body ached from this simple act of walking, but still he smiled and nodded back at them, determined they would not see the effort it required of him.

But it was when they passed the doors from the Halls into the palace itself that Fel'annár and The Company stopped short.

The entire front entrance, the corridors, the staircases and landings were brimming with people, silently watching as The Company and the commanders slowly stepped into their midst.

One, lone elf began to clap, hard and furious. He was soon followed by another, and then another, until the entire hall erupted. The clapping then was joined by shouts of glory and praise, and the warriors looked about themselves, at the shining faces that thanked them, the citizens of Tar'eastór that had so desperately wanted to thank them. Tears welled in their eyes and shy smiles blossomed on the lips of The Company, even as their hands discreetly held on to Fel'annár's belt. They climbed stairs and navigated corridors and still, they were followed by claps and shouts of thanks. The commanders and Handir had then left for their own quarters, and by the time The Company had made it to Fel'annár's corridor, their hold on the back of his belt was stronger.

The people stopped at a respectable distance from Fel'annár's guarded rooms, but they could still see the door, still see what lay around it and all along the other side of the corridor. They stood silent and expectant as Fel'annár cast his eyes over it all and the true impact of what they had done finally hit him.

The place was littered with plants and packages, bottles and boxes, wrappings of all shapes and sizes, reels of luscious material, scrolls . . . and for a moment all he could do was stand and stare at the gifts that had been carefully laid there. The Company had already known, though, had seen it all when they had come to bathe and change. The people of Tar'eastór wanted to show them, show Fel'annár how grateful they were for the sacrifice The Company had been willing to make.

Sontúr stepped forward and opened the doors, but before they passed through, Fel'annár turned back to the now silent people of Tar'eastór. Tears had welled in his eyes and he smiled softly back at them. With a slow nod, he turned back and disappeared from their sight.

Inside, the room was not cold and unused but warm and inviting, candles flickering in the sconces and upon the tables. They had been expected, and had Fel'annár ventured into the bathing area, he would have seen the hot water that lay steaming in the tub, would have smelled the flowers and herbs that suffused the air.

It was Llyniel and Sontúr who led an already exhausted Fel'annár into the bed chamber and settled him, watching as he lay back, eyes half-closed.

"Rest," said Sontúr as he turned and pulled his friend's boots off and covered him with the bedspread. He turned to Llyniel, a silent question in his eyes, one she understood perfectly. Nodding, she sat by the bed and gestured that he should go and join The Company—and Sontúr thought he would have chosen no other for his friend to love.

Sontúr sat—and then heaved a mighty breath of relief and fatigue, eyes turning to the mountain of offerings that had been brought inside, piled up on one side of the room. Normally, Galdith and Carodel would be poking through it all and Ramien would be admiring the silky cloth. Galadan would be watching as Idernon read through the scrolls and Sontúr himself would be opening the wine. But the battle and its aftermath, and then the events that had taken place at the Sentinel, had affected them all deeply, so much that they had not yet spoken of it. But now that they knew Fel'annár would recover, that they were *alone*, clean and comfortable and with fine wine in their hands, they could no longer remain silent.

"I am centuries old, have seen my share of rarities. But I will never be able to express what I saw at the Sentinel that dawn when Fel'annár returned," said Galdith, eyes fixed on the flickering flames. "I need to know . . . if you saw what I did; I need to know if you saw the *figure* . . ."

They remained silent, didn't even move until Ramien sat forward in his chair, forearms resting on his thighs.

"I saw her."

"And I," said Carodel. "I saw the space before Fel'annár shift, as if something floated in my own eye, distorted my vision, and for one moment, as the sun rose, I thought I saw . . . I thought perhaps it was a lady."

Again they were silent, but Galdith was smiling and a tear rolled from his eye. He swiped a hand across his face and sniffled.

"I saw what Carodel did," began Sontúr. "But I cannot be sure what it was," he said, shaking his head. "Perhaps some phenomenon

—the warmth from the sun and the dew upon the ground . . ." Idernon nodded slowly as he contemplated Sontúr's suggestion.

"I suppose we each of us saw what we believe we did. But one thing you can't deny, Brothers. We *all* felt something beautiful brush our souls. Strange that simple energy can achieve such a wonderful thing," said Carodel.

They sat in silence once more, thoughts of existence and beliefs, of faith and reason swirling in their minds, but it was not an uncomfortable silence, not now that they had spoken of it.

Idernon turned back to the fire. "For now, we concentrate on getting Fel'annár back to his usual self—and we guard him. We cannot forget the danger that still stalks him. He still needs to speak to his brother about his acceptance to join this plan he speaks of. After that, I don't think it will be long until we return to the Forest."

"I wonder what we will find," mused Galdith. "Fel'annár says Handir has painted a dire picture, speaks of some Summit the king has held, and I can't help wondering what his enemies will say on his return—what they will *do*, even."

"The king will hold our land together, Galdith," assured Ramien.

"The king has been absent for many years, Brother," said Galadan. "But whatever the state of the Forest we return to, we must be vigilant. We must trust no one, not even our own people, not until we understand what is happening."

"I agree," said Idernon. "You know, when our people see Fel'annár now, when they come to realise what it is he can do . . . I cannot rightly say how they will react."

The others looked at Idernon's profile as he stared into the flames. They knew he was right, and yet, all they had were suppositions, suspicions about how their land would welcome them—or not. They had no way of knowing the depth of Band'orán's treachery, of his desire to subjugate the Silvan people.

Not until they returned would they come to understand what they were walking into.

EIGHTEEN
NIGHT OF A THOUSAND DRUMS

"Hope drives ambition, fuels passion, brings optimism, leads to great deeds should the stakes be high. In Ea Uaré, they were, but it was hope that we did not have, and for all that Lord Erthoron tried, he failed to unite his people, failed to garner their patience to wait for the vote to be taken once more. We had waited for too long, had been driven too hard, and the tether had broken. The hope the Silvans had nurtured from birth was absent and silent, but still these forests were ours, forests that were slipping from our grasping fingers and into the ample pockets of the greedy.
We would not tolerate it. Not anymore."
The Silvan Chronicles, book IV. Marhené.

~

Three days later, Fel'annár's incessant fidgeting was unbearable. He walked with difficulty, grimaced often, was quick to tire and hesitant to eat. Still, he wanted to visit the gardens, and after what had happened at the Sentinel, they would not keep him from it—indeed, it would surely accelerate his recuperation, they said.

However, his wish had been granted under strict orders from both Llyniel and Sontúr. He was to use his *crutch*, he was to *sit*, and he was to *eat* when ordered to. He had agreed to it all, and then Llyniel had asked The Company to grant Fel'annár a modicum of privacy. There were things she needed to say, questions she needed to ask. Idernon had nodded in silent understanding and then had spoken to the others. Funny, she mused, because she had never thought to find a friend in the Wise Warrior. Yet now, of all its members save for Sontúr, it was him she felt closest to.

And so, they had taken Fel'annár to the gardens and had sat him in his favourite spot beneath the Sentinel. His pale and strained features eased slowly as his muscles relaxed, and Llyniel covered his legs with a blanket. With a grateful nod at Idernon, The Company fell back, out of sight but within walking distance should any danger approach.

They were alone at last—save that Handir stood watching them from afar, and Llyniel closed her eyes in frustration. She had not had one single, waking moment alone with Fel'annár since he had been cognizant enough to maintain a conversation. Yet to look at Handir now, she could not send him away. She gestured to the prince with her head and he walked to them, taking a moment to observe his brother as he stood over him.

"May I?" he asked, and Fel'annár looked up at him, nodding. Handir sat, stretching one leg out before him while the other was bent at the knee, one arm resting on it. It was a distinctly Alpine posture to adopt, thought Fel'annár. He had seen it in books, great lords sitting on plush cushions around low tables, picking at food and drinking wine. He smirked at his fanciful thoughts, but it soon faded, because Handir did not speak—instead he seemed to be warring with his words. Fel'annár wondered if he knew what his brother was thinking, and he spoke first.

"Before the battle, I had resolved to speak with you, but then I met Llyniel in a tree and then..."

"Yes, yes. Spare me the details, Fel'annár," smiled Handir.

"I wanted to speak with you about Lainon's plan." He felt Llyniel stiffen beside him, for the right reasons he hoped. "I and The Company want to be a part of it. We would help you in this endeavour to keep King Thargodén on the throne, to pull our people together."

Handir's intensely bright eyes gave him away, despite his cool features and the unmoving posture.

"What changed?" he asked, shrewd eyes boring into his brother's strangely confident gaze.

"During my time in Tar'eastór, I have come to love this place, love the Alpine side of myself. Racial discrimination does not exist here—I have received nothing but friendship and good will from these people. I even wondered once if I could stay here, not have to go back and face it all. But then a part of me needs to hope that our own lands can be just like this. Diverse, just, proud.

"And then Lainon's last wishes were always in my mind. He wanted us to do this together, and I would honour that, but my heart..." He faltered for a moment, grappled with his words. "I needed to understand, Handir, understand that I would not be used because of what I seem to represent to some. I needed to know that I would serve some purpose beyond the symbolic, that I could make a difference in some way that was justified, do something that others could not." He stopped, had said enough, and so he turned his eyes back to Handir, who was staring back at him as if he should continue. The prince leaned back, and Fel'annár had the distinct feeling that he knew he was holding back, that there *was*, indeed, something else that had tipped the balance.

Aria had charged him with uniting the Forest—as her Ber'anor, because he himself was Ari'atór. But he couldn't tell Handir that, not yet. Not even Llyniel knew about that.

"Perhaps this gift of mine will help us in some way," he continued. "Not to turn the Forest against anyone, but perhaps through the mind of the trees, things I can perceive, warnings I can heed . . . these things will be helpful to us."

Handir nodded. Fel'annár had tried to dissipate his suspicions and had failed, but still the prince did not press for now.

"I am glad, Fel'annár, glad that we can finally honour Lainon's wishes. He was a brother to us both, one who strangely has stepped into the space between us, brought us a little closer together."

Unfamiliar feelings came over Fel'annár. He didn't know if it was his weakened state or perhaps some effects from the herbs he was forced to take. Whatever the reasons, he felt light, strangely unburdened. He felt safe, like a child home from a storm. It was a strange thought. Handir snapped him out of it.

"I am considering speaking with Pan'assár of this plan, Fel'annár. His time in Tar'eastór has tempered his dislike of the Silvans, and although I cannot see him ever completely warming to them, he *is* loyal to the king. We would gain a formidable ally."

"Let *me* do it," began Fel'annár. "I have come to . . . *understand* . . . our commander. He does not hate the Silvans, Handir."

Handir's eyes turned to Llyniel, who had remained silent throughout their talk. If anyone would protest the inclusion of Pan'assár in their plan, it would be her, yet she said nothing at all, and Handir turned back to Fel'annár. "Then things have, indeed, changed, it would seem. Perhaps it is your initiation in the Kal'hamén'Ar . . ."

"Perhaps," said Fel'annár, once more leaving Handir with the uncomfortable impression that his younger brother knew much more than he let on. "It is Gor'sadén who has brought our commander back, Handir; he, too, is coming with us to Ea Uaré."

Handir's brows rose high on his forehead. "*Is* he now . . . that would certainly help us to get Pan'assár on our side. You are close to Gor'sadén and . . ."

Fel'annár chuckled. "Always scheming, Handir. But yes, I *am* close to him, and yet I will *not* use him to garner Pan'assár's support. I will have it . . . or I will *not*."

"Spoken like a true warrior," nodded Handir with a stifled smile, "Or should I say *lieutenant*?" He smiled and then breathed deeply, and for a moment, Fel'annár saw him as just another elf, no longer standing to ceremony, no longer scheming and second-guessing, no longer reading between lines and manipulating. Handir his *brother* suddenly sat before him, and of a sudden Fel'annár understood what those strange feelings were.

It was a sense of belonging. It was a sense of *family*.

He leaned back against the tree behind him and then closed his eyes, thankful for the first time that he was still injured and that his emotions would be interpreted as tiredness. It worked.

"Well, I have much to do then. Keep me informed, Fel'annár. I would speak with Pan'assár personally once you have told him what we intend to do."

"You trust me then to do this?"

"I do. I can see there are things you have not said, things you keep to yourself, and I will not delve into the wherewithal of that. You will tell me when you will," he said, rising to his feet. "Our return is imminent, Fel'annár. I wait only for you to be fit enough to travel. There are plans to be made, a route to be agreed on, a *safe* route, and there are missives that must be prepared and then sent with the utmost secrecy. There are dangerous times ahead, Brother. I would have us do this together."

Fel'annár smiled, open and genuine for the first time.

"Handir."

"What is it?"

"Lainon. He is not dead. He has found himself—he is *alive* across the Veil. Hobin has told me so."

He froze where he stood, eyes flickering wide even as they filled with tears. He turned to Llyniel, voice quiet and strangled. "I will leave you two alone then, to talk and to . . . be *Silvan* . . . if you must."

He smirked through the shock on his face, and with a wave of his jewelled hand and with eyes that were far too bright, he turned abruptly and walked back to the palace.

"Will you not comfort him?" asked Fel'annár.

"Not now. He needs time alone. I will see him later. Lainon's return is to be celebrated." She smiled radiantly.

Fel'annár watched her as she leaned sideways and plucked a single buttercup, and then twirled it between two fingers, eyes watching as the petals merged into a buttery ribbon of radiant yellow. He loved the way she looked at things—with deep curiosity and shining eyes. He loved her compassionate heart and sharp mind. He loved the gentle curve of her nose and her well-defined upper lip and . . .

"I love you."

Her head snapped to him, eyes searching, the corners of her mouth twitching upwards, but there was wonder in her honey-coloured eyes, a hazy sort of peace that warmed his heart. He watched her face until she was so close he could no longer focus, and then the touch of soft lips caressed his own. He felt her breath on his face, a hand smoothing reverently down his hair. She moved back, just enough for him to focus.

"And my heart is here," she said, her hand covering his chest over the simple linen shirt he wore. "It *has* been—for longer than I care to admit. I told myself it was your *body* I wanted." She smirked, and Fel'annár cocked an eyebrow at her. "Well, it *was*, but there was more. And yet I ignored it, told myself it was not the time for romance. I have a dream, one I will never relinquish. And then you told me yours, to be a Silvan captain. How could we reconcile our dreams with any kind of future together, Fel'annár? Always parted, never knowing if you would come back, and if you did, in what state I would find you. But then I saw you, I saw what Lainon had seen, what The Company see in you, and for all that I tried, I could no longer resist. When they brought you in from the battle I thought . . . I thought you would *die*."

Her voice faltered, and Fel'annár raised a hand, reached for her face, fingers combing into her hair.

"I didn't die. You saved me."

"I stopped you from dying. Aria brought you back. I bless that dawn, Fel'annár, the dawn of my eternal love for you."

Joy of the kind he had never felt surged through his body, and the Sentinel behind him raised its voice to the lands beyond. He wanted to run, open his arms to the world, and scream his joy, but he couldn't do that yet, so he imagined it, and then her lips were upon him, hand tracing down his neck and to his chest. She shifted forwards until her body pressed against him. The kiss deepened, and Fel'annár moaned in bliss. She needed to stop—but not yet. He pulled her to him, sunk into her lips, felt the pulse of blood in her neck, hot and irresistible.

She leaned back and smiled saucily, cocking her head to one side. "Soon, when you are better, we can show each other." She smiled that Silvan smile that had always managed to melt him like butter in the sun.

"Oh yes. I will show you." He smiled. "Show you what it is to be *Silvan*."

She laughed and batted him on the shoulder, and for a while they simply sat, shoulder-to-shoulder, while Fel'annár drew her in his journal, but it wasn't a buttercup he placed in her hands—it was his namesake. The vivid green flower after which he was named was in Llyniel's hands, just like his heart.

"So we are both going back to Ea Uaré, I to a family I do not know and you to a family you left behind. Can you forgive them, Llyniel?"

She thought for a moment before she spoke. "Perhaps. And you? Can you forgive yours?"

He stared back at her. Could he? Forgive Thargodén for creating him for the simple purpose of saving the one he loved? Months ago, the answer would have been a resounding *"no"*. But then he had met Llyniel and his heart had chosen. She had shown him what it meant to love, to know how it would feel should he ever lose her in the circumstances his father had lost Lássira. He wondered what he would *not* do to save her from death.

"Forgive him, yes. But whether we can erase the years between us, whether we can ever be father and son . . . " He shook his head. "I cannot say."

"We'll do it together, then, shall we?" she said, knowing that they would need each other in the months to come.

Fel'annár's hand splayed and he intertwined his fingers with hers, squeezing almost painfully.

"Together."

He pulled her to him and they kissed, long and languid, sealing their pact of friendship and nascent love, a union of kindred souls poised to fly away on a dangerous path of life. *Together* they had said, and as the soft breeze ruffled the pages of Fel'annár's diary, the capricious wind chose a page upon which another lady gazed into infinity, her eyes just as bright and green as Fel'annár's. She too had confessed her love, had held her own Green Sun in her hands, a Fel'annár of the Deep Forest, Silvan symbol of eternal love.

That flower still existed, sitting between the aging pages of a similar diary—a diary that King Thargodén would open every day and remember his own, eternal love beyond Valley.

∼

Shadows made no noise and Macurian was no exception, even though he was blind in one eye and his left arm hung useless in a sling.

He watched with keen, shrewd eyes as the lord standing before him sipped his wine and contemplated the privileged view beyond his window, framed with rich drapes. Sulén was rich—and he was ruthless. Dangerous in his aspirations, ones Macurian could well guess at. Just days ago, he would have respected the lord, but now, all he felt was pity for Sulén . . . and for himself.

The lord turned from the window and then sat, depositing his jewelled goblet to one side and taking up a parchment in the other, obviously re-reading something he had already seen. He sighed and took his goblet in his hand.

Macurian stepped from the shadows, and wine spilled over Sulén's manicured hand.

The Shadow smiled. "Lord Sulén."

"How dare you," he murmured. "I could have you thrown in the dungeons for this trespass."

"But you won't, of course."

Sulén stood, dabbing at his hand with a silken handkerchief. "What do you want?" he asked slowly.

"A good question, my lord. As you can see, battle has left me . . . *impaired* . . . for a while at least. I must think on an alternative way to earn my keep."

"I think we can come to an arrangement. I will have my treasurer see to it."

"I would rather you saw to it personally, my lord."

Sulén stared back at Macurian, reading his cool, steady eyes.

"Name your price, Shadow," he murmured, turning away, eyes darting here and there for anything that might help him should he need to defend himself.

"I want a fair price."

"But you failed. The Silvan bastard still lives."

"Yes. Yes, he does . . . and so do you. Perhaps you would be dead now, were it not for him, and still you call him bastard."

"Are you telling me, now, that you have scruples, Shadow?"

"Not really. I admire him, but that would not stop me from killing him."

"Then won't you finish him?"

"Perhaps, if you pay the price."

"I have already paid."

"You will pay tenfold should I tell your king all that I know."

"You dare to blackmail the House of Sulén?" murmured the lord, staring hard at the twisted Shadow.

"I prefer to call it a transaction, my lord. But in answer to your question, yes."

It had been an attempt to intimidate Macurian, but he had not flinched at all.

"Name your price."

"Your gems."

Sulén opened his mouth to protest, but Macurian stepped closer and the lord remained silent.

"Don't," said Macurian. "Open it." He gestured with his head to where he knew Sulén had stashed his fortune. He would rather have the coin, but he would never be able to carry such weight.

Before long, Sulén was handing over his family's considerable collection of diamonds, emeralds, and sapphires, jaw clenched and bloody intent in his eyes. Macurian had wrapped them in filthy cloth, nodded and then left, as silently as he had come. Sulén stared after him, his sharp mind enumerating the various things that Macurian could possibly do, but all of them contemplated the possibility that the Shadow would betray his trust. He looked about his study and then to his desk and the scrolls that lay there. There was sensitive information inside them, details he would need to replicate and hide away. He left the room in a whirl of fine cloth, in search of his secretary and his son, Silor. They would extract only the necessary information and eliminate all traces of names and then burn the scrolls. There were contingency plans to make, missives to write.

Minutes later he was back with Silor and his secretary. As Sulén strode to his desk, his heart plummeted to his boots, because where before there had been three scrolls upon the carefully waxed surface, now there was nothing—but wood.

"Oh gods."

The others watched him in confusion, but Sulén saw the words floating before his mind's eye, saw the orders and the promises, the names that would incriminate *him* but not his lord. He briefly wondered if the Shadow had taken them only to ensure that Sulén did not have him arrested or killed. But there was another possibility —that Macurian did have scruples, that he would present those scrolls as evidence against Sulén.

"We leave for Ea Uaré at dawn."

"What . . . *why*?" asked Silor. "Macurian has our jewels; he'll finish the job. Why would we leave?"

"You fool!" spat Sulén, grabbing his son by the front of his tunic and shaking him, eyes round and trembling. "He has more than our jewels. He has the *missives*, the ones Handir never received, but more than this, he has my unfinished missive to Ea Uaré."

Unfinished . . . *uncyphered*. Silor finally understood, and Sulén released him.

Straightening his tunic, he bowed. "I will see to it, Father."

~

Macurian would ride to Prairie, he decided. Humans would pay a pretty price for the services of one such as him, mutilated though he was.

He was still dangerous.

He had told Sulén that he would kill the Silvan in exchange for his family gems. It wasn't the first time he had lied—wouldn't be the last. He patted the bag of jewels that lay heavily in his panier and then kicked his mount into a canter. He passed through the gates and then cantered down the slopes, and as he passed the ruined trees, he bowed his head in silent respect and left the Motherland behind. As for the scrolls he had taken from Sulén's desk, he had left them upon an elegant table, inside an elegant suite of rooms, designated to a prince of the Great Forest.

~

"Is he dead?"

"He may be, but at the time Lord Sulén wrote this he was still alive," replied Councillor Draugole.

"Damn that baseborn Silvan," said Barathon. "Still, I am sure our allies will see to it soon enough."

"Perhaps," murmured Band'orán. "Still, we must assume the worst and prepare for the possibility that he *will* try to return."

"And we will be waiting for them," said the warrior who shared in their council. "We wait for Pan'assár's return—if he returns, and then we make sure our captains vote against the return of the warlord. In all truth, there is merit to the idea of waiting these two months. It gives us more time to persuade the reticent . . . and for the Silvans to calm down, let their anger subside before we deny them once more."

"Well then, it is all but done," said Band'orán as he stood and turned to his avid audience. "Our long years of planning and strategy are finally coming to a head. We have the majority vote of the Merchant's Guild and the overwhelming cooperation of the Inner Circle," he said, nodding at the formidable warrior, who returned his look with a smile. "Lords Sulén and Ras'dan have only to complete the task entrusted to them and then they will join us. That is when the second colonisation can begin. The seeds of discord have germinated and the Silvans grow weaker by the day. All is in place for when our prince tries to return, and if the bastard is with him, we will deal with them both once and for all.

"Take my hands, my friends, for it is time to make of Ea Uaré a land of Alpine splendour—with new lords, new princes, and a new king that will take our glorious people into a prosperous future, the likes of which Elvendom has never seen."

The warrior stood, a gleam in his eye that spoke of pride and hunger for a power that had been denied him . . . but that would soon be his. Whether or not Pan'assár made it back alive, he was finished. The Three were a relic of the past.

It was time for General Huren to shine now—beside his new lord and king, Band'orán.

~

Amareth watched Erthoron and Lorthil from where she sat at a small fire, which crackled and hissed in the early evening twilight. Golloron and Narosén were there, too, heads bent over as they listened and shared silent understanding. She knew of what they spoke—of a new Silvan council, one that truly represented their people.

The king had vetoed the result of the royal council, had been brave and had promised much in doing so, but the Silvans no longer believed him, no longer saw him as the leader of their nation. It was Band'orán who held sway over the majority of Alpines, they said. To the Silvans, the second vote was meaningless, predictable, just like the vote the Inner Circle would take on the return of the warlord.

A part of her wished that they would just accept things for what they were. But then she knew that was wrong, just as she knew that, in following their hearts and striving for justice, they might be forced to isolate themselves inside the woods, close them off to the Alpine invaders. They may have their Silvan Council, but who would *lead* them?

Stay away, my son. Don't come back.

She had no way of knowing whether Fel'annár was still alive. If he was *dead*, she would take the Long Road, leave the forests of her home for good, even knowing that they would, eventually, succumb to the power and wealth of the Alpines. But if Fel'annár was still alive, should he step into this conflicted land it would sentence him to a life of persecution by those who followed Band'orán, and only Amareth knew the extent to which Band'orán would go. The first time he had tried to kill Fel'annár, Lássira had fooled his assassin and paid the price. But they *would* find him the second time around.

She cast her eyes around their camp. They were just inside the forest proper, on the outskirts of Sen'garay. They had been met by crowds of Silvans come to hear the outcome of their demands, but questions had not been necessary.

Their patience had come to an end.

She closed her eyes with the first beat of a base drum. Deep and hollow, like a lost elf, alone in the dark.

The lonely beat continued until it was joined by a double drum, a higher tone, a faster rhythm. No longer alone, a timid light in the cold of night.

The Silvans called for *unity*.

Another beat joined the base and double drums, a melodious descant that shifted in tone, lending a complexity to the weave of tribal music.

The Silvans called for *justice*.

The higher tonal drums began their own lilting beat, interchanging rhythms and tones, and the chorus surged louder, defiant, like a wave rising to meet the cliffs.

They proclaimed the return of the Silvan people.

Representatives of the once noble houses of Oak and Beech, of the Winter Wolf and Silver Deer stood defiantly around the fires, hearts swelling with pride for who they were—what they had once been and would once more be. Their souls flared in their chests, like silver blades under the midday sun: a *Silvan* blade held boldly aloft. Theirs was an angry challenge from a proud people who had found their voice, a people who called for a leader to take back what was rightfully theirs . . . what should never have been taken.

They all stood now, even the children, not just here in their makeshift camp but everywhere, thundering drums spreading throughout the Forest, their message travelling far and wide, over oak and beech, fir and ash. From Oran 'Dor to Ea'nanú, Lan Taria to Abiren'á and Sen'oléi, even unto the barren wastes of Sen'uár where none were left to hear. Cups and plates, twigs and stones, clapping hands and stomping feet, their riotous clamour was a reflection of one collective heart, a Silvan scream of defiance, of rebellion, of proclamation.

But so too did it travel south and to King Thargodén's palace. It wove around the high spires and domes like a wind of change, of warning, a hand outstretched, not in harmony but rejection.

Your votes mean *nothing*.

King Thargodén stood like a marble statue before the vast expanse of forest beyond the windows of his offices, his crown prince at his side, equally silent. Aradan's head turned away, the face of his only child in his mind's eye, looking back at him in disappointment. Barathon and Draugole sat plotting while Lord Band'orán smiled into the distance, in his eyes a gleam of satisfaction and determination, anticipation for the conclusion of his plan, which had spanned almost a century. To him, those drums were not the rebellious cry of a people shaking free from their subjugation. They were the sounds of impending celebration. Thargodén's Silvan spawn would be crushed under his thumb and Band'orán would rise a king, as it should always have been.

Within the Inner Circle, General Huren made plans should the Silvans close the Forest, and the lord councillors of the king's court sat talking of the shameful council, of the vote the king had vetoed and whether he had been right to do so.

But the Alpine warriors and teachers, craftsmen and musicians, the farriers and the bakers, the *people* lifted their faces into the strange night and listened to the talking drums of Ea Uaré, and they asked themselves . . .

What have our leaders done?

And still, the Silvans beat their drums, clapped their hands, thumped their chests, and stomped their feet into the night, a night that would always be remembered as the *Night of a Thousand Drums*.

Their subjugation had come to an end. Their debasement and their humiliation would vanish into a shameful past. The Great Forest Belt was the home of the Silvans, and all that was left to do was reinstate their own Ruling Council and then bring forth the

Silvan warlord to defend the Forest from their enemies, whoever they may be.

They did not *need* Alpine lords. They did not *want* them.

They were no longer *welcome*.

FIN

Coming 2020. Rise of a Warlord

FROM R.K. LANDER

If you enjoyed the story, please consider reviewing. It would mean so much to me.

Review Dawn of a Legend on Amazon

And if you are on Goodreads or BookBub, would you share your thoughts with friends and followers?

The Silvan is an ongoing saga, so if you would like to keep abreast of the latest news on upcoming releases, or simply participate in the discussion, why not join my readers club? You can do that by visiting rklander.com.

Also, why not visit my website and follow my blog? You'll find me at www.rklander.com You'll get all the latest news, and the extras on the series, like the map, character sketches and the music especially composed for the series, by the incredible Will Musser.

Book 4 of The Silvan Saga is due early 2019.

ABOUT THE AUTHOR

I have always loved fantasy, especially of the epic kind. It's all Tolkien's fault, and then Ursula Le Guin, and perhaps Ray Bradbury - oh and Arthur C. Clarke.

Give me battles and exotic creatures, magic and faraway lands, but above all, give me a great story with characters that I can relate to.

I write in my pyjamas and drink far too much tea. I love my dogs and hate cockroaches. I enjoy cooking spicy stuff and my garden is my haven. But whatever I am doing and wherever I am, I am always thinking about my next book.

I hope you will enjoy them.

facebook.com/rklwrites

twitter.com/rklwrites

instagram.com/rklanderwrites

bookbub.com/authors/RKLander

goodreads.com/rklwrites

ACKNOWLEDGMENTS

As always, this work would not be what it is without the incomparable help of my life-long beta reader, M.Y. Leigh. We will see this through to the end, my friend.

I would like to express just how lucky I feel at having such a wonderful team behind me, but I would especially like to thank Kate, Kadie, Sharon, Tim, Claudia, Susan, Ken, Marilyn, Jen, David, Bruce, Anthony, Sherrin, Naomi, Ellen, Rebecca, Paul and Pearl.